Radiance

A lightness of spirit often draws the darkness.

Shayne McClendon

Radiance by Shayne McClendon
The Barter System Series
Copyright © 2010-2017 Shayne McClendon

Updated Edition: July 2017

Published by Always the Good Girl LLC
www.alwaysthegoodgirl.com

All rights reserved.

ISBN-13: 978-1548737191
ISBN-10: 1548737194

Dedication

I dedicate this book – my favorite in *The Barter System* series – to my beloved friend, Angela Mink.

A lot changed in my life in the last few years. Angela was one of several women who rallied behind me and kept me moving forward, personally and professionally, no matter what was happening in her own life. She was small in stature, huge in personality.

Cancer took her from me and the *many* people who loved her desperately (people she loved back *hard*) in May 2017.

I keep forgetting she's gone.

This book was one she read before I started seriously working on it. I sent her the bones of it and she was *giddy* to see the final. There were many late-night conversations about the story, the characters, and future developments.

Jana and I gave her lots of behind-the-scenes information months later when the cancer came back with a vengeance. She asked questions and we answered all of them because she wanted to know "just in case" she didn't get to read everything that came next.

It hurts that she had to "read" them that way, before many were even written. She was glad of it but it wasn't enough for her.

She deserved so much more.
More years, more laughter, more words.

Angela, I'm so grateful to you, for you, even though you weren't in my life *nearly* fucking long enough. You're deeply missed.

All my love,
Shayne

Note from the Author

I talked through initial ideas for this book with my friend Jordana. She hated the title (it stuck anyway) but *loved* Brie's story.

I hope she likes where things ended up.

You'll have a chance to visit with characters you've grown to love and meet some wonderful new ones that just might blow you away.

Brie is special to me. Since her initial appearance in *Hudson*, I've been unable to shake her from my brain. She showed up in *Liberation* and *Backstage*...but it still wasn't time to tell her story.

Her time is now. I hope you love her journey as much as I do. I've *always* had a soft spot for the ones who glow.

Shayne

Table of Contents

Table of Contents (continued)

Table of Contents (continued)

Prologue

September 2014

As much as Gabriella Hernandez loved each and every one of her friends, she was grateful to return to her silent apartment in the hour before dawn.

Natalia Roman, her best friend's fiancée, insisted on helping her out of the formal gown she'd worn to the Bishop Foundation benefit and into something comfortable. She gently brushed her hair and loosely braided it down her back.

Then Hudson Winters and his ladylove kissed her goodnight and she locked up behind them.

Racing thoughts made it impossible for her to sleep. She sat staring out at the skyline, watching the sun come up over the city.

When the apartment phone rang at eight in the morning, she picked it up in surprise.

"Brie, this is Carlo. You have a delivery. Is it alright for the men to bring it up?"

"Of course."

"They're on the way."

Disconnecting, she used her walker to make her way to the front door as the freight elevator beeped. She watched as the enormous whale fashioned from scrap metal she'd fallen in love with the night before was carefully wheeled out of the interior and across the hall.

Barely able to speak, she directed the men to set it up in the corner of her living room.

It was even more spectacular sitting majestically in her apartment. The tip of the whale's nose was barely a foot from her ceiling.

When they finished, she told the men, "Wait just a moment and I'll grab my bag…"

"No, ma'am. We've been taken care of already. Have a good day." The last man handed her a heavy linen envelope with her first name written in masculine scrawl. He nodded as he closed the door.

The sculpture stole her breath. Lowering slowly to the edge of her sofa, she opened the envelope and felt her heart hit a hard gallop.

Gabriella,

You're captivating.

My brother was thrilled to learn you were so taken with his work. I couldn't risk it falling into less-appreciative hands.

May it continue to bring you pleasure.

Harper

She re-read the words several times. Then she picked up the phone and called Natalia.

"Darling, why are you awake?"

"I haven't been to sleep."

"Is everything alright?"

"Harper bought me the whale from the auction. They just set it up in my living room. Is this, I mean, if I keep it am I committed to something?"

"You mean is it similar to my collar?"

"Something like that."

"No, darling. It's simply a gift. An extravagant one but nothing more than a gift." There was a long pause. "Do you *want* it to be more?"

"I have no idea."

"Brie, give it some thought. You'll be pursued more openly going

2

forward. I've known them for two decades. He won't stop until you either tell him no or agree to belong to him…and his oldest friend."

"I'm not sure what *belonging* would actually mean, not with him."

"Let's have lunch." There was the sound of rustling in the background and Brie heard Natalia sigh. "Make that dinner. We'll answer any questions you have, darling."

"Thanks. Enjoy naked time and send my apologies for interrupting."

"No, Brie. I'm *so glad* you woke me up. I'll call you later."

Her attention was drawn back to the note and she allowed herself to remember the way the two men, the lifelong friends, she'd met the night before had affected her.

Harper Delkin was the eldest heir to the fortune accumulated by Delkin Acquisitions, a company started by his grandfather. Physically similar to Hudson, he was six feet tall with a muscular build. Their warm skin and black hair caused many to mistake them for brothers.

It was their eyes that set them apart. Where Hudson's were pools of black, Harper's were an ethereal gray she'd struggled to match artistically.

Elijah Eklund was his best friend, his bodyguard, and presumably his partner in the ménage lifestyle. Slightly taller than Harper, his build was lean and sculpted. Golden brown hair streaked with platinum blonde and pale green eyes made him a striking counterpart to the man with whom he spent most of his time.

Making her way into her studio, Brie unclipped the sketch she'd drawn of Harper and Elijah the night of the building commemoration from her easel.

While she spent the evening sitting in the chair she was unable to leave on her own, Natalia unveiled Hudson's gift from Gabriella. A large canvas of the building painted in oils. It was something she'd worked on before her accident. Her best friend had loved everything about it.

Throughout the evening, the two men stood side by side and watched her. For the most part, they didn't speak and they didn't mingle. They simply watched her.

Eventually, feeling self-conscious and more than a little off-balance, she'd removed her sketching supplies to capture the moment. When she returned home later that night, she took a long time to get the shade of the men's eyes just right.

It was a sketch her friends noticed but didn't question.

She'd gradually added to it over the past weeks, including splashes of color and giving it more substance.

Much like the drawing of Hudson and Natalia that she'd given her friends recently, the level of detail announced it to be a project she returned to often.

Brie hadn't examined why she didn't put it away too closely. Most of the sketches she did were stored or gifted to the subjects in them. Removing stationary from her desk, she set down the picture and quickly wrote a note.

Harper,

Thank you for the sculpture and the compliment.

I didn't make the connection that Harrison was your younger brother. I last saw him when he was barely a teenager. His work is truly remarkable.

Please accept a far simpler gift from me in thanks.

Brie

Before she could second-guess her decision, she sealed the envelope and placed both items in the pouch that hung on the side of her walker.

Stepping into her sneakers, she made her way to the first-floor business center. She could see the concern on Carlo's face when he realized she was alone.

"Good morning, Carlo. I'll be right back. Well, as *right back* as I can be."

He smiled and she cursed the amount of time it took her to traverse forty feet. Selecting a large padded envelope that would fit the sketch without bending, she printed Harper Delkin's name on the outside. Then she returned to the front desk to speak to the concierge.

"Can you help me find a mailing address?"

Taking the package, the young man's expression was confused as he read the name. "You don't need to *mail* this, Brie."

"I don't, what do you mean?"

"Mr. Delkin owns an apartment on the floor below Mr. Winters. He rarely uses it but as it happens…ah, here he is now."

Chapter One

Brie was acutely aware of two things as she faced Harper and Elijah. The first was that she was wearing yoga clothes that showed every inch of her body. The second was that the two men looked even *better* in daylight.

Elijah pushed his shades on top of his head, capturing the blonde strands. She registered that they were dressed semi-casually in jeans and button-down shirts with light jackets but she couldn't have described the details if pressed.

Struck speechless at their appearance coupled with the news that Harper owned an apartment in *her* building, she gripped the rails of her walker with white-knuckled hands.

They stopped within inches of her and neither hid the way their eyes tracked down her figure.

"Gabriella." Harper's eyes flicked to his name printed in neat, bold letters before finding hers again. "May I?"

Somehow, she managed to nod.

He reached past her and accepted the package from Carlo without a word. Tearing the tab, he shook the note into his hand first and read. His mouth lifted in a half smile before he removed her sketch.

When she looked back on the moment, she'd never forget the way he inhaled sharply before fixing her with an expression of pure hunger.

Elijah's eyes glanced at the sketch quickly and then returned for a longer examination with his lips slightly parted. His eyes landed on her and she was fascinated by the expression on his face.

Harper's voice drew her attention. "You drew this." It wasn't a question but she nodded. "I appear angry."

Breathing deeply, she replied, "I thought you were. I don't really *fit in* at such functions. I lack the...ability to blend in that most people in your sphere possess. I thought you were annoyed by my presence." She lifted one shoulder slightly. "I draw what I see."

He didn't blink. "You thought I felt you didn't *belong* at the event?"

"I wasn't sure what else it could be."

"Not *that*, I can fucking guarantee." He took a step closer and she looked up into his face. "You clearly belong wherever you decide to be." His focus was incredible and she couldn't look away. "I wasn't angry." There was a pause. "You exist in the same sphere as I, Gabriella."

The way he said her name reminded her of Hudson.

"We couldn't *be* more different."

"Perhaps we're alike in ways you've not yet discovered."

Elijah took the drawing from Harper's hand and let his eyes roam the details. "It's perfectly executed. This is outstanding."

"Thank you."

His gaze captured hers and, though he seemed the gentler of the two by nature, she felt a shiver of response climb her spine. "Is this what you were drawing the night of the party?"

"Yes. I often get distracted in such ways."

He didn't blink. "Are you so thorough with all of your work?"

"Not usually. No." Her legs were weakening and she *did not* want to show vulnerability to the friends. Gripping the walker tighter, she confessed through gritted teeth, "I can't, I need to sit down. I can only use the walker for short periods."

Carlo came around the counter. "Brie, can I call one of the girls to go up with you?"

"I'm fine. Thank you so much. Do *not* call the penthouse." She smiled at his guilty expression. Returning her attention to the two men, she asked, "Would you like coffee?"

Placing the sketch and note in the envelope, Harper handed it to Elijah. "Yes."

Then he stepped around the walker and gently lifted her into his arms. Startled, her arm went around his shoulders.

"You can't *carry* me."

"On the contrary." He said nothing else as he headed for the bank of elevators.

Elijah was a step behind him with her walker in hand. They selected her floor and made the trip in silence. She stared at the curve of Harper's hand beneath her knees and found herself enthralled by the strength apparent in it.

The bodyguard preceded them into the apartment. He leaned her walker against the wall and checked each room quickly as Harper placed her gently on her living room sofa.

She murmured, "Coffee…"

"Unnecessary. Rest a moment." He sat beside her, his gaze focused on her face. "What is the extent of your injuries, Gabriella?"

Elijah lowered himself to the coffee table in front of her.

"I was immobile for…quite some time. I'm building my strength back. I get better every day. Some…injuries will take longer to heal completely but I'll get there." She met Harper's eyes. "I think you know everything about me already."

"I do," he admitted. "I was curious if you'd exaggerate your condition. Clearly, you downplay it."

"I don't focus on the negative."

"Does it bother you that I had you checked out?"

After a long pause, she shook her head. "Hudson did the same. It's a necessary precaution I imagine all powerful men are required to exercise." Letting her mind return to their conversation downstairs, she thought about the night of Hudson's building commemoration.

"At the party, you thought I was a paid mistress or something similar."

"Your position confused me. Your painting as well." It was a lot for a man such as him to admit.

Elijah leaned forward. "There was obvious emotion in the painting you did for Winters."

Her smile was slow. "You're dancing around the question you really want to ask." Carefully adjusting herself on the couch, she cleared her throat.

"I had a brief sexual relationship with Hudson and Natalia. I don't regret it. When I was released from the hospital, I learned he'd deeded this apartment to me. He's my best friend and I love him. I'm not *in love* with him and feel intense happiness now that Natalia holds her true role in his life."

Harper's frown made her shake her head.

"I doubt you'll ever be able to understand our friendship. To be fair, it confuses most people. You've spent much of your adult lives in competition. I'm not part of your game nor would I *ever* give him up."

"You're brutally honest."

"It's a fault." She shrugged. "He changed everything about how I viewed the world, my place in it, and what I considered for my future. I don't take such things lightly."

"His brother…"

"Don't." She blinked back instant tears. "It was as horrific for him as it was for me. More, in fact. He takes protection of the people he cares about seriously. He loves rarely but fiercely. You may know Hudson, you may know everything about me on paper, but you have no idea how the entire situation affected both of us. I won't discuss it."

There was a quick knock a moment before her front door swung wide. She'd disengaged the auto-lock when she went to the lobby.

Hudson stood in the entry with Natalia's hand in his. They'd clearly just rolled out of bed. Brie was grateful they'd managed to put on clothes.

The blonde exclaimed, "Fuck if you weren't right." Her blue eyes were huge.

"I'd do the same." Hudson's voice was low and dangerous. "Point it away from my woman or I'll snap your fucking neck."

Turning her head, she realized Elijah held a wicked handgun pointed at the couple in the doorway. Brie hadn't heard him draw it nor had she seen him move.

"Put it away, please," she said softly. He immediately returned the gun to a holster beneath his jacket.

She gave her friends a careful smile. "You've checked, satisfied your curiosity, proven Hudson's gut should always be followed, and seen I'm fine. Go back to bed."

"Gabriella."

"Hudson." Her no-nonsense tone made him smile. "I'm *fine* and you know it. Don't get up until both of you have plenty of sleep. No less than eight solid hours."

"She's right. I'm exhausted, darling." She winked at Brie. "Perhaps finally go to bed yourself?"

Waving her hand, Brie said, "Ridiculous notion, sleep. Highly overrated. Go and we'll have dinner."

Hudson stared at both men for a long moment before tightening his hand around Natalia's. He engaged the auto-lock and the door clicked shut behind them.

Harper's expression was unreadable.

To Elijah, she said, "I-I understand your position but I've never been around guns. Perhaps we can find a compromise?"

"I'm proficient with knives and my bare hands as well." Elijah kept his gaze somewhere over Harper's shoulder.

He didn't look or sound proud of his skills. The line seemed rehearsed. His fists were clenched on top of his thighs.

Reaching out, she gently lifted one of them and turned it over. She brushed her fingers lightly over his until he opened them. His hand was strong, the fingers long and blunt at the tips.

She laid her smaller one on top. "What instrument do you play, Elijah?" His green eyes snapped to hers. "I noticed your callouses last night. One of the strings?"

Voice barely audible, he replied, "Violin."

"That's lovely. Music was hard for me. I was horrible but never lost my appreciation." She gave him a smile. "I imagine your hands are proficient in *many* beautiful things."

His fingers curled around her wrist, his thumb stroking the side. They stared at one another for a long time.

Finally, he exhaled the tension he'd gathered around him in the single instant a possible threat to his boss and friend invaded her space. "I'm sorry, Brie."

"You have nothing to apologize for, Elijah. Your job as your best friend's bodyguard must be stressful sometimes."

"Sometimes," he agreed. He applied gentle pressure and pulled her forward. Planting a kiss on her forehead, he said softly, "I like what makes you different. Thank you."

"You're welcome." Leaning back, she turned her attention to Harper. "Tell me what you want from me." His eyes went wide in surprise. "Allow me to state my position so there's no confusion." She stroked her fingers over Elijah's hand and returned it to his thigh, sad to lose the contact.

Inhaling deeply, she looked back and forth between the men. "I imagine you're confused, as Hudson once confessed to being, that I'm not interested in money or position. You look at someone like me and see the *perfect* submissive. I admit it's a role that seems to come naturally."

Both men stilled.

"You figure I'm a woman who will allow you to dictate terms, be waiting to fulfill your needs, and show proper gratitude for your attention."

Shaking her head slowly, she said, "It's important that you understand a few things about me. I don't need any man to take care of me financially."

"There's no such thing as too much money, Gabriella."

"There's such a thing as *enough*, Harper. I certainly have no interest in *your* money or assuming the position of your whore."

Elijah growled, "You'd *never* be such a thing."

"Isn't that more about state of mind, Gabriella?" The man was far more exasperating than Hudson was in the beginning.

"Since I only have *my* state of mind as reference, I wouldn't know." She inhaled carefully. "I've got *months* remaining of physical therapy."

She told Harper, "My personality will probably annoy you as often as it intrigues you. The notion of a ménage relationship doesn't offend me in any way, but my bones are still too weak to handle the…pressure I imagine would be involved." She was distracted by the intensity of Elijah's gaze for a moment.

"Jesus, you're blunt." Harper had the angry expression on his face again and she grinned.

"I am. I'd apologize but I wouldn't mean it." She reached out and smoothed her fingertip along the crinkle in his forehead, startling him. "You get frustrated easily. You should smile more, Harper."

He captured her hand. "Perhaps you could help me do that."

"Perhaps." She shook her head and tugged from his grasp. "Why are you interested in me? I doubt I remotely resemble your usual fare when it comes to women."

"Explain."

"I'd guess the women you typically choose are tall, slender, and docile. Much like Hudson's former lovers, they're almost universally grasping, greedy, and willing to fake emotion in exchange for *gifts*, preferably of the sparkly variety. You don't have any desire to talk to them nor do you give a single fuck about who they are as people.

They're permitted in your orbit for sex and discarded when you're done. Paid for services rendered and quickly forgotten."

"Damn." Elijah's single word told her she was right.

"Why invest your valuable time," she gestured at the whale, "and money in someone like me?"

"Winters."

"Tell me what you mean," she pressed.

"You changed him. You…liked him."

"I didn't change him. He's the same man he's always been. I didn't like him at first but I quickly saw the man he was behind his gruff exterior." Pausing, she asked, "Do you find yourself unlikeable?" He nodded. She looked at Elijah and back to him. "Elijah likes you."

"In the beginning, he had no choice."

"There's *always* a choice and I doubt his loyalty is easily earned." She felt the bodyguard staring at her and swallowed hard. "Hudson and Natalia speak highly of you."

"You respect their opinion." She nodded. He curled his fingers into a fist on his thigh. "I can't love you, Gabriella."

She let the words hang in the air without addressing them. She needed a moment to process a statement that made her inexplicably sad.

Elijah was clearly upset. He turned to look at her.

"Did you…argue about me this morning?" The blonde didn't answer but his eyes held incredible emotion. "Natalia mentioned you're Harper's oldest friend."

"Yes. Since he was born."

"You share a lot of history then. Something tells me you're not as tolerant about some of his choices as Natalia has been of Hudson's. After so many years, you *must* know he has no desire to love a woman or receive her love in return."

"You're different from most women."

Unsure how to interpret the statement, she looked at Harper. "Life is short. Every second counts in ways even I was unaware of before my accident. I don't want to waste mine."

"You value *love* so highly?" he asked her abruptly. The mere word held contempt when he said it.

"No. I value *myself* that highly. I don't judge you, Harper. I also don't judge my need to love and be loved."

"You deserve to have everything you need, Brie."

Elijah's words shook her foundation and she blinked back tears. Staring at her lap, she inhaled carefully. When she lifted her face, she gave Harper a smile. "I'm not complex. Your attempts to *unravel* me are an exercise in futility. There's no mystery, no ulterior motive, no desire to play hard to get."

Hating to ask, she turned to the bodyguard. With a heavy sigh, she whispered, "Will you please get my chair from my room?"

Elijah rose instantly and returned pushing the wheelchair she'd left beside her bed. Without a word, he lifted her and placed her carefully in it. He smoothed his hand over her head and she tried not to lean into the simple touch.

"Th-thank you."

Returning to his previous position, Elijah stared into her eyes for a long moment. "I *can* love you, Brie."

The words made her heart tremble. Harper visibly stiffened.

"I suspect you *could*, Elijah. You strike me as a man who loves deeply and quietly. You ask for nothing, expect nothing, and aren't surprised when that's exactly what you receive."

"It would be an honor to love you."

"*Elijah…*"

Every word he said managed to penetrate to the innermost part of her. It had her *completely* off-balance. Much longer in his presence and she'd likely throw herself into his arms.

"My existence already causes issues between you." They were *not* Hudson and Natalia, their relationship held a note of aggression she didn't know how to navigate. "You've presented yourselves as a package deal. I respect that but ultimately, it would hurt me to be loved by one and considered hired help by the other."

"Fuck." Harper growled the word.

"You've stated you'll be unable or unwilling to love me. That means I'd serve a specific purpose. A sexual conquest, perhaps a person to facilitate in ways Elijah is not permitted to do."

Looking at the bodyguard, she sighed. "Something tells me you enforce rigid distance publicly."

"You've spoken to Hudson about us."

Frowning in confusion, she shook her head. "He wouldn't share information about you nor would I ask. It's just a vibe you both give off that I can't quite define."

To herself, she murmured, "Employee, employer...? I don't know. Something." She shrugged. "I'm pretty observant."

"No one is *that* observant."

"I'd say no one could be so *arrogant*. We'd both be wrong."

Harper sat back and rested his chin on his thumb, his elbow on the arm of the sofa. One finger rubbed back and forth over his upper lip as he watched her.

She hoped she successfully hid the sexual effect it had on her.

It was important to choose her words carefully. These two men had her twisted up in all sorts of ways.

"I'm *not* incapable or unwilling to love. Time spent in your company would make me see the good, the beauty in both of you. It's in my nature, both a strength and a weakness. I'd become emotionally attached, accept it wasn't reciprocated, and end up with a broken heart."

Harper didn't get it. "Did Hudson break your heart?"

"I knew almost from *day one* that my role was meant to be a bridge between their past and their future. I guarded my heart and managed to keep it safe."

"That must have been hard for you," Elijah said.

"There were moments I worried. They're incredible, separately and together. Too much time receiving *everything* they offered would've tipped me past what I could resist. I was getting too close already. After my s-surgery, I knew I had to set a time limit. They respected my decision."

"How long?"

She didn't pretend to misunderstand the question. Green eyes held hers as she whispered, "One night."

"You spent *one night* with them, in every way?" Harper sounded as if he didn't believe it but she nodded. "They didn't attempt to talk you into more?"

Twisting her fingers together, she said softly, "The last pieces started falling together for them that night. The following morning, I was hit and spent a long time in the hospital. That's when they saw what they shared."

"You're all close. How was that accomplished in one night?" Harper frowned.

"We built friendships first. I gave them a fresh perspective. In exchange, they helped me reconcile the person I felt pressured to be with the woman I really was on the inside."

"The woman you *are* is beautiful, Brie," Elijah told her.

"That's good of you to say. I have days of doubt."

She pointed at the whale. "The sculpture makes me feel wonderful because when a whale is removed from its' home, it's vulnerable, helpless, an object of pity. In the water, the one element in which it can survive, it's a creature that's fierce, beautiful, and powerful."

Closing her eyes, she murmured, "All my life, I've been out of my element." Gray eyes waited for her when she opened hers. "During my brief time with them, I experienced *water* for the first time."

She gestured down her body. "I find myself on land again, a creature that's once again an object of pity."

"I don't pity you, Gabriella."

"You find me *weak* as most do whereas I see you clearly as one of the strongest and most brilliant men I've ever met, Harper."

Looking at Elijah, she added, "You're the one who confuses me. There's *something*, I don't know. It's just beyond my line of sight and I can't put my finger on it."

"Does it frighten you, Brie?"

"Not remotely. I'm pretty much mesmerized by it."

"I've *never* met a person so honest."

"My mother used to tell me I was so distracted I'd forget lies if I told them." She stared at the bodyguard, struggling to nail down what it was about him that escaped her. "I feel as if I'll figure it out and laugh at myself for not seeing it sooner."

"Perhaps your reaction won't be laughter."

"That's...intriguing." She pulled her gaze from him and gave the darker man a careful smile. "I can almost guarantee you don't need or want a woman like me in your life, Harper."

"Why?"

"You don't dislike me but you don't like me either. I'm more trouble than I'll be worth to you and it'll be a long time before I can even be considered as a sexual distraction."

Harper insisted, "You'd be more than a distraction."

After a long pause, she nodded. "I guess we'll see." He looked victorious so she clarified. "When I'm back on my feet, if you're still interested, I'll spend time in your company."

"Your terms?"

The question caused her to stiffen. "There are no *terms* on my side,

Harper. I'll guard my heart, help both of you in whatever ways I'm capable, and hopefully see you happy. Then our time will end and you can get back to your usual selection of vapid supermodels."

Backing up, she made her way to the door. "Thank you again for the whale, Harper. I very much wanted to have it."

The men rose and walked to stand in front of her.

Elijah lowered to his knees. "There's no supermodel who could compete with all you offer, Brie."

"That's sweet of you, Elijah."

"That's the *truth*." His hands reached up to cup her skull, his fingers lightly stroking her hair. "It's like silk." Staring into her eyes, he traced his thumbs over her brows. "Your eyes are *blue*. I just realized."

"You're a lovely human being, Elijah." She brushed her fingers along his jaw and she watched the green of his eyes darken. "I'm happy to be your friend without conditions."

"Will you be my friend as well, Gabriella?"

"You've *no desire* to be my friend, Harper." Though it was the truth, it hurt her to say it aloud. He also didn't deny it.

Elijah gathered her carefully in a hug and planted a kiss on the skin beneath her ear. Meeting Harper's eyes over his shoulder, she knew he saw the physical reaction it inspired.

Against her hair, he whispered, "I'll wait for you, Brie."

Such a simple thing to say that affected her deeply. Inhaling the scent of her hair, he pulled back and pressed a kiss on her lips. Then he stood, picked up the envelope holding the sketch from her foyer table, and left her apartment.

Harper stared at her. "You fascinate me."

"It'll pass."

"You make me hard."

"I doubt I'm unique in the ability."

Despite himself, he laughed. "Your mind is quick. I'm giving you six months."

"You make it sound like a stay of execution. I'll still be under medical care and unable…"

"Eight months." She shook her head. "Ten months and then you'll *agree* to an arrangement with Elijah and myself."

"Harper, *why* is this so important to you?"

"Do you *agree*, Gabriella?"

Exhaling slowly, she thought about giving the two men the same privileges to her body as Hudson and Natalia. A single image played across her mind that made her entire body heat in response. This time, she *knew* she couldn't hide it.

"*Agree*, Gabriella." His words were low, fierce.

Unable to deny her awakened nature, she nodded and replied softly, "Alright."

The expression of victory on his face made her smile. He bent, lifted her from the wheelchair, and supported her weight.

Shocked, she stared up into his face. "I…"

Then he kissed her and Brie knew instantly she'd made a horrible mistake. He'd leave her wrecked.

Issuing a soft gasp, his tongue stroked inside her mouth and coiled against her own. His lips moved over hers and she felt the pull deep in her chest toward a man who'd already insisted he wouldn't love her.

You're a foolish woman and you'll get exactly what you deserve.

She didn't know how long he kissed her and had no memory of lifting her hands to stroke through his hair. The instant her fingers met the silken strands, his hold around her tightened.

With one arm, he kept her secure. She felt the hand of the other pet from her hair to her ass. Squeezing once, he returned to deconstructing her with his lips and teeth and tongue.

Unwilling to question the warmth and physical contact her best friends had inspired her to crave, she pressed her body more firmly against his.

Harper's kiss made her wonder what else he could show her. She stopped the train of thought and broke the kiss.

Gray eyes that seemed darker with his passion stared into hers. "Ten months, Gabriella. Then *nothing* will stop me from discovering if the rest of you is as addictive."

Planting kisses along her jaw, he whispered at her ear, "Get better quickly. Let me know if there's anything you need."

Returning to her lips, he kissed her again roughly. With a final hug, he lowered her gently into her chair and held her face in his palms.

For a long time, they stared at one another in silence. "I understand Winters' protectiveness toward you."

"Okay." Her mind was in chaos.

"Rest, Gabriella." It was no less than an order.

Harper left and she caught a glimpse of Elijah in the hallway before the door closed and locked behind them.

To her empty apartment, she muttered, "Oh shit."

* * *

Elijah felt as if he'd stumbled from a dark cave into full sunlight. Brie was spectacular.

As Harper exited her apartment, he saw the shell-shocked expression on her face and knew he'd kissed her.

"She agreed to an arrangement when she's released from medical care," he said smugly as they stepped into the elevator.

Frowning, Elijah stared at him. "After all she said to us, you seek nothing more than *sex* from her?"

It made his blood boil.

"What *else* would I seek, Elijah?" He shook his head. "She makes you behave like a lovesick teenager." Their eyes met as he stilled.

"I…didn't mean that."

"Yes. You did." He faced forward. "I seek more than sex from Brie. You're fixated on keeping score with Winters."

"I want to know *why* he guards her so fiercely."

Once inside Harper's apartment, he answered, "It's because she's kind and giving. She set a chain of events in motion that made him see Natalia as he was meant to see her."

At the door to his room, he added, "He guards her because she doesn't guard *herself* and he knows the world is harsh and unforgiving of gentleness."

Alone, he removed the sketch Brie did and smiled.

There was no doubt he wanted her sexually, but she offered so much more.

Chapter Two

When Hudson entered her apartment several hours later, Brie sat staring at the sculpture.

"You're alright?" His tone told her he'd waited as long as he could to check on her.

She nodded but didn't meet his eyes. "Off balance but okay." Over the hours she'd been staring at the whale, she'd found so many lovely little details she hadn't noticed. "Hudson?"

"Yes, Brie?"

"I don't think I'm strong enough."

He lowered to the couch beside her and lifted her hand. "You were strong enough for me."

Meeting his eyes, she whispered, "You're just *different*. I know you don't believe it when I tell you but, you're gentle. Once I got past the sharp exterior, it was so easy to see. You'd *never* hurt me."

"I hurt you, Brie."

"Never intentionally, never to be mean."

For a long moment, he stared into her eyes. "You're afraid?"

"Terrified."

"Tell me why."

Swallowing hard, she said, "It would've been so easy for someone like me to fall in love with both of you, Hudson. I knew early not to get attached romantically. I was careful because I knew I *had* to be. No two people belong together like you and Natalia."

She closed her eyes. "I don't know why it seems harder *already* to maintain the same detachment in this. Harper seems to barely *like* me but Elijah, good lord."

"Darling, he's Hudson without *me*." Natalia closed the door quietly and walked across the room to sit on the coffee table. She held Brie's other hand. "Hudson is everything you need in your life and you admire him, *love him*, deeply."

She nodded. "It sounds bad, I know."

Her best friend's fiancée stroked her face. "Not even a little. You think I don't understand?"

"It's hard for *me* to understand. I don't know how *you* do."

"There have been times over the past twenty years, periods when Hudson was otherwise occupied, when I *felt* his draw, Gabriella." Shocked, she processed the information. "He's the *only* other man who ever could've tempted me."

Staring at Hudson, Brie realized the confession came as no surprise to him. His black eyes held hers resolutely.

Tilting her head, she considered before looking back at one of the smartest women she'd ever known.

Gathering her courage, she said, "I want my *own* Hudson."

"Naturally, darling. Who wouldn't?"

Frowning, she asked, "That...doesn't make me seem like an awful person?"

"You know *exactly* what you want. You allowed yourself to gain the knowledge that will keep you from settling for less than you deserve. You're well ahead of the majority of the female population." She winked. "I've always found Hudson to be an outstanding example of the male species. I never understood why he wasn't tackled in the street."

The imagery made Brie laugh. "He's so good with women. Can you imagine his conflicting reaction?" One side of his mouth lifted in a smile. "Hudson?"

"Yes, Gabriella?"

"You set the bar *really* high with all men. If he doesn't meet your level of awesome, I'm going to fuck him up."

Standing, Hudson bent to kiss the top of her head. "You're not the only one." Straightening, he announced, "You need to eat. We'll talk more at dinner."

* * *

An hour later, they were settled in a quiet corner of one of her favorite little bistros.

When their drinks were delivered, she murmured, "He kissed me." Glancing up, she inhaled carefully. "Harper kissed me."

Natalia sat back with a smile. "To be honest, I'd be surprised if he hadn't. You have incredible lips and he's not a man to allow such an opportunity to pass him by." Brie giggled nervously. "How did you feel after?"

"Like a demolition site."

"Hmm. That's promising." Folding her hands in her lap, Natalia asked carefully, "What about Elijah?"

"He's more *dangerous* but the gentler of the two men, I think. That doesn't seem exactly right but, I feel as if he's been instructed to *manage* me somehow."

Thinking back, she added, "Kind of like the way you soothed me after my first Christmas here in New York."

Glancing away from the table at a painting across the way, she let her mind play over her interaction with the two men. "Elijah said h-he'd *wait* for me. It made me feel amazing."

Hudson met her eyes. "He wants you badly."

She nodded. "Harper told me he couldn't love me."

"Such an unmitigated *ass*," Natalia murmured.

"Elijah admitted that he *could* and I believe him. I'm drawn to him in an almost agitated way. I can't figure out what it is." Frowning, she mused, "The love of one wouldn't be enough and it would cause a rift between them. I'm *sure* of it."

"Women have never received the love of either man. Perhaps they think to compromise." Natalia sipped her wine.

"I want it all. I think...there's *something*. It has to be both."

Her friends were quiet for a long moment. "Did you make your position clear, darling?"

"I thought I did but, then I didn't stick to it."

Natalia's eyes widened. "What *exactly* did you agree to?"

Taking a deep breath, she explained, "That I'd entertain a sexual relationship with them and guard my heart, as I did during my time with you."

"Oh, shit," Natalia breathed.

"Yeah, I realized the error after the kiss and everything. To be honest, if I'd gotten the kiss *first*, I probably wouldn't have had enough functioning brain cells to make a different choice."

Hudson leaned his arm on the table. "You *cannot* be a sexual arrangement for them, Gabriella. You lack the mercenary gene. Your heart will end up shredded."

"I thought I could remain distant, like I did before." She shrugged. "Then he kissed me and I knew I'd messed up."

Looking down at the table, she admitted, "I appear to have something of a weak spot for people who scare me a little bit."

Hudson laughed. "Gabriella." She looked up with a sigh. "It'll be alright. I'll make sure of it."

"You can't. The two of you are combative on good days. You have to let me stumble through this one on my own. Just, you know, don't be surprised at some of my questions or weird ramblings as I work some shit out."

"Do you have any questions right now?"

Something about the way Natalia asked made the hair stand up on the back of her neck.

"I can't ask you specifics. No matter how curious I am or how much I want to know, it wouldn't be right. All of you have history and I'm not going to fuck that up."

The server set her plate in front of her and Brie met Hudson's eyes. "I'd like to keep my excellent record."

"I suggest you see how it unfolds. You're stronger than you think, Gabriella."

"I hope so." Picking up her fork, she stabbed a piece of lobster ravioli. "Enough about me. Fill me in on *your* day."

"Hudson suspended me from the ceiling and whipped my ass."

She laughed so hard she almost choked. "Your day was *way* more interesting." Waving her hand, she said, "Continue."

"We bought dinnerware."

Stunned to complete silence, Brie stared back and forth between them. "Stop it. Seriously?"

"True story."

"Can I *see* it?"

Hudson stated, "You'll be our first dinner guest."

Taking a sip of her wine, Natalia winked. "It's so refreshing that talk of fine china gets more of a response than flogging. I can't explain how much I adore you for that."

Grinning, Brie quipped, "You get spanked on the daily but *dinnerware* is a once in a *lifetime* kind of thing."

For two hours, they talked and laughed together. Any evening in their company was time well spent.

When they escorted her home, she hugged them hard. "Thank you for dinner and always being honest with me." Hudson kissed her forehead and Natalia gave her a smacking kiss on the mouth. "See you tomorrow."

Only when the door closed behind them did she let her smile drop from her face.

Nights were always harder.

Chapter Three

It was close to midnight when someone knocked softly on Brie's door. Using her walker, she opened it, stunned to see Elijah on the other side. Harper was nowhere in sight.

"Are you okay?"

"What an interesting question. You're a kind person, Brie."

"Thank you." Her confusion grew.

"I thought if you were asleep, knocking quietly wouldn't wake you. I'm always up late. I don't sleep much. I thought I'd play for you." He held out the violin case he'd partially concealed behind his body.

A huge smile broke over her face. "I'd *love* that. Please come in." She led the way to her kitchen and he closed her door. "Did you eat?"

"Earlier."

"Are you hungry?"

He frowned. "Isn't that the same question?"

Stopping, she turned to look at him. "No, Elijah. Just because you ate earlier doesn't mean you might not be hungry *now*. I've got tamales I made yesterday and apple bread."

The way he seemed to ponder her words told her much about how he'd been raised without him saying anything about it.

"Have a seat. I'll make coffee and heat you a little snack."

Walking to one of the barstools, he placed his violin on the counter and sat. He watched her as she placed the walker where she could get it and used the counter for balance.

"I'm happy to help you."

"I'm okay. Sometimes, I'm afraid not to have the walker when I'm in the apartment alone." She gave him a bright smile. "With you here, I'm more confident."

"I'd never allow you to be hurt."

Brie didn't answer as she made him a plate. When it was hot, she put it in front of him and started coffee.

"Are you tired?" he asked.

"Rarely. I feel like I sleep all the time. It makes me angry."

"Why?" He took a bite of the tamales and closed his eyes. "These are delicious." His smile was careful. "I didn't know I was hungry."

"I cook all the time. I always have leftovers."

"Why does sleeping make you angry?"

"I was active before the accident. I walked everywhere. I got a good night's sleep but I accomplished a lot during the day." She shrugged. "I don't feel as if I really *do* anything. Being tired feels ridiculous."

"You're healing. It's okay to be tired."

Smiling, she replied, "I'll try not to be so hard on myself."

He nodded and she watched him eat with her chin in her hand. He had the best manners of any man she'd ever seen. He ate rapidly but without a single wasted movement.

When he was done, he walked to the sink and washed his dish and fork. "Thank you."

"You're welcome."

"Things that seem small to you are big to others."

"I guess that's true sometimes. I feel that way about things my friends do for me."

"Hudson and Natalia?"

"Yes, and my other friends." She turned and poured herself a cup of coffee, adding sugar and cream. Taking down another cup, she asked, "How do you take your coffee?"

"May I taste yours?" Surprised, she held out her cup. He took a sip and she saw the pleasure on his face. "I'd like it that way."

"How do you normally drink it?"

"Black."

Such a small piece of information that spoke volumes.

"Would you mind taking our coffee to the living room? It's hard with the walker."

He quickly placed them on her coffee table and returned for his violin. He stayed with her as she made her way to the sofa.

"You have many friends."

"I do now. I'm grateful so I try to be a good one. I feel kind of inoperable right now, not good for much."

"I'm certain time in your presence is sufficient to make your friends feel glad to call you one."

"What a *lovely* thing to say. Thank you."

She lowered to the sofa and he sat beside her. "What did you do after we left, Brie?"

"I sketched, did some thinking, and then went to dinner with Hudson and Natalia."

"Did you talk about us?"

"Yes." She inhaled carefully and admitted, "I explained how much I truly liked you but told them I was nervous." After a small pause, she added, "Hudson said to go with it."

"I respect him more than most."

"I respect you for saying that, Elijah." She reached out and took his hand. He gripped her back firmly and her mind wandered. "I'm not sure I'm the right choice."

"I think you're the perfect choice."

"Why?

"A couple of years ago, my cousin Eira talked about you when she returned to school after her summer internship. She suggested I ask you to dinner. I didn't make the connection when I heard your full name. She always called you Brie." She nodded. "Would you have said yes if I asked you to dinner?"

"Honestly, I don't know. I was self-conscious." He tilted his head. "I looked...different then, Elijah. I felt bad about myself. I still do but the reasons are different now."

He stood up and removed his t-shirt. Her eyes widened at the scars all over him but she was amazed at the unbelievable fitness level of his body.

"Do my scars bother you?" She shook her head and he turned to show her his back. "Mine are very old."

Reaching out, she placed her palm flat on his skin. His back was covered in overlapping marks that she recognized from her night spent with her best friends. Hudson had barely reddened her skin.

The lashes delivered to Elijah had broken skin repeatedly.

She couldn't imagine the pain he'd been in and didn't realize she was crying until he knelt at her feet.

"Don't cry, Brie. It was a long time ago."

Pulling him close, she wrapped him in a hug. He was careful about how hard he hugged her back.

"I hate that someone put you through such pain. I hate it."

"I showed you because you shouldn't be self-conscious about your body, Brie. You're beautiful."

His skin was warm and she rested her cheek on his shoulder, happy when he rested his large palm on the back of her head. Taking her with him, he continued to hug her as he sat on the couch and settled her on his lap.

Sitting back, Elijah held her firmly. "I imagine a gentle person like you needs regular hugs. Do you get lonely?"

"More than I like to admit."

"Me, too. Let's stay like this and be less lonely together."

The words made her tighten her arms. He kissed the top of her head and she listened to the slow beat of his heart.

It lulled her to sleep.

* * *

Opening her eyes to sunlight, Brie was immediately confused. She was in her bed, covered in her blanket, the walker nearby.

She wondered if she dreamed Elijah's visit but then noticed a piece of paper on her bedside table.

Thank you, Brie. I'll play for you next time. E

To the quiet room, she murmured, "It's your innocent heart that will trap me in the end."

Chapter Four

Elijah stood at the window while Harper poured himself coffee. He thought about the taste of Brie's and smiled.

"She's a good person, Harper."

"I realize. I'm not an ogre."

Turning, Elijah placed his hands on the back of one of the dining chairs. "The night of the building commemoration, I didn't recognize her name. She stayed in the background at the winery. I only ever heard her referred to as Brie."

"She looks nothing like she did when I glimpsed her several years ago." Harper shrugged. "Isabella attended public events with her parents. Gabriella did not."

"She was embarrassed. Shy but, something else." Gripping the heavy wood, he added, "She's *still* embarrassed." He didn't look away from gray eyes that knew him well.

"You talked to her."

"I couldn't sleep."

Harper walked out of the kitchen and paused in front of him. "You went to *see* her." Elijah didn't respond. "Tell me."

"She fed me tamales and let me taste her coffee." A frown formed between his oldest friend's eyes. "I showed her my scars."

"Why?"

"She told me she was self-conscious for different reasons than she used to be. I assumed it was the accident." He shrugged. "She could have *no* scars worse than mine. I wanted to put her at ease."

Turning back to the window, he crossed his arms at his back. "When I followed them from the party, I realized she hadn't left the chair because she *couldn't* on her own. Unable to walk, she didn't want her wheelchair or walker beside her."

"Vanity perhaps."

"No. She wanted to pretend for one night that she was better. The exhaustion took her earlier than expected." He inhaled carefully. "She begged Hudson to send her home and return to his celebration. He refused as did Natalia." More to himself, he murmured, "She's desperate to be well again."

"Elijah." He met silver eyes. "Do you *love* her?"

"I've never loved a woman. I'm unsure." Facing the window again, he wondered. "I meant to play for her but then she cried for me, hugged me, when she saw my scars."

"Gabriella *cried* for you?"

He nodded. "I hugged her back and held her until she went to sleep. I made sure she was safely in her bed and locked the door before I returned here."

There was a long silence. "You'd *play* for her?" Elijah nodded again. "You've *never* played for a woman." The silence drew out between them and he didn't fill it. "You *love* her."

"In the past two months, I've learned everything there is to know about Brie. What I discovered surprised me, pleased me. It didn't prepare me for interacting with her face to face." He turned fully to face Harper. "I love her. You'll love her."

"I *refuse*, Elijah."

"Then you're a fool."

Elijah walked around him to pick up his jacket. Harper grabbed his upper arm roughly when they were side by side.

It was a move they both recognized as dangerous.

They stared at one another with *decades* of history, shared experiences, and loss between them.

Harper hissed, "She's just a *woman*."

"You don't know what you're talking about. Brie has the capacity to save us, we have the capacity to destroy her. I crave the former, I'll protect her as well as I can from the latter." He pulled his arm free. "Ready when you are."

Whipping his jacket off the chair, he shrugged it over his shoulder holster. At the front door, he waited at attention for his boss to approach. As Harper stood in front of him, he kept his gaze slightly over his shoulder as he'd been trained.

"Elijah…"

"You'll be late for your first meeting if we don't leave now."

He opened the door of the apartment and led the man he'd always sworn to protect through it. He cleared the elevator, the lobby, the sidewalk, and nodded to the driver who was as well-armed, if not as well-trained, as Harper Delkin's longtime head of security.

When they were inside the limo, Harper tried to return the conversation to Brie. He shut it down.

"We're outside the confines of secure space. You have several meetings today; in locations I've never cleared. Place your additional commentary about Gabriella on hold until we're once again in secure space. I have a job to do."

"We're not done. Know that, Elijah."

* * *

Harper stared at the man he knew as well as he knew himself.

In all the years they'd known one another, all the women they'd shared between them, Elijah hadn't loved any of them.

He involved himself physically but never emotionally.

Looking back, he wondered if he'd joined Harper in ménage pursuits out of loyalty, duty, rather than independent will.

Gabriella Hernandez was the first woman to affect him. She made Elijah think differently. She had him rattled, twisted up inside, and acting out of character.

Harper didn't like it.

Elijah was careful to keep his gaze averted, in full bodyguard mode as they crossed Manhattan for meetings that would consume the entire day.

For now, Harper allowed him the distance he required to do a job he'd never truly enjoyed, despite being the most highly trained and dangerous man in the world.

It was impossible to shake him when he was like this but in the end, Elijah would share his every thought to help convince him of Gabriella's worth to their lives.

Harper admitted his curiosity about Winters' former paramour and his lust to experience what she had to offer.

Other than that, he *refused* to allow her under his skin.

Chapter Five

Beginning October 2014

More than a week after Elijah's visit, he returned. He wore track pants, a t-shirt, and running shoes.

In his hand was his violin case.

It was only when she heard his soft knock on the door that Brie realized she'd been waiting, hoping for it. Seeing him on the other side of the threshold made her smile happily.

"Hi."

"Hello, Brie. How are you?"

"Good. Come in." When he closed the door behind him, she led the way slowly to her kitchen. "I bet you're hungry."

"How do you know?"

Winking, she quipped, "You're *male*. Have a seat."

He watched her in silence for almost a minute. "You're in pain. You're moving more slowly today."

"I started the next level of physical therapy. I'll be fine."

Walking around the bar, he lifted her in his arms and placed her on the padded stool. "Tell me what to do."

Unsure how to react, she told him to make a plate of seafood lasagna she'd prepared the day before for Riya and Tawny.

"You're not allergic to seafood, are you?"

"I have no allergies."

The way Elijah stated it made her think that if he'd discovered he had an allergy, he'd have found a way to crush the weakness.

Removing the warm plate, he joined her at the bar. She watched him eat and smiled at his obvious enjoyment. He quickly ate every bite and wiped the corners of his mouth.

"You're an incredible cook."

"Thank you, Elijah." Moving to get off the stool, she said, "I'll get us some coffee."

Lightly, he tugged her back. "Tell me how."

Nodding, she watched him wash what he'd used and follow her instructions exactly for coffee the way she liked it. Sitting beside her again, he smiled as she took a sip and sighed.

"What have you been doing since I saw you?" she asked with her chin in her hand. "Anything interesting?"

"Meetings. A lot of meetings."

"Do they bore you? I was barely able to stay awake during my business classes in college." Chuckling, she added, "I'm shocked I received my degree actually."

"I didn't go to college."

"You might not have a *degree* but I bet you attended every class with Harper. Am I right?"

"How did you know?"

"You've overseen his protection for what seems like most of your life."

"I was groomed for the task from birth. I'm almost two years older. Upon news that he'd be born to Hunter and Hope, my true training began."

Brie inhaled. After a long silence, she reached out to hold his hand. He'd subconsciously tightened it into a fist as he talked. Opening his palm, he clasped her back hard.

"I met Hunter and Hope when I was a teenager." She was cautious about her wording. "Did they know about your training?"

He shook his head once sharply. "Only my father. He presented me to the Delkins upon my eighth birthday with a promise to continue my training."

"Presented you?"

"Gave me to them to protect Harper when he started school."

Oh god.

Frowning, she struggled to wrap her mind around what he was saying. "Elijah, did *they* understand why you were with them?"

He turned his face and she stared into beautiful light green eyes that she imagined had experienced more pain in more awful variations than anyone she'd ever met.

"No. They believed they were fostering me. A task they were happy to assume to ensure I received the best education."

"But, you knew you were there for one purpose?" He nodded. "I can't pretend to understand. To hear these things makes me hurt badly for you."

"I won't speak of it."

"That's not what I want. I want you to feel comfortable talking to me. Maybe it'll help you heal from that time in your life. Nothing you tell me will *ever* go beyond us."

"What about your friends?" It wasn't an accusation. He seemed genuinely curious.

She shook her head. "No. Hudson and Natalia know not to share any details about anything with me and they understand my need to keep things private. There's too much history. It wouldn't be right." Shrugging, she added, "I've got to kind of stumble through on my own."

Elijah stood and wrapped his arms around her. She hugged him back and loved the clean male scent of him.

"If I admit the need to heal, I acknowledge my weakness."

"No," she told him softly, "you just let it happen. There's nothing *weak* about you. Even the toughest people experience pain and trauma. No matter what happened, you made it to this moment as a man who's strong, beautiful, and kind. You could've turned cold or uncaring. You didn't. You won."

Leaning back, his eyes roamed over her face. A strong hand lifted and stroked through her hair. He seemed fascinated by the texture, rubbing a thick strand between his fingers.

"Could you love me, do you think?"

"Yes, too easily," she confessed without thought.

"You're honest without pause. It places you at a distinct disadvantage." She shrugged. "Could you love Harper?"

"That's a harder question to answer."

"Why?"

"I'm drawn to you for reasons I can't define yet. I'm attracted to Harper but he clearly has no interest in more than a sexual relationship and that will probably carve out my insides."

"Is your attraction due to his similarities to Hudson?"

Brie paused with a frown. "No, though I admit it was interesting to me initially. Kind of fascinating. He's similar in looks and mannerisms but different in ways I don't fully understand. The *differences* entice me, even though it'll be those that hurt me in the end. Both of you are enigmas."

"You're more astute than even I realized." The silence drew out between them. "You offer us the possibility of love that asks for nothing in return."

"Love should be given freely, without condition."

"I'd like to feel what that's like, Brie." She didn't know how to answer. "I'll protect you."

Inhaling deeply, she gave him a small smile. "You won't be able to, Elijah. No matter how capable you are in the physical world, the emotional element is outside your comfort zone."

She watched him consider her words. There was no doubt in her mind that much of what she said confused him.

"You possess strong emotions."

"All my life, yes."

"You've been hurt." All she could do was stare at him. "I promise to be careful with you. I'll try to temper Harper."

Smiling, she replied, "You're only responsible for *yourself*. Harper made his interest clear. I proceed at my own risk."

He stroked his fingers from her temple to her jaw and her eyes drifted shut. She *craved* his warmth.

"You're tactile like a cat. I like that about you."

She needed a moment to think without looking into the eyes of a man who inspired powerful emotions already. Since his first visit, she'd lain awake nights hoping he'd return.

When his lips touched hers, she gasped softly. One hand wrapped around her as the other cupped her face.

Elijah's kiss was unlike *anything* she'd ever experienced. It was a play to both sides of her nature.

It called to the softness inside her that wanted to *give* love and *receive* love more than anything else. She also understood that he was a man capable of snapping her neck. He *wouldn't* but his ability to do so was strangely stimulating.

His focus was *incredible*. The way his mouth worked over hers made her want it absolutely everywhere.

Lifting away slightly, he whispered, "You're an unknown to me, Brie. I *want* to know you."

Deep inside, her heart tripped, felt as if it stopped, and then resumed beating. As it did, it felt fuller.

There was a *new inhabitant* as he returned to kissing her.

Pressing her palm to her chest caused him to break the kiss. He stared at her hand for a long moment before raising his eyes to hers. She didn't realize she was crying until he stroked a tear away with the pad of his thumb. The smile he gave her lit up his face, his eyes, his entire *being*.

Brie was *stunned* by it.

Without a word, he gathered her carefully in his arms and carried her to the living room. Placing her on the couch, he knelt at her side and reclaimed her mouth.

She wanted to climb inside his body with him.

The strength of her emotions regarding him seemed irrational but her heart was on its' own timeline.

Resting his forehead against hers, he gently massaged the back of her neck. He whispered, "I want to play for you."

Holding his wrists, she nodded but couldn't speak. He walked to the kitchen and returned with his case, setting it on the coffee table and removing his violin.

Then Elijah Eklund, a bodyguard known to many as the most dangerous man in the world, began to play.

Within ten seconds, Brie felt as if she was in a trance.

Based on references to his childhood, she knew without asking that he'd never received lessons. Like all child prodigies, he'd probably picked up someone else's violin one day and the instrument showed him what to do.

The notes flowed over her and Elijah clearly *loved* the way the music made him feel. As he played, his entire body relaxed.

It wasn't until she was forced to inhale that she realized she'd been holding her breath. The first song drifted away and he lowered the violin to stare at her.

"I-I've never heard *anything* so beautiful, Elijah." Her words were barely audible. "Please don't stop yet."

Bending, he brushed his knuckles along her cheek and kissed her forehead. "You like it."

Pulling him closer, she hugged his neck tightly. "More than I can explain. Your playing fills me with hope."

He planted a kiss on her neck and murmured, "Your heart is racing." She nodded against him. "I'm glad you like it."

Kissing his way along her jaw, he claimed her mouth and she was breathless from everything about him. He put the instrument down long enough to retrieve a blanket from her bedroom.

"I want you to be comfortable, Brie."

"It soothes me," she told him as he encouraged her to recline and covered her with the cashmere throw. "I don't want to fall asleep. I don't want to miss a single note."

Positioning the violin on his shoulder, he gifted her with another brilliant smile. "You should rest. I'm honored to help you do that. Hope is a good emotion to carry you to sleep."

One song to the next, Elijah played. Every note settled him deeper in a heart that had been painfully lonely.

She watched him, listened to him, opened herself to loving him, and didn't realize when she slipped into deep sleep.

* * *

After carrying a sleeping Brie to her bed and leaving her another note, Elijah turned off the lights, folded the blanket he'd covered her with, and ensured the auto-lock was engaged.

Pulling the door closed, he met Harper's eyes. He leaned against the outer wall of her apartment.

"She sleeps?" Elijah nodded. "This will break you if you allow her too close."

"I want her *closer*. I believe she already loves me."

Frowning, his lifelong friend said, "Impossible."

"Only you'd suggest such a thing about her."

Straightening from the wall, Harper faced him. "She'll poison you against me, Elijah."

Stepping closer to the man he'd willingly give his life to protect, he whispered, "She fears what you represent to her heart but will knowingly sacrifice her wellbeing for your needs. She wants you despite understanding that you seek nothing more than sex from her. I think she senses your dislike."

"I don't dislike her."

"You went to such *lengths* to secure her yet have nothing positive to say about her." Inhaling deeply, he handed Harper his violin case. "It's *you* who'll break *her*. It's *your* fear that will poison what she could mean to us. You'll not lay those sins at her door."

Walking to the stairwell, Elijah descended to the lobby and went for a run.

Chapter Six

Brie's Birthday – End October 2014

When Marciella Canfield left *Trois* with Fahad and Nuri Ghonim, Brie smiled at Hudson. "I like her *very* much."

"She'll benefit from your friendship." He kissed the back of her hand. "I do."

"You slay me."

He winked. "How are you?"

She knew what he asked and censored her answer. "I haven't seen either of them in two weeks. Natalia let it slip they were traveling." She laughed. "I'm not privy to schedules."

"How are *you*, Gabriella?"

"Hopeful." She tightened her fingers around his. "He plays the violin, Hudson."

Eyes wide, her best friend asked, "Elijah?" She grinned. "What an interesting gift for one such as him." He stared at her intently. "You love him?" Biting her lower lip, she gave a shy nod and he smiled broadly. "That explains why you're glowing more than usual. I try not to pry."

"Since *when*?" She lifted a brow and he chuckled.

Just then, Natalia appeared and she looked *rattled*. "Brie. It's getting late. You should let me take you home."

Frowning, she started to reply when movement on the floor above caught her eye.

Harper escorted a stunningly beautiful woman along the balcony to a corner seating area. She was barely dressed so her flawless skin was clear to see from thirty feet away.

When she sat, the dark man joined her and spoke to the server who approached. Elijah took up a position at one side staring into the distance.

Though his face was blank, Brie could *see* the tension around him. She watched him for almost a minute before he gave a slight frown and let his eyes track the room.

He found her gaze on the floor below. He unfolded his hands as if to make his way to her side. She shook her head.

Turning to Natalia, she murmured, "I really *am* rather tired."

Quickly saying goodbye to her friends and deflecting Tawny's always perceptive questions, she allowed Natalia to push her chair through the club.

At the entrance, Stav lifted her carefully and deposited her in Hudson's car. Her best friends slid in on either side of her.

Before they could attempt to reassure her, she whispered, "Don't say anything. Not tonight." She couldn't meet their gazes and couldn't control her hurt. "I'll *never* fit. I don't possess the necessary emotional detachment."

They escorted her home and when she was changed into comfortable clothes, she saw them to the door.

"Thank you for a beautiful birthday. You make everything amazing. Go back to the club and make up an excuse that Riya and Tawny will believe."

"Darling…"

"I can't discuss it right now. I love you both so much but I need to be alone."

"Gabriella." She fought and won the battle to meet Hudson's black eyes. "I'm taking you to breakfast."

"Stop trying to feed me all the time."

He hugged her tightly and she looked at Natalia for help. She didn't know how long she could keep her composure.

"Goodnight and happy birthday, darling. I'll call you."

Wrapping her arm through Hudson's, Natalia pulled him into the hall and Brie closed the door behind them.

Only then could she release the tears of hurt, confusion, and frustration she'd kept tightly restrained while in the presence of a man who seemed to be a mind reader when it came to her.

* * *

Brie should've expected the light knock an hour later but somehow didn't. There was no way to hide she'd been crying.

Opening the door to Elijah, she watched his expression change from one of worry to one of pain.

"I'm sorry. I'm so sorry, Brie."

Tiredly, she shook her head. "It doesn't matter."

"It matters."

"Not enough. Why are you here?"

There was a long pause. "He does what he can to keep you in a box." He shook his head. "I refuse to acknowledge the box. It makes him angry."

Brie tried to understand what he meant.

"He lashes out in a way he knows will hurt you to make me follow the rules. Let me come in, Brie."

Stepping back, she gestured him inside. When the door clicked shut, Elijah lifted her into his arms and walked to her couch. Sitting there with her on his lap, he hugged her tightly. They remained silent for several minutes.

"You need affection." The words confused her and she sat up to stare into his eyes. "You're still healing. This is a challenging time for you and I want you to have peace."

"What are you suggesting?"

"Give back as good as you've gotten, Brie. Take the offense rather than defense."

She let the statement play through her mind. "Like a fling?" He nodded. "Wouldn't that *hurt* you?"

His fingers clenched in her hair. "You worry about *me* when *your* heart suffers." He wrapped his arms more snugly around her. "Brie."

"I don't want you in the crossfire, Elijah. You've done nothing wrong and it isn't right." The thought of hurting him made her physically ache.

"Seek the comfort you need while you fight through your rehabilitation." He smoothed his hand over her skull to cup her neck. "You won't hurt me by taking what you need."

"I'm jumbled."

He took several deep breaths. "I'm caught between my history and what could be my future. It's a position that causes conflict on many fronts."

"I make it worse." She watched him consider his answer.

"I'd rather be the person who comforts you, Brie. I can't be that person right now. Despite my own situation, I sense what you need and there's no shame in it. Affection and touch will help you heal faster and protect your gentle emotions."

"I didn't expect you to suggest something like this."

He stroked a strong hand down her back. "I know Harper well. Seeing you change direction will shake his foundation."

"I don't like to play games, Elijah."

"It isn't a game. If you become involved and commit your heart, it's *our* loss, Brie. I *want* you for myself. I can't *take* you for myself. My hands are tied in ways I can't explain."

Swallowing hard, she knew she had to let go of the possibilities with Elijah until she was physically stronger. Handling Harper at her best would present enough of a challenge. There was *no way* to win in her current condition.

"The thing is, it's not likely to happen anyway."

"Why do you think that?"

Lifting one shoulder, she whispered, "Even if I *wanted* to find something like that, I'm no use to anyone. I…" She dissolved into tears and covered her face.

"Brie. *No, Brie.*"

For several minutes, she sobbed brokenly in the arms of a man who bore it differently than any other person in her life. He held her hard and let her cry until she was raw.

She was ashamed that she'd hoped to have *him* as her primary companion while she healed. Even though he had better things to do than babysit a woman in rehab, Elijah was wonderful company and she already loved him.

His relationship with Harper forbid her to ask or expect it of him. She wouldn't put him in such an awkward position but…

Letting him go *hurt*.

Chapter Seven

Harper stood in his kitchen wearing the sleep pants he'd pulled on after his shower.

He was pouring a glass of wine for his *date* when Elijah entered and slammed the front door hard enough to elicit a scream from the woman wearing nothing but her panties.

His bodyguard looked at her and said through gritted teeth, "Get dressed and get out."

Shocked, Harper shouted, "Elijah!"

The look his friend turned on him caused a shiver of fear to skate up his spine. Only an *idiot* wouldn't fear the man when he was in a rage.

Harper was well aware that he was armed at four locations on his body. None of the weapons were as deadly as his hands.

To the female whose name had slipped his mind, he said, "There's a threat. Dress and my driver will take you home."

"A threat?" She put her shoulders back to exhibit her fake tits and widened her eyes like a baby deer. "Oh, *no*. I want to stay with you. I don't know *what* I'd do if anything happened to *you*, Harper."

Her words were said breathlessly, at an unnecessary pitch, and it was so fucking familiar that he hated himself for a moment.

"Dress and my driver will take you home." She started to speak again and he couldn't bear it. "*Now.*"

While she scurried into his bedroom to find her clothes, Harper stayed where he was and maintained eye contact with his best friend.

Elijah opened the door when she reappeared and the instant she cleared it, he slammed it behind her.

"What the fuck is *wrong* with you?"

Crossing the room, the bodyguard stopped a foot from him. He wore the same clothes he'd been wearing when he escorted him and the woman to the door of the apartment and walked away without a word two hours before. Already an inch taller, being barefoot in front of him made Harper feel vulnerable.

He didn't appreciate it one fucking bit.

"Give me a few minutes and we can talk about your tantrum." Keeping his tone flip, he said the sentence he should've held back. "This one had a lot of energy and you missed out by spending time with your pet *rabbit*."

Faster than the eye could track, Elijah wrapped his large hand around Harper's throat. "Ever refer to Brie with such blatant disrespect again and I *will* hurt you."

"*Jesus…*" In forty years, Elijah had never threatened to hurt him. It was Gabriella's influence.

"Not even *he* would save you, Harper." He tightened his fingers slightly and released him. "I gave her up to protect her so *fuck you* and your energetic whore. Send her a bigger bracelet in compensation."

"She's just a *woman*."

"You have no clue how wrong you are and on the day you learn, I hope the emotional pain is *immense*. Perhaps then you'll learn some fucking humanity. I'm unsure when you lost it."

"Elijah…"

"Your capacity for cruelty toward a gentle human being sickens me, Harper. Did you purposely *slice at her* on her birthday, in front of all her *friends*, or was that a fucking *bonus*?"

It wasn't cruel to establish boundaries.

"Elijah…"

"Don't try to fucking *speak* to me when I have the salt from Brie's tears on my goddamn *shirt*." He backed from the kitchen, his body vibrating with fury.

Then he turned and walked to his own room, slamming a door for the third time in less than five minutes.

Harper had *never* heard him slam a door in his life. He lifted a shaking hand and raked it through his hair.

She had a far stronger hold on Elijah than he'd realized.

* * *

When Brie opened her eyes, again placed carefully in her bed by Elijah, she reflected on the fact that she'd grown weak.

Physically incapacitated for the first time in her life, she'd allowed her injuries and recovery to sap her confidence, her hope, and her positive nature.

To her reflection, she said firmly, "Snap out of it. Today."

Using a cream to bring down the swelling around her eyes, she dressed carefully. She needed all the armor she could muster when Hudson arrived. The man saw everything.

Considering she hadn't been much of a crier before the day she landed in New York, she cried far too frequently these days.

The trait disgusted her.

After she dressed, she picked up the cane and did a few test laps in her bedroom. Slow but doable.

Making her way to the kitchen, she started the coffee pot and stared at nothing.

Harper had deliberately shown up at *Trois* with a spectacular woman on his arm to hurt her for spending time with Elijah.

The question was, *why?*

To do such a thing meant he *knew* it would affect her. He was aware she was unguarded where he and Elijah were concerned.

Frowning, she said aloud, "What a douche move."

The man wanted her but only on his terms. Sex *only*. None of that messy *emotion* she was known to have.

His display the night before was the equivalent of a sharp slap to show her who was in control. A hateful reminder that while Elijah might have told her he'd wait, Harper had no intention of putting his life on hold for someone like her.

The more she thought about it, the angrier she got. When Hudson tapped on her door, she made her way to it, and threw it wide.

His eyes widened. "Are you alright?"

"I'm fucking *angry*."

"You're using a cane."

"I'm done looking like an old woman. It takes a little more time but the upside is I can use it as a weapon to beat the fuck out of emotionally stunted people." She returned to the kitchen.

He closed her door and followed. "Gabriella…"

"No. I'm sick of being *sweet little Brie*. Sick of it. I'm going to do something crazy and not feel the least bit bad about it."

"Does this involve eggs or spray paint?"

Turning to him, she lifted a brow. "Would you talk me out of it if it did?"

"No. However, I'd enlist Tawny's assistance to keep you from getting caught. She loves mayhem."

The *fury* evaporated from her but the desire to fight didn't and she laughed. "I don't know how she stays out of jail."

His expression was gentle. "What can I do?"

"Hudson…I want to be like you."

"In what way?"

"Less…*me*. More you."

"Gabriella, you're perfect."

"I'm too soft. Things make me cry when they should make me flip people off." She growled. "I *hate* crying."

"You've had reason to cry."

"I'm *weak*, Hudson."

"You're *gentle*, Gabriella. There's a difference."

Lifting her eyes, she told him, "Elijah came here after you and Natalia left last night."

She watched him carefully control his expression. Then she explained their conversation and he was unable to hide his shock.

"Elijah told you to seek comfort elsewhere?"

Nodding, she whispered, "What do you think?"

"One, you're standing perfectly upright with that cane and seem steady on your feet. You'll be back on your own steam in no time." The observation made her grin. "Two, I agree."

"You think an affair is a wise choice?"

"You must consider it. You cry because your heart hurts and you're lonely. I don't want you to be lonely. I hate it."

"I-I wouldn't know where to look for…casual." She shrugged. "It's never been my thing and I'm limited. You know?"

"Avoid anyone involved in the lifestyle until you heal. Someone new may neglect to consider your injuries." He mused, "I know attractive young men who are biddable. They work for me."

The suggestion made her laugh. "No matter how much I love you, gonna have to reject your offer to pimp out some nerdy hotties at your company."

He snickered and it made her feel a lot better. "Guard your heart a bit longer, Gabriella."

"Agreed. The fucking thing *clearly* has performance issues." Exhaling roughly, she added, "Losing Elijah is painful, Hudson. I love him. I don't want him to suffer."

Warm hands cupped her shoulders. "Trust him. He wants you and he'll *find* a way to have what he wants. It's the way of such men. For now, focus on you and let Delkin twist."

Smiling slowly, she nodded. "For once, I'm starving."

"Excellent. Feeding you and Natalia particularly pleases me."

"Lord, why?"

"As a boy, food was too often a luxury. Feeding the people I care about always reminds me how far I've come."

"You're awesome. Just fucking awesome." He kissed her hair, guided her to the door, and they descended to the lobby.

Carlo came out from behind the desk. "Brie! Look at you!" He hugged her tight. "Henry!"

The doorman peeked through the glass and his smile covered his whole face. He rushed in and took her shoulders. "There's the bright and happy girl I remember." He bent to kiss her cheek. "I can't wait to tell the others."

"My stomach is going to eat my face. I'll chat when I get back."

"Of course. Enjoy, Brie. This is going to be a *good* day." Carlo hugged her again and returned behind the desk.

Henry held the door with a huge grin. "Mr. Winters. Miss Hernandez."

"Thank you, Henry." The words from Hudson filled Brie with pleasure and when they were on the sidewalk, he glanced down and winked.

Leonard waited at the curb and said, "Lola is going to lose her shit, you know. Kickass results, Brie."

Behind them, Harper's car pulled to a stop. Elijah stepped out and stood stiffly to the side as his charge exited the vehicle.

Brie called out, "Good morning, Elijah. Kiss my ass, *Delkin*."

Then she got in the back of Hudson's car and didn't look back.

When they were a block away, Hudson started laughing and it was highly contagious.

* * *

Harper feared he'd irreparably damaged his relationship with Elijah by his actions.

They unexpectedly returned to the building so he could use his apartment's secure system for an emergency call to a small outpost in eastern Africa.

As he got out, he was shocked to see Gabriella preparing to get into Winters' car. She looked incredible.

Clearly, Elijah overstated her distress.

In tandem with the thought, she called, "Good morning, Elijah. Kiss my ass, *Delkin*."

He blinked at the pissed off side of her he'd been unaware she possessed. She ducked into the limo and a ripple of awareness shot through him.

Gabriella didn't look back. Winters didn't acknowledge him.

Seeing her inner fighter emerge, he recognized that he'd hurt her far more deeply than he intended.

The woman had been an impulse decision, one meant to show he wasn't waiting around for Gabriella's attention.

How his date for the evening *looked* hadn't even crossed his mind since she resembled so many others who were similar in nature. That she was barely dressed was also common.

In hindsight, he'd ignored Elijah's comments about Gabriella's embarrassment about her scars. He'd forgotten her insistence during their first conversation that she wasn't Harper's *type*.

How the fuck was he supposed to fix the cluster he created?

Elijah's eyes flicked to his and away. Sighing, Harper got back to work and knew he'd have to figure it the fuck out if he ever expected his oldest friend to talk to him again.

Chapter Eight

Mid-November 2014

Two weeks following her birthday party at *Trois*, Brie found herself restless on her first night back at the club.

She missed Elijah constantly and hid her sadness.

There were no more nightly visits but she continued to listen for his knock, just in case. She hadn't seen the bodyguard since the night he told her to seek the comfort she needed.

She didn't cry but she worried about her newfound anger. It wasn't an emotion that sat well on her shoulders.

Riya and her men looked vibrant and happy, whispering together, and laughing quietly. Zach and Quinn waited for Tawny, talking to Hudson about recent changes to the market.

Other members frequently approached and she'd smile and converse for a few minutes but she wasn't really in the mood.

Brie was frequently lost in her own thoughts.

Though Riya and Tawny inquired, Brie remained unwilling to share information about Harper and Elijah. It seemed over before it began but…she *hoped*. Her mind drifted to the two men constantly and she was furious with Harper's callousness.

She wasn't sure how to go about finding, much less *pursuing*, a casual relationship at this stage of her rehabilitation.

Looking around, she wanted to explore the unique space on her own two feet. The cane was too slow and she needed both hands while she sketched.

She itched to see *everything* inside the historical building. There was an elevator to the second floor but she was embarrassed to use it.

"Gabriella." Hudson's voice pulled her from her unusual introspection. "Would you like a tour?"

She shook her head with a sigh.

"The upstairs…"

"I'll *wait*, Hudson. When I see it, I want to *walk*. To explore and be able to sketch without having to make sure I don't fucking *fall*." Her eyes widened. "I'm so sorry…"

"Ssh. I understand." His voice was gentle as he reached out to place his hand over hers. "I'd have already gone mad."

Turning hers over, she gripped him like a lifeline. "I need this to happen *faster*."

"Your recovery?" She nodded. "You're doing remarkable. Your doctors are blown away by your progress."

"I can do *more*."

"You will. I know you're impatient. What can I do?"

"Forgive my behavior."

"You've done nothing wrong, Gabriella."

Rubbing her temple, she whispered, "I feel like a raging bitch."

"*Never.*"

Tawny collapsed in the chair beside her. "Did you call me? I distinctly heard raging bitch." Grudgingly, Brie laughed. "Hating this shit, huh?"

"I mean, *fuck*." Releasing Hudson's hand with a final squeeze, she gave the redhead her full attention.

"You feel helpless and that must chafe like nipples in winter."

Laughing, Brie nodded. "Something like that. I don't mind putting in the work. I just want more headway. I want, I don't even know what the fuck I want."

"I get it." Tawny sighed. "Bet it doesn't help that your last experience before all this was being crawled over by the dynamic duo of dirty sex. Must make you antsy."

Hudson choked on his scotch.

"Tawny, *lord*." Brie couldn't contain her grin. "I'm stuck in limbo. Truthfully, I could use a distraction."

Considering, she asked, "What about that sexy motherfucker who gave you the penis sculpture?"

Her heart contracted painfully but she covered it. "It's a fucking *whale* and you *know* it."

"Sure, but it's definitely *phallic*. I mean, seriously. From the shape to the blowhole, I see penis."

"Bitch, you see penis in *everything*."

"A-fucking-men. Anyway, what about calling him and his hot bodyguard to work your pretty ass over and remind you why you need to keep getting up in the morning?"

Brie closed her eyes and took a deep breath. No way could she share the complexities of Elijah and Harper with Tawny. The woman was *way* too unpredictable.

"I'm can't handle them right now."

"Why not? I thought these were *done deal* orgasms."

"I'm not strong enough physically or emotionally." She chose her words with care. "I offer nothing of value at this point."

Tawny stared deeply into her eyes. Brie got the impression the woman saw more, knew more than most. "You're not just a hole to fuck. If either of them don't see the value in every goddamn thing *else* you have going on, fuck them."

Twisting her hands in her lap, Brie murmured, "I'm not firing on all cylinders. I'd probably get sex mixed up with love."

"You need some disconnected play time."

"I've got no clue what I need. I'll be fine. I just need to be on my own feet for real. I couldn't even *handle* full on sex yet."

Tawny made a funny tapping motion on the arm of the sofa. "Want some good news?" Brie nodded with a smile. "Joshua and Jessica are here. They're heading this way."

"Oh *god…*"

"Chin up, buttercup."

The outgoing and adventurous couple who'd been part of Riya's dissertation ignored everyone else as they approached and knelt on either side the chair where Brie sat.

Hudson's eyes were huge.

Joshua took her face in his hands. "You're fucking gorgeous. What's this I hear about you feeling bad?" He kissed her full on the mouth, licking inside and following with several small kisses that trailed along her jaw to her neck.

Jessica stroked her fingers through her hair. "Injuries couldn't snuff you out, pretty girl. Looks like you're kicking ass and taking names to me." She gently cupped the back of her head and delivered a kiss that made Brie's breath catch in her throat. The blonde moaned. "You're delicious."

"You look overheated, Brie." Joshua worked her light sweater off her shoulders with a wink. "I really want to see as much of your skin as you'll let me until I'm given permission to pet you everywhere."

She wore black jeans and a turquoise shell top with flat boots that ended just below her knees. The weather was turning cool but he was right. Brie suddenly felt *very* warm.

In tandem, the couple ran their palms over her shoulders and down to her hands.

"Still silky and golden. Soft and tempting." Jessica's eyes lifted. "You think a few scars makes me want you less, Brie?"

"I…"

"They make me want you *more*. You're a fighter. Nothing makes me hotter than a fucking fighter."

Joshua ran his hand up her inner calf to her knee. "What's different? Something's different." Rising, he cupped the outside of her breast. "Are these smaller?"

Brie nodded, overwhelmed by their attention and unable to form a coherent sentence.

"I thought you were hot before but *damn*. I bet you like yourself better now. That's what matters, you know? They'll still taste as good as I imagined."

He kissed her again and she felt dizzy.

When he broke it, Jessica waited and they traded her mouth back and forth for a couple of minutes. The entire time, their hands stroked over her body through her clothing.

Finally, they hugged her hard. "You should let us love you down, Brie. You don't have to do anything or worry about our pleasure at all." Joshua raked his hands through her hair. "We'd be so careful. What do you think?"

She confessed, "I can't think."

The blonde traced her cheek with the back of her knuckles. "You don't have to think. What you need is pleasure without being flooded with emotional stimulation. We'd be great friends for you, Brie. We'd make sure you had fun and remembered you're still young, without twisting you up inside. Just the ticket, I think."

Glancing over her shoulder, Jessica grinned. "Hey, Riya."

Blinking away the sensual fog the couple wove around her, Gabriella realized her friends were watching the three of them with their mouths open. Natalia sat quietly on Hudson's lap, having joined them at some point.

Riya struggled to find words. "Hey, you guys. Um, you know Brie is still recovering, right?"

Joshua and Jessica smiled at Brie while they lightly traced her face. "We heard she was feeling a little down, frustrated with her recovery time. No fucking *way* were we going to miss a chance to show her how sexy we found her from day one. We can be gentle, lick her from head to toe, and remind her what pleasure is all about without doing anything to set her physical therapy back."

The imagery immediately sent signals to Brie's nipples and womb. *Just the thought...*

"We've masturbated to the thought of you many times. That's the kind of impression you made last year when we met. We heard you hooked up with the hot stoic guy and his delicious girl. Sadness like you wouldn't *believe* at the missed opportunity." Jessica shrugged. "We got it though, they telegraph *we'll-fuck-your-brains-out* real subtle."

Natalia and Hudson stared at the younger couple. It was one of the few times Brie had ever seen them truly speechless. Natalia's eyes met Brie's and she issued a shaky laugh.

"We heard they're engaged, totally your BFFs, and you're back on the market. Fucking awesome news and we'd like to cover you in some much-deserved pleasure."

They lowered their lips to the skin beneath her ears and planted warm kisses along her shoulder.

Brie met Tawny's eyes. The redhead stared back, the only one not shocked by the couple's appearance or hard press.

"Did you do this?"

"Sure as fuck did. They talk about you every time I see them." She shrugged. "They wanted you before the accident. They restated their desire to lick you unconscious without going against doctor's orders so I brought them tonight."

Winking at Hudson, she added, "I concur with all their accidental compliments."

"*Tawny...*"

"Brie, shut up and let them touch you." She smiled as her men scooped her up and settled her between them. "You deserve to remember ecstasy. They can remind you and ensure you end up a quivering mass of nerve endings." Blowing her a kiss, she added, "Just hush and let it happen."

Taking a deep breath, Brie let herself fall into the way the couple caressed and murmured to her.

Their voices were low enough that no one else could hear them and so soft that her mind layered them over each other. Smooth Texan accents turned her insides to melted butter.

"You forgot how beautiful you are but we can remind you. Touching you, making you feel amazing, is such a small gift we can provide that's completely selfish. We won't hurt you, won't take more than you can give. We'll make you feel so good. Let us show you what you need."

They pulled back to look at her face. Holding her hands, they placed them on their faces and guided her over their necks and shoulders.

She whispered, "You're both in amazing shape…"

"We have stamina for *days*, Brie. We want you to touch us. Take whatever you want, whatever you need."

They moved closer to give her more access to them and she relished the chance. The temptation to *touch* and *be touched* was almost overwhelming.

Joshua was still in *incredible* shape and Jessica reminded her of Natalia, slender and almost delicate.

Her gaze met Natalia's and her friend winked.

"I'd love to…sketch you together." Brie looked at them shyly. "Would you let me do that?"

Their smiles were brilliant. Jessica asked excitedly, "Could you draw one for us to keep?"

"Oh yeah. I can do that."

"Whatever you like, we're open to, Brie." They resumed kissing her and said at her ears, "Any position you want to see. We can hold back for a *long* time. We can do that between licking and sucking you." More touches. "Maybe you could tell us *exactly* what to do so we get it just the way you want it."

Holy shit, the possibilities.

"How'd you get here, Brie?" Joshua asked the words quietly as he massaged the inside of her thigh. "I'll get you safely anywhere but the destination should feature a bed. We're going to lay you down and spend *hours* feasting on every inch."

Jessica added in a whisper, "Where's the closest place to get you naked?"

* * *

Harper watched a fit young couple crawl over Gabriella and thought his brain would explode.

He moved to stand up and Elijah ordered, "Do *not* draw attention to your presence. She needs to be touched."

"Then *fetch* her, Elijah."

"She's no more a *dog* than she is a *rabbit*. She's a kind and beautiful woman who deserves better than what you'd do to her. *Sit there.* Enjoy the result of your fucking games."

"Your mouth..."

"Says far less than it could. You're many things. A hypocrite was never one of them. Two weeks ago, you flaunted a woman in front of her who's *everything* she knows she's not. Your *type*, as she so accurately described it."

Shame curled in his belly. He lashed out, "Your *type* as well."

"Never. I could barely tolerate them. It was made only slightly more bearable if they were gagged."

The shock of the admission rocked him. "*All of them?*"

"Each and every one." He broke protocol and met his eyes. "You rubbed your lack of care in her face. You hurt her. I told you you'd lost her. That night, I told her to seek comfort wherever it could be found."

There was no doubt Elijah wanted her desperately. "Why didn't you..."

"Shut *up*. For once in your fucking life, shut the fuck up and *think* before you speak to me as if I only met you today."

Crossing his arms at his back, he faced forward and did his best to disconnect from Harper's presence. It had been many years since he'd attempted it.

Harper's gaze returned to the image of Gabriella in the grip of a focused assault on her sensuality.

Where she'd seemed nervous and hesitant initially, she gradually gave in to a nature that craved human contact. Her hands drifted to the back of one dark head, one light. He watched her eyes close and her lips part slightly.

She was fully involved and it was spectacular.

After half an hour of public making out that had him harder than he'd been in a long time, they helped her stand and walked with her to the exit.

Harper held his breath as he realized she was truly going to let the couple take her home.

His eyes connected with Hudson's and the man smiled tightly. There was no doubt in his mind that his somewhat friend and rival had been aware of his presence from the start.

He *wanted* Harper to witness the fact that Gabriella wasn't without options of her own.

"I hope they give her everything she deserves," Elijah said quietly. "I also hope they don't steal Brie's heart. For that, I might never forgive you."

He meant the words.

At the apartment, his bodyguard checked the house, pronounced it clear with a nod, walked into his room, and closed the door.

In his own bedroom, Harper's body was in chaos. He pictured what the couple was doing to Gabriella. He wondered if they were tasting her at that moment. Eating her pussy, sucking her nipples, and touching her everywhere.

He quickly undressed and stepped in the shower. Fisting his cock, he let the pleasure build slowly as he considered the image they made. When he came with a gasp, he remained under the spray for a long time.

There was no way he could stay in New York. He needed to get Elijah out of the city as well.

His friend wasn't the only one who hoped they'd get another chance in the future to touch Gabriella. The woman spun out his brain, made it hard to think.

* * *

Elijah showered and sat in focused meditation. One day, he'd have the chance to touch her. For now, he hoped she took *everything* she needed and deserved.

Calming his mind, imagining the happiness Brie would feel receiving touch, allowed him to sleep deeply for the first time since the unfortunate events on her birthday.

The following day, they returned to Washington.

Chapter Nine

Early December 2014

Harper had been off-balance for weeks. It was unfamiliar and unwelcome. Upon their return to the Delkin family estate, Elijah settled into the routine he'd held since he was a child and all but ignored his oldest friend.

The bodyguard spoke to him in his capacity as his head of security. Otherwise, the man refused to interact on any level.

Harper finally had all he could stand. On the way to their meeting, he said quietly, "I'll talk to Winters."

"Regarding?"

"Gabriella." When Elijah didn't move or respond, he nodded. "I know I messed up. I'm sorry."

"I wonder how he'll react to your *second* apology."

Harper sighed. "Don't let him kill me, if you don't mind."

Ascending to the top floor of a high-rise in Salt Lake City, he braced himself to face his most formidable business rival in a deal that benefited them both.

He'd arranged dinner afterwards to gauge the waters outside of the business realm.

The dozen people at the conference table stood when Elijah preceded him into the room.

Hudson Winters did not.

One of the rare men who had his respect in the world they inhabited watched him, still and unblinking. He'd be lying if he said it didn't affect him on a gut level.

For several hours, Harper engaged in a financial battle of wits with someone who never failed to make it interesting.

When the documents were signed, they shared possession of a small abandoned town, forgotten in the fifty years since the last of the population moved away.

Set in a secluded valley in Utah, it would be the future testing site for educational, environmental, and sociological technology being developed through their own companies as well as those of their friends and colleagues.

As the others gradually made their exit, Harper found himself alone with Winters. Elijah hadn't moved or spoken in hours. He barely blinked.

"How did this project come to your attention?"

"A conversation I had with Gabriella before she was hurt." Harper hid his surprise as the man stood and walked to the windows. "She saw an article about abandoned towns around the world. Her idea was for several clean slate locations. Projects that focused on bringing out the best mankind had to offer in all areas. I purchased three of them in Europe, South America, and Australia."

"The others?"

"Marciella Canfield now owns three in Canada, Central America, and Iceland. Owen Douglas purchased one in Oklahoma before I could grab it. I was displeased."

He inhaled carefully. "I'll send you a list of those that remain for analysis. This is the only other viable site of those available in the United States."

"Why bring me in? You certainly didn't need my money."

"Gabriella suggested we attempt a joint venture with only positive and far-reaching outcomes. She said it would be good for us. I believe the phrase she used was *bonding experience*."

He couldn't hold back his snort of amusement and was shocked to hear a stifled one from Elijah as well.

Joining Winters to take in the view, Harper was silent for a long time before he murmured, "I fucked it up."

"Yes."

"I'm sorry."

"Noted."

The silence drew out between them. "Any suggestions?"

Winters didn't answer for so long that Harper didn't think he would. "Why should I help you?"

"I have no idea."

"I warned you she was different."

Nodding, he replied, "I didn't realize how different." Clearing his throat, he sought information. "The couple…?"

Turning to face him, Winters clasped his hands behind his back. "Gabriella ended their arrangement after two weeks."

"The reason?"

"Their similarities to Natalia and myself. A deep love for one another without the capacity to include others in it." Black eyes held his unsympathetically. "Your actions were childish and needlessly hurtful. She felt it deeply."

Harper accepted the deserved reprimand with a nod. Even *he* couldn't deny the words.

"Joshua and Jessica's youth and sense of adventure stopped her from spiraling into despair. However, it's another situation that ultimately left her without what she needed." To himself, he murmured, "I hate seeing her unhappy."

Unable to handle Elijah's silence any longer, Harper made a decision. "Will you discuss it over dinner?"

"Within boundaries, yes."

* * *

Elijah cleared the private room at the exclusive restaurant and took a position beside the door.

As Hudson Winters passed him, he stopped and said clearly, "Join us, Eklund. Your role is not that of *employee* when Gabriella's name is involved."

Meeting the man's eyes, they took the measure of one another for the third time in twenty years.

The first involved Harper's reputation. Winters proved himself a man of honor who could be trusted. Their interaction was a *draw* with an outcome of mutual respect.

The second involved Natalia Roman. Seeing the man's love for a woman Elijah had always admired but *did not* love convinced him to concede. He could *count* the number of times in his life that he'd done so.

This time, the woman who stood in the space between them was Brie. It was critical Winters understood there'd be *no concession* this time.

"You love her," Elijah stated without animosity.

"Naturally. I won't see her harmed. I see your desire to ensure she's not." Gesturing to the table, Elijah nodded and all of them took a seat.

Winters wasted no time.

To Harper, he said clearly, "You *must* set aside your *pride* and your *jealousy*. If you're powerless to do so, don't toy with her."

Turning his gaze to Elijah, he stated, "It was you who suggested she seek comfort elsewhere."

"She needed things I was unable to provide."

Winters sipped his scotch. "Your position now?"

"I'll see her when we return to New York." He felt rather than saw Harper stiffen beside him.

For a long time, they maintained eye contact.

Elijah didn't blink.

"You're prepared to care for her?"

A hundred scenarios rapidly filed through Elijah's mind.

Caring for Brie in ways she understood as well as ways she did not *yet* understand had been at the forefront of his mind since watching her leave with a couple focused on her pleasure, on soothing her, on reminding her that she was alive.

"I'm prepared to wait until she's cleared from medical care. At that time, yes." Looking deeply into the black eyes of a man he knew would kill to protect Brie, Elijah made his feelings clear. "I love her. I believe she loves me."

"You're correct. It happened quickly but it isn't reversible, Eklund. She hurts at the loss of you."

The words filled him with fucking *bliss*. His desire to go to her immediately was almost overwhelming.

Switching attention, Winters asked, "Your position, Delkin?"

"I don't want to love her. I don't want *her* to love me. I have neither time nor patience for such tender emotions."

Tender emotions would change his life if he'd allow them the opportunity.

Winters didn't seem surprised. "Your interest in Gabriella remains entirely sexual."

"Yes."

"I call *bullshit*." Harper's eyes went wide. "No matter your *words*, you're attracted to her beyond mere sex."

"No. I..."

"Harper, so help me god." He sat forward and put his arm on the table. "I get your initial need to fuck someone who was temporarily mine."

Elijah watched Harper's face still with shock.

"I also understand the attraction to a woman quite *other* from the women in your history as well as my own." He shook his head. "You lie to us *both* if you tell me you don't feel the fucking draw of her heart."

The room was silent for almost a minute.

Clearing his throat, Harper murmured, "I'm too cold for a woman such as her."

"As I once thought of myself. Yet she wants you any fucking way," Winters shot back.

"She's drawn to me because I look like *you*."

"It isn't my *looks*, Delkin." He sat back and sipped his scotch. "As an artist, she must find our physical similarities fascinating. As a woman, she's drawn to something she *feels*, not something she *sees*."

Elijah agreed. "It's the *puzzle* that fascinates her."

Winters and Elijah shared a silent communication and Winters smiled slowly. "She's mentioned feeling as if there's something she's missing about both of you."

Harper was annoyed. "It's not complicated. I look like you. She wanted you and it didn't work out."

"How *little* you know her." Sitting up straight, Winters drew who he was around himself. "Gabriella seeks a lover who will provide strength, knowledge, and safety. Who will appreciate who she is without judgment. Simple *touch* and *love* are what drive her. In return, she's willing to give all of herself. Mind, body, and heart."

"You were able to provide all but love," Elijah mused.

"It was a bitter truth."

Taking a long pull of his drink, Harper stated, "Her emotions are frustrating."

Winters shook his head. "No. It's frustrating to be *incapable* of loving her. Natalia and I speak of it often. We'd take her into our lives but it would ultimately hurt her more than help her. I wouldn't present her with an offer that's less than she deserves nor would she accept it."

"I don't understand this woman."

"It isn't for you to *understand* her, Harper. You don't have the emotional capacity. It's only for you to *accept* her and provide the little she needs."

"She requires more than any woman I've ever met."

"Not *more*, merely *different*. What she offers in return is priceless." Winters leaned forward. "She's pulled toward what she senses from both of you." He paused. "She *will* love you, Harper. Every aspect of who you are as a man. She'll accept you, love you unconditionally. You can trust her."

"I don't trust women."

"Untrue." The words hung between them.

Finally, "Natalia was different."

"Gabriella and Natalia are the *same* in every way that matters." Elijah watched Winters inhale carefully. "You're the obstacle. You deny yourself, as well as the other two involved, out of misplaced *fear*." Leaning forward, he growled, "Slay the fucking *weakness* and get the fuck on with it."

Chapter Ten

Christmas Eve 2014

Tawny shook Brie awake sometime after three. "I brought some of those little gourmet brownies Max whipped up like it was fucking *nothing* earlier and I need an accomplice."

Grinning, Brie rolled over and retorted, "No tequila this year."

"I snagged you that sparkling non-alcoholic shit." The redhead made a gagging sound. "By the way, we need to up the security on your front door."

"How long did it take you to get inside?"

"Girl, four *minutes*. However, in my defense, I was holding a tray of brownies so I had to improvise."

"You didn't put them down?"

"On the *floor*? Not sanitary and these are *Max's* brownies! That's like, sacrilegious and shit." Bouncing off the bed, Tawny sang, "Come on! I picked movies."

To the room, Brie murmured, "Don't we have to be at Riya's in a few hours?"

Sitting up, she took stock before grabbing her cane and following her friend into the living room.

Stopping in the doorway, she let her mind absorb the blanket fort that spanned her living room furniture, anchored at the top by the whale sculpture.

"Tawny, how *long* have you been here?"

"More than an hour. You sleep deep. I could've absconded with your sculpture and painted it like a penis – *because it is* – by the time you rolled out of bed."

"Whale. It's a whale." The woman always made her laugh. Rubbing her eyes, she added, "I took a pill. I've been having trouble sleeping."

Skipping to stand in front of her, Tawny put her hands on her hips. Her hair was in pigtail braids and she wore footy pajamas covered in *Hello Kitty*. "How are the Wonder Twins?"

"Joshua and Jessica are wonderful. They flew back to Texas yesterday to attend his dad's wedding. They'll be there through the holidays." She made her way to the kitchen and started coffee.

"Still providing crazy monkey sex on the hour?"

"Um, no. After two blissful weeks, I needed to get some distance. They're young and fun, easy to like, and incredible for my ego." She lifted one shoulder. "Ultimately, they're like Hudson and Natalia. They're open to everyone and everything but they only truly *love* each other. I took our time together for what it was and enjoyed it."

"Shit. Sorry, girl."

"Don't be sorry. They helped me when I was truly sad. I think it's my new calling in life to be the kick in the ass couples need." She winked. "They flew to Vegas three days ago and got married."

"Shut the fuck *up*!"

"I can't." Taking a seat at her bar, she felt the effects of her insane physical therapy session. "They're perfect together. I imagine they'll have lots of great experiences. I doubt they'll ever be truly monogamous but the love, *that* they'll only ever give to each other."

Tawny seemed lost in thought for a long moment. "You think Hudson and Natalia fuck outside their couple-hood?"

"I've got no idea. I know they'd need to have someone, I don't know, less emotional than me. Someone they could be with and walk away from without guilt. They could never cross that line with me again."

"Make you sad?"

"Hell no. They're *holy shit* in bed." Brie crossed her eyes and Tawny chuckled. "I like them better as friends. No confusion and they're fucking *happy*. That makes me happy."

By dawn, the brownies were gone, they'd consumed an entire pot of coffee, and screamed themselves hoarse through two action movies.

"Quick nap and then we'll go harass the cranky threesome."

Climbing in her big bed, Brie rolled to her side when Tawny climbed in beside her. "Where do Zach and Quinn think you are tonight?"

She shrugged. "I needed some distance myself."

"Why?"

"They asked me to marry them." Brie's eyes went wide. "They have no clue what fuckery I'd bring into their lives. Going too public is dangerous, for all of us." For almost a minute, the redhead simply looked at her. "I can't tell you all of it now. I need a raincheck."

"Done."

"You're the only person in my life who lets me just *be* without a hundred questions, worries, and accusations. I want you to know I really appreciate that."

Reaching out, she took the other woman's hand. "Anytime. Get some sleep and recharge. You can paste on your *good time Tawny* persona when we head upstairs."

* * *

Riya's annual holiday party was packed as usual. After two hours, Brie found herself laughing almost non-stop.

She chose a long-sleeve red dress that ended in uneven layers at her ankle. Underneath, she wore a lingerie set Natalia bought her in ethereal white lace that made her feel incredibly sexy.

Despite having to wear *flats* and walk with a *cane*.

Micah took a seat beside her with a grin. "How are you doing, Miss Hernandez?"

"Better every day."

"That's the spirit. I can't tell you how much I look forward to dragging you out on the dance floor again. We grumble like small children on a long car ride." He winked. "I saw that in a movie."

"You're *lovely* as usual and gave me a tiny brain scramble with the words you said."

"Liar."

When she could stop laughing, she told him, "Maybe by this time next year I'll have a hope of keeping up with you again."

"I'll hold you to that." He accepted a glass of champagne from a passing server for each of them. "I know you're still on lots of medications but I wanted to toast the work you did on my website." Clinking their glasses together, he leaned forward and kissed her cheek. "Outstanding on all fronts."

"Thanks. I'm so glad you liked it."

"The developers who implemented your changes said it was the smoothest transition they'd ever seen."

She crossed her eyes. "Thank god. I hate the back end."

For a few minutes, they sat together and people watched, adding commentary that verged on silly. When he met her eyes, she saw a serious topic change on the horizon.

"Riya mentioned your possible arrangement." She didn't pretend to misunderstand, wondering what was coming. "In this world, the rules are clearly defined, Brie. Your safety must be paramount."

"I'm unsure it'll happen but, do you have any advice?"

"Clear and concise communication at all times. Leave no doubts about what you seek and refuse to take less than you want. As with Riya, your heart is your most powerful weapon but it can leave you at a disadvantage with men who don't understand how it *functions.*"

"Hudson said the same."

"I find he and I are more similar than I'm comfortable with sometimes." There was laughter in his honey eyes. "I know he guards your back and respect him highly for it. If your past relationship – or his dealings with Delkin – ever make you hesitate to go to him, I'm happy to help."

"You're such a good man, Micah." Riya settled herself on her husband's lap and leaned forward to kiss Brie. "I worried a little about Hudson having the detachment to advise you."

"He's protective. I need to deal with this on my own, no matter which way it goes."

"I agree and commend your consideration of everyone involved." Riya glanced over her shoulder and her face lit up.

Two couples walked around into Brie's line of sight.

"I finally get to introduce you! This is Victor and his wife Shay." With her arm still wrapped around Micah's shoulder, she accepted kisses on the cheek. "This is Lucas and his wife Amelia." Smiling brightly, she said, "This is my *wonderful* friend, Gabriella Hernandez."

"Ma'am. It's sure a pleasure." She moved to stand, feeling like a little girl with the huge man standing in front of her. He had to be almost seven feet tall. "Nah, honey. We'll come on down to you. You're an itty-bitty thing like my sweet girl."

He crouched and settled Shay on one knee. She was pretty and practically glowing with happiness. "Riya told us so much about you I feel like we're already friends."

Stunned, Brie managed, "Um, I-I feel like I know you, too." The couple laughed warmly and she was struck a little stupid. "I mean, *shit*."

Lucas sat on the sofa beside her and brought his wife to sit on his lap. "You bubble over with goodness."

A nervous laugh escaped Brie and she put her hand over her mouth. "Exactly as described, good *lord*."

Amelia grinned. "He gets that a *lot*. Kind of panty-meltin', huh?" Unsure how to respond, Brie tried to smile. The tall woman chuckled. "No need to be embarrassed. Who doesn't love Sam Elliot?"

"I mean, really," Brie said deadpan.

"Riya mentioned you've been fightin' your way back from a major car accident." Shay reached out and held her hand. "I'm impressed as all hell."

Victor gave her a wink and she was struck by the fact that he had almost the same eyes as Hudson. "When you're back on your feet, you need to trip on down to Georgia. The local boys would follow you like puppies and we'll stuff you full o' fried chicken and peach cobbler."

"A long way from New York City but a nice little timeout," Amelia added. "You'd love our place in Montana, too. Nothin' for miles and miles but sky, trees, and mountains."

"They sound lovely." Brie's mind suddenly exploded with a hundred questions and she started talking a mile a minute.

The couples didn't seem to mind.

Eventually, Max hauled over a couple of chairs for himself and Victor. They were some of the most open and honest people she'd ever met.

It was surreal to meet two more of the men from Riya's dissertation. The ones Brie had more than a little crush on while she was reading.

The reality was even *better*. She talked to them for hours and she felt as if she'd found kindred spirits.

* * *

Hudson and Natalia appeared after the staff party at *Trois* ended and hugged her between them. They presented her with another sculpture from Hudson's collection and the memory of the first made her hug them for a long time.

At her ear, Natalia whispered, "You have to join us tomorrow. We're going to test out the new dishes."

"I'm not intruding on…"

Placing her finger over Brie's lips, the blonde arched a brow. "We're going to vegetate *all day* and you're going to hang out with us so trying to resist us is pointless." Plumping her lower lip, she winked. "Still love them. I can't help it."

The confession made Brie snicker and she puckered comically for a kiss that she received. Natalia swooned dramatically and Hudson caught her with a grin.

Clearing her throat, she said, "Um, you should let me cook."

Natalia huffed indignantly. "We *catered*." Releasing a sigh of relief made her friend put her hand on her hip. "I can *cook*. Some stuff. Maybe."

Rubbing noses, Brie told her, "You're a fucking *gourmand* with tea and cookies."

She was so grateful to friends who went above and beyond to include her in their lives.

There were times she felt as if she had nothing to offer but they always made her feel welcome, protected, and loved.

They'd always be the ideal Christmas gift to her.

Chapter Eleven

New Year's Eve 2015

Brie was determined to feel good. She *refused* to dwell on her sadness.

She was about to begin a brand-new year. She was nine months past the accident that almost killed her and getting stronger every day physically.

Riya and Tawny insisted on taking her shopping and for an extended spa day to prepare for the outrageous annual party.

The outfits they tried to put her in made her giggle maniacally.

Finally, hand on her hip, Tawny huffed. "The hunters will be out *en masse* tonight and we're presenting you accordingly."

"First, no. I'm not interested and I'm not cleared for sex if I was interested, which, I repeat, *I am not.* Second, there's no *way* I'm exposing that much skin. Especially when I can't wear appropriate shoes. Three…" She held up her cane. "Figure it out, Red."

Stomping away, she mumbled, "Nobody lets me do *anything!*"

Grinning, Riya asked, "You're *sure* you're not interested? The inquiries at *Trois* are growing."

Her eyes widened. "No."

"Oh yeah. Natalia didn't tell you?" She shook her head. "Probably because most of them are too young."

Tawny landed between them. "Blondie is a firm believer in *seasoning.* Especially where you're concerned. Doesn't like the twenty-somethings sniffing around her *baby girl.*"

"Shut up," Brie said laughing.

"Fine. After you try on this jumpsuit."

"No."

"It lights up!"

"Fuck you, no."

"Come on, it's *festive*!"

In the end, they compromised on a bronze sweater that was softer than a hundred baby kittens, brown leather pants, and matching riding boots.

Tawny was somewhat appeased, Brie was comfortable, and Riya looked as if she'd spent the day running a daycare.

They did her hair and makeup. It took the friends trading off to straighten her hair. She kept shaking her head and saying, "I *warned* you. Did I not *warn* you?"

When it was finally done, they stared at her in stunned fascination. "Brie. Holy *shit*. That's gorgeous."

"Thanks." The lowest layer brushed the top of her ass. In its' naturally curly state, it was around her bra line.

Tawny wrinkled her nose. "You're absolutely *sure*..."

"Positive. I don't need any more dicks in my life."

"Ha! I see what you did there." Clapping her hands, the redhead announced, "Let's hustle. Zach and Quinn promised to play hide-n-seek their penises with me."

"Tawny..."

"I know, I know. It's not fair. I always know their hiding spots." She shrugged. "Somehow, the game never gets old."

Laughing, they headed downstairs and climbed into the M's Towncar. They chatted with Rodney all the way across town.

None of the men would arrive for a couple of hours so they went early to help Natalia with any last-minute details. She always outdid herself and *Trois* was stunning.

Lights and fabric descended from the massive chandelier to the four balcony corners. They watched her order staff like a pretty, sexily dressed drill sergeant.

Straps of black leather crisscrossed her narrow body in strategic places and formed what appeared to be a precarious mini dress. Leather stilettos tied up her ankles.

Hudson entered and greeted their group but when he caught sight of Natalia, he did a comical double-take that made them all snicker as he kidnapped the blonde to her office.

Brie called out with a grin, "Anything you need us to do while you're...busy?"

"Bowls." It was all she could manage before they heard a door slam.

The three of them were *gutted* with laughter. When her stomach stopped hurting enough to talk, Brie said, "I assume snack bowls with all the chocolates and stuff?"

Riya carefully blotted her makeup. "We can do what we want. She'll be so fucking mellow when she comes back she won't notice *shit*. Oh god. Did you see the cartoon wolf thing he did? I fucking died..."

Then they were off again.

When the couple emerged an hour later, Tawny pointed two fingers at Natalia and said, "Bitch got *blowjob Botox.*"

Retaining their composure was impossible, especially after the blonde blew them a kiss. It was no use.

Other members started drifting in and the club filled with conversation and celebration.

When the *third* pair of men approached her *just to chat* around ten o'clock, Brie wondered what the fuck was going on.

She accidentally said, "You know I'm still out of commission, right?" She tapped the top of her cane.

A big man with dark red hair trimmed high and tight winked a bright blue eye. "Aye, lass. I'm Gerard Weatherford. My friends call me Gear."

Blinking at the heavy Irish accent that disconnected her central nervous system for a second, she managed, "I mean, I'm still in physical therapy."

His friend was as tall but leaner. The smile he turned on her was lovely and showed his dimples. Gentle brown eyes and hair made him seem friendly.

Also in a heavy Irish accent, he told her, "Several months more, accordin' to the grapevine. Finnan Brodie."

Shaking hands, she glanced back and forth between them, waiting for one of them to explain their interest.

"Pretty girl, we're not lookin' to tackle ye to the nearest bed. Met yer redheaded friend in Amsterdam. She and her men spoke highly of ye. Business brought us here and we seized the chance to introduce ourselves."

"I don't…are people trying to *set me up*?"

The auburn-haired man laughed loudly. "Not at all. There's idle chatter that Eklund claims ye." It made her heart skip and he stepped closer. "However, should it not work out, know there are other…opportunities."

Tawny appeared at her side. "Gear. Finn. I see you've met Brie." She planted a smacking kiss on Brie's cheek.

"Red. No more home cooked meals."

She rolled her eyes. "You love feeding me. You'll never cut me off." With a smack on her butt, she added, "I'm returning the favor. My girl will *never* starve."

Both men laughed. They each took her hand and kissed the back. Finn winked, "No pressure, lass. It was a true pleasure."

"Keep us in mind if ye get lonely, pretty girl. We'll make ye laugh and treat ye right."

She watched them walk away and turned to Tawny with a frown. "Stop trying to fix me up."

"When those assholes who have you dangling on a string get their shit together, I will. Until then, you need to know there are many men out there who would love to get you in their clutches. They need to know that shit, too."

Sighing, Brie nodded.

Their usual group got a little bigger when Marci showed up after eleven with the Ghonim cousins. She looked frazzled and was still wearing a business suit with a classy chignon.

Kissing all their cheeks, she explained, "I literally just stepped off the plane an hour ago. You guys look fantastic. I look like one of those women in the Excedrin commercials."

They caught up with everyone's latest news and Brie kept her attention firmly fixed on the friends she desperately needed as midnight approached.

Natalia rang a bell when there was one minute remaining in a year filled with incredible revelations, trauma, and the beginnings of a new life she never thought she'd have.

At the ten-second mark, an arm wrapped her waist and gently pulled her around. She stared into green eyes she'd missed even more than she realized until she looked into them.

"Happy New Year, Brie."

Elijah kissed her and didn't stop until the room erupted in cheers and the sound of party favors.

Breathing him in, she reconnected to the taste and texture of his mouth as his hands held her close. She held him hard and took the moment for what it was.

When he lifted away, she followed him for an instant before she caught herself. His smile liquefied her brain.

Harper stood at his side but Elijah didn't release her.

They stared at one another for a long moment before she whispered, "Happy New Year."

"I'm sorry, Gabriella."

Inhaling carefully, she asked, "Do you know why you're apologizing?"

"Some but...not completely."

"It's a start."

Lifting her hand, she held his shoulder and tugged him down for a kiss. It shook her the hell apart. He ate at her like a man starving with his hand on her ass until Elijah tugged her away and claimed her mouth again.

At her ear, Harper murmured, "Your *hair*. I'll probably dream about it dragging over my bare skin later."

She moaned into Elijah's mouth.

For an hour, they kissed her, held her, and gave her the contact she was *desperate* to have. Every minute she spent in their presence put more of her heart on the line, but she couldn't care about her need to touch them. She wouldn't pass up the chance to do so.

Elijah stroked her and she let herself fall down the spiral of love and hope he represented.

Harper was rougher. There was a desperation, a confusion, that surrounded him and she did her best to offer him solace.

Brie *forgave* him. She *gave* to him.

It was who she was.

* * *

Elijah initially insisted on going to the club to check on Brie. He hadn't planned to take her focus from her friends.

Then he'd watched from the second floor as two men he knew well approached her and openly flirted.

"Fuck."

"Is that *Gear* and *Finn*? What the fuck are they doing in the States?" Harper asked quietly. Straightening, his fingers clenched on the balcony railing. "Elijah..."

"Wait. She's constant, true. Brie won't entertain the *thought* of others when she's unsure of us."

Brie was polite but clearly not engaged.

When the two men kissed her hand and walked away, her effervescence winked out.

Harper straightened his suit jacket. "We need to go down there. Now. There are too many circling her tonight."

Smiling slowly, Elijah said, "Moths to flame."

* * *

After spending a couple of hours reminding Brie how much they wanted her, they prepared to leave the club. They purposely passed the mercenaries who worked for Delkin Acquisitions regularly.

Gear and Finn were highly sought after, effective, and much appreciated by the few women in their circles.

"Eklund. Delkin. I assume ye've appropriately marked the lovely Miss Hernandez. A pity." Gear met Elijah's eyes with a smile. "I was hopin' ye'd treat her like the others."

"No. She's *nothing* like the others."

The smile faded from the big man's face. "Ah, Elijah of the granite heart, ye've fallen at last?" He didn't respond. "I bid ye well. She's a pretty lass with *many* interestin' friends."

Winking, he turned back to the bar and held up a hundred-dollar bill. Tawny skipped up to grab it and gave him a smacking kiss on the cheek.

"Thanks, Gear. Don't bet against me."

Played so easily by a woman everyone underestimated.

"Dump the coffee tycoons and come away with me, lass."

"Nope. They were gymnasts."

She walked sedately to Elijah and Harper. "I'm curious, how *tempting* do you think Brie would be to our mutual friend?"

87

Elijah growled and Harper flinched.

"He has a soft spot for the ones who *glow* and he's a veritable smoothie of the two of you. Fuck with her and I place her squarely in Hollow's path." Drawing herself up to her full height, she added softly, "You know she'd be good for him."

There was no doubt in his mind Brie *would* be good for him but Elijah *refused* to give her up.

"Tawny."

"*Elijah.*"

"Don't." It was the closest a man like him ever came to begging and both of them knew it.

Her green eyes stared into his for a long moment. "Okay. Don't let him hurt her again."

Then she walked away and Elijah took a relieved breath.

* * *

Three days later, Brie was supposed to fly to Washington to visit her parents but all flights were grounded.

She didn't admit her relief to anyone. She couldn't confess her fear about returning to a place that held memories of her weaker self.

Though her parents were sad she wouldn't make it, they were thrilled with the remote meetings she held with the winery staff and the growth of the entire division.

That she hadn't touched the principle of her trust fund stunned them and they openly questioned her about it.

"I still work. I earn a salary from the winery and take on projects with clients. That's a safety net I'm grateful for but I'd never abuse it."

"You and your sister humble us, Gabriella."

Her mother and father visited her often and she met Isabella for lunch once a month or so but going back to her home, to the place where she'd always felt *less* was a difficult step.

Instead, she found herself hanging out with Tawny at the club.

"Where're your men tonight, Red?"

"Traveling. They're closing on that chain Hudson turned them onto out in Utah. I told Quinn it was better if I stayed behind because I'd offend the locals."

"An unfortunate truth. You really have to keep your number of arrests within reason, Tawny."

She released a heavy sigh. "I know. The lawyer the guys put on retainer for me is so awesome though. I think the sweet thing secretly wants to go straight to be with me."

"You're a *mess*."

"Yes, yes I am."

For a couple of hours, they talked randomly and it was always enjoyable to spend time with a woman who seemed to know interesting facts no one else knew.

Suddenly, Tawny froze and gave a low whistle. "Look who *just* walked in."

Following her line of sight, Brie gasped when she saw Harper and Elijah choose a table diagonal from theirs and order drinks. The corners of the club were dim and intended for privacy.

The men were more relaxed than she'd ever seen them. She let her eyes take in their movements as they shrugged suit jackets off their shoulders and hung them on the backs of their chairs. Elijah's shoulder holster stood out starkly against his crisp white dress shirt.

"In all seriousness, they're fucking hot."

Brie was unable to form a rational response but wholeheartedly agreed. She held herself immobile, knowing too much movement would draw Elijah's attention. She wanted the opportunity to observe them without their knowledge.

As if she read her mind, her normally energetic friend was motionless and quiet as well.

For a long time, they watched the pair.

Finally, Tawny said softly, "You should go over there. They want you more than you realize. I kid you not."

"What do you mean?" she asked, almost breathless.

"I know people who know them." There was a pause. "They're committed to you."

"Elijah, perhaps. Harper is uninterested in my emotions."

They settled into silence again and Brie was enthralled. Gone was Harper's scowl and she was happy to see a smile on Elijah's face as they talked with their heads a few inches apart.

Harper reached out and curled his palm around the back of Elijah's neck. The men stared at each other intently and Brie realized she held her breath.

The move was *sexual*. Of that, Brie had no doubts.

Her vague suspicions that the two men shared a far deeper relationship than the world knew were confirmed. Finally, clarity over a question that hadn't consciously fully formed. She gave a low moan.

Tawny whispered, "Jesus. That's stimulating."

"Oh my *god*…"

"Did you know?"

"I think, part of me wondered. I didn't know for sure. There was a little thing but I kept losing it."

"You didn't ask Hudson? He and Natalia must know."

Brie shook her head. "Whatever Elijah and Harper want with me is between the three of us. I can't discuss them with Hudson. They've known one another too long and their relationship is often antagonistic as it is. I want to be careful."

"Excellent approach." Tawny was quiet for almost a minute. "Does it turn you off?"

"God, *no*. Not even a little bit. In fact, I had no clue how much it would turn me *on*."

They were silent as the men spoke softly to one another, Harper maintaining his hold on his lifelong friend. Then he pulled him nearer and whispered at his ear.

Elijah's face was nearer the women watching. His eyes closed as Harper pressed close.

Every cell in Brie's body was hot.

Suddenly, Elijah's eyes opened and he found hers across the room. His lips moved and Harper pulled back. They stared at her.

Faces side by side, almost touching, the darker man's hand tightened on Elijah's neck.

Until she rubbed her palm over her lower belly, Brie didn't know she was telegraphing her reaction. Releasing her lower lip from between her teeth, she took several careful breaths.

"They've got you in their sights, Brie. I hope to fuck you're ready for what happens next. I think you'll be just fine."

Then her friend got up and walked *away*.

Her heart beat twice before the men stood and headed in her direction. Alone, watching them make their way around the dance floor, Brie tried desperately to contain her response.

It was futile.

Heart racing, breathing too fast, and filled with sexual need unlike *anything* she'd ever experienced, she stared at them as they stopped beside her table.

They were beautiful, partially broken, and she understood so much more about them. She also wondered why they sought her out as a third to a well-established relationship.

Harper and Elijah weren't simply friends. They were *lovers* and she imagined they had been for a long time. They lived a double life, hiding their relationship, and probably eaten alive with stress about their secret being leaked.

Somehow, she managed to say, "Please sit down." They sat but remained silent. "How have you been?"

Harper's eyes stared into hers and she fought down the urge to look away and protect herself.

"You're Natalia's maid of honor." She nodded. "I'm Hudson's best man."

"He told me. I wasn't surprised. You were the ideal choice." Looking at Elijah, she asked, "Have you been practicing?"

"Yes." He leaned forward, crossed his arms on the surface, and looked as if he physically *ached*. She hated that their relaxation before seeing her was gone. "I thought you were out of town."

"My flight was canceled. I didn't mind, to be honest. I'm still nervous about going home."

There was a long silence and Elijah growled, "Fucking *say* something."

Matching his position brought their faces close across the small space. "What do you think I'm *not* saying, Elijah?"

"Is it negative?"

"You know *better* than that. I know you do." Reaching out, she took his hand and he gripped hers almost painfully hard. "I don't have a single negative thought in my mind."

His green eyes held hers. "You didn't know?" She shook her head. "Did you suspect?"

"Something, I wasn't sure."

His frown deepened. "You still...?"

"It changes nothing, Elijah."

He pulled and she leaned closer. Resting his forehead against hers, he whispered, "Why?"

"I think about you too much to ignore." She sighed. "You clearly have more than most." She swallowed hard, "I don't understand the point of *me* at all."

"We *need* you, Brie."

Moving back, she cupped his cheek in her hand. "I'm sure there are reasons the secrecy is necessary. I hate that you're clearly conflicted and I'm sorry you hurt."

"How do you know I hurt?"

"Your eyes. I didn't understand all the reasons why." Inhaling carefully, she turned to look at Harper. "You always allow the gentler man to *handle* me in some way. Why?"

He didn't reply at first but something flickered in his eyes. He sat forward, rested his elbow on the edge, and seemed to look deep inside her. "I need to be certain."

"Certain of what?"

"Of *you*, Gabriella."

Frowning, she tilted her head. "You've had…problems." He didn't answer but continued to stare at her. She closed her eyes. "Oh my god."

The world of wealth was a fairly small circle in Washington. Though she hadn't been close to the Delkins personally, her family's relationship with them stretched back two decades.

Two years after graduating college with his master's in business, Harper officially assumed the reins of his father's multi-million-dollar company. Over the course of the following three years, his management resulted in their first billion-dollar fiscal year.

The year he turned thirty, the Hernandez family received invitations to his wedding. Brie declined attending, far too embarrassed to shove her chest into formal attire.

Izzy talked for days afterward about the extravagant affair. She didn't hide her instant dislike of the new bride. Sucking her teeth, her sister summed up her feelings regarding the woman.

"Flighty, self-absorbed, and has obvious entitlement issues. I wish the man luck because he's going to need it with that one."

One year later, she overheard her mother whispering to a friend about the tragic circumstances surrounding the death of Harper's wife.

The woman took her own life. Only a few people were aware that she was pregnant at the time.

Opening her eyes, she stared into those of a man who faced unique challenges most of the world wouldn't understand. Unable to stop the tears that slipped over her cheeks, Brie placed her hand over his forearm.

"I'm sorry. So sorry, Harper." She gripped the muscle through the fabric of his shirt.

The enormity of the situation rolled over her in a wave of sadness. He made his choices based on history and fear of exposure. No one should live their life in such a way.

She covered her face with her hands. She needed a moment to adjust, to find her way back.

Suddenly, she understood her role and it broke her heart.

Then they were standing on either side, their arms wrapping around her. Harper lifted her face. Elijah held her hand.

For a moment, she had a glimpse of confusion and something else. He brushed his fingers over her damp cheek. "You cry for me, Gabriella?"

"I'll do it, Harper."

"Do what?"

"No one will ever know. I swear it."

For almost a minute, he stared into her eyes. "You'd give up your *life* to create a *front* for me?" She returned his gaze without blinking. "Why?"

Her tears continued to fall but she ignored them. "You already possess what I'll never have. I won't allow you to lose it."

"*Brie.*" Elijah's voice broke as he gathered her in his arms and held her close. She didn't break eye contact with Harper.

His scowl deepened and his hand curled around her neck. "People like you should *not* exist." He leaned down and whispered across her lips, "The world will seek to *crush* you, Gabriella."

"I'm still *here*," she insisted.

"Yes, you are."

Then he kissed her and she whimpered. It was the most aggressive kiss she'd ever received, filled with messages she didn't know how to decipher.

It went on and on as Elijah stroked her back with his lips pressed to her hair. The bodyguard continued to hold her hand. She didn't register what he was doing until he placed her palm over his cock and pressed her firmly against him. Reflexively, she squeezed before registering the implication.

He was *hard*.

Breaking the kiss, she stared into bright green eyes filled with lust he'd carefully hidden every time he'd been near her. Harper placed her other hand over his length and growled when she lightly stroked flesh that was equally hard.

She met Elijah's eyes and nearly lost herself in his expression. Moving closer to block her from view of the room, their palms crossed her body and cupped her breasts.

Her heart stumbled. Perhaps she didn't understand their interest after all.

"Firmly *bi*sexual," Elijah murmured. "The confusion comes from wanting you more than other women, Brie." Lifting his face, he added, "We didn't seek you out as a front. I'd *never* allow you to be used in such a way." Flattening his palm over her heart, he held her gaze. "This would break badly."

"Gabriella." She looked at Harper. "Six months remain before we come for you."

"I don't understand."

Elijah's lips pressed against her temple. "I promise you'll understand *everything*."

They passed her mouth back and forth between them, holding her hands on cocks that throbbed with need while they massaged breasts that ached for so much more.

"You're a creature unlike anything or anyone I've ever known." She heard the strain in Elijah's words. "Until you're naked, sweating, and coming apart between us, I won't stop. I'll show you no mercy."

Her moan vibrated into Harper's mouth and his hand lowered to press against her low belly.

"You're shaking, Gabriella."

Then their hands slipped lower, stroking together over her mound through the thin fabric of her pants. The resulting orgasm was instantaneous, unexpected, and violent.

Her fingers curled around them through their slacks and tightened hard. She pulled her head back to stare at them, panting heavily.

"You still think me weak. I have images in my mind I never realized would make me wet." She stroked her palms down to cup their balls firmly. "I want to know how you taste."

Staring at Elijah, she whispered, "I wonder what it'll feel like to have you both inside me." Leaning up, she licked over his lips. "To feel you both come. The heat of you filling me up with pleasure I can't even *imagine*."

She watched as they stilled, jaws clenched against climaxes she could *feel* them having beneath her hands. Elijah's head dropped back on his shoulders.

Turning to look at Harper, she gave him a slow smile. "You continue to underestimate me."

"I'll work on breaking the habit." Dragging his hand up her torso, he settled over her breast and tweaked her nipple. She gave a low moan. "Think about us when you touch yourself later, Gabriella."

She sighed as they bent to trade her mouth once more. The need on Harper's face made her ache.

Elijah raked his fingers through her hair and clasped a handful firmly at the base of her skull. "There's more to tell you. Only when you're firmly in my hands will you know the answers to the questions you haven't asked."

He nuzzled her cheek and whispered, "I'll dream of you, Brie. I'll think about you touching yourself with my name on your lips. Lips that will be wrapped around my cock before I die of the wanting."

At the muscle between her shoulder and the column of her neck, he bit her gently with his teeth.

"I wait for you." Straightening, he held her gaze for a long moment. "Goodnight, Brie."

With a final kiss, they walked back to their table, collected their jackets, and left the club.

Tawny's voice behind her made her grin shakily. "I bow, bitch. I motherfucking *bow.*"

* * *

In the car, Harper's mind ricocheted from thought to thought. He stared at Elijah with wide eyes.

"How did we *not know* she was still in town?"

"It doesn't matter now. All is well, Harper."

"All is..." He raked his fingers through his hair. "How can you say that? All is *not* well!"

"You can trust her. I know you know that." His half-smile didn't match the panic in Harper's heart. "Only I have ever made you lose control in public."

"You've *never* lost control in public for anyone, Elijah."

"The culmination of all things I desire most. It won't happen again but it's telling that she was able to accomplish it."

Harper leaned his head back on the seat. His heart ached.

Chapter Twelve

February 2015

That she hadn't seen Elijah and Harper in more than a month had Brie ready to vibrate out of her skin.

The only thing that helped the insane sexual tension was physical therapy. She upped her routine to five days a week.

Intense pain and buckets of sweat but finally…progress.

She'd been practicing walking without the cane in the apartment. Sometimes she was afraid because her leg felt too weak to support her but twice, she'd almost forgotten the hated crutch when she left the house.

On Valentine's Day, she received three dozen white roses with a note from Elijah.

I'd rather be there. E

After placing several in her studio to dry, she arranged the others around her apartment. It made her feel closer to him.

Riya relayed information from Micah that Harper was in Europe overseeing the purchase of a textile factory.

No one seemed to know when they'd return and it made her wonder about the future when both men were gone for months at a time.

To the apartment, she said in disgust, "You haven't even seen them naked. Dial back the Suzie Homemaker vibe."

Brie didn't ask others about the two men. She smiled when they passed along news but inside she felt like she was cheating.

If they wanted her to know, they'd tell her personally.

On a day when the weather was positively *mild* for February, she decided to take a walk to her favorite coffee shop. The baristas were thrilled to see her and insisted on bringing her order to the table she chose out of the way.

Distracted, she smiled when Natalia took a seat in the chair opposite. "Hello, darling."

"You look lovely. How did you know I was here? Does Hudson have me fitted with a tracking device?"

"Not yet. I harass poor Carlo and tip Henry enough to pay his mortgage to keep a sharp eye on you."

"Thank you but you know I'm *fine*." She frowned. "You're up pretty early, aren't you?"

Leaning on the table, Natalia quirked her brow. "The man *barely* rests, I feel like a slacker if I go back to sleep after he leaves for the day."

Brie laughed. "You work *very* late hours. No guilt required. Sleep when he leaves until your body tells you to wake up. He likes taking care of you and doesn't resent that you need it."

"You're fucking brilliant." She pointed at the blank sketchpad. "I rarely see a page that isn't filled with something."

"Natalia…" She swallowed hard. "I-I know. About their relationship."

Electric blue eyes lifted to hers and widened. "I assume they didn't *intend* to reveal their little secret."

Brie explained the night she'd watched them at the club.

One of the staff set Natalia's coffee in front of her with a smile. "I thought you'd left. Enjoy."

Mechanically, she sipped the brew. "Darling, how do you *feel* about this latest information?"

"Curious. At first, I thought they meant to use me as cover." A warm shiver passed over her as she remembered their attention. "Apparently *not*."

The blonde blinked. "To my knowledge, no lover has *ever* been privy to that detail, Brie." She cleared her throat. "They never *meant* for me to know."

Processing what she implied, Brie sat forward. "Natalia."

"We hadn't known them more than a couple of years. All of us belonged to the same club in Dallas but weren't aware."

Lifting her eyes, she murmured, "You know the particulars of The Playground?" Brie nodded. "We…ran into them there. The circumstances left no doubt regarding their relationship."

Mind racing, Brie said softly, "Don't give me details."

"Well *done*, darling." Natalia sipped her coffee. "For a while, I'm certain Harper feared Hudson would use the knowledge to gain an advantage."

"He's not a dirty fighter."

"When Harper realized neither of us were sharing the information or shunning them in social situations, it became an unwritten piece of history between them. It changed the way Hudson was considered from that moment on."

"He was taken seriously as an up and coming business talent with a strong core of honor."

Natalia nodded. "Exactly. From then on, it was easier for a young man from nothing to get meetings with the most powerful people in the world."

Sitting back, Brie's lips parted in shock.

"Without Harper Delkin, Hudson would've continued to accumulate money and power because he *never* quits. However, it would've taken longer. Harper's nod of approval for an illegitimate boy from the basest poverty opened doors that would've been *forever* closed to him."

"Give me a second. Give me just a second."

Her mind reeled with the knowledge that Harper helped her best friend when he was starting out because he was grateful for his discretion about the man he loved.

Brie had another revelation. "It also led to the correct assumption that you weren't disgusted by the thought of their relationship. It made *you* more appealing." She grinned. "You wouldn't have thrown up pesky emotion all over them."

Natalia laughed and the beautiful sound drew smiles from around the café. "I *adore* your pesky emotion."

"That they can keep their two worlds separate shows an incredible strength of will."

"Neither of them would risk Harper's reputation on the kind of women wealthy men tend to pick up like lost pennies." She shook her head and blonde curls bounced. "Without the luck or, you know, the ability to read."

Brie lost it completely for almost a minute. "That's so wrong. I'm sure *some* of them are smart."

"They're few and far between. It's enough to make me grind my teeth at social functions." She winked. "You're the kind of trophy powerful men should want. The perfect package."

"Hardly, Natalia."

"Men like the flash, sometimes the Victoria's Secret label on their ass, and then bitch like children when the poor dumb thing turns out to be all fluff, no filler. You have lots of good filler with your brain, heart, and *pretty boobies*."

The blonde mouthed the last bit and Brie didn't know if she'd be able to pull herself together.

"Gabriella." Her laughter strangled and she glanced up to meet Harper's eyes. Elijah stood beside him. "Natalia, always lovely to see you."

"Hello, gentlemen. Did your plane set you down on the roof? I've been keeping my ear to the ground."

"We wanted to surprise Brie." The addition from Elijah visibly stunned Natalia. "I do *speak*, Lady Roman."

"Beautifully, as a matter of fact," she answered. "I'm going to take

Brie's advice and nap."

"Allow us to escort you back to the building," Harper said. Natalia looked as if she'd object. He added firmly, *"Please."*

Frowning, the blonde nodded. To Brie, she said, "Come, darling. We need to go."

Confused at her friend's change of mood, Brie quickly gathered her bag and the four of them left the cafe. Everyone was strangely quiet and she *hated* being so slow with the cane.

"I'm sorry I'm holding everyone up," she murmured.

"Nonsense, Brie." Natalia tugged her hair from behind where she walked side by side with Harper.

Both men were quiet and she wanted to ask if they were okay as they approached the building awning.

A long black van sped toward them, a front wheel jumping the curb. The side doors started to open before it rocked to a complete halt.

Elijah said coldly, *"Cover."*

Harper grabbed Natalia roughly and wrapped his arm around Brie's waist, carrying her to the front doors. Henry opened it and he all but threw them into the lobby as the concierge came out from behind the desk.

He barked, "Safe room. Call Winters."

Then he raced back to the street and Brie shoved grabbing hands away from her. Distantly, she heard Natalia scream her name. Her leg gave way at the front glass and she stared through the window on her knees.

Several men wearing masks, dressed in black, were in a battle with Elijah and Harper on the sidewalk. She watched the men fight back to back, the bodyguard moving faster than her eyes could follow.

It seemed to go on forever.

They disabled several of the attackers before the rest of the security team landed in the thick of things.

"You need to come with me, Brie." Carlo tried to lift her but she fought him. "I have to get you to safety."

"No! I'm staying *here*! I've got to stay here!"

Just then, Harper met her eyes over Elijah's shoulder. The bodyguard's body protected his completely, pressing him against the van. Elijah's other hand held one of their attackers suspended by his throat against the vehicle.

She watched Harper's lips move and Elijah glanced over his shoulder. His eyes went wide when he saw her at the window. He dropped the assailant and kicked him in the head.

His hand on the back of Harper's neck, the bodyguard walked him close to the front of his body, barking orders at his team. They stepped over several downed figures and entered the building lobby.

Elijah dropped to one knee beside her. He kept Harper with him, forcing him to kneel as well.

"Brie. Let go, Brie." It was only then she realized she still held the metal framing around the front glass. "Come away from the windows. Let's get you to safety."

Lifting her fingers away, she nodded. Her head felt dizzy and her stomach felt upside down. "I-I don't think I can get up."

"Let me help, Brie," Carlo told her gently.

Turning to the concierge kneeling at her side, she noted a bruise forming along his jaw. "Did I, did I *hit* you?"

"You were upset. It was an accident. Let's make sure you're safe." Nodding to Elijah, the concierge helped her stand. "You landed on the floor pretty hard. Wrap your arm around my shoulders and I'll try to find your cane."

"I'm sorry, Carlo. I didn't mean to hit you."

"I know, pretty girl. No harm done. Natalia is probably about to lose her mind so let's get to her as quickly as possible."

The trim man helped her to a space behind the lobby desk she'd never noticed. The tile pressed in to reveal a safe room.

The moment she entered, Natalia grabbed her from Carlo and collapsed on a padded bench.

"I'm *telling*, darling. You scared about ten years off my life." Holding her shoulders, she gave Brie a sharp shake. "When trained people with *guns* tell you to get to safety, you fucking *do it* and let them do their *job*."

"I didn't know what was happening and it made me panic." Then she burst into tears and Natalia hugged her tightly. "I need to be told things so I don't react badly."

"It's alright. Everything is alright." To someone else, her friend said, "Get a blanket. I need to warm her up."

Instantly, a soft blanket wrapped around her but Brie couldn't stop shaking.

Lifting her hands, Natalia hissed. "Jesus, Brie. You snapped your nails to the *quick*." Electric blue eyes lifted and there was a long pause. "I didn't know it was so powerful already. Now I understand your reaction."

All the adrenaline left Brie's body in a whoosh and she zoned out, shaking and confused.

She didn't know how many minutes passed when she realized Hudson crouched in front of her. He held her shoulder hard.

"Gabriella."

She blinked. "I-I messed up."

"Everyone messes up." He smoothed a lock of hair from her face. His other hand held Natalia's so tightly his knuckles were white. "You're both safe. That's the important thing."

"Those men, they were after Harper." Hudson nodded. "They'd have kidnapped him, *hurt* him. He and Elijah could've been *killed* fighting back."

"Violence is an unfortunate side effect of money."

Brie rubbed her temple hard. "I didn't realize. I thought Leonard was a *precaution*. I'm so naïve. I didn't think, I never thought it would touch people I care about."

Hudson tried to reassure her. "The people trusted with our safety are well trained, Gabriella. Don't worry. The main goal is mostly money."

"This attack was in retaliation for my purchase of a factory that laundered money for the Albanian mob." Harper's voice drew Brie's gaze. "It's always something but Elijah is *very good* at what he does and he hires other people he trusts."

He sat beside her. "How are *you*, Gabriella?"

"I'm okay."

"You're a *horrible* liar." He lifted her fingers and took in the damage to her nails. "You fought hard." She didn't know what to say. He lifted silver eyes to stare into hers. "Thank you."

She frowned. "For splitting everyone's attention during a crisis and potentially making a dangerous situation worse?"

"No. For *caring*." He gathered her close and kissed the top of her head. "Elijah will be back soon. He'll demand you join us and I agree that you must."

"He's going to be angry."

"That won't be his reaction. Rest."

Listening to the beat of his heart, she fell asleep.

Chapter Thirteen

Warm hands smoothed along Brie's face and neck, bringing her out of a bad dream in a wonderfully peaceful way.

Meeting Elijah's lovely green eyes, she whispered, "I'm sorry."

He shook his head. "Come, Brie."

Bending, he lifted her in his arms and walked out of the safe room to the elevators. Several armed men accompanied them. They were clearly hardened fighting men.

"Soldiers?" she asked aloud.

"Most of Elijah's team is ex-military," Harper replied. "They're the best at what they do."

"I'm glad." Meeting the man's eyes nearest to her, she said, "Thank you for getting there so fast."

Surprise crossed his face. "Of course, ma'am."

Three members of the team went room by room in Harper's apartment while the other half remained with them in the hall.

"Clear, sir."

Elijah nodded. "Help with containment and bunk downstairs. We'll meet in the morning."

Without another word, he carried Brie inside.

"You can take me to my apartment." He didn't respond.

Walking into a bedroom, he set her down carefully on a platform bed and shrugged off his jacket. He opened a concealed cabinet and removed a black metal box.

Resting it on the bed beside her, Brie realized it was a sophisticated medical kit.

Harper stood in the doorway with his arms crossed.

Removing nail clippers, Elijah carefully trimmed her broken nails. With a tweezer, he extracted several metal splinters. When he was satisfied, he cleaned the tips and applied bandages to two that took skin and bled badly when they broke away.

He unlaced her boots and took them off. When his hands settled over the closure of her pants, she numbly lifted so he could shimmy them from her lower body.

Her eyes widened at the heavy bruising and swelling around her knee. Elijah broke an ice pack and wrapped it there. Reaching behind her, he pulled a blanket around her shoulders.

Settling back on his heels, he watched her intently. Swallowing hard, she asked, "Are either of you h-hurt?"

"Minor scratches. Nothing serious."

She nodded and exhaled. "Are you angry?" He shook his head slowly. "I didn't know what was happening. I reacted badly." Scrubbing at the tears that slipped down her cheeks, she added, "I'll do better."

"You do everything *exactly* as you should."

He raised himself and put his arms around her. Cupping the back of her head, he held her as she cried out her stress and fear. After several minutes, she wrapped her arms around his neck and hugged him hard.

"Thank you for being so good at what you do. I'm really fucking happy you trained Harper."

"How do you know I trained him?"

"You wouldn't have trusted it to anyone else and he fights like you." She inhaled deeply. "Had I not been acting like those ridiculous women I can't stand in movies, I'd have registered how fabulously fluid you are when you fight together. I'll just point that out now."

He chuckled and hugged her harder.

A while later, she leaned back to look at him. "I'm glad you're both safe, that you weren't hurt. I want to ask questions but I'm terrified of the answers."

Elijah used a damp cloth Harper handed him to wipe her face and smoothed her hair behind her ears with his fingers.

"Most threats are thwarted before they're carried out."

"That's a relief." Tilting her head, she frowned. "Elijah, why were you at the café? How did you know I was there?"

"Carlo told me you'd gone for coffee."

As understanding dawned, Brie put one hand over her mouth. "Y-you *knew* about the threat and you wasted precious time to get me back to the building." Shaking her head, she was suddenly angry. "You can't *do* that. You can't!"

"Brie."

"Either of you could've been *hurt* or *killed* and it would've been *my fault*." She reached out to hold his shoulders. "Elijah, you can't *ever* do that again."

"We agreed we had to get you," Harper told her. "We came in covertly and the team was on their way. He wanted me in the safe room. I refused."

"Of course, you did! You couldn't let *him* go out there alone while *you* were safe. Not after, oh my god." She shook her head. "You can't let *me* mess up your routine. I can't distract you! Neither of you would *survive* without the other."

"Gabriella…"

"Brie…"

They addressed her at the same moment but she was shaking again. "No! I'm fucking *new* here. I don't fucking *count!*"

Elijah gripped the back of her neck tightly, his gaze intense. "You fucking count to *me*."

"I don't have priority over a relationship that spans *forty years*. Some woman who's been around *five minutes* doesn't get saved first. Not today, not ever!"

"She damn well does if you *know* she fucking *loves* you."

His kiss shorted out her ability to think. It was rough, almost savage, and it went on and on. It blanked out everything but the feel of him, the taste of him.

When he broke it, she pulled him back in a frenzy and took another. He gave her exactly what she needed. He kissed her until her anger and anxiety began to lessen.

It took a long time.

Leaning back, he whispered, "A woman has never loved me."

She held his face, stroking his cheeks with her thumbs. Resting her forehead against his, she replied, "You're a man who's ridiculously *easy* to love, Elijah."

"You're the only person who's ever thought so."

"That's not true. Harper just hides how easy it is to love you. He doesn't want to seem weak."

"Gabriella. How the fuck do you *know* so much?"

Most would've thought he was angry but Brie knew he wasn't. All the time she'd spent with Hudson helped her navigate his mannerisms.

"I'm astute." She shrugged lightly. "One day, you'll see that."

He didn't answer but she could *feel* his stare.

Gathering her close, Elijah kissed her head. "I'm going to feed you. It helps with the aftershocks."

She nodded against him and he lifted her to her feet.

Wearing a sweater that brushed the top of her ass and fuzzy socks, she cleared her throat in embarrassment.

"Um, I need to put pants on."

Harper raked his eyes down her body and took in her delicate pink boy shorts. "That would be a shame. Eat, *then* pants."

Looking at him, she raised a brow. "That sounds kind of shady, Harper."

He shrugged. "You have a remarkable ass. You shouldn't cover it just yet. Let me get my pleasures where I can."

Laughing, she went to take a step and almost hit the floor. Elijah caught her. "Fuck. Fuck. *Fuck.*"

"You banged it pretty bad," Harper said softly.

"If it wasn't already *weak* it wouldn't be a problem." She was so angry she wanted to cry. *Again.* She growled under her breath, "You start bawling and I *swear to god*, you silly bitch."

Gritting her teeth, she straightened and took a deep breath. "Do you have my stupid fucking cane around here?"

"I like your feisty side." She grunted and Harper winked. "I particularly enjoyed *kiss my ass, Delkin.* That made me hard."

"You're obviously a glutton for punishment."

"You have *no* idea." Bending, he picked her up and carried her into the dining room. Setting her on a chair, he explained, "I don't know what happened to your cane."

"I hope it got run over by a bus," she mumbled.

Elijah walked in the kitchen and started removing the makings for sandwiches. "You'll have another one in the morning."

Tilting up her face with the side of his hand, Harper kissed her and she forgot what she was about to say. She reached for him and held the back of his head.

A long time later, he lifted his face, changed his mind, and took another kiss. She moaned softly as her tongue coiled with his.

Eventually, he let her go and stared into her eyes. "Don't love me, Gabriella."

She sighed. "I'm doing my best."

"Elijah will love you. You love him." She didn't respond. "That will be enough."

"You really have *no idea* how the human heart works, huh?" She shook her head. "Go be stoic, Harper. I'll watch."

A few minutes later, they joined her at the table with positively enormous sandwiches and drinks. She stared at the creation for a long time before picking up her knife and cutting it in half, then cutting the half into two equal pieces.

Pushing her plate across the table, she gestured at it, "I don't move around much. I'll tackle this side." Grinning, they each accepted a section. "This is less overwhelming."

She placed her napkin over her lap and Elijah followed the movement with a frown.

"I have to maintain *manners* at least." His eyes flicked up to hers. "I shall expose myself the moment I'm done."

"We don't eat with women." The statement from Harper surprised her.

"At all?" She tilted her head when he shook his head. "How the hell have you managed to avoid it?"

"They aren't here long." He lifted his glass of wine.

She burst out laughing before she could stop herself. "Well, that's one way. Do you keep little snacks they can take with them?" She winked. "I imagine they must not have much strength left when you shuttle them out the door."

Watching the infamously stern Harper Delkin snarf white wine was one of the best experiences of her life.

Elijah grinned at her. "I never considered snacks."

"You need granola bars, dried fruit, and juice boxes for nutrient replenishment. Maybe those packets you get on flights. Hope you enjoyed your trip, have some pretzels."

Both men laughed and it was incredible.

"Okay, I'll stop or you'll never get to eat. I'm the worst choice for your first female dinner guest."

"You're the best choice," Elijah said. "You have a gorgeous laugh."

"So do you."

They focused on their food and she managed to squash the sandwich to a size that fit in her mouth.

When she was done, they took her plate. Harper frowned at her wine glass. "You don't drink?"

"Are you kidding? My share of the umbrella corporation is a winery and distribution facility." She inhaled the scent of the wine and her lips parted in surprise. Taking a small sip, she confirmed. "This is one of mine."

"Yes. You make some of the best wines in the United States."

Sighing sadly, she said, "I can't drink yet. Too many meds."

"Ah, I forgot." He reached to take the glass and she held it with a small dog bark that made him laugh.

"I'll just *smell* it." Bracing his hand on the table and the back of her chair, he stared into her face. "Relaxation looks good on you, Harper."

He whisked away the cloth in her lap. "That napkin did *not* look good on you."

She rolled her eyes dramatically. "It was *so* last year's fashion anyway. The in-crowd prefers hemp napkins handwoven by arthritic natives."

"Your imagination and quick wit are fascinating."

"Thanks."

"I want to fuck you."

She fluttered her hand. "You say that to all the girls."

"Tell me about your time with the couple."

"No actual sex. Well, *they* had sex."

Harper's eyes darkened. "You didn't fuck them."

"Not technically. I received mad orgasms and they took care of each other. They took requests."

"You *told them* what you wanted them to do?"

"Mm hmm. In detail." Her smile was slow. "I rather enjoyed the picture they presented and had to sketch it. They're *outstanding* at following directions."

"You sketched them fucking?" She nodded. "Did you touch yourself while you watched them?"

"Yes. Then we'd watch movies and snuggle on the couch." He frowned and she tilted her head. "It wasn't only about the sex, you know."

"It's *always* about the sex. They had you naked. How did they keep from taking you?" He seemed legitimately confused.

"I wasn't strong enough. M-my bones. I have to be sure they're healed." She cleared her throat. "Harper, I explained why I was unable to commit to any sort of arrangement earlier. I wasn't just making you wait."

"Four more months."

"About that, yes. Joshua and Jessica wanted me to feel human, to remember why it's important to keep going. I was lost."

"They helped you emotionally?" She nodded. "I don't know how to do that. Elijah was never emotional before you."

"Does it bother you?"

"Sometimes."

"I appreciate your honesty." Inhaling carefully, she whispered, "I won't hurt him. I won't hurt you. I won't ruin what you have together. I'd never do that."

"You can't hurt me."

"Okay." She steeled herself against his repeated insistence that he *would not* love her. "Now that we've had this lovely chat and you've clarified how you're the modicum of control and immune to me, may I have my pants?"

"No. I like you without pants."

"It isn't socially acceptable to go without pants. Eventually, I'll have to wear them."

"I'd rather you not."

"You're a little frustrating, Harper."

"I know." He kissed her roughly several times before walking to his bedroom. "Goodnight, Gabriella."

"You're *leaving?*"

He paused and turned. "I lack the gene to resist a warm woman in my bed. Elijah is better at self-denial."

Then he closed the door.

Glancing at Elijah, she realized he'd been leaning against the bar with his arms crossed while Harper marked his territory and stated his conditions.

"That was…interesting." She pressed her fingers along the bridge of her nose. "*Now* can I have my pants?"

"No."

He picked her up and carried her back to the room where he'd doctored her. Placing her gently on cool linens, he worked her sweater up her torso and over her head.

"You're taking my top now, too?"

He nodded as he pulled the blanket over her and turned off the lamp. Walking around the bed, he climbed in beside her.

"Brie."

"Yes?"

"I left your bra but I regret doing so."

"Fine. You can have it." Instantly, he worked the clasp free and tossed it to the floor.

Beneath the blankets, he wrapped his arm around her and stroked a warm palm up and down her bare back.

"This is better." He kissed the top of her head.

"You should take off *your* clothes in a show of solidarity."

He chuckled and stood long enough to strip to his boxer briefs.

When they were skin to skin, she asked quietly, "Why did you keep me with you, Elijah?"

"The look on your face. In the lobby when I thought you were already in the safe room."

"What look?"

"Fear of loss." He held her closer. "I could *see* your love for me, your worry for us. I needed you near."

Rolling to her side, she slid her arm over his stomach and nuzzled her cheek against his chest, kissing the skin there. His arm crossed her back and the tips of his fingers brushed the side swell of her breast.

"I wanted to be near, Elijah. Tomorrow, I'll go home."

"Sleep, Brie."

Brie soaked up his presence like the rare gift it was in her life and she was grateful. Glad to be able to touch him, that he was in town to touch her, and that no one had stolen the opportunity through the earlier violence.

His warmth and steady breathing gradually put her out.

* * *

In his own bed, Harper stared at the ceiling with his hands crossed behind his head.

He replayed the day. From the moment he'd seen Gabriella laughing openly with Natalia to her fear for them to her obvious pain when he reminded her not to love him.

She was funny, smarter than he realized. The more time he spent in her presence, the more he liked her.

The fear inside him grew.

Chapter Fourteen

Third Week of March 2015

One year to the day of her accident, Brie woke from an awful nightmare. Shaking and distraught, she sat up to catch her breath. A warm palm settled on the skin of her back.

"It's alright. You're safe." Elijah's voice anchored her to reality. "Today will be hard."

"You knew," she said without looking at him.

"Yes."

Since the day of the attack, when the men were in town, Elijah sometimes stayed the night with her. Having him hold her and the ability to touch him made it possible for her to sleep.

It wasn't as easy when he wasn't with her.

Laying back down, she inhaled carefully. Turning her head on the pillow, she whispered, "Thank you for staying."

"I enjoy sleeping with you, Brie. It's an unusual experience for me. It's rare in my life that I haven't slept alone."

She wanted to ask why he didn't sleep with Harper but didn't feel as if she had the right.

Rolling to his side, he propped his head in his hand. "You're somehow even more beautiful when you sleep." He stroked wild curls away from her face.

"Thank you."

They returned late from a business trip. On edge, she hadn't been able to sleep. Elijah's knock in the middle of the night filled her with relief and happiness.

As she opened the door to him, he took her in his arms, kissed her senseless, and carried her to her bedroom.

Removing everything but her panties, unbraiding her hair, he placed her in bed and joined her in nothing but boxer briefs.

In the morning light, his eyes were bright and his smile made her heart thump loudly in her chest.

"I missed you while you were gone." Moving to her side, she tucked one hand under her head and stroked the other over the lines of his face, neck, and chest. "It always feels longer than it is."

"Do you hate that we travel so much?"

She shook her head. "It's the way it is. I understand. I worry more now…that you could be hurt or k-killed. I know there's real *danger* so I send you all the good vibes I can when you aren't in my line of sight."

"I *knew* I felt something."

Brie tried to smile. "Natalia said you're the best in the world at what you do and I'm glad. Keep coming back, Elijah." Stroking her fingers over his sternum she whispered, "Keep this beautiful heart beating."

His hand held hers to his chest. "I'll always come back to you. I'll always bring Harper back to you."

Her smile faded. "He doesn't *want* to come back to me. I'll take what I can get in the form of rough kisses and verbal sparring. He resents even the *suggestion* of more than that."

Time spent with Harper made her ache to help him. She didn't know all the reasons he resented love, perhaps even women in general, but she knew she could help if he let her in.

"Do you love him, Brie?"

"I…it's not easy for me, Elijah. Knowing Harper doesn't *want* me to love him hurts because I want to help him see that loving me is safe. He loves you so he's *capable* of it."

"Give him time."

"He's warned me and now it'll be my own fault if I don't heed those warnings." She shook her head. "He may only have room to love you and I can't resent it because I understand. It feels so *good* to love you."

Then he was kissing her and there were no more words. His hands roamed her skin and she panted into his mouth.

Holding and kissing her seemed to please Elijah as much as it pleased her. Though he was *always* hard, he never remarked on his need for relief.

"Let me taste you," she whispered against his lips. He went still. "Show me the best way."

Unable to kneel or crouch, she wasn't sure how to accomplish what she wanted. She was *desperate* for him.

"I'll wait, Brie."

"You *have* waited and you've done it with more patience than any other man would've had. I'm not sure of a safe position. Help me, show me how." While she watched, the green of his eyes darkened. "Please, Elijah."

"Why is this important to you?"

"You offer comfort and care *no one* has ever been able to give me. I want to give back, to please you." She smiled. "Just having you here pleases me more than you realize."

His thumb traced her lower lip. "I dream of it."

"You dream about me sucking you?" He nodded and her nipples furled. She was wet just *thinking* about it. "Let me do this for you."

His voice was low. "I'm not what you think I am."

"What do I think you are?"

"Mild. Gentle."

Hugging him tightly, she kissed him. Pulling back, she stroked her fingers over his face. "Then show me who you really are, Elijah. I *love* you. I *trust* you."

He wrapped his hand around her throat.

Brie held his gaze without blinking. When he gradually tightened his grip, she wasn't afraid. Even when she *knew* she'd lose consciousness, she *could not* fear him.

* * *

Elijah knelt naked at the side of the bed, watching as Brie woke. Her reaction would determine more than she realized.

She tried to lift her arm and discovered she couldn't. She experienced a moment of confusion. Turning her head, she found his eyes. Confirming his presence, he watched her entire body ease.

Silently, she simply stared at him. He let the silence draw out between them and she didn't fill it. He saw questions in her eyes but she didn't ask them.

"I won't *ever* do that again." She didn't respond and he reached out to stroke her face. Her eyes closed and she nuzzled him. "I had to test you. I had to know."

Midnight blue eyes opened and he could've drowned in them. "You may speak, Brie."

"Teach me, Elijah."

That they were the first words from her mouth caused a ripple of shock to go through him that he hid from her.

"The bindings are symbolic, tied loosely, meant as a reminder." She nodded. "I didn't bind your lower body. I worry about your healing injuries. Only one hand to the headboard, one to the base. There's a simple bow on the inside of each wrist that you can untie yourself if you need to."

She was completely relaxed and it made him love her more.

"Your safe word is whale." One side of her mouth lifted in a smile. "Tell me when you should use your safe word."

"If I'm in actual pain or feeling real fear."

"You're still mending. Listen to your body carefully, Brie. What you're capable of now may be different than six months from now but I *will not* set your progress back."

"Thank you. I trust you."

The statement filled him with pleasure. "Do you have any questions?"

"How can I please you, Elijah?" He kissed her possessively, roughly, and she moaned into his mouth. When he broke it, she tried to follow him and caught herself. "Sorry."

For being such a fast learner, he kissed her again.

Standing up, he put his hands beneath her arms and carefully moved her head just off the edge of the mattress. He lightly massaged the back of her neck.

"I'm okay. Please."

The height of her bed was ideal for the position. His only regret was that he'd be unable to see her face. Resuming his full height, he traced the tip of his throbbing cock across her lips.

"Open." She did so instantly.

Giving her just the head, he called on every control he'd ever learned to keep from coming.

It wasn't just the heat. It wasn't the wetness. It wasn't that he'd maintained abstinence for months in honor of her.

It was the first time a woman made him feel *welcome*. She sighed and her breath skated along his length.

He fed her a bit more and she took him gladly. When half of his cock was in her mouth, she pressed her thighs together.

"Spread your legs. Let tension build." Without hesitation, she separated her legs and inhaled carefully. "Excellent."

Pulling back, she whimpered. When she realized he wasn't taking his cock from her mouth, simply beginning to thrust, she moaned around him. He watched as he disappeared between her lips and wondered at the intensity.

Many women had sucked his cock over the last two decades. A few were tied up at the time.

Eventually, he came but it was usually out of boredom. Tired of playing games with grasping females, he performed sexually as if from a script and quickly scrubbed all trace of them from his skin.

Everything with Brie was different.

He watched her nipples pebble tightly and *knew* she was wet from the act of sucking him. Her heart rate was through the roof and he stroked his fingers through her silken hair.

"When I can't hold back another second, I'm going to come down your throat. Then I'm going to eat you until you're screaming, Brie." The mere thought made his mouth water.

Her body tensed with a long whimper and she gripped the bindings with tight fists.

"You deserve to come," he growled. "I deserve to taste you."

The moans she made around the flesh of his dick sent chills up his back and he increased the force of his thrusts. He felt her breathing catch and pulled back slightly.

She *growled* and tried to move her head to take more of him. He gave her what she wanted and watched his cock move the skin on the underside of her jaw, the top of her throat.

He gradually built the depth and speed of his strokes and she adjusted. For several minutes, he tried to remain detached enough to extend the ecstasy he'd been desperate to experience since the first time he was close enough to see the beauty of her mouth, the fullness of her lips.

Then she swallowed around the crest and he was lost.

"Take me, Brie." Her entire body shook as she swallowed everything he had, easing the vise around his balls for the first time in months. "*Fuck.*"

His legs trembled and he locked them out, riding every second of the bone-deep pleasure no woman had ever inspired.

Balls empty, satisfied on a level he didn't even recognize, he pulled from the heat of her mouth and crouched beside her. She panted, whimpered from her chest, and he kissed her.

Brie ate at his mouth and he untied her, knowing she needed to touch him. The second she was free, her hands stroked over his face, neck, and shoulders.

She wanted to hug him but shook too badly. He sat on the side of the bed and lifted her to a sitting position.

"Don't let me go, Elijah." The words were whispered against his neck as she hugged him as hard as she was able. "Harder. Hold me harder."

Bringing her fully into his lap, he wrapped his strength around her and she absorbed it.

After several minutes, she started to cry softly. Elijah knew why, he understood. He held her tighter.

* * *

Brie rode the most powerful sexual experience of her life, made so by the perfect blend of circumstances.

Her mind was in complete chaos.

The way the two men *looked* was a red herring. It distracted her, kept her off balance, and blurred reality.

It had been Elijah all along.

He was her Hudson. He was the man who spoke to her personality and understood how to evoke her true sexuality.

She held him as hard as she could, taking what he offered for as long as possible because there was no denying the truth.

Brie would *never* be allowed to keep him.

Chapter Fifteen

Unaware of falling asleep, Brie blinked in confusion when she woke up and stared into Elijah's eyes.

"I waited until you were awake. I have to leave." She nodded. "When I return, I'll thank you properly."

Remembering a conversation with Hudson in her sunny kitchen eons before, she smiled. "I'm not keeping score."

"I am." He kissed her until she was breathless and stroked his hand over her body. "Are you alright?"

She raked her fingers through his hair and nodded.

"I'll be back, Brie."

"Be safe. I love you."

He kissed her again. Then he was gone.

As the door clicked into place, she rolled to her back and stared at the ceiling. On the bedside table, she grabbed her cell phone and dialed the only person who might understand her turmoil.

"Darling. I was *just* about to pop down and invite you for brunch." The soft click of Natalia's heels as she walked through the first floor of the penthouse made Brie smile.

"Fucking excellent. Give me ten minutes to dress and I'll leave the door unlocked."

Brie walked out of her bedroom in leggings, a long sweater, and flat boots. She pulled her hair into a semi-neat bun at the back of her head.

Natalia was dressed to perfection in a caramel business suit and matching heels. Hair and makeup flawless as usual. She stood in the studio looking at one of Brie's paintings.

She could see her friend's curiosity about it and cut her off at the pass. "More on the painting later." Brie grabbed her cane and headed for the door. "Let's go. I need twelve hours of advice and I *know* you don't have that long."

"Did something happen?" Natalia paused in the doorway and examined Brie's face for a long moment. "Aah, the *reveal.*"

"My brain is scrambled. Help."

"Come, darling. I'll help put your mind to rights. How well I remember the mental anarchy. Discovering the *need* isn't half as shocking as discovering the man who can *fulfill* it."

Wrapping her arm through Brie's free one, they walked to the elevator and Brie frowned when she saw Leonard waiting inside the doors of the lobby. Henry stood beside him.

"Hey there, Leonard. What...?"

"A temporary precaution to put Hudson at ease," Natalia explained cheerfully.

At the restaurant, Leonard parked the car and appeared beside their table.

"Okay, what's going on?" To the driver, she said, "Sit down and eat with us. I'm about to freak out."

"Sorry, Brie."

"Don't apologize. You're awesome and I love seeing you. Join us and somebody tell me what's going on before I rattle apart."

Lowering into a chair, Brie noted that he chose one that enabled him to see the entire restaurant.

Natalia told her, "There were some...repercussions from the situation last month."

When she offered nothing else, Brie crossed her arms on the table. "I know I panicked. I know I'm considered fragile and everything.

Natalia, *tell* me."

"Photos were taken of us."

"When?"

"As Elijah and Harper escorted us back to the building. We looked like a foursome and the implication is that we're two couples. They surfaced this morning."

Sitting back, Brie let her eyes track around the room. Her suspicions about several men were confirmed when she recognized the member of Elijah's security force who'd ridden with them in the elevator.

"How many people are guarding us?"

"Possibly a dozen. Between Hudson and Harper, they share a lot of manpower." Natalia shrugged. "It's a safeguard."

"I'm sorry you got mixed up in it." Brie reached out and grabbed her hand. "Why come out? *Natalia…*"

The blonde leaned over the table and turned her hand over to grip her back. "Darling, listen to me. This isn't the first time I've been under lockdown. I've been photographed with Hudson thousands of times over the years. Leonard and I once spent six hours playing rummy in the limo when we were unable to leave a parking garage."

"Nothing can *happen…*"

"Ssh. It's alright. Nothing will. We *cannot* hide. It makes us seem more valuable. Leonard is good at his job as are the other men who work with him and Elijah. I'm going to be fine and so are you." Her eyes held Brie's. "Take a deep breath and trust them. You know you can."

Nodding, Brie took a sip of her orange juice. Natalia squeezed her hand firmly. "We're going to eat, pick up coffee, and return to the apartment. You'll feel more comfortable talking there."

An hour later, after behaving as if they were in no rush, Brie breathed a sigh of relief when Natalia was back in the lobby.

In the elevator to the penthouse, she hugged her friend tightly. "Nothing can *ever* happen to you. It would *kill* him."

Leaning back, she stared at the lovely features of her best friend's woman. "Regular checkups." Patting Leonard's suited chest, she added, "Plenty of iron."

The driver laughed.

Arm around her waist, Natalia led her into the apartment and sat with her on the sofa. "No more stress today or talk of negative things. Let's talk about something fun. Spill it."

Blushing several times, Brie described her morning with Elijah.

Snickering, the blonde said, "I *told* you those skills would come in handy."

"They really did." She twisted her fingers in her lap. "You knew Harper's looks distracted me, made me assume he was like Hudson."

"Yes. His personality adds to the confusion since he's similarly abrupt. I had every confidence Elijah would choose the right time to show you who he was but your intense attraction to him from the start made me wonder at your blind spot."

Considering, Brie nodded. "The way Harper looks and behaves was so familiar." She grinned. "You know I enjoy a little bit of *asshole* in a man."

Natalia laughed warmly. "As much of a puzzle as you originally were for Hudson, I believe he was the same for you. Once you figured him out, you gave as good as you got and that made him *respect* you. Protectiveness is in his DNA but he doesn't give respect lightly."

"I'm damn proud of that, I'll have you know. I'd put that shit on my resume if I still worried about keeping one."

"I can't wait to tell him."

Brie was quiet as something niggled at the back of her mind. Talking aloud, she mumbled, "Elijah is clearly dominant. Two dominant males can share a submissive. An arrangement with someone like me would make sense but…"

She stared at the black marble floor, thinking it through. "They've had a *sexual* relationship for more than twenty years and haven't committed to women in any capacity, so…how did that work?"

Frowning, Brie traced the threads, replayed conversations, and when the answer came to her, her eyes felt as big as saucers.

Natalia reclined on the couch with her arm across the back, her legs crossed. She looked utterly relaxed as their eyes met. "I *love* watching you discover fascinating new data."

"Holy *shit*." Rubbing her palms over her thighs, Brie laughed nervously. "I *never* saw that coming."

* * *

At thirty-thousand feet, Elijah watched the clouds pass. His mind was focused on his morning with Brie and his regret that he hadn't left her fulfilled.

When he received the update that the team had seen her safely from and back to the building, he exhaled.

"You stayed with her again," Harper said sharply.

Turning his head, Elijah met pewter eyes that had captivated him since he was eighteen. He knew the man's moods, likes, and dislikes better than any other person on earth.

In the forty years they'd known each other, Elijah had witnessed him in states of fear, pain, happiness, sadness, grief, fury, and passion.

Harper's continued refusal to see what Brie offered them separately and together was a source of intense sorrow.

A storm brewed and for a man who saw the world in black and white, Elijah struggled to feed both sides of who he was while remaining true to old promises and new ones.

"Have you figured out a way to fuck her yet?"

Sitting forward, he rested his elbows on his knees. "Why, Harper? I don't understand your changing moods." He shook his head. "One day you're bantering with her and seem relaxed for the first time in ten years. The next, you make snide remarks as if those moments never happened."

Slapping the financial paper into the seat beside him, he ground out, "We *fuck* them and they *leave*."

"Winters would've castrated us both. You *knew* she'd be more from the start. You sought his fucking approval *twice* and received it. You told me to pave the way and I did so. It's *you* and what *you want* that changes by the fucking day."

"You'll *always* be mine."

Tiredly, Elijah nodded. "And you'll always be a spoiled child that I must placate in whatever way you see fit if I'm to have any peace." Raking his hand through his hair, he stood up and stepped into the aisle.

Harper grabbed his hand. "*Elijah*."

"I tire of your inconsistency. Your childish tantrums bore me. I'd rather let her go, lose her myself, than try to protect her from your spiteful attempts to wound her."

"She'll end up making you hate me."

Bending, Elijah gripped the hair at the base of his neck. "Your misplaced jealousy, Harper. Your cruelty. Your inability to compromise even knowing how good she'd be for *you* as much as me. It's *you* who'll accomplish what you fear."

He let go and stepped back. "All she wants to do is *love* you. You fight the best thing to ever happen to us, selfishly dooming me as well as yourself to decades more of the same tedious bullshit with the same tedious women who *offer* nothing and *take* as much as they can grab with both hands."

In the bathroom, Elijah stared at his reflection as he gripped the sides of the sink.

Closing his eyes, he struggled to lower the rage, the frustration, the sadness that churned inside him.

He replayed his morning with Brie in his mind and felt everything settle, fall into place. It was the memory of Brie begging him to *hold her harder* that calmed him.

Aloud, he whispered, "I need good vibes. I need you."

Elijah straightened and put his shoulders back.

Harper would *stop* fighting the only woman who could bring them the life they never thought to have. He'd stop disrespecting the potential for every gentle thing they'd always talked of being out of their reach.

This bullshit had gone on long enough.

Returning to his seat, Elijah spoke calmly but firmly. He outlined the reality of *his* wants and needs for a change and Harper listened, shocked and combative.

In the end, his best friend, his lover, would *submit*.

Elijah had *always* been stronger.

Chapter Sixteen

First Week of April 2015

The final night of the weeklong celebration for Riya and Tawny's birthdays had kicked everyone's asses.

The year before, no one celebrated. They'd been too worried about Brie's condition, waiting to see if she'd pull through from the hit-and-run that almost killed her.

It was important to her that they celebrated *hard* to make up for it. Before the festivities began, Brie went to her follow up appointment with the team of specialists Hudson hired to monitor her rehabilitation progress.

They took her off half her medications and reported that the healing of her skull was far better than expected. The worst of the broken bones were knitting strongly and they determined she'd regain full mobility of the affected joints over time.

The best news was that she was on track to meet *her* release date of June rather than the September date she'd originally received when her doctors sent her home from the hospital.

Cleared for alcohol consumption within reason, Brie could party like a big girl again.

The last evening, their entire group of awesome women gathered at the same place, at the same time.

They promptly tore some shit up.

Tawny and Brie were the only ones in any condition to meet for drinks the following night at *Trois*.

When they walked in, Natalia kissed them lightly and issued a small glare. "I feel like shit but I'm *here*, damn it."

"You look so *pretty* despite your condition," Brie assured her.

"Don't placate me. I'm too old for this shit. It wasn't until I was awakened to *screaming* sunlight this morning that I realized I was the fucking *matron* of our little gathering last night. Hudson laughed at me."

Tawny elbowed Brie. "Then there was screaming of a whole different kind, I bet."

Deadpan, Natalia stated, "True. The absolute *best* cure for a hangover, girls." She waved her hand at them. "Go away now. You're both too chipper and adorable."

Stepping closer, Brie placed her fingertips along the sides of Natalia's neck and massaged the muscles leading to her skull. In thirty seconds, the blonde looked as if she was melting.

"You need a massage and a soak. I'll text Hudson."

"I adore you, darling." Natalia kissed her lightly and held her gaze. "You have the *best* hands. Thank you."

Brie winked. "I adore you, too."

As they walked into the main room, Tawny said, "I've got this cramp right *here*..." She pointed to her ass. "Can you massage it for me?"

Laughing, they chatted until they collapsed on a comfortable sofa to partake in their favorite pastime of people watching.

The redhead handed Brie tequila, grinned, and clinked their glasses. "So fucking glad to have my drinking buddy back. You talk to the twins?"

Brie nodded. "Isaiah and Ezra are relieved that the girls recover quickly. Poor Teddy is *still* in bed. Kiefer isn't sure he'll ever release her to our care and keeping again."

"Totally saw that one coming. I talked to Marci earlier. Her men sent her to an all-day spa to detox from the booze. They personally cleared her schedule to make it happen. She was in heaven." Tawny shrugged. "Told you, princesses."

"You could be a princess if you wanted to but you'd likely slice people up with your tiara."

"Truth." She paused. "You know, you *could* be Hudson and Natalia's princess. They adore you even though they don't have all that ooey-gooey love you like. If you wanted, they'd take you right under their...bodies."

Laughing until she was actually crying, Brie shook her head. "Love that isn't reciprocated equally eventually hurts. I love them too much to love them that much." She sighed heavily. "I only have one life and I want to make it count."

"Brie, I'm sorry."

"I'm willing to love hard. Is it *wrong* to want that back?"

"It isn't wrong. No one deserves it more."

She looked at her hands. "Everyone always says I'm *unique*, like it's a good thing. It's really hard to be different, Tawny."

"I thought, fuck. Things aren't going well?"

"I won't get to keep them. No matter how this has been presented as a package deal, it isn't." She closed her eyes. "Eventually, when Harper has what he wants, he'll be *done* with me and will disconnect from everything I represent. I know he resents my relationship with Elijah. I'm prepared for it but it's going to hurt really bad."

Leaning forward, Tawny took her hand. "You ever need me, I'm there, Brie. If you need to recoup, come to my place."

She nodded. "Thanks. I didn't mean to get emotional."

"Reality is pretty fucked up. It intrudes when we least expect it. Best to deal and get it out."

Tilting her head, she added, "Take *everything* you can from this experience, bitch. Soak up the love, the sex, and the crazy. However, if shit goes down, save *yourself* first."

* * *

When Tawny's driver pulled to the curb in front of the building, he helped her out with a smile. "Have a lovely evening, Miss Hernandez."

"Thank you, Bobby."

Tawny got out of the car tense when three men stepped from the shadows to escort Brie in. Glancing around, she noticed a car idling behind them.

The redhead put her hand on her hip. "Boys, you should identify yourselves or you're going to get *fucked* up." Inclining their heads, Tawny kissed her cheek. "Call me if you need me."

Then she returned to the car and drove away.

Gesturing to the lobby, one of the men murmured, "Ma'am."

Inside, Brie stopped at the front desk and removed a heavy linen envelope from the bag she carried with her everywhere.

"Donald, can you please make sure Elijah gets this wh-whenever he comes in? Leave a note for Carlo?"

The nightshift concierge nodded. "Of course. Your progress is wonderful to watch, Brie. You barely need the cane."

She glanced at the hated thing and gave him a smile. "I can't wait to be rid of it for good. Have a great night."

In the elevator, the three men stood at her sides and in front of her. Brie didn't even know who they worked for.

"If this were a movie, you could be the bad guys and I'd be the dumbass who had no clue." She pitched her voice high. "Come on in, make my murder look like a suicide, and I'll fall seductively over the balcony."

The men tried not to laugh and failed utterly.

As the doors opened on her floor, Elijah stared at the men with a frown. All of them went to immediate attention.

"They can protect me and still be *human*, Elijah. I like when people laugh. It lessens the awkwardness of anyone thinking I'm worth offing in some ghastly, front-page manner."

Stepping between them, she glanced back and smiled. "Thanks, guys. Be safe."

Leading the way to her apartment, she held the door for a man she hadn't seen or heard from in more than two weeks.

"I'll make coffee."

"Brie?"

She pressed her hand to her heart. "It's been a weird night. I'm sorry. Give me a second to get my balance."

In her kitchen, she conducted mindless tasks and fought tears she didn't want to cry.

"You're moving so much better."

"I had my appointment last week. I'm doing great. Should be on track for June like I hoped. I shaved three months off their initial estimate. I'm proud of that."

A warm hand slid along her upper chest and pulled her against him. She stared at the skyline across the room.

"Riya and Tawny had their birthdays. Yesterday we celebrated with like forty security guys covering the bar we went to. I'm off a shit ton of meds so I can drink again."

"Brie."

"I worry about Natalia. She told me about the photos the day you left. I was glad to be brought up to speed at the same time I found out my best friend's soulmate could be kidnapped or shot in the head because she joined me for coffee."

"Brie."

"I think that's about it. What's happening with you?"

"I'm new at this part. The only person I'm accustomed to truly communicating with is always with me. I'm sorry." Turning her, he held her face in his hands.

She'd ached to see the beautiful green of his eyes.

"I missed you. I talked to Winters but I should've talked to you. Your progress is incredible and I'm so proud of you. You've worked hard."

He stroked the pads of his thumbs over her brows. "You're handling everything better than anyone else would."

"I won't bother you. I know you're busy." She reached up to hold his wrists and silently cursed the tears in her voice. "If you could let me know you're alive once a week, that would go a long way to helping me not freak out."

"Fuck. I'll get you a secure cell."

"I don't care if it's a smoke signal just, let me know you're breathing so I don't assume the worst and lose my mind. I need to know you're *breathing*, Elijah."

"I'll do better."

He bent his head to kiss her. It was so easy to fall into his kiss and forget what planet she was on. It didn't matter.

Whatever planet he was on, that was where she wanted to be.

* * *

Elijah watched Brie sleep. She had his hand tucked between her breasts as she laid on her stomach.

He'd held her, hugged her, for a long time after she told him everything he'd missed in her life over the two weeks he hadn't thought to pick up a phone.

He knew every move she made throughout the day if she left her apartment. He forgot she didn't have the same resources to know he was okay.

Other than Harper, no one else had ever been concerned if Elijah's heart was beating at the end of the day.

Seconds after he laid down beside her, she slipped into deep slumber she clearly hadn't been getting. There was a small pout on her lips and her curly black hair flowed over her pillow and down her back.

Sighing softly in her sleep, she scooted closer to him and sealed her naked body along his side. For a moment, her eyes fluttered open. "I love you, love you, 'Lijah."

Wrapping his arms around Brie, he allowed himself to stop the world for a few hours and just *be* with her.

* * *

Elijah let her sleep when the sun came up and went down to the lobby to brief his team in the conference room there.

Carlo smiled as he stepped off the elevator. "Good morning, Mr. Eklund. Brie left something at the desk for you last night."

Taking the envelope, he broke the seal and a key dropped into his palm. She'd included a note.

> *Elijah, use this whenever you're around. I don't want to miss your knock. I listen for it. I miss you. Brie*

In the conference room, he briefed his team, left instructions to contact him by text with any updates, and informed them he was taking the day off.

Then Elijah returned to the apartment of a beautiful sleeping woman, using the key she left him to get inside.

He had promises to keep.

Chapter Seventeen

Brie woke slowly, rested for the first time in *weeks*, and took in the empty space beside her. Reaching out, she touched the pillow where he'd slept.

Pulling it closer, she wrapped her arms around it and inhaled deeply. The clean, male scent of him lingered.

She wanted to cry but she didn't.

Instead, she took a deep breath, put it back, and turned over to get up. Elijah knelt on the floor beside the bed.

Unable to play it coy, she wrapped her arms around him with a gasp and pressed her face to his neck.

"You're still *here.*"

He hugged her tightly, totally involved the way Hudson always was, and she accepted the fact that she'd found another man she really wanted to hug her for the rest of her life.

"Good morning, Brie." She tightened her hold. "You love *hard.* It makes me feel stronger."

Leaning back, she blinked back tears. "It does?" He nodded and she stroked his face. "That's what it's *supposed* to do."

Raking her fingers through his hair, she whispered, "Your hair is longer." One fingertip traced a brow that was lighter than it had been. "You've been in the sun. You soak it up."

"You see me in ways no one ever has."

"I love you. Every part of you matters."

Rising from the floor, he pushed her back to the mattress and she knew she'd accept the risk if he wanted to make love to her. One arm held his weight above her, the other stroked from her neck to her breast.

"I made you a promise. We were interrupted. I always keep my promises, Brie."

Then he was gone and she watched as he stripped his clothes away for her. When he was naked, she got up and stood close to him, her palms spread on his chest.

* * *

Brie's voice was quiet. "I've never seen you all at one time. I just want to touch you, take you in." Raising her gaze, he stared into her dark blue eyes. "Is that alright?"

Elijah nodded and remained still as she explored him.

Raking her fingers through his hair, she traced the outline of his ears, the lines of his face, and down his neck.

Gentle hands ran over his chest and shoulders, down his arms to his hands. She petted him, squeezed muscle, and compared the size of his hand to her own. Her short nails raked his nipples, pressed the planes of his abdomen, and held his hips.

"I can't kneel yet," she murmured in disappointment.

She touched the tops of his thighs, lightly caressed the skin of his cock, and cupped his balls. Walking behind him, she repeated her exploration over the marred skin of his back and planted a kiss between his shoulder blades.

He felt her fingertips trace the indentations just above his waist and warm palms smoothed over his ass, squeezing lightly.

Returning to stand in front of him, her smile was heart stopping. The pleasure on her face at the simple opportunity to *touch him* almost sent him to his knees.

"You're such a beautiful man. Thank you." With her palms on the sides of his neck, she whispered, "I'm yours to command, Elijah."

He kissed her.

The simple act of kissing Brie was more earthshaking than sex with women in his past. She was fully involved, *present* in a way he'd never known to miss.

Palms cupping her face, he gave her what she deserved. Only when she was shaking, whimpering into his mouth, did he lift away to look at her. She always followed his lips, seeking him.

It was who she was.

She held his gaze for a long minute of silence. "May I ask a question?" He nodded. "Should I not look at you? The things I've read, I'm not sure." One side of her mouth lifted in a smile. "That one might be hard for me. I love your eyes."

"The way your mind works is one of the most beautiful things I've ever had the good fortune to witness." Holding the back of her neck, his thumb stroked the skin beneath her jaw. "Submission is the *will*, not the rules. Your desire to love and submit is evident in everything you do."

"You'll tell me if I'm doing something wrong?"

"I'll tell you if there's something I need from you. There's no right or wrong, Brie. There's you and me." He placed his palm over her heart. "Every beat *here* means you're doing it right."

Tears slipped from the corners of her eyes and he knew he'd burn down the world to protect her.

He stepped forward, backing her to the edge of the bed. Holding her shoulders, he encouraged her to sit. He lowered to his knees between hers, held her hips, and she smiled.

Almost a foot taller, he knew Brie liked when he was close. She started to reach for him and lowered her hands with a small frown.

"Touch me, Brie." Her eyes lit up and she did so instantly. "If I want you to remain still, I'll tell you or I'll bind you. I love your touch."

"It's *wonderful* for me."

He allowed her to pet him for a couple of minutes and plant kisses over his face. Her toes traced the skin of his calf while her fingers kneaded the muscles of his shoulders.

"Your similarity to a kitten is adorable."

Hugging him, she whispered, "Your similarity to a hot as hell bodyguard with a dominant nature and a gift for the violin makes me pretty damn happy, too."

Her ability to make him laugh was always a surprise.

Reaching to the top of the bed, he grabbed her pillows and stacked them behind her.

"Lay back, Brie."

She did and kept her eyes on his.

Resting his palms on her thighs, he said, "The first night I saw you, your hair hung loosely, framing your face and shoulders. You didn't move from the chair you sat in all night but others flocked to you."

Smoothing his hands over skin that had been ripped and torn as a car ran her down in the street, Elijah watched her hold her breath. He bent to kiss the worst of her scars.

"I remember thinking you seemed to light up the space around you. People are drawn to your natural iridescence, to the smiles you offer in welcome."

Trailing his hands down her legs, he cupped her feet and massaged gently. Working his way over her calves, he kissed her knees.

"Even Harper was drawn to it though he didn't understand what it meant. He wanted you initially because of your relationship with Winters. They've always been in silent competition. One can't have more than the other."

Holding her hips, he pressed his lips to the bend of each. Her breathing stuttered softly.

"I warned him, as did Winters, that you were outside his frame of reference. Women hold one place in his mind and it was clear to me you'd never fit such a small classification."

He rubbed his cheek over her slightly rounded belly and knew her hands itched with need.

"You can touch me, Brie." Instantly, fingers stroked through his hair and he closed his eyes at the pleasure of it.

"At the theater, I saw the same glow. It struggled against sadness, loneliness that was getting harder for you to hide. It pressed darkly, trying to snuff you out, but you fought. I wanted to soothe you, but I wasn't sure what you needed."

Rising over her, his fingers smoothed the outsides of her breasts and her nipples furled even tighter as he watched.

"At the after party, you showed me how easy it was. Simply holding your hand lit you up in a way I'd never seen. You give so easily of yourself and accept others without condition."

Taking a furled peak in his mouth, he suckled it firmly and her fingers curled tight in his hair as she held him to her.

The taste and texture of her pushed his own need higher than it had ever been. He released her with a soft pop and blew over the damp tip. A shiver passed over her skin.

"Every interaction with you teaches me, Brie. You find pleasure in the smallest things. It makes me want what I've never wanted before and causes me to think about my future in ways I thought were closed to me."

Taking possession of her other nipple, she moaned softly. Her hands drifted to his shoulders, lightly scratching and rubbing his skin.

He was a glutton for this woman's touch.

"You've touched me more in our time together than I've ever been touched in my lifetime, by any person. I didn't realize how addictive it would be."

Kissing his way over her chest and up the column of her neck, he claimed her lips. She opened herself to him, gave to him, and made him feel worthy.

Her hips lifted slightly and brushed her bare mound over the heated skin of his cock. He broke the kiss with a growl.

His forehead against hers, he murmured, "You'd give to me at risk to yourself. Your love humbles me, Brie."

Moving back quickly, he buried his face between her legs and tasted the only woman to *ever* made him hunger.

She gasped his name into the quiet room.

Gently placing the back of her thigh over his shoulder, he closed his eyes to savor the musky tang of her pussy.

For the rest of his life, he'd crave the delicacy.

Within a minute, she trembled, clenched her thighs, her breathing rapid. He pulled back enough to glide three fingers over her, circling gently, before trailing them to the snug entrance that made his cock throb painfully.

Pressing inside, he turned them, raking the tips along her inner walls as he set his mouth to the task of breaking her down to the simplest part of herself.

The first time she came, he pushed deeper inside her, resting his other palm over her belly to feel the way her womb pulsed under her skin. Her upper body arched, her fists tangled in the bedding and his hair, he watched her absorb all he gave.

His voice hoarse with need, he told her, "When my cock is gifted with the honor of taking you, I hope I can withstand the pleasure, Brie."

Sitting up, she cupped his face and kissed him in desperation, licking away the evidence of her release.

"Now, take me now. I'll be okay."

"I won't endanger you."

He gripped the hair at the back of her neck and kissed down the column of her neck. Sucking her nipple hard, he let her feel his teeth while he continued to thrust deep with his hand.

She touched him everywhere she could reach. "*Elijah,* take from me. Let me please you."

"You'll please me by giving me more of your come. Lay back." He watched as she collapsed against the pillows, her hair a wild tangle around her upper body. "Watch me eat you."

He returned to licking and sucking her, the blue of her eyes darkening further as her lower lip trembled.

Slickness flowed from her body. He removed his hand to rub it into her folds so he could lick it away. Holding her gaze, he dragged his tongue between swollen lips and circled her clit.

She held on for three minutes before her body took over.

"C-coming…"

The sight of Brie's torso lifting from the pillows, her eyes closing as her orgasm stole her ability to control anything made him want to drive his cock inside her until they were unable to move.

Her body shook, his name was a chant on her lips, and she gripped the sheets to anchor herself.

Need too great to deny caused him to stand. Wrapping his fist around his length, he used her juices to stroke himself.

Pulling her lower lip between her teeth, she whispered, "Yes. Please god, *yes*."

She probably didn't intend to cup her breasts or realize that she rolled her nipples while she watched him fist his cock.

Her thighs pressed the outside of his legs and he ground out, "I won't come until you do, Brie. Touch yourself for me."

Releasing one of her breasts, she settled her fingers over her mound. She used her thumb to stimulate her erect little clit while two fingers slipped into her pussy.

He could hear how wet she was and it made the skin on the back of his neck tighten.

Panting as she watched him, Brie pushed herself to climax, and he enjoyed seeing the way it rolled over her.

Her voice begged, "Please let me have it." Her eyes glazed. "Come on me, mark me, let me feel it."

Rolling his head on his shoulders, Elijah stroked himself faster and harder. The first stream splattered over her ribcage and nipple. The second covered her hand and belly.

Then she sat up and took him deep into her mouth, swallowing everything he had left.

Breath sawing in and out of his lungs, he watched as she took him as deep as she could.

When he'd have pulled back, she wrapped her arms around his ass and took him a little further. Even as her eyes watered, she swallowed around the head.

Slowly sliding her mouth from him, she laid back on the pillows. She licked his release from her hand while her other massaged it into her nipple and skin.

"I love the taste of you, Elijah."

As his breathing returned to normal, he took in the image she made sprawled, satisfied, and covered in his come. A single thought made him smile.

Harper had *no clue* what he was missing.

Chapter Eighteen

Harper Delkin fucked the mouth of the woman his fill-in security team escorted into the apartment and watched her fake tits bounce with the force of his thrusts.

She still wore the slinky little dress and stilettos she'd arrived in. Her makeup and hair were less than pristine as he gagged her with his cock and gripped her head to take it.

Within thirty seconds of entering his space, he sent his staff out and instructed her to get on her knees.

She did so with a knowing smile.

The diamond bracelet in his pocket ensured she'd take whatever he dished out and *beg him* to do it again if he wanted.

"Pull your dress down," he ordered. "I want to see your nipples on either side of my cock."

She obeyed without an instant of hesitation.

The silicone implants meant her type never wore bras. He doubted she wore panties. He wanted to know. Taking his cock away, he reached down and pulled the flimsy material over her head.

He watched her try to catch her breath. *No panties.* Part of him wanted to laugh. The rest of him ached.

"Spread your legs. Put your fingers in your pussy."

Pressing his cock deep again, he stayed there as she followed his direction. He went back to using her mouth, watching as she fingered a pussy he had no interest in tasting or putting his dick in.

Angry, he growled, "I might fuck your ass when I tire of your mouth."

She moaned around him because she'd agree to anything he wanted. "Fuck it hard while you make yourself come. Would you like that?"

"Mm hmm..."

"Of course, you would. You like everything." He hated *himself*, he hated *her*, and he didn't even remember her name. "Make yourself come and don't fake it. Imagine whatever you have to but I better know it's real."

She nodded as the heavy makeup around her eyes slid over her cheeks. He pulled back enough for her to breathe and watched as she frantically played with her clit.

She was thin and blonde. Her eyes were a pretty brown but he could only see them as calculating.

Harper closed his own to block her out.

He imagined Gabriella in the woman's place. Elijah would *slit his throat* if he treated her like his usual women.

His thrusts would be slower, not so hard. He wouldn't want to hurt her. He'd let her adjust, let her see he could be decent, he could be a good man.

That he could be gentle with a woman.

Stroking his fingers through her hair, smoothing over her cheek, he'd smile she took him. He'd show her he was grateful to have time with her. So many people loved to be in her presence.

She'd touch him and he wouldn't be afraid. He'd plan how he would touch her back after he came, licking and massaging every inch of her skin in thanks for the pleasure she provided.

The tension would build but he'd drag it out, doing everything he could to hold back, because the privilege of her body shouldn't be wasted.

When he couldn't take it anymore, when she moaned around his cock and made his balls ache with the need to come, he'd let himself go.

She'd take everything because it pleased her to please others. His climax would be powerful and he'd pump himself dry between her fantastic lips.

Exhaling roughly, he opened his eyes.

The blonde's eyes were still closed as she rode her own orgasm. When she was done, he pulled from her mouth.

An unfamiliar sense of shame rolled over him as he zipped up his slacks. Bending, he lifted her to her feet and dropped her dress over her head. From his pocket, he removed a linen handkerchief and carefully wiped her face.

"Harper?" He met her eyes. "Whoever you imagined, that's the person you *need* in your life. Stop fucking around with women like me. Someday, I hope a man treats me with the respect you obviously have for her."

She picked up her purse and he tried to give her the bracelet. She shook her head and took a bottled water off the bar cart.

"This is all I need."

"Wait. Wait. I *need* you to take it." He pressed it into her hand and watched a blush tint her skin. "Use it for something you really want or need." After a pause, he added, "I'm sorry."

She nodded. "Don't call me again, Harper. I just whored myself for the last time. See ya."

As she left the apartment, he thought about the stack of similar bracelets in his safe.

He'd never been so tired in his life.

Pressing his palms against his eyes, he took several calming breaths. Then he made a call and asked for help.

* * *

After a shower, a nap, and another round of mind-melting orgasms, Brie and Elijah sat at her dining table eating a simple lunch of steak salad she'd prepared.

She wore a t-shirt and panties, a napkin in her lap.

Grinning, she told him, "This thing you have with pants could be a problem."

He frowned. "I see *no* problem with you not wearing pants."

The knock on the door surprised her. As she stood to get it, he gently tugged her back to her seat.

"No pants means no answering of front doors."

She laughed and shook her head. "I forgot."

Watching him walk across her apartment in jeans and a t-shirt, barefoot, was one of those moments that settled in her heart.

Opening the door, he paused before stepping back. Harper, Natalia, and a young woman in scrubs entered.

"Hello, darling." Glancing at the man in front of her, Natalia added, "Elijah. How relaxed you look. I *like* it."

Clicking across the room, her friend placed a hand under her elbow. "I need a minute of your time privately." When she stood up, Natalia took in her half naked appearance with wide eyes. "Good *lord*, you're lovely. Come."

As she passed Elijah on the way to her bedroom, Brie said, "I told you the *no pants* thing was going to bite me on the ass."

Both men's eyes settled on the body part and the darker man told her, "Absolutely understandable."

Natalia closed the door softly. "Darling. I've had the most unusual request from Harper. I confirmed with your doctors that it wouldn't be a problem but it's totally up to you."

Frowning, she asked, "What sort of request?"

As one of her best friends explained what Harper Delkin wanted her to consent to, it was hard to calm the erratic beat of her heart. When Natalia finished, she walked to her closet and selected a pair of stretchy capris. She needed armor.

Opening the door, Brie approached the young woman and lifted the sleeve of her t-shirt. The girl removed a syringe and Elijah took two steps in her direction.

"It's alright." She never looked away from Harper's face as the girl swabbed her arm.

When she was injected, the man who'd spent the morning worshipping her body demanded, "What the *fuck* is that?"

"Birth control." Blinking, she broke eye contact with Harper and met Elijah's green eyes. "My doctors cleared the safety of the injection."

Natalia bent and kissed her cheek. "This was the most unusual liaison position I've ever been asked to fill. I'll call you later, darling." She took the young nurse with her.

Left alone with Elijah and Harper, she said, "You could've asked *me*. I have no interest in getting pregnant. I'm sure you already know I've got sparkling blood work. No nasty little STDs to worry about."

Walking past them, she murmured, "All the minute details, squared away neatly and done by your own hand. Smart move. All rich men should be so clever." In her kitchen, she picked up the bottle of wine and refilled her glass.

"I've offended you." Harper approached the counter and watched her. "I didn't mean to offend you."

Elijah stood perfectly still just behind him. Tension vibrated from him in waves.

"Harper, allow me to clarify. You haven't *offended* me. This isn't a board meeting. *You hurt my feelings.* I'm just *bursting* with obnoxious emotional tendencies so if you could keep your goddamn feet off them, I'd consider it a solid."

Setting down her glass, she pressed her fingers against her eyes. No fucking *way* was she going to let him make her cry.

"It was meant as a precaution."

Inhaling carefully, she shook her head. "Jesus. I don't *want* anything from you. I'm not going to trap you or blackmail you. I don't take what doesn't belong to me, no matter how *badly* I fucking want it."

Lowering into a chair, she said, "Why the hell you're so fixated on someone you clearly don't trust or even *like* as a person confuses me."

Cupping her breasts, she hissed, "It's just a *body*, a collection of female parts. I assure you, mine isn't all that special. And *as you fucking know*, there are far better."

Barely hanging on, she whispered, "Your looks fooled me, Harper. I never imagined a man who looked so much like my best friend would be so different."

He sat in the chair beside her. There was a frown on his face. "Winters didn't worry about pregnancy?"

Brie stared at the man for a long time. "We practiced safe sex. There was no actual discussion but he didn't arrive with a nurse to inject me."

Leaning forward, she said coldly, "He realized I wasn't a gold-digging cunt out to score the prettiest bauble in Tiffany's front window. Then again, he sees me as a *human*. You see me as a receptacle to deposit your next load of come."

She stood and walked to her front door, holding it wide. "I'll call when I'm cleared to be fucked so you can make an appointment and check that off your goddamn list."

"Gabriella." Whipping her head to the side, she met Hudson's eyes in the hall. "What in the *fuck* is going on?"

Chapter Nineteen

Hudson entered the room and stole all the oxygen.

He gently set Brie away from the door and slammed it hard enough to crack the wood of the frame.

Stepping just ahead of Harper, Elijah murmured, "*Fuck.*"

"Hudson?" She kept her voice low and calm.

Black eyes met hers and she could *feel* his rage on her behalf. Like gentling a wild horse, she touched his forearm, sliding her palm over his suit jacket to the cuff of his dress shirt to his hand. He held it hard, his jaw clenched.

"Breathe for just a second. Please don't force Elijah to fight you. He can't let you hurt Harper."

"Gabriella…"

"There's too much testosterone in the room right now. I'm okay and I know you know that."

Pinning Harper with a livid glare, he ground out, "You think she'd *trap* you? Have you learned *nothing*?"

"He makes choices based on his history. You didn't know what to make of me either but we built a solid foundation and you learned I wasn't like other people. It hurts my feelings but I understand where it comes from."

"You *defend* him? How *dare* he insult you."

"He doesn't *know* me, Hudson." She shook her head. "There's a good chance he never will but I can't let it damage things between the two of you. I won't."

She held his hand between both of hers. "I'm a woman always on the outside of what most people think of as normal. Your life can't be defined or impacted by the chaos in mine. I'll be okay."

"I don't want you *hurt*, Gabriella."

Inhaling carefully, she whispered, "I know but I'll survive it."

Hugging her to his side, he growled at Harper, "You *pound* at her spirit with fists when a *whisper* is all she requires."

Cupping her skull, he kissed her forehead. "Call me later so I know you're alright."

She nodded and felt him take a deep breath. Stroking his palm over her hair a couple of times, he released her.

As the door slammed again, she flinched, exhaled roughly, and rubbed her temples firmly.

"Thank you for diffusing the situation, Brie." Elijah's voice was tightly controlled.

"Of course. I don't want anyone hurt because of me."

Harper said, "I'm sorry."

Staring at nothing, she asked, "Do you know why you're apologizing?"

"Not entirely. No."

"I thought not," she murmured and turned away.

"Gabriella…"

"Escort him home, Elijah."

In her bedroom, she leaned against the door, hurting.

* * *

Harper tallied his list of mistakes and knew shit was beyond fucked up. Glancing at Elijah, green eyes stared back in fury.

"I only meant it as a precaution."

"She has a *brain* and a powerful sense of self. Why didn't you ask her personally? Why involve Natalia?"

"I wanted her presence to lessen the coldness of it." He swallowed. "I handled it badly."

"You handled it as if Brie's a paid courtesan. As if her heart wouldn't see that you consider her as nothing more than another pussy to plant your flag on."

"I don't. I *know* she's different." Raking his fingers through his hair, he tried to explain. "Faced with her half-dressed, I couldn't think. I was distracted, confused, and wanting."

He shook his head. "The more she verbally thrashed me, the less mental capacity I had to form rational sentences."

"Tell me now." Gabriella's voice was quiet as she stood in her bedroom doorway with her arms crossed over her torso.

Black curls fell around her and she inspired more lust in a t-shirt and leggings, her feet bare, than women had while dressed in gowns and accessories worth tens of thousands.

He nodded. "I'm not, it isn't about you trying to trap me, Gabriella. You aren't the type. I know that about you."

She inhaled and then nodded once. "Thank you, Harper."

Crossing the room, Brie poured him a glass of wine and gestured to her dining table. He sat and she placed the glass in front of him.

She encouraged Elijah to sit as well. She ran her hand over his hair before she took her own chair.

"I'm listening."

"Ten years ago, I met Danielle at a society function. She was well-bred and lovely. I was the oldest and assumed I needed heirs. In the beginning, she did what she was told and knew how to be silent."

Inhaling carefully, he said, "She met a concise list of requirements. I ignored her fragile mental state and her emotional instability because it didn't matter. I had what I thought I needed and it was all I cared about."

He took a long drink of his wine. "Like other women I'd known, I kept her supplied in gifts to leave me alone. She got pregnant and I congratulated myself on handling things quickly. Things went wrong in the fourth month."

"The hormone changes worsened her emotional problems."

"During a party, she screamed my name and I saw her on the third floor above the foyer. My first thought was that she wasn't *dressed* for the event. My second was that she was *embarrassing* me. I was *annoyed* with her, *angry* even."

Reaching out, Gabriella placed her hand on his forearm.

Swallowing hard, he struggled with the memory and closed his eyes. "She climbed up on the railing, sobbing as she pointed at me. Elijah is the fastest man I've ever seen on stairs. He made it to the second-floor landing when she screamed *I'll never be enough. I hate you. I won't give birth to the devil's spawn.*"

He whispered, "Then she jumped. She broke her back and killed our child instantly. Elijah tried to save her but she died on the way to the hospital. It was impossible to hide the details. There were too many witnesses to the horror of it."

"Did she know about your relationship?"

"The moment I became engaged, his sense of honor forbade one. I *never* trusted her with our history." Harper's expression was pained. "I traveled constantly and Elijah was always with me. She resented that he had time and attention she didn't."

"Losing him must have made it so much harder for you."

"I deserved the loss. I never even told him my plan to marry her. He found out when my family did."

"Oh god, *no*, Harper."

Taking a long pull of the wine, he focused on the glass. "Danielle used to call Elijah my *puppy*. Don't you have to train with your *puppy*? Your *puppy* probably likes trips."

He shook his head once hard. "It fucking *infuriated* me. I hated her by the end." He closed his eyes. "I hated the mother but I *wanted* the child."

She stared at him for a long moment before sitting forward with a sigh. "I understand. I should've thought about birth control earlier. I figured condoms or something. Either of you are more knowledgeable about preventing pregnancy than I am. It hasn't been a big *threat* in my life, you know?"

He watched her stand and tug down the leggings and pull up her t-shirt on one side. "It would be dangerous for me to become pregnant, Harper. Parts of my pelvis, thigh, and knee had to be reconstructed."

Pulling her clothes back in place, she continued, "I've been on high grade narcotics for most of a year. My blood doesn't clot well, sometimes not at all, because of blood thinners to prevent aneurysms. The doctors stopped my cycles because I practically bled to death in the hospital and they haven't reappeared."

She shrugged and there was a sadness to it. "I have no clue if I *could* conceive or if my body would carry a child now. I've got several years left of drugs and scans and probing before it would be safe."

Her smile was self-deprecating. "Not that I'm asking you to sign up for the task." Harper found the thought strangely stimulating. "I'm saying that if you'd talked to me, I wouldn't have argued. I'd have understood and agreed with the safety measure."

For a long moment, she was quiet. Then she stood up, stepped between his legs, and held his face.

"Talk to *me* in the future, Harper. I'll listen."

"I can barely *think* when I'm near you."

She smoothed gentle fingers through his hair. "We'll come up with some sort of signal so I know you want to communicate but might be having trouble." She winked. "The heart can only pump blood to one head at a time, I've heard."

"I'm trying. I don't know how to deal with you."

Lowering her face, she rubbed her lips across his. "I'm not complicated." He closed his eyes as she planted three kisses over his mouth. "Touch me, talk to me, and try not to be mean. It hurts me more than most, Harper."

"I'm sorry, Gabriella."

Staring into his eyes, she whispered, "Do you know why you're apologizing?"

"Yes."

"Progress." She kissed him again. "As far as your deceased wife, we wouldn't have gotten along." Sucking her teeth, Gabriella added, "Puppy, my *ass*. I'd have slapped the shit out of her *for you* because domestic violence is wrong."

Despite the weight of the topic, both men chuckled.

Staring at a woman who offered something he didn't understand wanting, Harper said softly, "Thank you."

Wrapping his arms around her, he accepted the genuine affection she gave so freely and wondered what ripple effect she'd have in his life.

Shutting off thoughts of the future, he held her and embraced his present.

* * *

Just after dark, Elijah escorted Harper from Brie's home and they prepared for a midnight flight to Africa.

In the apartment, Harper said, "She's a good person, gentler than anyone I've ever met. I'm sorry I hurt her, Elijah."

"I need you to be careful, Harper. She's breakable."

After Brie and Harper settled things between them, she made them dinner and asked a hundred questions about the life they lived. She focused on things no one ever asked.

Her interests were people and places. Their favorite place to travel, if there'd ever been someone who made them "fangirl," and how did they cope with jet lag were just a few of the things she wanted to know.

Smart, funny, and loving, time with her gave Elijah a glimpse of normalcy he'd *never* experienced.

They took turns kissing her goodnight and she told them to be safe. She was the first person to say it in Elijah's life, the only woman to ever be invested in his return.

It made it difficult to leave her.

When his bag was packed, Elijah stood beside the door, waiting for Harper. Checking his phone, he received the updates for the day from the security team.

Frustrated, he wasted no time when his friend appeared with papers in his hand. "Stop fucking random women." Silver eyes met his in shock. "You play roulette with her body and her safety. She's *clean*, Harper. I won't have her contaminated by your drive-thru fucks."

Opening the door, he handed their bags to the men waiting in the hall. "I can't imagine how *hurt* she'd be if she knew."

Defensive, Harper replied, "It doesn't *mean* anything."

Elijah closed the door and stepped closer. "It seems few things *mean* anything to you anymore. She *trusts* us. You can't keep sticking your dick in anything with a pulse. It's fucked up and you know it."

"Ah. I'm to add abstinence to my life. Understood, Elijah. Forgive me for filling my time with unapproved recreation while you woo the lady fair."

"Am I to *pity* you? There have been *seven women* in the last twenty days on three continents. The equivalent of *all* Brie's sexual partners in her lifetime."

"Is that true?"

He could see the surprise on Harper's face and refused to address it. "You mock the small amount of time I give her when we're in the same time zone when you could easily *join* me. Painting yourself the *victim* is beneath you."

"Abstaining is *easier* for you."

"How is it possible that you don't know me after so many years, Harper? Brie is medically *incapable* of actual sex. I wait as *she* is forced to wait. There's nothing *easy* about it."

"I didn't realize…"

"Sex means *nothing* to you. Those with whom you have sexual relationships mean *nothing*. You require instant gratification in all things. I should be accustomed to it by now." He swung the door wide, his heart aching. "Let's go."

Hours later, he arranged for a courier to deliver Brie a secure cell phone. The moment it was active, Elijah called her.

"We left at midnight. Return isn't set yet but I'll let you know. I miss you, Brie."

"I miss you, too. Once a week. Don't forget."

"Never again. I promise."

Hanging up, he focused on catching up on paperwork and tweaking training itineraries for his team. There were several new additions he was interested in testing.

He had no idea what else to say to Harper.

Nothing he said seemed to make a difference. Elijah was beginning to wonder if he'd *ever* accept Brie or if she'd end up hurt as she feared.

The possibility filled him with anguish.

* * *

On the plane, Harper stared at his laptop screen and tried to settle his racing thoughts.

He admitted he was a selfish man. Since he was a child, he'd been coddled, protected, and indulged.

Elijah had been his guardian all his life. A voice of reason, of logic, who thought only of Harper's interests.

The one time he hadn't trusted him, hadn't shared what was in his mind, he'd ended up marrying Danielle and caused what he feared was irreparable damage to their relationship.

Acting in haste, he did what he wanted. The night he'd shared the news of his pending marriage, his parents were happy for him, if a bit hesitant over his choice.

His best friend, his lover remained still, silent.

His parents and siblings assumed he'd already known. While they celebrated, as Harper smugly accepted congratulations and teasing, Elijah excused himself.

He didn't return for two days.

Realizing he was back, he tried to gain access to Elijah's space and discovered he'd been locked out.

He waited just outside to confront him. When he emerged, his bodyguard calmly explained that everything between them on a personal level was finished.

Panicked, filled with regret, he tried to change the mind of the strongest and most honorable man he knew.

"You made your choice, Harper. Had you bothered to discuss your plans with me, I'd have made my position clear. I won't dishonor myself, I won't live a lie, so that you can indulge yourself at the expense of a woman who doesn't know anything about you beyond your net worth."

"We can be with her together," he insisted desperately.

"I respectfully *decline* your offer. I have no attachment or attraction to the woman you've chosen to marry."

"Elijah. I'll call it off."

"You'll *dishonor* the promise you made to her? No. She was your choice a week ago. You wanted her enough to hide the purchase of the ring as well as the proposal."

He stepped closer and said quietly, "Have I earned so little of your respect, your consideration, that you'd have me find out in a gathering of friends and family?"

"I'm sorry. I should've told you. I didn't want to hurt you."

Green eyes looked deep and Harper knew Elijah saw *everything* about him, the good and the bad.

"You failed."

Then Elijah went around him and walked downstairs.

The eighteen months that followed were filled with wedding planning, trying to adjust to his new wife, and his desire to get her pregnant as quickly as possible.

Harper hid his pain over the loss of the only person who loved him despite his mistakes, his selfishness, and his inability to show adequate appreciation for anything in his life.

When he wasn't with his wife, he sated himself, soothed his pride, by fucking women in every location.

Elijah refused to interact outside of his position as personal security and Harper's attempts to gain his attention were futile.

Soon after Danielle's death, his mother died and his father withdrew into deep grief.

Lost, alone, and confused, Harper started drinking and whoring. Barely able to maintain his daily responsibilities, it was Elijah who prevented his complete ruin.

He dried him out, banned him from women, and forced him to take a vacation to pull his shit together.

On the fourth day, Harper *begged* Elijah to take him back, swearing everything would be different if only he'd reconsider.

That the dangerous man accepted his apology was amazing. That he didn't *kill* Harper when he returned to cycling women in and out of his bed was a shock.

Elijah started acting as a third to limit how much access the greedy women who gravitated to him had to Harper while he was at his most vulnerable.

That his best friend never wanted *any* of them was information he'd only recently received. It *broke* part of him to know he'd been no better than the tyrant in Elijah's childhood.

He'd pushed him, all but *forced* him to engage in ways he wouldn't have chosen for himself.

All of it, he'd done out of love for Harper.

If he didn't fix what was wrong with him, he'd lose Elijah again. He knew the next time the loss would be permanent.

Chapter Twenty

Mid-May 2015

The day Brie and Harper came to an understanding of sorts, she finally saw the potential of what the three of them could have together.

She tried to rein in her *hope* without success.

Elijah provided her with a secure cell and it would've been hard to explain her pleasure when he checked in with her at least once a day.

They'd been gone a week when she received a text at one in the afternoon that asked, "Are you busy?"

Three seconds after she responded she wasn't, Elijah called.

"Hi. I miss you."

"I miss you, Brie. What are you doing?"

"Painting. What are you doing?"

There was rustling in the background. "Just finished training a new unit in the middle of nowhere."

"That sounds fascinating. Are you tired?"

"No but they are."

It made her laugh. "Of course they are because you're superhuman. What are you going to do now?"

"Just got out of the shower and will attempt to get some sleep for the first time in two days. I wish you were here." He grunted. "Strike that. There are bugs the size of my forearm. I wish I was *there*."

She listened as he prepared for bed somewhere else in the world.

Something told her not to ask too many questions.

"Ew, *yuck*. So do I. Hold on for a minute. I'm going to set the phone down." She locked up the apartment.

In her bedroom, she stripped down and climbed in her bed. When she was settled, she picked up the phone.

"You're in bed."

"I'm keeping you company."

"Fuck, that's a *lovely* image."

They talked and laughed for more than an hour. Finally, she told him, "You need sleep, Elijah."

"Too hard to sleep."

"Is that a pun?" He chuckled. "Orgasms always help me sleep. It's the only way I get any these days."

"An even *lovelier* image. Tell me about this phenomenal new sleep aid."

"Well, I like to take a stupidly long shower before I get in bed. It relaxes stiff muscles. Once all the lights are off, I wonder where you are and what you're doing."

"Usually something boring."

She smiled. "I like to imagine you're just getting out of the shower. In my mind, you're always just getting out of the shower or waking up."

"Interesting."

"I like imagining you relaxed. You're always on the go. Sleeping and showering force you to settle for a moment."

"You have a lovely heart."

"Last night, I imagined you were just waking up and that we were all tangled together. You did that full torso pet over me that gives me shivers."

"Noted."

"You rolled us and held my wrists over my head with one hand while you stared down at me. Honestly, I was ready to come at that visual alone but I held back to make it last."

"*Brie…*" She listened to him inhale deeply. "Are you naked?"

"Yes."

"Are you touching yourself?"

"Do you want me to?"

"Yes." There was the sound of rustling. She slid her hand over her belly and settled her fingers over her mound. "Are you wet?"

"Very." She whispered, "Are you stroking yourself?"

"Yes." Thinking about the way his hand looked wrapped around his length made her moan softly. "You like watching me fist my cock."

"It fascinates me. The strength in the movements, not gentle like you are with me. The way the muscles in your arm flex, the veins visible under your skin. It's just so, *god.*"

"Don't come, Brie."

"Mm. Okay."

"Put two fingers in your pussy. Imagine they're my tongue." She gasped. "I love the taste of you. No matter how long I eat you, you're always slick and warm and inviting."

Sighing his name, she stroked herself steadily.

"One day soon, I'll experience it with my dick. I hope I don't embarrass myself."

"Don't worry," she told him breathlessly. "If you come quickly, it takes the pressure off. Hmm, you'll make more and more and *more* for me."

"Fuck. The thought of thrusting inside you, hard and deep, until you scream for me."

"I *want* that, Elijah. I want you wrung out from the pleasure of taking me in every way you need, any way you want."

"Come for me, Brie," he told her hoarsely.

Moaning, she allowed herself to let go of her need and came harder than she ever had alone. Gasping for breath, shaking, she murmured his name like a prayer.

His low growl on the other end of the line followed by her name made her climax last a long time.

"You're fucking spectacular."

"I feel the same way about you, Elijah." Sighing, she asked softly, "Do you think you can sleep now?"

There was a long pause. "You're so giving. Yes."

"I'm going to take a nap, too. Sleep at the same time so I feel like we're together." She wanted to ask when they were coming back but she didn't. "Goodnight, Elijah."

"Brie?" She hummed. "I miss you badly. Goodnight."

To her surprise, she fell into a hard sleep and woke up after dark. Taking a moment to center her thoughts, she sent Harper a text to say hello and tell him she missed him.

He wrote back, "Ditto."

Smiling to herself, she said aloud, "Gotta start somewhere."

Throwing back the covers, she went to shower and change. She wanted to hang out with her friends.

* * *

The men were gone for three weeks and Brie killed time with physical therapy, work for the winery, and several projects she'd taken on for Tawny's men. When she wasn't working, she painted and sketched.

Anything to keep her mind busy.

After wrapping her gift for Natalia's unorthodox bridal shower, she headed downstairs to meet the others for the drive across town.

Natalia, Riya, and Tawny were already in the M's car and she waved at Rodney as she left the lobby. He opened the rear door with a huge grin. "You look great, Brie!"

"Thanks. Better every day."

Harper's car pulled to a hard stop behind them and Brie's eyes widened in surprise. Elijah stepped from the back, lifted her into his arms without a word, and returned to the interior.

The moment the door closed behind them, they fell on her like starved men.

"I-I have to…"

They kissed her silent and kept kissing her until she forgot what she was going to say, what she meant to do, and where she was supposed to be.

Holding her between them, they slipped off her leather sandals and stroked their hands up her legs, gathering the Bohemian chic skirt she wore as they went.

"You smell *fantastic*," Harper said at her neck. His fingers slipped under her panties and stroked over skin that was freshly waxed, highly sensitive, and already wet.

Elijah pulled down the layered tops and bra she wore and exposed her nipples, taking one into the wet heat of his mouth while they worked their hands over her folds together.

The climax happened so fast, it was embarrassing.

Groaning low in his throat, Harper painted her lips with his wet fingertips and devoured her mouth.

Elijah murmured, "Again. We have time before she's technically late."

Sinking to the floor of the limo, Harper stripped her panties down her legs and buried his tongue in her pussy. Brie screamed, the sound muffled by Elijah's mouth. He held her breasts in strong hands and broke the kiss to lick and suck them.

They touched her everywhere and she *overdosed* on it.

When Harper lifted his head, his chin was slick with fluids from her body. He gripped her neck and sat her up. "Taste your pussy, Gabriella. It's fucking delicious."

He shared her flavor and her head spun from more stimulation than she'd ever received at one time.

"Switch." Elijah practically shoved Harper out of the way and took his place between her legs. Pushing his fingers deep, he lapped at her slickness with a low moan.

Releasing her clit with a soft suck, he growled, "Get it. I want to know she's wearing it when we drop her off. She's so fucking *wet.*"

Half her mind registered Harper removing something from a side compartment and handing it off as he cupped her breast and licked warmly over her aching nipple.

"I already cleaned it for you, Brie. I wanted it ready the moment I had your pussy exposed."

While she watched, Elijah carefully inserted a curved toy inside her that made her gasp in surprise and longing.

"It isn't about the size but the *shape*…and the little extras." He tied fine strings around her hips with a wink of one gorgeous green eye. "So it stays in place. You're slick."

A low vibration caused her to whimper. Gripping Harper's hair, she watched Elijah lap around the toy and circle her clit. She exploded, dropped her head to the seat, and shook so hard she held them to keep from falling on the floor.

The vibration stopped and she inhaled carefully. They watched her ride the orgasm and played with her hair.

When she could speak, she whispered, "Welcome back."

Chuckling, Harper said, "I had no idea you possessed the best place to eat in New York."

Laughing weakly, she managed to say, "I'll return the favor when I can lift my arms."

"You're going to the party. It's important to you." Elijah stroked her face.

"I don't, I'm kind of shaking and ridiculous right now."

Grinning, Harper commented, "Mm. You look fantastic."

"*Brie*." Sensing a different tone, she opened her eyes and stared into his as she tried to regain her composure. "Leave the toy in place. We'll pick you up in a few hours."

She nodded, practically delirious.

He gave her a wink and put her panties in place, pressing his flat palm against the wet skin through the lace. They sat her up and straightened her clothes.

The movement made her eyes widen. "*Fuck*...um, Elijah?"

"We'll see you in a little while."

They took turns kissing her stupid. Then she realized they were parked in front of the club.

"I'll never be able to pull this off."

Harper squeezed her breast and brushed over her nipple. "Enjoy yourself and please tell me your pussy stays open late. I *love* midnight snacks, Gabriella."

"You guys are diabolical. Holy shit."

The driver held the door with a smile as she stepped out. Glancing back, the men stared at her.

"I've been doing some...we'll call it *research*. This countdown is pretty much *killing* me." Taking a deep breath, she gave them a distracted wave and they chuckled.

Making her way slowly up the steps to the entrance, she smiled awkwardly at Stav as he held the door. The toy made it hard to focus on words and walking and remembering to breathe.

"Your mobility improves every time I see you."

She huffed air from her lower lip, praying not to have another orgasm in front of Natalia's head of security.

"I've sweat enough to fill a lake at this point."

"The progress is worth it. Enjoy yourself tonight. I think everyone is inside." He winked. "You're never the last one to arrive at these things."

"I lost track of time."

In the deserted lobby, she went into the closest bathroom to pull herself together. The secure cell rang and she answered it with trembling hands.

"Brie."

"Elijah," she sighed.

"Are you alone?"

"Yes, I needed to wipe myself down and spritz a bit of perfume. I smell like a horny teenager." She started to laugh when the toy vibrated inside her. Catching herself on the edge of the sink, she whispered, "Oh *god*."

"Your gift came with a *remote*. We're outside. Let me know when you're safely seated. I don't want to cause an accident."

"Diabolical."

"See you soon, Brie."

The line went dead and she whimpered at the implications. In the main room, Riya met her at the door.

"Seeing someone snatched right in front of you is a little jarring. Girl, you look…" Her eyes went wide. "Never mind. I *know* that look."

Brie chose a chair as far from the others as she could and lowered herself into it cautiously. The toy was so stimulating without vibration that she debated sending Elijah a text.

In the end, she knew it *wasn't* a request.

Moments later, she rested her head and worked to steady her breathing and avoid slipping from her seat.

Rejecting food, drinks, or holding anything she might drop or spill on herself, she engaged with her friends to celebrate Natalia's hustle into wedded bliss with her best friend.

For an hour, she rode the waves of pleasure as they crashed over her and did her best to hide what was happening from the women closest to her.

After another orgasm, Tawny sat demurely in the chair beside her. Resting her chin in her hand, she stared at Brie.

"The first time Zach got me to stay over at their place, they put this nifty contraption in my pussy. They made me promise to wear it, no matter what."

Brie could barely focus but she *tried*.

"The boys traded the remote back and forth all day. By evening, I wasn't able to support my own bodyweight. They arranged me like a doll all night and it was *awesome*."

Just then, the toy hit high vibration and Brie melted into the cushions as she struggled to speak.

"Your tag team took things up a notch since they knew you'd be hanging out with friends. I like their improvisation." She winked. "I shudder to think what they'll do to you once the doctors give the all clear. Good luck!"

Giving her damp brow a smacking kiss, the redhead skipped across the room and whispered with Natalia.

The blonde was still laughing as she approached. "They're so mean but you look like you're feeling no pain, darling." Taking out her cell phone, she petted Brie's head lovingly. "Yes, you'll have to come get her. She's toast. Mission accomplished."

"Sorry. So sorry," Brie murmured.

"Nonsense. I *demand* you have them find one for Hudson. Your face is priceless."

Through glazed eyes, she watched as Harper and Elijah walked through the door and made their way to her.

With a slight bow, the bodyguard presented Natalia with a small wrapped box. "Congratulations on your pending nuptials, Lady Roman."

Her happiness was obvious. "The way to a woman's heart is *not* through her stomach and I appreciate that you know that." Pausing, she asked, "Why do you call me Lady Roman?"

"My ancestors were Swedish Vikings. Many were rumored to be berserkers but I recognize nobility when I see it."

Natalia smiled slowly. "Thank you."

"Lady Winters will sound every bit as regal." He winked before crouching beside Brie. "Hey, pretty girl." Smoothing a damp tendril of hair from her face, he said, "You look gorgeous in your pleasure."

"I feel high."

Harper brushed his lips over her temple. "That speaks well of your future. No drugs required." He scooped her into his arms and her head dropped back. "Like a Victorian maiden."

"Help. Now I'm just *having* them. Don't talk to me. It makes me come harder."

Without saying goodbye to anyone and knowing every single one of them would understand, the men removed her from the club and into the back of the limo.

"Tonight, we please you together, Brie."

Substantial effort helped her mutter, "Pleasing you pleases me, Elijah. I've missed you both."

"Would you be willing to demonstrate how much you've missed us, Gabriella?"

"Always. As soon as I regain control of my muscles. Also, my vision. Possibly get a little of my brain cognition back."

They laughed and she soaked up the fact that she reclined in Harper's arms.

Chapter Twenty-One

They murmured to her while they drove to the building and Brie didn't object when they carried her to Harper's apartment and laid her on Elijah's bed.

As they stripped her clothes away, Elijah groaned. "You're *soaked*, Brie. I could wring out your panties."

Untying the toy and removing it pushed her into another orgasm and Harper kissed her while she rode it.

"Your tight ass is drenched with the fluids from your pussy, throbbing for something to fill it." Using her excessive wetness, Elijah smoothed his fingers around the pucker and pushed inside. "Your entire body is *primed*, Brie."

"*Please*, I want it."

"Soon enough. Tonight, we play safely. I admit I could hammer nails with the hardness of my dick."

"That sounds delicious," she whispered.

He stroked in and out of her ass for several minutes. "The thought of taking you in every hole, in every position, and watching you absorb pleasure as you have tonight will haunt me until I can have it."

"I've been haunted by similar thoughts for months. I'm glad I'm not alone," she replied.

Harper stretched out beside her, rubbed the flat of his palm over her clit, and slid his fingers into her pussy.

The resulting climax wracked her body tight, stole her ability to breathe, and shoved her into darkness.

* * *

Harper met Elijah's eyes over Gabriella's limp form. "I've never seen *anyone* so receptive to pleasure."

"She's incredible. I wouldn't lie to you." He planted a kiss on her belly, nuzzled her there, and stood. "She runs on touch. The simplicity fascinates me. I'll run her a tub."

Hudson stared at the woman in his best friend's bed. Leaning over, he confirmed that the scent of oranges came from her curls.

Raking his eyes down the length of her body, he took in the mixture of scars and soft, golden brown skin. The scars marked her as a survivor.

Much like Elijah.

Resting his head on the pillow beside her, he flattened his palm on her belly and felt the way her womb continued to spasm. He couldn't count the number of women who'd *faked* multiple orgasms in his history to feed his ego.

They never realized it had the opposite effect. It drove home their focus on cash and prizes rather than their desire to be with him because they wanted him as a man.

Gabriella's entire body trembled with aftershocks from her orgasms. He knew she was open, honest in her reactions.

Her full breasts were real, the nipples a warm mocha that were tight with stimulation. Her lashes were long and thick.

It was her *mouth* that made him imagine every decadent act. The same color of her nipples, he imagined her pillowy lips wrapped around his cock more often than he'd ever admit.

Harper didn't remember ever really *examining* a woman's body in such detail before, much less *appreciating* everything she had to offer. It made sense that the first one to make him do so was Gabriella.

Opening her eyes, he saw her confusion. She turned her head on the pillow and smiled.

The way it made him feel was alarming.

"My entire body feels like I'm still on a morphine drip. You guys are damned imaginative."

He grinned. "Thanks."

"You're a beautiful man, Harper."

"Ah, the similarities to Winters."

"No. You're a beautiful *man*. I love Hudson for many reasons that have nothing to do with his physical appearance or the short time we had a sexual relationship." Her smile was gentle. "I'd never mix you up. You're different to me."

"Winters?"

"He's my best friend, my confidant, the man my best female friend loves, my protector whether I need him to be or not, and the kindest person I've ever known."

"Do you think about your time with him?"

"Sometimes, a particular phrase or circumstance sparks a memory. We don't discuss it but I remember it fondly for bigger reasons than orgasms."

"What reasons?"

"They saw me. No one had ever *seen* me before I met them. I was the girl everyone depended on to be sweet. I worked hard to pretend I wasn't lonely. I let people mistreat me because I didn't want to fight. I was susceptible to the con because I thought I finally *mattered* to someone."

"I'm sure you matter to *many* people, Gabriella."

"No one of my own." Inhaling carefully, she turned her gaze to the ceiling. "I was *less* in every way that seemed important to the people around me and I pretended I didn't know that."

"They helped you."

"They *showed* me I had value. Even now, when I'm hurting, they don't let me forget."

"What do I represent?"

"Possibilities." Her expression turned sad. "I don't expect you to love me, Harper. I ask that you don't deliberately *hurt* me. I know the day will come for me to make a graceful exit and take the time I need to heal." She whispered, "When it's over, I want to look back fondly on *our* moments as well."

Elijah rested a knee on the edge of the bed and crouched over Gabriella. His palm slid along the back of her neck and he stared at her for a long moment. "You *matter* to me, Brie."

Harper watched her fight not to cry. She swallowed several times and inhaled deeply. "Thank you, Elijah."

Watching a man you'd known all your life kiss the first woman he'd ever loved shouldn't have made his heart pound hard in his chest.

Knowing their love was the same, yet *different*, from the one you shared with him shouldn't have filled him with hope, with the thought that *maybe this could work.*

It shouldn't have changed his mind about her presence *taking something* that belonged to him to the possibility that she could *add* an element they'd been missing all along.

Their kiss inspired those rapid-fire thoughts in his mind and he stared at Gabriella as if seeing her for the first time.

Then she turned her head and murmured softly, "Kiss me, Harper. Take what you need. I give it freely."

As his lips met hers, he allowed himself to let her in and he feared when all was said and done, he'd fall to her charms as Elijah had fallen.

The thought was terrifying.

* * *

Elijah carried Brie into the bathroom and lowered her into the whirlpool tub. She asked for a couple of pens and secured her hair before she reclined with a sigh, watching him undress.

As he slipped beneath the water, he was surprised and pleased when Harper entered the bathroom.

He sat on the edge of the tub with a smile. "You're a lovely woman,

Gabriella."

"Thank you." She asked him softly, "Aren't you coming in?"

"Alas, I'm not strong enough."

She sat up and slid her wet palm along his neck. "You are." He started to speak and she said, "Harper. *Undress. Join us.*"

A shiver worked its' way up Elijah's spine at the tone in her voice. Silver eyes met hers in confusion but she remained still, watching him. Then he stood and slowly took off his clothes.

Only when he was sitting on her other side did she smile and raise herself up to kiss him. She hugged him tightly, soft as a kitten again. "You're even better naked, as I expected."

Harper blinked the fog from his brain. He stared at Elijah in silent accusation but he shook his head.

He'd never discussed Harper's nature with Brie.

Relaxing back against the tub, she closed her eyes. "I feel like I've run a marathon. My muscles are jumpy."

Riveted by her, Elijah asked, "How many did you have?"

She laughed. "I lost count at the club. A lot. More than I honestly thought was humanly possible. Excellent little gadget. Next time, I need to be home. I must have looked like I was having *episodes* or something."

Taking her hand, Harper noted, "When we walked in, you looked like a puddle. You've recovered nicely."

"Oh, there was a puddle," she quipped. "I can't *imagine* what my friends think. Snatched right off the sidewalk. Show up looking and smelling like I've been on a three-day porn and masturbation bender." She shook her head. "You could've added *your* scents so I didn't give off a sad spinster vibe."

"Noted." Elijah winked when she looked at him.

Turning to Harper, she mentioned nonchalantly, "Elijah ate me until I forgot my name then painted me with his come."

Every muscle in Harper's body visibly tightened and he started to reach for her before he stopped himself. His nostrils flared with lust and need unlike anything Elijah had ever seen.

Brie wasn't done. "He also tied me to my bed *so* carefully and fucked my mouth. I didn't lose a single drop."

Vibrating with tension, Harper started to get out of the tub. "I'll hurt you trying to fuck you if I stay."

"*Stop.*"

Freezing with his arms braced on the edge to lift himself out, Elijah watched Harper trance out at the *command* in her voice. He was familiar with the expression and the results.

Brie's ability to inspire it was brand new.

"I want to taste you, Harper. I *want* it." She ran her palms over his chest and whispered, "I *know* you want me to suck you until you come down my throat. You're tense. I can make that better. *Give me what I want.*"

Elijah was fucking spellbound. "Brie." She glanced over her shoulder and smiled at him. "Let's get out of the tub. It's dangerous in here for you."

She nodded and held her hands out to Harper. "Can you help me? Falling would seriously suck."

Dragging air into his lungs, he pivoted and stood on the rug beside the tub. He rubbed his hand through his hair and turned back to her.

Rather than taking her hands, he lifted her out completely and set her on her feet. Elijah followed and stood behind her.

"What are you *doing*, Gabriella?"

"Blending two things you need that cause conflict."

"Explain."

She held his face. "I *see* you, Harper. You're a powerful man. You love a willing, even *docile*, female to purge your real stress. On the other hand, you wouldn't maintain a long-term relationship with a man like Elijah if he didn't provide something specific you needed."

He frowned. "How do you know these things?"

"I wouldn't pry or break your trust by talking to anyone. I told you once I'm observant. I also happen to be rather clever."

"I don't *like* you knowing."

Trailing her hands over his shoulders, she kissed the skin over his heart. "I'd never abuse your trust. I know it'll take time for you to believe that."

"What do you *want?*"

"For you to *feel* free when you're out of the public eye. For you to smile more because you *feel* like smiling."

"You have to want more than that, Gabriella."

"Yes. I also desperately want to touch you."

Harper wrapped his hand around her throat and held her firmly against Elijah's chest. "You *confuse* me."

Brie telegraphed no fear. "I know. I hope it lessens over time." Raising her hand, she placed it over Harper's heart. "Let me touch you, give to you. I'd *never* hurt you."

His fingers tightened. "Elijah wouldn't *let* you."

"I know. He loves you and his loyalty is unshakeable but he'd *never* have to protect you from me, Harper."

They stared at one another and Elijah held his breath. "I'll break your neck *myself* if you're lying, if you betray me."

"I wouldn't. I couldn't."

"Why?"

"You *know* why."

"Say it. I *dare* you to say it." He stepped closer and Elijah poised himself to protect her.

"I love you, Harper."

His expression contorted to one of pain. He pulled her forward by her throat before pushing her into Elijah again sharply. He whispered, "I *told* you not to fucking *love* me."

"I can't help it. I'll still walk away when you let me know it's time." The words filled Elijah with unspeakable agony.

Eyes that had deepened to dark gray met his. "I *trust* you, Elijah."

"I've *never* betrayed your trust. Not once in forty years."

To Brie, Harper ground out, "You've brought chaos with you."

He felt her shrug one shoulder. "I'm an artist. We tend to be eccentric on the whole."

Grudgingly, he gave her a smile. His hand dropped away and he took a deep breath. "What do you want from me?"

"Have you ever allowed a woman to explore your body?" Harper shook his head after a hesitation. "I want to learn you."

"I don't let women touch me. I don't…generally like to be touched."

She stepped in his direction and brought his face down for a kiss. Against his lips, she murmured, "You've never been touched by me."

Truer words were never spoken.

Chapter Twenty-Two

Taking Harper's hand, Brie backed into the bedroom, leading him gently. "I never thanked you."

"For what?"

"The day you called Hudson about the building, I was in his office. Your mention of Natalia gave me my first opening to encourage him *not* to let you have her."

His eyes went wide.

"It was a critical first step to really pushing them toward each other. They fought hard for a while."

"You're so…*odd*, Gabriella."

Her smile felt huge. "Thanks. You're the first person to use the real word. Most people say *unique* or *original* to avoid telling it like it is." She shrugged. "It's not like I don't *know*."

Elijah laughed and she stared into beautiful green eyes.

"You know him best. Guide me." Harper didn't hide his surprise. "This isn't about making you uncomfortable. I want to know you but I also want to please you."

"I want to fuck you so bad my hips hurt."

"Soon you'll have that. I'm sorry I'm not able to give you everything you need." She sighed. "It's hard for me, too."

"You want me to fuck you?"

"I want *both* of you to fuck me. *Hard.* For *days*." She tilted her head. "Did you think I just enjoyed heavy petting? Dear god, I look forward to being fucked into a coma." She put her hand on her hip. "Then you can do it again when I'm revived."

"I want to take you. I want to watch Elijah take you."

Moving close enough for her nipples to graze Harper's chest, she stared up into his face. "The feeling is *mutual.*"

Both men gasped but she was tired of talking.

Reaching up, she slid her fingers into black hair. She gently raked his scalp, massaged his skull, and watched his eyes close. Imitating the way she'd explored Elijah's body, she worked her way over his torso slowly until he swayed on his feet.

When her fingers slipped over the skin of his cock, their eyes met. "Don't come yet. I want you in my mouth."

She continued moving over his skin and he started leaning into her touches. For half an hour, she scratched him, massaged him, tested the resistance of his muscles, and absorbed the warmth of him through her hands.

Returning to the front of his body, she wrapped her arms around him, pressed her cheek to his skin, and whispered, "Thank you, Harper."

He hugged her back hesitantly at first and exhaled hard. Such a simple exploration hadn't been easy for him.

Elijah instructed, "Brie. Sit on the side of the bed."

Gradually loosening her hold on Harper, she moved to step away and he tilted her face up for a kiss she gladly accepted. His fingers smoothed gently over her neck and shoulder.

Settling her ass on the mattress, she noted the platform bed was lower than her own. The possibilities made her smile.

Elijah inhaled slowly and reached out to hold the back of Harper's neck. It was the first time they'd touched while naked in front of her. Even the simple interaction made her tug her lower lip between her teeth.

"She won't hurt you. She's incapable of it. *Don't hurt her.*"

Harper nodded and allowed Elijah to guide him across the room until he stood just beyond her bent knees.

"May I touch him while I suck his cock?"

"Yes."

The sight of his dick a few inches away made her mouth water. She licked her lips and started to close her legs.

"Spread them, Brie." She obeyed instantly. They waited for Elijah's instruction. "Experience her mouth, Harper. You're not to come until I give you permission."

The moment he stepped between her knees, she smoothed her palms up his thighs. Lifting her gaze, she stared into storm gray eyes that wanted things he didn't understand.

She opened her mouth and Harper sucked air through his teeth. Pressing the head inside, she stared at him as she suckled it. His body tightened and his lips parted with rapid breaths.

Her gaze moved to Elijah's and he smiled at her. "Hot, wet, welcoming. She gives because it's what she was born to do. Let her have more of you, Harper."

Pushing his length deeper, he groaned. "So…different."

Elijah raked his fingers roughly through Harper's hair. "It's because she expects nothing but your pleasure. She loves to be touched."

Around Harper, Elijah reached to stroke from her head down to her shoulder. She closed her eyes and sighed.

"Feed her another inch of your cock. She wants more."

Unable to contain her moan, she massaged the muscles of his upper legs, enjoying the flex as he thrust.

Needing to see his face, she opened her eyes again.

"See the way she looks at you. In no hurry, nowhere she'd rather be. Focused on nothing but taking everything you'll give her. For you to enjoy what she offers in return."

"I want to come so bad," Harper groaned. "It's too much."

Elijah rested his forehead against the other man's temple. "Not yet. Draw it out. Relish how good it feels. Take the time to *feel* everything. The way her lips suckle around you, how her little tongue moves over you with every stroke, the sensation of her exhale on skin damp from her attention."

Harper's head dropped back on his shoulders. "I can't…"

Reaching between his legs, Brie applied pressure to his balls and squeezed the base of his cock in her fist.

The air stumbled in Harper's lungs.

"She helps you. Keeps you from coming." Meeting her eyes, she watched Elijah's gaze move over her body. "Look how tight her nipples are, the slickness easing from her pussy. She could come from the pleasure she feels in taking your cock, from how much stimulation she's had tonight. Instead, she holds you back, allows you time to truly enjoy it."

Pressing his lips to Harper's ear, he ground out, "Show her your power. Show her your control. She's the *only* woman who will ever appreciate this side of you. There's no greed, no selfishness. There's only *her* pursuit of *your* pleasure."

Elijah fisted one hand in Brie's hair, the other wrapped around Harper's waist, his cock pressed against his lover's hip.

Brie worried the sight would cause her to lose control and moaned around the throbbing flesh in her mouth.

"Everything is stimulus. Every touch, every word, every image." He pressed a kiss to Harper's cheek and she whimpered. "The act of me simply *touching* you makes her desperate for knowledge and experiences."

"*Elijah…*"

"Yes, Harper?"

"I need. *I need.*"

"Then *take* what she wants to give you. *Fuck. Her. Mouth.*"

As Harper slid his hands along her skull, she felt the way they trembled. His thumbs smoothed along the line of her jaw. The mixture of pleasure and fear on his face called to her, made her ache to show him the life he could have.

Then he moved harder, faster, deeper, and all she could focus on was breathing and taking him.

"Like nothing before...give me permission."

"Do you want to come down her throat?"

"Yes, god yes."

"It's what she wants. To taste you, drink you down." His hand tightened on his waist, in Brie's hair. "What will you give her if I let you come?"

"Anything. Fuck. *Anything.*"

"The only thing Brie requires, *needs*, is touch."

"I want to. I want to touch her." He clenched his jaw. "Please, let me come."

"Look into her eyes. See *her* while you take your release between her willing lips. Know *who* it is that swallows your seed and finds *your* pleasure more important than her own."

Harper opened his eyes and stared into hers. His movements slowed. His thumbs slid over the skin of her cheeks. Then his hands moved and she moaned around him as he traced her brows, along her temples, to the corners of her mouth.

"I want to come, Gabriella. I need to come."

She nodded around him and released the pressure holding him back. One hand gripped his ass, her other rested over Elijah's cock, pressing him, stroking him between her palm and Harper's hip.

Exhaling shakily, he cried out, "Oh god, yes. Fuck *yes.*"

Elijah held him harder as the climax exploded and he pumped jets of hot semen into her mouth. "Give Brie all of it, Harper. Every drop. Experience satisfaction, satiation."

She worked to swallow him but never looked away from his face, watching his orgasm take away the lines of stress and worry that were always present.

"So good it hurts."

Elijah stared at her with his forehead against Harper's temple. "I know the feeling well. Let her help you. Let her show you how worthy she finds you."

A tremor traveled over him and he exhaled roughly. She let her hand coast over his leg, ass, and stomach while he came down from the high. As he softened, she took more of him, sucked him clean of his own release.

Finally, his shallow thrusts stopped and he blinked.

His hands stroked through her hair as he pulled from her mouth and bent to kiss her. He rested his forehead against hers. She listened to the sound of him dragging air into his lungs.

"Thank you."

"Thank *you*, Harper. That was wonderful."

"You're so *clean*, Gabriella."

Her hand cupped his cheek. "You deserve to experience pleasure with a woman that isn't a transaction. You deserve to be welcomed and appreciated for the man you *are*, not what you *possess*."

"I've never had that."

"You have it with me. When I say I want nothing from you, that's not entirely true. I want to see you at peace, to see you smile, and perhaps be one of the reasons for it. You're a good man, Harper. A worthy man."

His hand tightened in her hair. "I hope so."

"I *know* you are. I wouldn't be here if you weren't. Breathe and just *be* for a little while. I have no expectations. There's no ulterior motive. Just *be* with me."

"I want to, Gabriella."

She nodded as her hand continued to smooth over Elijah's cock pressed against the skin of his hip. The bodyguard was hot, hard, throbbing under her palm. His large hand held Harper's shoulder while she kissed him again.

Inhaling carefully, silver eyes stared into hers. "I can't. I'm not ready to share it. We haven't…no one has ever been with us like that."

"I understand. There are no expectations, Harper." She kissed him again, stroking his face, and he straightened. "It makes me happy to make Elijah happy." Lifting her eyes to brilliant green, she murmured, "I'm yours to command."

"Sit behind her." He winked at Brie. "I'll guide you."

Watching as Harper sealed himself to her back, his legs outside her own, Elijah bent to kiss her until she was breathless. Her hands held his face, her thumbs stroking features she knew better than her own after months of sketching him.

Standing up, his knuckles glided along her cheek and she absorbed the love apparent in his expression.

"Let me please you, Elijah."

Softly, he commanded, "Open."

* * *

Harper absorbed the warmth of her body and closed his eyes as one of her hands settled on his thigh at the moment her mouth closed around Elijah's cock.

His own was nestled along the crease of her ass, more satisfied than he'd been in years. He gathered her hair and slid it to one side of her body, dropping his mouth to her shoulder.

Elijah's voice mesmerized him as it had for more than half his life and he allowed himself to fall into the words.

"Watching your pouty lips around Harper's cock was almost as good as feeling them on mine. Your eyes sparkle darkly, always focused on the moment, the pleasure." He smoothed a fingertip along her brow. "So giving, loving. You deserve more, Brie. All the touch you can handle."

Harper slid his palms over her shoulders, her upper back, and around to her belly. He watched the way Elijah's body flexed as he rolled his hips, thrusting gently in and out of Gabriella's mouth.

"You're one of two people in my life to make me *hunger*. Who make me want to spend days feasting on every inch of you, taking you again and again until you literally can't come anymore."

She moaned around him and Harper slid his hands up to cup her breasts, flicking her taut nipples with his thumbs.

"Watching Harper touch you draws my balls so tight. The way he stares at me while you suck me, I fight not to come."

Gabriella's hand slipped between his legs and cupped his sac with a sigh. Withdrawing from her mouth, he put one foot on the bed beside Harper's leg.

Fisting his own cock, he told her, "Suck them, Brie. Let me feel your mouth on me."

Without hesitation, she took his balls between her lips and sucked. Her hand moved around to his ass, pulling him closer so she could access more of him.

Elijah's gaze lifted to Harper's, knowing how much he wanted to join her. "That feels incredible. Take my cock." Releasing him with a pop, she immediately took as much of the length as she could.

"Lay back on Harper's shoulder, Brie." She did and Elijah followed her, fucking her mouth harder, deeper, inches from *his* mouth, making it water. "That's it, pretty girl. Relax the muscles of your throat."

She never looked away from Elijah's face, never stopped touching him while her other hand smoothed frantically over the muscle of Harper's thigh. He could feel the way she trembled between them.

"Hot, wet, beautiful Brie. Do you want to come?" A small whimper. "Do you want to wait?" She nodded. "Would you like me to eat you to make you come?" There was no mistaking her moan. "I'd love for you to come for my mouth."

To Harper, he murmured, "Touch her. Brie, hold it back. Let it build."

His palm slid along the side of her neck while Harper moved his hands over her breasts and belly, down to her mound. She gasped, pressed into him, and he was hypnotized by Elijah's focus, by her responses. He used the flat of his fingers to smooth the slick folds, to circle her clit.

"Are you ready, Brie?"

Shaking, moaning, she relaxed even further as he pressed deep and stilled. She swallowed around him, struggled to take even more, and Harper slipped his fingers inside her as her eyes watered.

"Take me." Elijah's head dropped back on his shoulders, his body tightened, defining every muscle beautifully, and he growled as he released his control. "*Yes.*"

At the last moment, he pulled back and Harper watched with a sharp inhale as Elijah's come splashed across Gabriella's tongue and lower lip. She closed her mouth, kept her hands on both of them as she turned her head to stare into Harper's eyes. She didn't blink, didn't push, didn't lick away the drops on her lip. Simply waited in silence.

So, Harper kissed her.

Elijah's flavor exploded on his tongue. It was a taste he knew well. As he claimed Gabriella's mouth roughly, holding her harder than he intended, he wondered at this new *layer* to sex that he'd never experienced before.

It was something he'd never truly considered. The possibilities made him hunger, made him ache, and frightened him to the core of who he was.

Gabriella Hernandez was a dangerous woman.

Chapter Twenty-Three

End-May 2015

After spending ten hours in the company of Elijah and Harper, the men departed for Australia.

Physically, sexually, and emotionally exhausted, Brie slept for eighteen hours straight when they escorted her home and kissed her goodbye.

She took the teasing of her friends in stride at brunch two days later by pointing out similar disappearances and recovery times she'd witnessed in their relationships.

Tawny nodded sagely. "Remember when Riya got back from her conference and the M's wouldn't let her out of the apartment for three *days*. I thought we were going to have to have emergency personnel break down the door."

"Man, the *show* they'd have gotten," the brunette sighed.

As they left the restaurant and parted ways, Tawny pulled her aside and took her for coffee. Settling at a table away from the windows so the security who followed her everywhere wouldn't freak out, Brie sipped and waited for questions.

"Are things better?"

Inhaling carefully, she considered her answer. "The pleasure climbs. I'm deeply in love with Elijah and the love I have for Harper has the potential to be just as strong. The pain is going to be worse but I *believe* it'll be worth it. The memories without a doubt."

"You think it'll end? They're *so* focused on you."

"I hope it doesn't." *The hope would make it worse.* "I wasn't able to protect myself. I don't think I would have if I'd had the choice. They speak to my personality, all sides of it, in ways I didn't expect."

"It might work out. Elijah, girl, he's powerful."

Sensing a story but feeling wrong about chasing the bait, Brie controlled the tears that desperately wanted to fall. "He is but, he's also a man of his word. Promises were made long before I came into the picture." She shrugged one shoulder. "It's too late for me to pull back. I've got to see what happens and hope my love is enough in the end. It would be nice to have a happily ever after to our story."

Tawny was quiet for a long time. "You hope for it but…you don't think there will be."

"No. I don't."

* * *

One month before the wedding, Natalia hosted a party at the penthouse to celebrate with friends and family outside her usual circle. Brie and Riya finished last minute details as Hudson picked up his mother from her apartment and Natalia met hers at the airport.

Brie watched as Camille Truing entered on Hudson's arm. She was *lovely* and it was visually stunning to see the petite light-featured woman standing beside her powerful, dark son.

Their relationship filled her heart with hope. Their life could've been different had Hudson not *refused* to allow it.

Shortly after Camille's arrival, Natalia's mother entered to celebrate her daughter's life and love. Watching as mother and daughter approached Hudson and Camille held Brie enthralled.

He was formal with his future mother-in-law, taking her hand and kissing her cheek. After a big smile, she hugged him tightly and he smiled softly as he returned it.

Jane Roman held Camille's hand in her own and they spoke softly for several minutes. Tears were shed by both women and then they hugged for a long time.

Sipping a glass of wine, Brie grinned.

"Fascinating, right?" Tawny stood at her side staring at the small group with wide eyes.

"Like seeing a unicorn or something," she answered truthfully. "Have you met either of them before tonight?"

Clearing her throat, the redhead hedged. "No, I've never *officially* met them, but I know *of* them."

"One day, you'll spill."

"You're the third person to say that to me this week." She shrugged. "You're the only one who's patient for me to do it."

Brie chuckled. "I imagine."

She linked her arm through her friend's and they clinked their glasses. Tawny's observations on people and situations could leave her gasping for breath.

They visited with Marci, Fahad, and Nuri who'd taken their relationship to the next level in the prior months. "The three of you are so dignified all the time." Shaking her head, Brie added, "I don't know how you do it. I'm such a spaz."

Marci chuckled. "Nonsense. You're lovely, Gabriella."

She crossed her eyes. "Total spaz." Looking at the cousins, she whispered, "The graphics prototype kind of makes me weep with happiness."

Fahad gave a slight bow. "Your opinion means much to us. We knew you'd be the right person to test it."

"I'll write an essay filled with inappropriate adjectives for you. Holy crap, the pen is so responsive, it feels like I'm truly drawing." Hand on her hip, she gestured at Tawny with her wineglass. "This one tried to steal it when I let her play for a few minutes."

Laughing, Nuri said, "You'll have one tomorrow."

Dramatically trembling her lower lip, Tawny sniffed loudly. "That, yes, that."

"I'm going to excuse myself to talk to Max and Micah but it always makes me happy to see the two of you." Marci winked and the threesome walked away.

Tawny went still and muttered, "Shit. You're about to be introduced to the moms. I'm out so I don't scare them." She made a rapid retreat as Hudson and Natalia escorted the older women to meet her.

Camille hugged her hard. "Seeing you back on your feet makes me so happy."

"Thank you. I've missed you."

Leaning back, the blonde touched her cheek. "You're missed by everyone but your sister keeps us up to date. How *pretty* you look." After another hug, she stepped back to Hudson's side.

Natalia announced, "Mother, *this* is Gabriella."

Jane took her hand and held it in silence for a long moment. "You remind me of Hudson when he was a boy."

In absolute seriousness, Brie replied, "I take that as the *highest* compliment, ma'am."

"As you *should*. I've heard so much about you from these two." A huge smile spread over her face. "I hear it's *your* influence that made them pull their heads out of their asses and get the fuck *on with it* already."

Brie burst out laughing. "I should've known. It's a true pleasure to meet you."

Natalia's mother was a deceptively quiet woman who gave all outward appearances of being sedate and vintage. It was clear to see where her daughter inherited her quick wit.

After a few minutes chatting, Brie told her friends, "I beg you, *please* introduce them to Tawny. I need that in my life."

Chuckling, Natalia and Hudson bent to kiss her cheeks and led their mothers away.

This should be interesting.

Brie watched, holding her breath, as the foursome approached the redhead from behind. Hudson saying her name in his stern way caused her to whirl with a movie scream and put her hands up in a classic boxing style.

Then the silly bitch nodded earnestly and *curtsied* for Camille and Jane. It was a *damn* good curtsy.

Over his shoulder, Hudson winked at her and she grinned.

Few people would ever understand what a truly *fun* person he was and she was grateful to have the knowledge.

* * *

A warm arm circled Brie's waist through the thin material of her gown at the same moment Elijah whispered, "You look incredible. Good enough to eat and I happen to be *starving*."

He tugged her and she followed him without hesitation.

In the small alcove behind the kitchen, Harper waited with tension surrounding him.

"Is that vibration for *me* or because you've found yourself in Hudson's *lair*?"

He laughed and it made her feel *wonderful*. Elijah bodily lifted her, placing her between them against the wall. They instantly leaned in, their forearms braced above her.

Harper stroked the back of his hand along the strap of her dress, raking warm fingers over her skin. "Gabriella."

She didn't speak at first. Everything inside her wanted to *touch* them and after a brief hesitation, she allowed herself to do so.

"I didn't think you'd make it."

"We landed less than two hours ago and we're flying out again tonight. We wanted to surprise you." Elijah's lips trailed along her shoulder. "Are you surprised, Brie?"

"Happily." Placing her palms on the center of their chests, she stroked up and over their shoulders beneath their jackets.

A single fingertip traced the raw silk of their ties and she realized they were identical to the fabric of the gown she wore.

Flicking her eyes up, Harper smiled. "Natalia had them made when she ordered your dress."

"She always thinks about little details," she murmured. "Thank you for the easel. It's beautiful, Harper."

"You're welcome."

The day before, deliverymen arrived with a stunning art frame that featured built-in steps. She'd be able to position enormous canvases and raise or lower them to reach the top. It took up one wall of her studio and she'd already envisioned several pieces it would hold for her.

"You had it made for me."

He gave her a charming half-smile. "I needed to buy you *something* and you apparently *abhor* Tiffany's."

It made her laugh. "I can use the easel daily. Diamonds will only end up covered in paint. It was thoughtful of you."

"You're so fucking *refreshing*." He stroked his hand over her shoulder while Elijah rubbed his palm back and forth across her belly. "Your recovery proceeds quickly now. You need the flexibility to paint whatever inspires you."

"I've been painting a lot recently," she told him.

"Anything in particular?" Elijah nuzzled his face against hers and she sighed, her eyes drifting shut.

"Mm hmm," she murmured. She smoothed over them, touching skin she wanted naked more than she wanted her next breath. "How have you been?"

Their hands stroked over her sides and they bent to plant open-mouth kisses on her neck.

"Struggling, away from you," Elijah answered.

Brie nodded. "Stay focused. The thought of either of you distracted scares me."

"Harper keeps us busy. Don't worry, Brie."

"I'm familiar with the routine of twenty-hour work days. I try to stay busy myself. It helps."

Harper lifted his head to say, "I barely get a fucking thing *done*, Gabriella." Against her ear, he growled, "My mind is *consumed* by thoughts of you."

Her response was shaky because it wasn't something she expected Harper to admit. "I'm sure that annoys you."

"Not as much as being perpetually hard. That's more than a little inconvenience when you're meeting with dignitaries and shit." The image made her snicker. "If I don't have you soon, I'll lose my fucking mind."

Then Harper's lips were on her and she held him tightly as he demolished all rational thought about where she was and why. They massaged her skin through her dress and large palms cupped the cheeks of her ass. She tried to hold back her moan and failed.

"Do you think about us when we're gone, Brie?" She tried to nod and thought she might have succeeded. "Do you touch yourself when you think about us?"

"Yes. I think I'm developing a problem." They groaned. "I've never been so desperate. I need you."

Her nails dug into Elijah's back under his jacket as his fingers slipped beneath the bodice of her gown. A warm, strong hand cupped her breast and rolled her nipple between his finger and thumb. She pressed into the touch, needing more.

Harper obliged, gently gathering her hem in his hand until his palm rested directly on the skin of her thigh above her stockings. A blunt fingertip traced the line of her garter, moving higher until he trailed it along the outline of her panties. Nudging beneath the scrap of material, he rocked against her when he met the smooth, damp folds.

"Fuck, you're wet." He dragged his finger along the crease of her, dipping just the tip inside her pussy. Her heart beat too hard. "Hot enough to burn. My cock throbs for you, Gabriella."

Her forehead rested on his shoulder, straining for air as she tried to withstand lust these two men never failed to inspire inside her.

"Please…" She hadn't meant to say it aloud but they responded instantly.

Hands firmed on her skin as they increased their attention. Elijah maintained a firm hold on her breast and moved his other hand down, sliding under the back of her dress and inside her panties. From behind, he stroked two fingers into her pussy and she jerked in their arms.

Holding her tightly, Harper claimed her mouth as he made maddening circles over her clit. Releasing her lips, he stared down into her face. She watched him, breathing rapidly, as she fell over the edge of an orgasm that stunned her.

She struggled to get herself under control as they continued to touch her. When a second climax hit before she recovered from the first, she felt faint.

Harper never broke eye contact as they tore down everything Brie thought she knew about herself and replaced it with something new and different.

Where these men were concerned, Brie knew she was in *serious* trouble. More than sex. More than love. With a sense of dread, she realized she *needed* them and that made the stakes so much higher.

"You're the most naturally sensual woman I've ever met," Elijah told her as she stroked her hand up to hold the back of his head. "You *bask* in pleasure unlike anything I've ever seen."

The men removed their hands from her clothes and she watched as Elijah sucked his fingers.

Harper stroked his across her lower lip and watched as her tongue darted out to taste herself. Pulling him down, she kissed him slow and easy until he moaned into her mouth. Planting small kisses over his lips, she turned to Elijah.

Resting her palm on his face, she whispered, "Please kiss me."

"Gladly."

Their arms surrounded her, crossing at her back and neck. She liked that they were getting more comfortable touching one another in front of her.

When Elijah lifted his mouth away, she whispered, "I love having you touch me at the same time. Feeling the three of us so close to each other. I want so much more." She closed her eyes and inhaled carefully. "A few more weeks before I can experience everything. I can make it."

He murmured, "I wait for you, Brie."

Meeting his gaze, she saw the intensity there and understood what he meant. "You've always had your relationship and it's the *perfect* way to seek relief. It won't hurt me, Elijah."

"As I've attempted to explain several times without success." Her eyes darted to Harper's and he shrugged. "He refuses to break his word."

She could see that not having access to Elijah was taking a toll on him. Smoothing her fingers along his temple, she said softly, "I never want to cause you pain, Harper. I know a lot about loneliness."

"It's alright." She frowned and he added, "Don't worry, Gabriella."

"Your reward for your fight back is going to be incredible, Brie. I want to share that celebration with you." She stroked her fingers through his blonde hair. "I'm so proud of you."

Staring into his green eyes, she considered. "Thank you. Your opinion means more to me than you can imagine." He smiled. "You've given me hundreds of orgasms in the last months. I've had time with you together and time with you *alone*, Elijah."

"Gabriella." She met silver eyes. "The new rules are firmly in place."

"I like imagining you together. Don't deny yourselves. I've had *explosive* orgasms thinking about it. Take what you need. I-I wish I could give you more."

Growling, Elijah's entire body pressed her to the wall and he kissed her until she didn't know if her legs would keep her standing. Beside him, silver eyes practically glared at her with sexual need. The rawness of it made her heart skip.

The gentle rocking of his hips pushed the hardness of his cock over her clit through her gown and her eyes rolled back in her head.

"When you're healed, I plan to fuck you on every available surface until you're too physically weak to *consider* leaving my bed, Brie."

Harper breathed raggedly. "After the pleasure of your mouth, I ache to know what it feels like to fuck your pussy, your ass. To take you myself, to take you with Elijah. I want to see you sexually obliterated."

Inhaling sharply, she gripped the base of their necks tightly. "Then I hope to hell we have someone we can *call for help* because I'll make it my fucking *mission* to see both of you in the same condition. There may be two of you but I'm *starving* so *be prepared*."

Both men shook with their lust and took turns devouring her mouth. Touching her through her clothes, they pushed her into another climax and she rode the ecstasy and agony of it with her teeth gritted.

Her forehead against Elijah's chest, she mumbled, "I want to know *everything*. I expect the two of you to take until I've got nothing left to give, until I can't remember my name."

Working to slow her breathing, she smoothed her hands over them, her heart tender.

Shakily straightening from the wall, she checked the state of her clothing, smoothed her hair, and checked them over as well.

Adjusting their ties and jackets, raking her fingers through their hair, she stared at them for a long moment.

"I selfishly took all the pleasure but I think you know I'll make it up to you at a better time and place. I hope you think about me when we're not together but I also hope you love each other, touch each other, when I can't touch you. Both of you need that and I'll imagine you do either way."

She smiled but it felt funny on her face. "I have to get back. I love you and I miss you already. T-tell me goodbye before you leave."

Then she kissed them with all the pent-up passion, love, and uncertainty that was slowly driving her insane.

Returning to the party, she stopped in the downstairs guest bath to freshen up.

Her emotions were in *chaos*.

* * *

It took a couple of minutes for Elijah and Harper to pull themselves together enough to rejoin the gathering of more than forty people less than twenty feet away.

Shooting his cuffs, Harper said quietly, "She doesn't understand the strength of your will yet. As if you'd *touch* another." He shook his head.

"You've been strong, honorable, since I asked it of you. I know it doesn't come without cost."

"It's almost funny how little desire I have to find other women. I consider it sometimes but quickly dismiss the idea." Their eyes met. "I'll suffer the wait with you."

"Her touch lessens the agony of it for me."

Nodding, he turned to pour himself a scotch from Winters' bar. "Not having you with me around the clock would lessen my own, Elijah."

He saluted him with the cut crystal glass. "It's a form of heaven and hell. I've earned the punishment, I suppose."

"It isn't intended to be punishment."

"And *yet...*"

He shook his head and watched as Gabriella emerged from the downstairs restroom and was immediately pulled into a small group consisting of Chadwick, Scottsdale, their woman, and the redhead.

They were laughing warmly in seconds.

She was a woman who fascinated him, drew him, even as he resented her existence. He wondered if he'd ever understand how her mind and heart operated.

He wondered if he'd ever *want* her love as much as she wanted to give it to him.

As the days passed, Harper's fear grew.

Chapter Twenty-Four

June 2015

Bachelor parties with grownups like her best friends were far different than those held by young brides and grooms. Hudson chartered a yacht and everyone assembled to partake in an entire day of live music, alcohol, five-star food, and laughter.

Brie did her best to hide her sadness when she learned Harper and Elijah wouldn't make it before the small ship disembarked. Her sunglasses helped and the people gathered together eased her melancholy.

The warm weather and location called for summer clothes. She was happy to find an elegant ivory sundress that draped to the floor and pretty leather sandals.

She hated exposing the scars on her legs.

"Darling, your skin is positively glowing. Excellent choice." Natalia kissed her cheek as Brie stepped on deck. The blonde wore a coral sundress that draped to mid-calf and made her eyes glow brightly from her face. "Thank you for helping with the planning."

"I did very little. I accept my lack of event ability but chipped in for the graphic design. Riya and Lola pulled out *all* the stops." She winked. "They managed to keep Tawny out of the mix."

"I don't know if I'm sad or intensely relieved."

Her laughter halted abruptly as Hudson joined them from inside. "Oh, my sweet baby Jesus. You look wonderful...and *casual*."

Dressed in light linen slacks and a shirt in a lighter shade *without a tie*, Hudson's dark hair and eyes were a striking contrast. Then she looked down and realized he was wearing comfortable sandals on his lovely feet and thought she might faint.

"I need a picture of this shit. I want proof."

He grinned. "I've been on vacations, Gabriella."

The statement made Natalia laugh. "In a manner of speaking, darling." To Brie, she added, "He works on boats, balconies, and beaches. Dressed for the moment but very much in *tycoon* mode."

Brie snickered. "I bet that changes now."

"You're right," he answered stoically.

"This was an inspired idea. Once again, you're the *man*." Watching them happily, she nodded. "Always leave them laughing. I'm going to get my drink on. Yell if you need anything."

Trading kisses, she wandered away to explore.

They'd been on the open ocean for a couple of hours when she noticed people drifting toward the rear deck. Curious, she made her way there as well.

A small helicopter landed on the pad there. She stared in stunned fascination as Elijah and Harper stepped from inside.

The aircraft lifted into the air and the men smoothed their hair in a hypnotic synchronized movement. Elijah spotted her first and they made their way to her side as guests stepped aside in awe.

Practically incoherent from the blood rushing around her body, she murmured, "That was *quite* an entrance."

Harper took her hand. "Winters made sure the yacht had the capability. We didn't want to miss it."

Sliding his palm along her neck, Elijah said nothing as he claimed her mouth. He took his time, made her ache all over, and when he lifted away, she stared into green eyes that made her melt. They roamed over her body slowly.

"Caramel and cream. You're delicious, Brie."

Glancing back and forth between them, she admitted softly, "I know

I'll think of so *many* clever things to say later. Right now, I'm speechless."

"That's a first, Gabriella. I'll make a note." Bending, Harper worked his mouth over hers and she moaned. "I concur. Delicious."

She hugged them each tightly. "I missed you bad. I'm so fucking glad you made it."

They hugged her back and held her between them as they ordered drinks.

The day felt complete with them there. Watching Elijah and Harper attempt to adjust to her friends and their outgoing personalities amused her. Having them close enough to touch salved her heart.

They'd spent *another* nine days apart. Separation was becoming harder. She was careful to hide her need to see them and showed her happiness when they were in her orbit.

It would have to be enough.

Lola and Leonard approached and Brie held out grabby hands to hug Hudson's longtime assistant hard. "Girl, you outdid yourself with all this."

She shrugged one shoulder. "You know the king gets irritable if things aren't exactly so."

"Hmm, and I know what a perfectionist you are. Nice try." Looking at Leonard, she quirked a brow at his khaki slacks and casual linen shirt. "No suit. I think I may fall over in shock."

The driver and bodyguard laughed. "Still armed."

"Like I didn't know." He hugged her and she raised up to kiss his cheek. She felt Elijah stiffen at her back and internally rolled her eyes. "You know Harper Delkin and Elijah Eklund."

The siblings grinned and Lola winked. "Yup."

"I worked for Delkin Acquisitions after the military."

"Really? I didn't know that, Leo." She watched Leonard move his gaze from her to Elijah over her shoulder and give him a slow smile.

"So, old friends?" she said as cheerfully as possible.

"You might say that. Or you might not." Leonard returned his attention to her. "However, I'll admit you're in excellent hands. If you weren't, I'd be…angry."

Brie blinked and looked at Lola who struggled to hold back her smile. "Is that a *Hulk* reference?"

"Yes." Leonard said succinctly and bent to kiss her cheek. "That's enough flexing and glaring for one day. I'll see you later." He tapped the tip of her nose with his finger and she snickered as he walked away with a single incline of his head at the men behind her.

Lola added, "Stop by this week so we can finalize the reception itinerary."

"Will do and I'm so glad you're coordinating. I have no clue what I'm doing."

"Utter bullshit. You're brilliant. See you later, Brie."

Turning, she glanced at Harper. His expression was carefully blank.

Elijah followed Leonard's progress across the room.

Frowning, she asked, "Everything okay?"

"Yes." When she didn't look away from his face, he lowered his gaze to hers. "I dislike him around you."

"Why?"

"He's dangerous."

"I'm aware. So are you."

"*Exactly.*"

Her eyes went wide and she was *floored* at the implication. "You'd better *explain* that before I throw a stereotypical female hissy fit in the middle of this classy affair, Elijah."

He led her outside and guided her away from other guests. "Men such as us are…territorial, Brie." She placed her hand on her hip. "If you were angry, upset, he'd step in to protect you."

"I see and that's a *bad* thing because…?"

"I don't want him touching you."

Tapping her fingers, she inhaled carefully and looked at Harper. "Nothing to add?"

"I'll let him take this one."

"Excellent. It's my turn then. In the past ten months, there have been absences that lasted as much as a month. I haven't bitched or whined, I haven't in any way tried to change you or weighed in on the lives you lead." Meeting silver eyes, she added, "Even when you regularly had call girls escorted to your apartment."

"*Shit.* Gabriella…"

"Not to worry. It wasn't *Elijah* who told me the risks you were taking with *my* body. I *worked* in the building before I *lived* in it. I know people from the parking garage to the penthouse. All the workers and many of the residents. With your *frequency*, it was bound to be noticed."

Being honest with herself, Harper looked ashamed about his actions.

She shook her head. "I kept my mouth shut. I've asked for *nothing* from either of you. I possess a goddamn vagina but I happen to be picky about who I allow to access it. Something tells me your total number of sexual partners would *terrify* me. You're ten years older so you probably lost track a couple hundred pussies ago…*both* of you."

Elijah's eyes closed.

Putting her shoulders back, she said through gritted teeth, "As for being *territorial*, I notice it didn't change *Harper's* behavior in the goddamn slightest so if you think for one *second* that I'll censor innocent interactions with *any of my friends* who care about my personal safety and happiness to placate your egos, you can *fuck the hell off*."

She walked inside and avoided people who would've asked her questions she was in no condition to answer. Going into the ladies' room, she worked to calm her temper and settle her hurt feelings.

It took a long time.

* * *

As Brie left the restroom, Elijah pulled her out of the hallway into another room.

She had a moment to exclaim, "I'm still mad!"

Then they gripped her tightly and took turns annihilating her senses with kisses and touches. Minutes later, they lifted from her enough to stare into her face.

"I'm sorry, Brie. As drawn to you as I am, I know how other men *like me* see you." He inhaled carefully and slid his palm along the side of her neck. "You don't understand the way dangerous men perceive you."

"How powerful men in general perceive you," Harper said as he added his warmth to the other side.

"I'm nice to *everyone*. I like people. To me, it doesn't matter whether they're a pretzel vendor or a mercenary or the head of a multi-billion-dollar corporation." She scrubbed at her tears. "I'd never *betray* you, damn it."

"I know. I *know*, Brie. I'm sorry."

"My friends are all I have when you're gone. None of them talk about either of you because they know I have no clue where you are, what you're doing, or when you'll be back. They aren't a *threat* to you. They help me laugh when I really want to cry."

"Forgive me," Elijah murmured as he pressed his face to hers. "I was thoughtless."

Lifting her hands, she curled her fingers around their wrists. "No matter how lonely I get I'd never hurt you. I need you to believe in me, Elijah." He pressed closer.

Harper shook his head. "It's because of me, Gabriella. The way I've been hasn't been easy for him." He took a deep breath. "I'm sorry there was such a thing to hide from you more than your knowledge of it. Elijah demanded I stop and get full blood work to ensure your safety. He didn't want to hurt you whereas I hadn't even *considered* how you'd feel."

"It hurt but you never made promises so I let it go."

Harper kissed her temple. "I'm sorry. There's been no one else and there won't be."

"As long as we're together," she added. He looked at her with a frown. She shrugged sadly. "Don't make such an open-ended promise."

Elijah claimed her mouth for a long time and when he pulled away, he said against her lips, "Do you forgive me?"

She nodded and the last of her anger dissipated. It was impossible to hug them any tighter, to get any closer. Needing so much more, she wanted to cry in frustration and he noticed it.

Elijah gripped her hair and tilted her head back. "You're almost there. Another week until your appointment."

"I get why you worry. I can't hold you hard enough, I can't *show* you."

"Show us what, Brie?"

"How much I love you."

Picking her up, he carried her across the room and settled on a couch near the window. "I *never* doubt how much you love me. I don't worry about *you*. I know the *temptation* you present to men like me, to men like Harper." He kissed the top of her head. "You're *lonely*."

She nodded and he pulled her closer. Wrapping her arms around him, she drew her legs in to touch as much of him at one time as possible.

Her palm spread over his heart and she nuzzled her face at his neck, inhaling the scent of him with a shaky sigh. He smoothed her hair and ran his palms over her body through the dress.

"You're so sensual that I forget sometimes what you really need."

Harper sat on the other end of the couch. "What?"

"Touch. Connection." He kissed her forehead and Brie raked her fingers through his hair. "She's affectionate with her friends and it helps but not enough. It's why she was hurt by what I said."

"I don't, what do you mean?" The confusion in Harper's voice was clear.

"We show up, push her as far as we can sexually, then we're gone again. It's wearing on her." Nudging her face up, he said, "Why didn't you tell me, Brie?"

"It's pathetic."

"No." He smoothed his palm over her cheek. "Not pathetic. You're loving. We're taking a lot and neither of us noticed you weren't taking enough."

"I don't need much," she whispered. "Usually I'm okay."

"Okay isn't good enough, Brie."

After ten minutes, she didn't feel as if she was going to shake apart. Lifting her head, she stared at Harper. Crawling across the couch, she sat in his lap and wrapped her arms around him.

He tensed and held her awkwardly.

"You don't have to touch me back, Harper. Just...let me be like this for a little." She held the back of his head and inhaled the clean smell of him. "I know it's stupid to you. I know."

"You've been lonely?" She nodded against him. "I'm sorry. I'm not accustomed to women who have real emotions. I understand how someone like you would need to be hugged and everything."

"Someone like me?" She was almost afraid to ask.

"Gentle. Sweet. It makes sense."

"Just give me a minute to remember how you smell, how you feel." She hugged him tight and listened to him breathe. Rubbing her cheek over his shoulder, she planted a kiss at the hollow of his throat and moved to get up.

His arms tightened and held her in place. "You can stay."

Heart pounding, she relaxed against him and wrapped her arms around his neck, petting the hair on the back of his head. She was careful not to fidget.

Elijah moved closer, his arm stretching out on the sofa behind them and wrapping his hand around the darker man's shoulder. His other stroked through her hair.

Harper inhaled deeply. "You're kind of like a cat."

Looking at Elijah, she said, "I hope you *like* cats, Harper."

"They're not bad," he told her. "They don't usually like me."

Rubbing her hand over his chest, she whispered, "This one thinks you're pretty amazing."

"I'm sorry. I was selfish and inconsiderate, Gabriella. It won't happen again." Then he kissed her temple and settled her more fully in his arms. The lull of his heartbeat soothed her.

The sun was at a different angle through the window when she opened her eyes and realized she'd fallen asleep. Harper was asleep on Elijah's shoulder, his face fully at peace. She watched him without moving.

Meeting green eyes, she smiled softly and Elijah winked.

Only when Harper stirred did she pretend to wake up, stretching and rubbing against him. Sitting up, she took her time kissing them, her hands on both at all times.

Taking a deep breath, she held them close and said, "I really needed that. I hate that we argued. I'm glad we didn't leave it that way."

Elijah cupped her face in his hand. "We didn't *argue*. I was a misogynist ass and you didn't let me get away with it. I'm *more* worried about how lonely you've been. Talk to me when you start feeling disconnected, Brie. Things move fast day to day. I don't want to miss the signs."

Hand on the back of his head, she kissed him and whispered, "Thank you. I love you."

* * *

Back in the main room, everyone was starting to file in for dinner when eight male and female members of the crew stepped up on stage.

They stripped away their uniforms, music started to play, and they performed a highly skilled and decidedly raunchy dance routine to the shock – and clear enjoyment – of the guests.

Beside them, Tawny said, "As if there weren't going to be *strippers* at this thing. I don't fucking think so. That shit's sacred."

The redhead had her arms crossed, a smirk on her face.

"You're the coolest chick on the planet," Brie said with admiration. "You've *got* to tell me how you pulled this off."

Grinning, she replied, "Contacts. That one has a *lovely* rack."

When the music ended, the room went crazy clapping.

From behind them, Hudson said sternly, "Tawny."

The movie scream and boxing stance *never* got old.

* * *

Hours later, Brie said goodbye to Harper and Elijah at the pier. "See you when I see you. Know I love you. Coming back safely is important so, make that happen."

They nodded and took turns kissing her. Elijah held her and said firmly, "I never doubt you, Brie. I'm sorry I hurt your feelings."

One more kiss. "We're good. Call me."

Then she walked to Hudson and Natalia, grinned up at a smirking Leonard, and got in the back of the car with a shake of her head.

She carefully kept the conversation to the wedding and her friends didn't push. In the lobby, she hugged them tight. "We're getting close and I'm so excited."

"Seamstress tomorrow afternoon. I'm taking you to dinner after."

"Okay. Go celebrate your victory. I'm exhausted and I love you."

The moment the elevator to the penthouse opened, Hudson practically lifted Natalia inside and his mouth was lowering to hers as the door closed.

Waving at Carlo, she went to her apartment and took a quick shower.

Climbing into her bed, her phone went off. She was shocked to see a text from Harper.

"You looked beautiful today. Thank you for being gracious when we fuck up. It's a first. Sleep well, Gabriella."

She replied, "You looked beautiful as well. Love means forgiveness. Travel safe, Harper." Smiling to herself, she sent another. "Any chance I can get you guys to send me a selfie?"

Ten minutes later, Harper sent her one of them side by side on what she assumed was his private plane. "You'd have thought I asked him to sing a fucking show tune in Times Square. This is a first. Ever. For either of us."

The photo that downloaded was Harper giving his corporate smile and Elijah being his bodyguard self. They looked gorgeous and she loved it more than would've made sense to anyone in her life.

"You have no clue how happy I am right now. One of me."

She held up her phone and took one of herself against her pillows with silly pouty lips. Her hair was ridiculous but it was clear she wasn't wearing clothes so…no fucks given.

Seconds later, he texted, "Pan the fuck BACK, Gabriella." Laughing, she sent her first dirty photo ever, showing her breasts. An almost instant reply. "Pan back MORE, Gabriella."

Sighing, she stood and went into her bathroom. Using a couple of curvy girl tricks for best results, she took a full body nude and sent it, adding, "Don't make me regret this."

The phone rang and the instant she answered, Elijah said sharply, "One from the back." She laughed so hard she almost couldn't hold her phone as she told him to wait while she took and sent it. "Fuck. Yes. You're so lovely."

"I won't ask either of you to compromise yourselves and I've got my own sketches locked away that are super dirty."

"Miss you already, Brie."

"I miss you, too."

"I'll call you tomorrow. I love you."

"I love you, too. Tell Harper from me and then tell him from you."

"I will. Goodnight, Brie."

Turning off all the lights, she climbed under her blankets. She felt *much* better.

* * *

Disconnecting, Elijah sent the final photo to Harper and he moaned when it delivered.

"Dear *lord*, that ass."

"Agreed." He paused. "She said to tell you she loves you and remind you that I love you as well."

Silver eyes lifted to his. "Lovely of her." He saved each of the photos and tucked his phone in his suit jacket. "Where do you see *me* in this arrangement, Elijah?"

"I don't understand the question."

"Withdrawn."

Elijah considered. "Are you alright?"

"Of course." He opened his laptop as the plane lifted off.

"Harper." Waiting for his full attention, he murmured, "A little longer."

"Yes. Then we'll see what happens. I find myself more curious than ever before."

For a long time, he stared at his oldest friend and tried to figure out the emotional element of a relationship that had never discussed them, focused on them, or even cared about them in some ways.

Brie was right. He had no clue how to navigate it.

* * *

During last fittings for her bridesmaid gown a few days later, Brie's eyes widened in shock at the final result of Natalia's design.

"Um, this is…"

"You need to be pure sex, Brie," her friend explained. "It's black, classy, and going to lay over your golden flesh like a second skin."

She didn't usually show so much and her scars made her self-conscious. "I'm going to have a nip slip in this. I'm going to bend over and my tits are going to fall out."

Raising one blonde brow, Natalia's response was, "We can only hope, darling."

"I can't be a sex kitten at your *wedding*…"

"The fuck you can't. Leave me alone and let me work." She turned to the seamstress and mumbled, "Woman is getting laid if I have to supply the ropes to tie her ass down."

Unable to contain the fit of laughter the words provoked, Brie left the shop and waited across the street at the coffee shop.

She lost all decorum around her friends. It made her happy.

Chapter Twenty-Five

June 20, 2015 – The Wedding

"I don't think I should've worn white, Gabriella. I mean, really." Natalia stared at her reflection in the full-length mirror with a small frown between her eyes. "My mother is probably *scandalized.*"

Brie snorted. "Yeah, right. She's fabulous and ridiculously chic. Besides, she told you if you held a black and white wedding and then tripped down the aisle in *beige* – a color she looked ill to utter – it would throw off the entire thing. So! Rock that designer gown that looks like it was painted on your fantastic body and anyone who doesn't like it can fuck off."

Turning, the blonde took Brie's shoulders. "Are you sure you're okay? You pushed your recovery."

Lifting her hands, she cupped Natalia's cheeks. "You and Hudson deserve every single beautiful thing life has to offer. I'm as anxious and excited as you are and if I pushed myself a little bit, I consider the outcome more than worth it. I feel amazing. If I get tired, I'll sit down."

Turning the slim woman toward the mirror, she stared around her shoulder. "Look at you, Natalia. You're dressed in a wedding gown and about to become the wife of the man you've loved for more than thirty years." She blinked back her tears. "My happiness for you fills me up."

"Don't make me cry, darling," she whispered. Raising a long-fingered hand, she placed it over Brie's. "I'm so grateful for you, for your friendship."

Sniffling, Brie shook her head and gave Natalia's shoulders a hug. "We're so emotional. Okay! I've got to go check the lay of the land."

At the door, she paused and glanced back. "Natalia?" The blonde turned and the sunlight caught her just right. "You're the most beautiful bride I've ever seen. I can't wait to see Hudson's face when he sees you. I'm going to watch him watch you."

Two slender hands covered her friend's lower face and she smiled through happy tears.

"Don't get snot on your gown." She winked. "I'll be right back."

* * *

After reassuring her best girlfriend and making sure she had everything she needed, Brie almost started bawling at the damn beauty of everything to do with a wedding she'd been waiting for as anxiously as the couple getting married.

Closing the door of the bridal suite softly behind her, she walked as quickly as she could the other end of the hall and gave a soft tap on the door.

"Enter."

The abrupt response made her grin as she swung the door wide. "Oh, sweet *lord*, Hudson. You look fucking outstanding."

Her best friend, a title the man earned every day, was dressed in a tuxedo. His black hair was brushed back from his forehead and it was getting long enough that the natural waves were evident.

"Gabriella, I'm a goddamn *wreck*. You look lovely."

Her eyes widened as she closed the door and stopped in front of him. "Thank you and we can fix whatever it is."

It was then that she realized he was having trouble with his tie.

"I can't *count* the number of times I've performed this unbelievably simple task. This is bullshit."

She pretended not to notice that his hands shook and gave him a bright grin. "It's *clearly* the stupid tie. Let me." Shooing his hands away, she took over until it laid properly. "There. Now you're as perfectly perfect as your stunning bride to be."

His eyes met hers and she loved the way he gave his complete attention when he talked. "How is she? Any sign of cold feet?"

"You damn well know *better*." She smoothed his lapel and straightened his boutonniere. "She's a little nervous and her emotions are close to the surface but I imagine those are feelings many brides share."

"I wouldn't know."

She shrugged. "Nor would I." His eyes flickered with an instant of sadness and she cupped his cheeks. "If the two of you don't stop worrying about me, I'll marry the first man I see." Tucking a tiny stray hair behind his ear, she added, "I'm so damn *proud* of you, Hudson. For so many reasons."

"That means more than you realize, Brie. Seeing you back on your feet makes the day that much more special. I know you pushed so hard…"

One finger over his lips, she insisted, "I'm *fine*. Not ready to walk the streets yet…wait, that makes me sound like a hooker." He gave her a full laugh. "Anyway, I'm great and you aren't permitted to worry about anyone or anything on the most important day of your life. Promise?"

"You remain the most fascinating human being to me."

"As you are to me. In my case, fascinating is often a synonym for weird but I'm cool with that." She rubbed her hands together. "Now! What can I do to help before we get this show on the road? Any little tasks you need me to race out and do?"

Glancing around, she gave a small scream at the sight of Harper and Elijah standing at the far end of the room, watching her.

Neither had moved or made a sound since she walked in.

"Elijah and Delkin are here," Hudson explained. Rather unnecessarily, in her opinion.

"Jesus. Yes, *thank you*, Hudson." She inhaled carefully against the visceral reaction they caused. "Hello. I'm going to…*go*."

Pausing in the act of turning toward the door, Brie knew she couldn't allow the presence of men she thought about more often than was healthy, to stop her from saying what she needed to say.

Turning back, she gave her best friend a gentle smile. "I can't express how honored I am to be part of this moment in your life. You're the best friend I've *ever* had, Hudson. Thank you for a million things, big and small." She hugged him carefully but he wasn't having it and gathered her tightly to him. "Don't be nervous. It's all going to be just right because that's exactly what you deserve."

Releasing her, he cupped her face and bent to kiss her forehead. "It was you. We won't forget."

"Don't make me cry," she whispered. Squeezing his hand, she turned for the door.

"Gabriella." Glancing over her shoulder, she met his eyes. "Had Natalia not called dibs, you'd have been *my* best man rather than *her* maid of honor." He shrugged. "As it was, I had to go with my oldest…friend."

Looking at Harper, his pewter eyes called to her, as did the green ones beside him. She refused to think about how good the friends looked in their tuxedos.

She had shit to do.

"You made an excellent choice, Hudson." She laughed. "However, I'd have loved watching a seamstress struggle to get *my* ass in a tux. I'll see you out there."

Just outside, she experienced a fit of nervous giggles barely muffled by her hands. Finally able to calm herself, she returned to Natalia's side.

* * *

An hour later, Brie stood on one side of the altar while Hudson and Harper stood on the other. Elijah sat in the first row. She could *feel* his gaze.

As Natalia appeared thirty feet away, the guests gasped and murmured about her incredible beauty but Brie kept her eyes firmly on Hudson.

The love, the near *worship* he held for his woman was evident on every inch of his face.

It made her heart feel full to overflowing.

Watching every step Natalia took down the aisle toward him, Hudson never blinked.

Gabriella saw the shimmer of tears in his eyes and understood the journey the couple had taken to get to this place, this moment, in the history of their relationship.

It was knowledge she treasured and she was overjoyed to be a witness to it. Searing the moment into her mind, she knew she'd sketch it later.

Handing over her bouquet with trembling hands, Natalia turned to her fiancé. Within mere moments, after more than thirty years of friendship, they were married at long last.

Those assembled stood to clap and cheer.

The newly wedded couple turned and bent as one to kiss her cheeks. Natalia's voice trembled with emotion, "Did you *see?*"

Nodding happily, Brie was unable to stop a tear from slipping down her cheek. She replied softly, "It was the single most beautiful moment I've ever witnessed in my lifetime and I won't *ever* forget it."

They hugged her tightly between them. "I love you both so much. Congratulations. Now go greet your guests as *husband* and *wife*, because it's about damn time."

Laughing, they turned and spoke to Harper before walking up the aisle. Natalia's hand was through Hudson's arm and he held her there securely.

With her hands clasped over her heart and a smile that felt far too big for her face, Brie watched them take the first steps into their true future together.

"Gabriella."

Inhaling sharply, she met Harper's eyes. He held out his arm and she put her hand through it robotically. His warmth radiated through the expensive fabric.

He placed his other hand over hers and gently stroked her skin with his thumb. She glanced up at him and he smiled. It was the first time she'd seen an expression on his face that neared actual happiness when he looked at her.

It stole her breath.

"Naturally, we'll be required to dance." He winked. "I'll be careful with you, Brie."

Hudson's oldest male friend led her toward the waiting limo that would carry them across town to the luxurious reception. Elijah fell into step at her other side. They pretended not to hear Riya call her name across the room.

Brie wondered if it was possible for a human heart to literally beat out of a person's chest. She knew the next few days would test the theory.

As they gently assisted her into the supple interior, Harper murmured, "Your time is now *up*, Gabriella."

The limo door closed quietly and she found herself wrapped in a cocoon with two men who inspired her every sexual fantasy for ten months…and fulfilled many of them without even realizing it.

They were instantly on her, stroking their hands over and under the thin silk she wore.

Concealed from the outside world less than ten minutes after her friends said their vows, Brie determined that Natalia had been right about the dress.

"I want you naked. I'll settle for exposed." Harper's hands slid beneath the straps of the bodice that had a hell of a lot more support than it looked. He slid them off her shoulders, baring her upper body.

Her nipples drew even tighter and neither man hesitated to lower their mouths to them. Arching into them with a low moan, she settled her hands on the back of their heads.

Releasing the tip with a soft pop, Elijah's mouth claimed hers with ferocity. His body pressed along her side and his erection throbbed through the layers of their clothes.

Their hands stroked her everywhere and she chaotically wondered what they could accomplish before they reached the reception venue.

"Time. How much time?" She didn't recognize her voice.

"Too goddamn little, however much it is," Harper said sharply. She laughed unevenly and he rested his head above her breast. The heat of the breath sawing in and out of his mouth felt wonderful. "Fuck, Gabriella."

"A wonderful idea but not even a quickie is possible."

His answering laugh made her grin. "I feel like an adolescent. Complete lack of control."

"I'd like to officially say hello and ask how you've been."

Sitting up, she took them in. She hadn't seen them since the yacht party. She needed a minute to get her breathing under control.

Gripping her tightly, both men lifted their heads to look at her.

The skin around Elijah's mouth and eyes was tight. "I thought I was going to swallow my fucking tongue when I saw you in this dress, Brie."

"Natalia's selection."

"She's a fucking genius." Harper raked his hand through his hair. "Okay. We should get you together, Gabriella. No way are we escorting you from this limo looking freshly fucked."

"If *only*..." Her tone was wistful.

"Stop *talking*. Stop *looking* at me like that or we'll disappoint the newlyweds. I need to be inside you more than I require social acceptance."

"I'll behave." She shrugged the straps of her bodice into place and sat up to straighten the skirt.

"It's a crime against humanity to cover those tits," Elijah said with a sad shake of his head. He reached out to pet them through silk. "Don't worry, you'll be free again soon enough."

Laughing, she reached past him for a bar towel and club soda. "You have my lipstick everywhere."

"Not yet, but I will."

Whimpering, she wet the towel and wiped the traces of red from his lips. "Tell *him* to stop talking." Elijah took the towel and ran it over her jaw and neck where he'd trailed it.

Harper grinned. "I can't. He can kill me in twelve different ways."

She looked at him and quirked her brow. "While I can only think of *one*."

"Ouch."

Elijah used his thumb and forefinger to turn her face to him. "I'll teach you the others." Then he kissed the tip of her nose and smoothed a lock of hair behind her ear.

"The two of you are not to form an alliance."

Brie smiled as she looked into green eyes she dreamed about every time she closed her eyes. "Too late. You're toast and you're going to love every fucking minute."

Harper stroked his palm over her breast and nodded. "You possess an unfair advantage. They're just so pretty."

The limo pulled to the curb and she took a deep breath. Elijah left the limo first when the driver opened the door, followed by Harper who reached back for her hand.

On solid ground, she whispered, "I'm so wet. I feel as if I could come from a cool breeze." The men tensed to get back in the car but she called out, "Riya!"

"Your ass is *mine*, Brie."

"Elijah, I look forward to finding out *exactly* what you plan to do with it." As her friend approached with her men, she removed her hand from Harper's arm and kissed her cheeks.

Staring at the two men at Brie's sides, Riya's eyes went wide. "Well, okay then. I made Rodney break the speed limit to catch up. Wasn't sure you'd actually make it to the reception with the way they hustled you out of there." Clearing her throat, she murmured, "You missed a bit of lipstick."

Glancing down, a smudge of red glared along the inside swell of her breast. Max handed her a handkerchief with a smile. Riya clustered closer so she could remove it then took the linen and perfected her lipstick line.

Tawny appeared in their midst. "I assume they're going to officially pop your two-dude ménage cherry tonight now that you're all flexible and shit."

Brie rolled her eyes. "Oh, for god's *sake*, Red."

"It's been dude one, chick two so far and let me tell you *what*, the chick one, dude two dynamic is pretty fucking awesome. Side note, you deserve it. The tests they put you through were no joke so I'm glad that shit's over." Elijah frowned but Tawny had more to add. "I thought those bitches were going to break your bones *again* during a couple of those torture sessions."

"They had to be sure," Brie murmured. Finger under her chin, Elijah had questions in his eyes. "I'm fine. It's done."

"I didn't know, Brie. I thought it was just a checkup."

"Good thing you weren't there. That would've made it way worse. How much pain she was in would've fucked you up. She doesn't suck *any* of my body parts and I was ready to slit their throats."

Weakly, Brie said, "Thank god for Riya. Natalia threatened to call her lawyer."

"That's because Blondie and I were escorted out about halfway through. I love that classy bitch." Tawny cleared her throat. "Now, some advice I forgot to mention before because you weren't getting the D on the regular. Keep track of your panties, that's all I'm saying. Those fucking things end up *everywhere*."

Riya shook her head. "I never lose panties. I don't wear them anymore." Micah looked down at her with a growl. "I'm lying but I *love* to see their reactions. Let's get inside."

"I can see two men who *really* want to get inside so it's gonna be a long night for them," was Tawny's response.

"I'm staying away from you. You have no fucking decorum." Brie smacked Tawny's ass and the redhead shook it.

"Make me flinch or don't bother."

Micah clapped Harper on the shoulder. "You'll get used to it. What do you drink?"

When Brie moved to follow the others, Elijah held her to his side. "I should've been with you."

Once they were inside the building, she stopped and reached up to stroke his face. "It's better you weren't. I know you're busy. Both of you run constantly. Don't worry about me. I just hope you get a chance to rest sometimes."

Pulling him down, she pressed her cheek to his and whispered, "I don't want to get lipstick on you again. I missed you."

Then she joined her friends.

Chapter Twenty-Six

There'd be few things as beautiful in Brie's life as watching Hudson take Natalia in his arms and dance with her for the first time as a married couple.

It was breathtaking. It was the stuff of legends. When she had a moment, she slipped her sketchbook from the bag Tawny brought for her and quickly made her impressions.

She didn't know Elijah and Harper were beside her until she exhaled roughly and looked up.

"Gabriella, you're...incredible."

Blinking, she murmured, "I doodle a lot."

Harper took her hand. "All my life, I've had an artist in my family who couldn't focus until he brought the images in his mind to reality." He tilted his head. "I never understood his compulsion until this moment."

Elijah kissed her bare shoulder. "That isn't doodling, Brie. That's captivating, moving *art*."

Glancing down at the paper, she sighed. "It'll be better later. They'll have tons of photos I can look through. They like my pieces."

"Brie." She met green eyes. "It's *your* paintings that decorate their penthouse?" She lifted one shoulder in a shrug. "You're fucking magical."

The woman guiding the evening stepped up on stage. "We'll now hear from the best man, Mr. Harper Delkin."

Silver eyes held hers as he kissed the back of her hand and stood to take the stage.

"Elijah…"

"Ssh. Listen."

Brie knew Harper spent much of his life in one form of spotlight or another. Some of his speeches to corporations and governments around the world were on YouTube. She'd listened to many of them.

There was a small shiver of fear as he stepped in front of a microphone to talk about the man he'd competed with for two decades. Inhaling carefully, she held Elijah's hand.

"I've known Hudson Winters for slightly more than twenty years and his stunning bride for just less. We've argued, we've competed, and we've pissed one another off in our bid to go bigger or better. To be honest, I thought I knew him as well as I know myself."

Slipping his hands in the pockets of his slacks, he shook his head. "I was wrong. It's only in the last year that I've been introduced to the *man* Hudson is. One who helps those who are weaker, who earns deep loyalty and trust, who loves selflessly those who offer nothing in return but gentle friendship."

His mouth lifted in a smile. "Hudson, you captured the heart, the mind, and the hand of a beautiful woman who has *never* failed to impress me with her intelligence, elegance, and grace. You surround yourself with people who speak of you as protector, confidant, and source of steady strength."

Accepting a glass of champagne from the server beside him, he lifted it toward the couple. "May every year shine brighter, bring you more of those things you need as well as want, and fulfill the quiet promise of your first thirty years of friendship. Congratulations."

Every person in the room stood up and toasted them.

Hudson and Natalia met him as he left the stage and the two men shook hands. Then Brie watched in stunned fascination as Hudson brought the man in for a hug. Natalia pressed her cheek to his and hugged him as well.

Harper returned to their table and Brie stood waiting for him.

"Thank you. Thank you for understanding. That was beautiful."

Then she went into his arms and released a small sob as he crushed her to him.

Many stood to speak while guests danced, ate, and drank. She danced carefully with several people and was furious that she was so stiff in movements that once came easily to her.

As Micah returned her to her table, he kissed her cheek. "Brie, how *far* you've come in a single year. Well done, love." His honey eye winked. "I call dibs on the first dance at the Christmas party. You'll blow everyone away once again."

Riya gave Brie's shoulders a slight shake. "Tawny and I can't handle *all* the heavy lifting. Do you understand the uneven dance partner problem at *Trois*? Some nights I can't feel my damn feet." She rolled her eyes dramatically. "Knowing how well you shake your ass, we count the days."

Her husband nodded. "Natalia will eventually have to bus poor unsuspecting women in. The males *need* you, Brie."

She gave him a grin. "You know, people as pretty as you and Max make those around you a little stupid. Then you talk. Stop talking."

His laugh was warm. "You've never been susceptible and I find it so refreshing."

"The day those two college girls tripped right next to us, I thought I'd pee my pants laughing with Riya after we helped them up...lord. My jaw hurts to remember. I think Riya bit through her tongue." She waved at them. "Go. I need entertainment and the two of you provide it so well."

Brie watched as he dragged Riya out to dance. The way they moved was so fucking fluid.

At her side, Elijah asked, "You like to dance?"

She nodded. "I love their optimism but I'll likely never be able to move the way I used to." The thought filled her with sadness. Holding out her foot, she hissed at her shoes. "I still can't wear *heels* yet. Damn it."

Folding her hands in her lap, she took several breaths.

"Brie." She met Elijah's eyes. "Give yourself time." Leaning forward, he kissed her lightly.

It helped.

"You have many friends," Harper said.

"I try to be a good one."

The emcee stepped to the stage and said, "Now we'll hear from the maid of honor, Gabriella Hernandez."

She groaned. "Oh my god. Please don't let me throw up."

Standing, she made her way to the stage as if it was her execution. With shaking hands, she looked at the notecards and shook her head.

"I-I don't usually speak in front of people. I prepared notes but…they make me more nervous." She looked at her best friends as the room went silent. "I'm going to look at you and pretend no one else is here."

Taking a single deep breath, she started. "During our friendship, you've helped me in more ways than I can e-explain. I read that you're the sum of the five people you spend the most time with and I hope, so desperately, that it's true."

She twisted her hands together tightly. "Natalia, I'd love to be as poised as you are in every situation. You're gorgeous on the outside, stunning, but your brain and your heart are what make it *impossible* not to love you. Thank you for accepting me, for making me laugh, for your comfort, your care, your advice, and a hundred little things you didn't have to do but you did with true class and sometimes a hot cup of tea."

Swallowing past the lump in her throat, she stared into black eyes she'd sketched many times. "Hudson, I hope one day I have as much of the strength and genuine *goodness* that's a natural part of your biological makeup. Through my friendship with you, I've met so many fantastic people because they *gravitate* to who you are, even when you don't see that. Thank you for including me in your spectacular life. You earn my loyalty, trust, respect, and love every day."

Brie inhaled carefully. "You're two of the most brilliant and kind and funny and *exceedingly* patient people I know. Individually, you're awesome but *together*, that's where the magic happens. You share a love I never thought I'd witness. The kind everyone wants but few people ever find. Lifelong happiness couldn't happen to a better man, a better woman, to better friends. I love you and I'm so glad to see you attain the happiness you've *always* deserved." Smiling, she accepted a glass of champagne and added, "To Hudson and Natalia."

After the toast, she descended the stairs and they hugged her tightly between them with their lips pressed to the top of her head.

"Darling, I swear to god. You're the only person who has *ever* made me cry in public." Natalia cupped her face and tucked a tendril behind Brie's ear. "Thank you for entering my life and making so many things possible. I love you, Gabriella."

Hudson took her chin between his finger and thumb, staring into her eyes for a long moment. "You're still the one I never saw coming." It made her heart thump hard in her chest. "You're an *exquisite* human being and I love you."

Hugging them hard, she murmured, "Love each other balls to the wall and destroy anything or anyone who ever tries to fuck your shit up." They laughed and she huffed. "I couldn't say that up there but…you know."

She waved her hands. "I've got to go wipe my face and stuff. Go dance and eat because I know you're not going to think about food once you're on the plane." Turning to go, she paused to add, "Restraints and seatbelts are *not* the same thing." Quirking her brow, she hissed, "Arrive alive!"

They laughed as she crossed to the ladies' room. After pulling herself together, she sat in the small seating area just outside to catch her breath.

Riya and Max sat on the sofa beside her.

The brunette grinned. "How you holding up, Brie?"

"I've never talked in front of so many people. I'm happy I didn't puke on stage."

"It was beautiful, so beautiful. Even Tawny teared up."

"Shut. Up."

"Truth. Don't tell her I told you."

"Considering your first interaction with Hudson, I find it lovely that you've grown so close." Max's British accent scrambled her thinking long enough to cause a delay in hearing and comprehension. She crossed her eyes when he smiled.

Blinking, she frowned at Riya. "Why do you insist on bringing them out in *tuxedos*, woman? Ugh!" The couple laughed. "Okay, my brain's back online."

"You're adorable, Gabriella," he said.

She shook her finger at him. "No talky!" He grinned and she gave him a wink.

Thinking back, she replayed the first time she met Hudson. "If he hadn't been open to being my friend, things would've gone differently between us." She shrugged. "I confused him, made him curious. So many people *want* change but can't really see how to make it happen. I can't imagine my life without them in it now."

Leaning forward, Riya took her hand. "They're settled and happy. I almost fell over when Tawny told me about Joshua and Jessica."

"Life as a bridge. Lives changed, happiness achieved." The sentence made her feel sad for a moment and she shook it off. "I might have to write a book."

Riya gazed at her intently. "Make sure at the end, when everyone *else* has happiness, that you take some for yourself, Brie. It's okay to be selfish sometimes. Max and Micah taught me that and it's an important lesson."

Inhaling, she murmured, "Thanks."

"Now! You look recovered from your public speaking so let's get you back inside before all the security guys assigned from god knows who start closing in. Come on."

"There really are a lot, huh?"

Max told her, "They attempt to blend in but some of them are rather large and you're not very big. It makes me chuckle."

She stared into his brilliant blue eyes. "I'm glad there aren't men with accents in my life. I don't know how she gets a fucking thing *done*."

Pulling her to her feet, Riya linked their arms. "I do mental concentration exercises. It's been a slow process but a vast improvement over my initial blank staring and drooling."

"Love, you *never* drooled…outside of certain scenarios."

Brie started laughing until she was gasping for air.

Elijah's appearance in front of her caused her brain to hiccup and her laugh bubbled to a stop.

He inclined his head at the couple politely and turned his focus to her. "I'm stealing Brie. I apologize for the intrusion."

Wrapping his arm around Brie's waist, he led her away. When they entered a quiet solarium at the end of the hall, he pivoted on his heel and turned to her, his palm slipping along her neck.

Delivering a kiss that made her moan into his mouth, he pulled back to stare into her eyes. "Your speech was beautiful."

"Thank you."

"It made me see your relationship with Hudson and Natalia so clearly. They love you *deeply*."

For a long moment, she held his gaze. "They do…but it pales in comparison to the love they have for each other."

"You think our situation will be a repeat of that experience."

Inhaling carefully, she reached up to trace his face. "No. It'll be something completely different, Elijah."

Painting a smile on her face, she focused on bringing back the earlier mood. "Let's get back. I'm sure they'll cut the cake soon and we can send them off on their epic honeymoon."

"Brie." She paused in the act of turning. "Wait."

Stepping closer, she whispered, "I love you. Those aren't just words to me." She held her palm over her heart. "I hurt when I'm not near you. It won't disappear on a whim. I won't ever use it against you. I love you and no matter what happens, I'll have the joy of it, Elijah."

Hugging him, kissing him, taking his breath into her lungs was a place of bliss she knew wasn't hers to inhabit.

His fingers raked through her hair and he rested his forehead against hers. "I won't hurt you."

"I know you'll do everything humanly possible to prevent it. Thank you for that."

"I love you, Brie."

Taking her hand, he led her back inside and she worked to steady her mind and heart.

Everything was better when Hudson placed a fingertip of icing on the tip of Natalia's nose and laughed when she made him hold her first bite between his lips so she could eat it.

They made her heart feel *hope*. For them, for herself.

Chapter Twenty-Seven

Brie watched her friends dance and laugh. She randomly sketched from the table where she insisted on staying after making a round of the room.

"Are you done socializing?"

She turned to Elijah and returned his smile. "I'm a little tired and my attention span sucks. Too many quirks. I can't wait to sort through their photos and copy the ones I'll duplicate."

"I love your quirks. You're an outstanding date."

Her eyes widened and she grinned. "It *is* like a date."

Elijah stroked a finger over her cheek. "How easy it is to please you, Brie."

Lifting one brow, she whispered, "I'll let you test the theory."

"Hey there, little sister."

Whipping her head to the side, she smiled at her sister Isabella. The look on her face made Brie immediately nervous. She'd carefully avoided any talk of the men who sat beside her.

"Izzy, I thought you were still in Paris. You look great."

Similar in coloring and features, Isabella was a taller, leaner version. Izzy was extremely confident. It had been a source of sadness, even envy, for much of Brie's life but their relationship was strong.

Hand on the hip of her stunning blue gown, she stared at Brie for a long moment. "My meetings in New York were moved up." Her eyes landed on Harper before moving to take in Elijah. "You've made new friends."

Both men were still and silent.

"Yes. You know Harper Delkin and his head of personal security, Elijah Eklund. My sister, Isabella Hernandez."

"Miss Hernandez," both men responded robotically.

"We're acquainted." Her eyes pierced Brie's. *Oh fuck, no.* "Business, of course. I'm a little surprised you haven't mentioned them. You seem…comfortable with each other."

"I, that is…"

"It's okay. We can catch up later." Bending, she kissed her cheeks. "You're beautiful. Tawny told me about the tests. I'm sorry I wasn't here."

"It's alright." Swallowing hard, she added, "I didn't know you talk to Tawny."

"Mm hmm. We need a girls' weekend, Gabriella. You clearly withhold information in our weekly phone calls. I'll arrange it when you tell me your…schedule."

Straightening, she smoothed a tendril of Brie's hair behind her ear. "Enjoy your evening. I love you." Meeting the eyes of the men at her sides, she murmured, "Gentlemen."

Then her sister walked away and disappeared on the other side of the dance floor. Her mind was in chaos and she worked to regulate her breathing.

"Gabriella…"

"Brie…"

They said her name at the same time but she held up her hand. She needed a moment. Picking up her wine glass, she took a long sip.

Without looking at them, she asked quietly, "How long ago was it that you had sex with my sister?"

"Gabriella…"

"Answer the *question*."

"A few months after Danielle's funeral."

"You didn't feel it was relevant to mention it?" Inhaling carefully, she said sadly, "Definitely your type physically despite her ethnicity."

Elijah lifted the hand she'd clenched into a fist on her leg. "Brie." She didn't look at him. "It was ten years ago and they didn't suit each other *at all*. Isabella is quite different than you."

"I'm *aware*. Believe me, I'm aware."

"No, Brie. She's different in ways that have *nothing* to do with your outer appearance." Blinking against tears, she turned to look into his green eyes. "There are many reasons we didn't bring it up. It represented a couple of hours of their lives and I had to get involved but *not* in the capacity you suspect. I ask you to trust me."

"Gabriella. I'm sorry."

"Do you know why you're apologizing, Harper?"

"In this, there's no doubt." He reached out to take her other hand. "I didn't seek her out but responded to her focused, aggressive advances. I knew your parents but you and your sister weren't familiar to me because of our age differences. When I discovered later, I found myself in a problematic situation."

Frowning, she turned to look into silver eyes. "I don't understand."

"You love your sister. You're close." She nodded. "Let's keep it that way. Please don't ask me anymore questions, Gabriella. I won't lie to you but I swear on my life that *nothing good* will come of the knowledge."

Looking at Elijah, he held her gaze for almost a minute. "What is she...wait." She took several deep breaths. "Is she safe?"

"For the most part."

"Is there any way I can help her?"

Closing his eyes, his hand tightened around hers. "Brie, let me give that question some thought before I answer it. I don't want to lie but I can't risk your safety either."

"Elijah, if you find yourself able to keep her from being hurt, will you do that?"

"Yes."

Pulling her hands from theirs, she rubbed her temples. "Is there anything else that's going to fall out of the closet when we swing the door open?"

They laughed hesitantly. "Not that I can think of at the moment."

Exhaling roughly, she replied, "That was a big one. Talk about awkward."

Leaning in her direction, Elijah started to respond when the room quieted. Hudson and Natalia walked up on stage.

"We'd like to thank all of you for joining us. Hudson insisted I have a *real* wedding. I'd have happily married him at the courthouse." Hudson wrapped his arm around Natalia's waist and she leaned against him. "Special thanks to my circle of female friends for making this possible. I don't get up early enough to taste cake or meet with wedding planners. Without you, this wouldn't have happened."

The guests laughed and she grinned. "Harper, your words moved me. It's an honor to have you here after so many years of history. Hudson and I have always respected you, admired you, liked you...though he's hidden it rather well." There was another round of laughter and Harper reached out to hold Brie's hand. "*Thank you.* Truly."

Hudson kissed the top of her head and Natalia's eyes closed for a moment. "For most of my life, my best friend has been a man who *always* thinks I look lovely and *never* has a single criticism about my tendency to be late for positively everything. Feeling comfortable in a group of intelligent and funny women for the first time is something for which I'll always be grateful. I'm the oldest but they make me feel young when I'm around them."

Tilting her chin up with the side of his hand, he murmured at her ear. Clearing her throat, Natalia inhaled deeply. "Hudson is a fixture in my universe and has been since I was ten years old. Sometimes, you can be so *close* to something that you miss the obvious."

Across the short distance, she met Brie's eyes. "It took a particular woman to show me how deep my love went for the only man who's ever mattered to me. Gabriella hadn't known us long before she started working her particular brand of magic. Love, given selflessly, can heal wounds you didn't know you had, open your eyes to someone you'd been blind to, and change your life."

Brie struggled to maintain her composure.

To the room, Hudson announced, "We have a plane to catch and I'm going to celebrate with the woman who's put up with my bullshit for three damn decades. *Always* beautiful, *never* late, and addresses any situation with the perfect dose of sarcasm." He hugged her hard and whispered at her ear for a long moment.

"Harper. Outstanding to have you here. I admit you've made me work to keep up over the years. Knowing you were out there made me hungry and kept me focused. You have one of the most brilliant business minds in the world and bitch about my charity calls but always gives until it hurts. I'm glad to know you, proud to consider you a friend."

Then Hudson Winters looked into Brie's eyes and promptly destroyed any possibility of composure.

"I was an asshole the first time I met Gabriella. Two weeks later, she gently placed the first block in a friendship that remains difficult to define."

Elijah gave her a handkerchief and Brie wiped her eyes with shaking hands. His palm on her back, Harper's hand holding hers tightly, she inhaled.

"Had this fantastic woman not entered our lives, Natalia and I would likely have gone on as we had for *years*. There's a chance we *never* would've embraced the utter simplicity of what we have. That's a fact. Brie brings chaos in her wake and your reflex might be to fight it."

He winked. "I found it was best to go with it. She once told us she'd always have our back. She said she wasn't imposing but she offered a soft place to land. The words stayed with us and we'd like to remind our best friend that if you *ever* need a place to land, a moment to breathe, you always have a home. It's the home you encouraged us to create together." Natalia lifted her face and the couple shared a smile. "Thank you for the gifts you brought into our lives and we love you."

They stepped off the stage and walked to Brie's table. They hugged her and wiped her tears. "Darling, we'll let your men comfort you. Call us if you need any little thing and we'll see you in a few weeks."

"Gabriella. *Take until you're drunk with it.* No one deserves it more and you're fucking *due.*" Hudson stroked his knuckles over her cheek. "Text me when you arrive."

All she could do was nod and they kissed her with smiles. Then her best friends shook the hands of the men beside her and made their way to the exit.

It wasn't until they'd disappeared from sight that Brie asked in confusion, "Wait. Text when I get *where?*"

Elijah and Harper stood. Silver eyes stared into hers. "We leave for Washington the moment you say your goodbyes, Gabriella."

She blinked, speechless.

Bending, Elijah murmured, "Say goodbye *quickly,* Brie."

* * *

Forty-five minutes later, after several confused questions and shocked reactions to where she was going, Brie allowed Elijah and Harper to lead her from the venue.

Her mind spun as she boarded a private plane. When she was seated, she said, "I-I didn't pack."

"We have everything you need at the estate," Harper replied.

Swallowing hard, she stared out the window as the plane started to move. "I haven't been back to Washington in almost two years."

Elijah wrapped his hand around hers. "You're stronger than when you left, Brie." She nodded absently.

When they were in the air, the blonde unbuckled her and lifted her in his arms. "It's after midnight and the flight will take about six hours. You need to sleep."

"I don't…" Her words trailed off as they entered a small bedroom at the rear of the plane.

Setting her on her feet, he smiled.

From a drawer, he removed a soft t-shirt and sleep pants with fluffy sheep on them. Stripping her gown over her head, he helped her dress and took down her hair.

"You're adorable." He tucked her in and sat beside her. "You need rest. You've had a lot of emotional input today."

Brie frowned. "What about you guys? You're going to leave me in here alone?" His eyes widened. "I've never been on a plane like this. I *have* had a lot of emotional input. You can both sleep with me. I'm not the only one who needs rest."

When he stared at her in confusion, she sat up and called, "Harper!" The dark man appeared in the door with a frown. "Will you both lay down with me?"

"I don't…what?" His frown deepened.

"We have a long flight. I don't want to be back here alone. You need rest, too."

"I don't sleep when I fly," he said stiltedly.

She threw back the covers and climbed out of bed to stand in front of him. "Okay."

"Okay, what?"

"I'll stay up with both of you." She put her hand in his and smiled when he squeezed it. Glancing back, she held out her other hand for Elijah. "Come on."

He stood up and stared down at her. "Brie."

"Don't make me," she whispered. "I can sleep where you guys are." Her toes curled into the carpet. "Please?"

"Are you afraid of flying?" After a brief hesitation, she nodded. "Did you just lie?" She nodded again with a smile.

"You don't have to sleep, Elijah."

Green eyes held hers, considering. "Tell me. Tell me what you need. I don't always know, Brie."

"I-I'm really happy for my friends. Happier than I've ever been in my life actually."

"You feel off balance?" She shrugged her shoulder. "Brie, are you *jealous*?"

There was no way to stop the tears. "Not of one or the other. Just the overall happiness and their confidence in it. It sounds bad but it isn't, I don't know." She waved her hand and released Harper. "I'm ridiculous. Go work and stuff. I'm going to crash for a little while. I'm just overtired."

She climbed back in the bed and pulled up the blankets. Curling on her side, she closed her eyes and tried to talk her brain into calming the fuck down.

Her eyes flew open as she was lifted into the center and the men laid down along her sides.

Harper stared at the ceiling. "This is my side."

"Okay," she murmured softly.

"I've never slept with a woman."

"Ever? How did…never mind." She reached out and took one of his hands as Elijah curled against her back. Harper had always returned to his own bed on the nights she stayed with them. Holding it to her chest, she smiled at him. "I won't bother you. I don't move much."

"Sleep, Brie," Elijah said at her ear. He planted a kiss on her neck and nuzzled her hair. "I'll wake you up an hour before we land."

"Okay. Thank you."

Closing her eyes, her brain gently quieted. She didn't realize how quickly she fell asleep.

* * *

A soft tap on the door woke Elijah first.

Brie registered that she was sleeping on Harper's shoulder and he had his arm around her back and curled at her waist. Elijah's hand around her crossed it.

Quickly rising, he spoke at the door. Glancing up, she met Harper's eyes.

"I slept." She nodded. "You're soft and warm."

"Do I snore?" He shook his head. "Excellent. I think we all overslept. Even Elijah."

"That's never happened."

"It's my fault. I forget you have important things going on and I shouldn't distract the two of you. I'm sorry."

Elijah sat on the bed. "I'm training a team." Glancing over her shoulder, she waited for him to continue. "To cover Harper when we're with you. I have one that backs me up but I've always been present."

"Until you met me. I sidetrack you and that's dangerous."

"Things with you are different, Brie. We have to make changes before we're forced to make them on the fly."

Carefully, she unwrapped her body from Harper's and sat up. Raking her hair out of her face, she stared at an aerial photo of the Delkin estate affixed to the opposite wall.

"I don't fit, do I? The life you both lead, there isn't room in it for someone like me. I'm t-time consuming."

"Brie…"

"Don't lie to me, Elijah. Not on purpose." She inhaled carefully. "It's okay. I'll be more conscious of it. I'd never forgive myself if I put either of you in danger."

Swallowing past the lump in her throat, she plastered a smile on her face. "We're in Washington. I've got strange feelings about it. I'll get dressed." Climbing to the end of the bed, she stood and went into the bathroom. "Just going to take care of some necessities."

Closing the door, she experienced a moment of panic.

Then she reminded herself that she'd take everything she could in the time she had with them and be grateful for it.

By the time she stepped from the tiny space, she felt stronger.

There were clothes on the bed for her. Soft leggings, flats, and a pretty top sat beside a gorgeous bra and panty set.

As she dressed in the underthings, Elijah opened the door and paused to take her in. Harper leaned in the door behind him.

"Thank you for the outfit." Smiling, she finished getting dressed. As the top fell over her, she quipped, "No way in hell you haven't seen *plenty* of women put their clothes back *on*."

"You're a strong woman, Brie."

She stepped into the flats. "I work at resiliency. It's a good skill to have being me."

Looking around, she quickly made the bed and gathered her things. She was glad she always had her messenger bag. Everything she'd worn the night before fit in it. She removed a clip and pulled her curls away from her face.

After folding the clothes she'd worn to sleep in, she set them back in the drawer Elijah took them from and turned to them with a smile.

"Okay! Done. Lead on, gentlemen."

They stared at her for a long time and then stepped forward. Their palms cupped opposite sides of her neck, their wrists crossed, and they took turns kissing her.

She was distantly grateful for the mouthwash she'd found in the bathroom.

"Good morning, Gabriella. Welcome back to Washington. It's good to have you with us." Harper rubbed his thumb on the skin behind her ear. "I don't know how to talk to you."

Wrapping her fingers around his neck, she told him, "You're doing great. Good morning, Harper."

Elijah waited when they pulled apart. "You fit, you aren't time consuming. We'll adjust and make it work." She nodded with a bright smile and he tightened his fingers. "*Trust me*, Brie."

"I do." After another kiss that shook her foundation, she added, "I'm committed and I love you, both of you. I've gone too far to turn back."

"Let's acclimate you back to your old stomping grounds." Harper gave her a smile and added, "You're pretty."

Surprised, she managed, "Thanks."

Then her men, for as long as she could keep them, led her off the plane and she inhaled the Pacific Northwest for the first time in a long time.

It was terrifying.

Chapter Twenty-Eight

The trip from the airport was surreal for Brie. She watched familiar scenery pass and marveled at changes that had happened over the two years she'd been gone.

"Are you happy to be home?" The question from Harper pulled her from introspection.

"Conflicted. Despite the bad memories, I have good ones as well." Shaking her head, she stared at the deep green of trees that were different here than anywhere else in the country. "When you leave…"

"What do you mean?"

She met his gray eyes. "I'm aware that neither of you take time off. In a day or two, a bit more if I'm lucky, you'll have to leave. I'll check in at the winery. Spend some time with my family. See what still fits."

Returning her gaze to the window, she murmured, "I feel more at home in New York now. I'm ashamed of the weak person I was here. I can't wait for the awkward questions I'll get considering why I left in the first place."

"Brie." Inhaling, she met Elijah's gaze. "It'll be okay."

She nodded but didn't reply. After another few miles, Harper told her, "There's a gala at the estate tomorrow."

The very idea…

"I can't attend and you know that, Harper."

"Why not?"

Sighing, she rubbed her temple. "I've lived here all my life as have you. My family owns whatever your family doesn't in a solid twenty square miles."

Calming her thoughts, she sat up straight. "You're *Harper Delkin*, a name more familiar here than anywhere else. I'm sweet and chubby Gabriella Hernandez, the awkward artist and strangely business savvy youngest daughter of my parents. They once mentioned your name to me as an eligible male they approved of since I had no clue how to pick men for *myself*."

"Shit. I'm sorry, Gabriella."

"No reason to be." She folded her hands in her lap. "The suggestion was preposterous then and the fact that you'll be fucking me makes it no less preposterous now. Let's avoid intrusive questions neither of us want or need."

"Do you want to leave, Brie?"

Watching as they turned on the long drive into the Delkin estate, she replied, "No. I need to know I can survive being here. I can't let my past haunt me."

Elijah lifted her from the seat and settled her in his lap. "Look at me. *Look at me*, Brie." She raised her eyes. "You're hurting and I hate it. Tell me what to do."

"I'm sorry. I need to adjust. There've been so many changes, new information, a lot of emotional upheaval."

They pulled to a stop and a team of men waited outside to brief Elijah. "Brie…"

"I need somewhere I can decompress. Do what you always do. I'll be okay. I just need, I need to be still."

"Brief the men, Elijah. Gabriella can come with me." She started to object. "I insist."

Stepping to the shell drive, Harper took her hand and likely surprised himself as much as her. They left Elijah behind and he walked rapidly through the house, nodding at staff who greeted him.

Pausing at double doors, he stated, "This is my office. Elijah's is next door. So you can find us."

She nodded and he ascended a staircase that was partially concealed. At the top of the stairs, positioned above where the two men worked, he opened another set of doors.

Stunned, she stopped in the threshold. "*Harper.*"

"It used to be a sunroom when my grandparents were alive. It hasn't been used in decades but I thought the light might be good. I asked a family friend to prepare it for you. Caroline hopes to meet you one day."

"Caroline?" Brie was barely able to concentrate.

"A woman who helped Dad after my mom died. She's an incredible artist who owns a gallery in Boulder. I told her about you when I asked who could make your easel."

Squeezing his hand, she let him go to wander the long room that featured an entire wall of windows. Painted bright white, Harper had created an art studio for her complete with a replica of the easel he'd sent her in New York.

Circling the room, she touched the canvases and supplies, ran her fingers over the sheer fabric that covered the windows, and took in the most beautiful gift she'd ever received.

Returning to him, she hugged him tightly, glad when he hugged her back. "Thank you, Harper. How did you know?"

"I noticed if you're sad or tired or angry, you sketch and it helps you. I'm…not good at emotions, Gabriella. I wish I could communicate them like you do."

"You're better at it than you think." He smoothed his thumbs over her cheeks, taking her tears with them. "I don't mean to be emotional. I try to rein it in."

"I should've asked you before I brought you here. I didn't realize it would hurt you." He raked his fingers through her hair. "I'm sorry."

"I want to be here with you and Elijah. I have to work through some things but I want to be with you both."

"It's *not* a preposterous idea, Gabriella." She frowned in confusion.

"I wonder how different my life, Elijah's life, would've been if we'd found you a decade ago."

They stared at one another in silence.

She smoothed her fingers along his face. "I don't know. I'm glad to have time with you now. I'll appreciate every minute and I'll abide by the terms, Harper."

"You fall outside the *rules* we've always had in place. I don't mean to hurt you or be cruel to you. I *do* like you. I *do* see you as human, probably one of the kindest I've ever known. You also scare the hell out of me."

"I know." Brie was moments from crying all over him.

"Take some time to relax. Sketch or paint or just sit for a little while and let the jet lag settle." He held her as he kissed her and she returned it with every part of herself.

"One of us will come get you in a few hours if you haven't surfaced." Smiling against her lips, he added, "Harrison disappeared into his studio set up in the old carriage house for six weeks at one point. My father worried we'd have to commit him."

"My mother would've dragged me out by my hair." It made him laugh. "Go do all the business stuff you have to do. I'll try not to get paint all over the clothes."

He shrugged. "There's an entire closet for you. Splatter away." One more kiss and he headed for the door. "Enjoy, Gabriella."

As he pulled the doors partially closed, she gave in to the temptation to create. It was the only thing that would settle her mind and her heart. She needed strength and calm to handle the days ahead.

She loved Elijah and Harper too much to allow her fear and stress to ruin what time she had with them.

Setting a fresh sketchpad on a smaller antique easel by the window, Brie picked up a charcoal and stepped into her therapy session.

* * *

Outside the converted studio, Harper wasn't surprised to see Elijah waiting. He took him in from head to toe and felt the same love he'd practically forced on his unspoken bodyguard when he was too young and stupid to be subtle.

He *was* surprised when his oldest friend took his hand and led him to the small library next door.

When they were alone, Elijah hugged him tightly. "Well done, Harper. Fucking well *done*. Thank you."

Returning the embrace, he inhaled carefully, taking Elijah's scent deep into his lungs. He'd been unable to really touch him in months and the simple contact was almost overwhelming.

"I've missed you." Elijah's arms tightened around him. "I know why, I understand. I'm trying. I want it to work."

"That's all I ask. Just try."

"You've never asked me for anything, Elijah. I've taken, gorged myself, and never really stopped to ask what you needed." Gripping his shoulders from behind, he tried to control the feelings ricocheting inside him. "I'm sorry."

"We'll work through it. I won't leave you, Harper. I've loved you most of my life and I need you. I also need Brie. I need what she is, how she is, to show me how to feel worthy of the next breath, the next sunrise."

Leaning back, Harper frowned. "Elijah?" The expression on his face frightened him. "What do you mean?"

"I was at the end." He shrugged his shoulder. "The night of the building party. I was filled with rage over the woman you'd found the night before. I felt dirty, Harper. I felt out of control and saw more of the same stretching out for years."

Blinking against tears, Harper processed the fact that his oldest friend, the man he loved and spent all his time with, was so deep in despair and he hadn't even *noticed*.

He let his green eyes close. "She was *clean*. I could see it. I wondered if she could help me lance the rage, if she could help *me* be clean." Lashes lifting, he murmured, "I love you, Harper. I love Brie."

Nodding, Harper gripped his skull in his hands. "Why didn't you *tell* me? I almost drove her away!"

Elijah held his neck. "I know you're afraid. She's different from every person we've ever known. Try, for me. Don't make me choose. I don't want to live without her but I won't break my promises to you."

The pain in Harper's heart was a tangible thing. "I'll do anything. Tell me what to do."

Pulling him close, Elijah slanted his mouth over Harper's and kissed him for the first time since the morning in Gabriella's apartment when his best friend promised to wait for her.

Breathing him in, Harper gave a gasping sob as he took what he'd needed so badly.

This man's strength had taught him how to be strong. His loyalty made him feel worthy. His love filled a heart that felt incapable of it.

The only thing Elijah had *ever* taken from Harper was his submission. Even then, he gave back far more pleasure than he received.

Holding him tightly, the only person he'd ever admitted to loving gave to him again.

Forgiveness.

Harper hadn't known how desperately he wanted it until it was given freely. He soaked up the warmth, the passion, and the safety Elijah inspired. The kiss was incredible and all-encompassing.

When he broke it, their foreheads met and Elijah murmured, "I've missed you, too."

"I don't know if I'll ever love her the way you do. It doesn't matter. I don't care. Let her love you, Elijah. Let her show you the things I'm incapable of showing you. You need her."

For the words, Elijah kissed him again, devouring with his lips and teeth and tongue until Harper moaned into his mouth.

Walking him back, he was pinned to the wall, the hardness of Elijah's body sealed against him. As a strong hand stroked over his cock, he couldn't hold back his whimper.

Their eyes met and Harper whispered, "As much as I *want* you, Gabriella *needs* you." Kissing him roughly, he ground out, "Go. Find me tonight and we'll please her together. I can wait. I deserve to wait."

Lust glowed from Elijah's eyes. It wasn't easy to send him to the woman who confused him in so many ways but Harper knew it was the right thing to do.

Reaching up, he held the face that was anchored in his first memories. "I know *nothing* about love but I've loved you every day of my life. Let her give you love that's clean and good. Don't forget me, Elijah. Don't leave me behind."

Quiet for almost a minute, green eyes stared into his and strong fingers raked through his hair. "When the time comes, I need you to *trust me* as you've always trusted me, Harper. I need you to *believe* how much I love you, to know I could *never* forget you. I won't leave you behind. I'm taking you *with* me."

Another kiss, gentler than the others and Harper murmured, "Pave the way. Settle her heart the way you did in New York. When she fully belongs to you, I know you're strong enough to love us both, to protect two rather than one, to take what *you* need and give us what *we* need." He smiled. "I'll get to work and imagine the pleasure you wring from her. It will raise my own anticipation."

Stroking his hand over blonde hair he'd always loved, he gave Elijah another kiss and left the room.

His cock was harder than it had ever been and as he returned to his office on the first floor, he smiled.

When he was finally able to come, he hoped his heart could take it.

Chapter Twenty-Nine

Breathing raggedly, Elijah took a moment to calm his mind before walking to the studio Harper created for Brie.

It was an unbelievable gift, selfless and kind.

The men had loved each other forever and though they'd have to rebuild much of their relationship, Elijah knew it was possible.

So much was finally possible again.

Standing in the partially open door, he watched Brie sketch the small garden outside her window. Directly above Harper's office, they shared the same view.

It was incredible to see her standing on her own two feet. Her hair was haphazardly contained in the clip as her hand flew over the canvas.

He'd never wanted a woman with such desperation in his life.

Approaching her silently, he watched as she paused mid-stroke. Sighing, she murmured, "Elijah."

"You're remarkable."

Setting down the charcoal on the small table beside her easel, she turned to him with a smile.

"Were you worried about me?" He nodded. "I'm better now. I felt funny in my skin. Drawing helped." Twisting her hands, she added, "I didn't mean to get melancholy."

"You're human. You adjust faster than most. I love the person you are in any mood, whatever you're wearing – or not, and no matter what you're doing. You fascinate me."

Approaching him, she wrapped her arms around his waist and rested her face on his chest. "Thank you. I love you, too."

Tightening his arms around her, he said quietly, "I need you, Brie. I ache for you."

Lifting her face, she stared up at him. "I ache for *you*...I don't want to hurt Harper."

"He told me to come to you."

"He's trying to accept me, to share you. It isn't easy for him." She lifted one shoulder in a slight shrug. "I'd be the same in his place. I understand."

"How do you see things so clearly?"

She shook her head. "For a man as strong as Harper to love you the way he does, that runs to the *bone*. You're the *reason* he gets up in the morning. He doesn't show that but I know it's the truth. I've caused so much damage between you already, Elijah."

"You haven't. You *saved* me, Brie."

Kissing her was like taking a breath after holding it for a long time underwater. It filled him up, made him feel whole, and gave him a glimpse of true beauty.

Breaking it, she sighed his name with her eyes closed. He took another and loved the way she opened herself in every way.

Distracted, she let him back her across the room. He supported her as he laid her down on the plush sofa covered in heavy white linen. The moment they were reclined, she wrapped her entire body around him.

"Brie." Her eyes fluttered open and she focused on his. "Do you trust me?" She nodded. "I had a vasectomy when I was twenty and I'd *never* touch your body unless I was clean."

Her fingers traced his brow to his jaw. "One day, will you tell me why you did that so young?"

She was the most perceptive person he knew. "Yes."

Arms and legs tightening around him, she whispered, "I don't want anything between us. I trust you with all of me, Elijah. Take what you need."

He took his time undressing her, baring her to his eyes and touch. He took the clip from her hair and watched the curls tumble around her. Arms over her head, she waited for him to undress. The way she followed his movements made him feel fucking powerful.

Crouching over her, she smiled as she stroked her palms over his shoulders and chest. "Looking at you is a feast for the eyes."

His slid his palm along her side, pausing at the bend of her hip and upper thigh. It was the area of her body that had sustained the most trauma. The scars showed the surface damage but the breaks in the bones of her pelvis and upper leg were what worried him.

"I'm okay."

"The slightest pain and you *say something*, Brie. Do you understand?"

Lifting at the waist, she wrapped her arms around his upper body. "You won't hurt me. I made them do additional stress tests to be sure." His eyes widened. "I had to know."

Pushing her back to the couch, he followed her down. One hand between her legs, he growled when he confirmed how wet she was. "Thank god."

"*Please*, Elijah."

Notching his cock at the entrance of her, he held her gaze as he pressed forward. She tugged her full lower lip between bright white teeth and moaned. He worked his way into the body of the only woman he'd *ever* taken bare and worried about being able to last.

Finally seated, balls flush to her skin and her cervix cupping the head of his cock, she trembled in his arms. Her snug walls clenched around him and he held her tightly.

Resting his forehead beside her, he inhaled deeply several times. She hugged him as hard as she could, the sole of her foot stroking the back of his leg.

"I'm not empty anymore. I love you, Elijah."

Raising his head, he stared into magnificent eyes that shimmered with unshed tears. He stroked her hair away from her cheek and kissed her gently.

Holding her gaze, he started to move. She never stopped touching him, connecting to him, *loving* him. He knew even if he lived to a hundred, her complete trust and acceptance of him as a man would have the same ability to move him.

He took her up slowly, steadily, watching her take every thrust and hold her breath each time he withdrew. Watching her face, staring into her eyes, he saw the first climax climb until she embraced it with a gasp.

Never slowing, he loved her through it, clamping down on every ounce of control he had not to join her. Only when she stopped shaking did he go harder.

Her slow smile almost made him lose it.

Bending his knee, he spread her wider and stroked his hand over her skin. Trailing up her side, he cupped her breast and squeezed the nipple firmly.

Her nails pressed into his skin. "More. I'm okay, Elijah. Take what you want. Don't be afraid. You won't hurt me."

Inhaling carefully, he raised his upper body on his hands and stared down at her.

"Stunning." She followed the word by stroking her palms over his torso and down both sides of his groin. "I want all of you. Fuck me, Elijah."

"I worry about hurting you."

She lifted and held the back of his head. "How will I know if I can handle *two* cocks pounding into my body if I'm not sure I can handle *one*?" The imagery made his blood boil and he drove deep and hard. Brie nodded. "Yes, god *yes*."

Then he let her have who he really was.

Fiercely driving his cock into her willing pussy, he watched her breasts bounce with the impact and listened to the small moans from her throat.

"How desperate I've been for you. Every second of agony, of want, was worth it, Brie." So quickly, she was on the cusp of another climax and he growled, "Cream all over my dick. Then I'll fill you up."

Breath stumbling, her body locked and she let it take her. He enjoyed the way her skin flushed, the tightness of her nipples, and the way her pussy spasmed around his length as he continued to thrust brutally hard and deep.

It held her captive for a long time.

She murmured his name like a prayer. "Give it to me. Every drop."

Coming hard, she wrapped herself around him, holding him as close as she could while he pumped his semen directly into a woman for the first time.

"So hot. I didn't expect it to be so hot. That feels amazing."

Understanding that he was the first man to ever have access to her skin-to-skin made him hug her tighter, still stroking as he gave her all of him, inside and out.

"Loving you makes my heart so fucking happy, Elijah. Don't let me go."

He couldn't. He wouldn't. She made him want to keep waking up.

* * *

Brie dozed for a few minutes and woke to Elijah staring down at her with a smile. He pressed his hips against her and she realized he was hard again, or *still*, she wasn't certain.

Then he was fucking her and she didn't care about details. "You're the most beautiful woman I've ever known, Brie." His fingers played with a strand of her hair. "Being inside you, part of you, helps me understand your need to be closer."

The kiss he gave her went on for a long time. "I'd like to mention that you have an outstanding cock and it should be inside me often."

He chuckled and took her harder. "Before we get completely carried away, the moment you give me another dose of you, I have an idea."

Outlining her plan made him fuck her even harder and it made her grin.

When she fell apart in his arms and he emptied his balls, Elijah left her long enough to retrieve the robe she requested and then carried her downstairs to Harper's office.

Also at her request.

Setting her on her feet just inside the door, Brie depended on him to close and lock the door while she approached the dark man who watched her in surprise. Elijah sat in a chair on the other side of the room, silent and watchful.

Pausing beside the desk, she carefully moved everything out of the way and sat on the surface in front of Harper.

Opening the robe to reveal her nakedness, she leaned back on her hands and spread her thighs. She watched him take her in, his nostrils flaring in a combination of shock and lust.

His eyes tracked over her while the rest of him remained perfectly still. Then he focused on her pussy. Reaching out, he rubbed his fingers over folds slick with her release as well as Elijah's.

"He came inside you." His eyes flicked up to hers. "You let him fuck you without a condom?" She nodded. "He fucked you *hard*. It eases from your pretty swollen pussy like fresh cream." His fingers played over skin that was already sensitive and she whimpered.

"How many times did he come?"

"Twice," she replied breathlessly.

"Filled you up so nice. How many times did you come?"

Thinking carefully, she told him, "Four."

Using both hands, he spread the entrance with his fingers. He was mesmerized by the way Elijah's come seeped from her body. "Look at you. That's beautiful." Scooting closer, she watched him inhale the scent of her. "You smell so fucking good."

Pushing three fingers inside her, she could feel the wetness sliding from her body. "Harper." Silver eyes glazed with passion met hers. "Let me have your hand." He held out his slick fingers. While he watched, she sat up enough to suck them clean. Returning to her original position, she murmured, "I needed to know how I tasted *before*…"

"Before what?"

"You add *your* flavor."

Harper vibrated with need. Voice barely audible, he asked, "You'd let me pump my come inside you bare?" She nodded. "I want to fuck you until you scream for me." He pulled her roughly to the edge of the desk and placed her feet on the arms of his chair. "I'll do that…*after* I eat this succulent pussy."

He buried his face between her legs and she didn't know if she'd be able to keep from screaming as he growled against her flesh. Watching him lick away the evidence of their combined release made her want so many things.

Lifting away slightly, he reinserted three fingers and stroked deep several times. They shimmered as he took them out and rubbed them on her clit.

As Harper sucked the little bundle of nerves hard, she inhaled sharply.

Pushing his tongue as deep as he could, he returned to suckling her clit. "Come for me so I can bury my cock in this soaking wet pussy, Gabriella. I want to soak it more."

From the other side of the room, she knew Elijah watched them and it added another layer of the forbidden. Then she was coming apart and watched as Harper stood, still fucking her with his fingers as he tore at his pants with his other hand.

Covering his shaft with her fluids, he held her knee in the crook of his arm and wasted no time driving deep.

Head thrown back on his shoulders, he took several deep breaths before he lowered his eyes to look at her. "What a fantastic pussy you have, Miss Hernandez."

Sitting up, she wrapped the tie he still wore around her fist and brought him closer. "Then I suggest you *fuck it* immediately, Delkin." She kissed him and moaned. "Elijah is delicious. I can't wait to taste the three of us on your cock."

Leaning back on her hands again, she murmured, "Fuck me *hard*, Harper."

"Yes." Pulling back, he drove into her pussy brutally and stared at his length disappearing into slick heat. "Hot, bare pussy. You feel fucking amazing."

"I wonder what it'll feel like with two cocks fucking me." She smiled at him. "The wall is thin between my ass and my pussy. Can you feel Elijah's cock rubbing against yours when you take a woman together?"

"Yes." He fucked her harder still.

"I imagine that's as stimulating as whatever hole you happen to be fucking." Brie moaned as he wrapped his hand around the back of her neck and thrust faster. "A hot pussy and the feel of his hard dick pounding a tight ass. God, if I didn't have two of those sources of pleasure, I'd *almost* wish I was a man."

He tried to hold back his laughter and failed. "You're out of your fucking *mind*, Gabriella."

"I'm aware."

His thrusts slowed as her hands roamed his upper body. Sitting up, she stroked her hands over his shoulders, pushing his jacket off. Loosening his tie, she pulled it over his head. Staring into his eyes, she unbuttoned his shirt and shoved it away as well.

Pushing to the root, he stilled and stared at her. "I was doing it again."

"Doing what?" she asked with a gentle smile.

His hands coasted over her shoulders, slipping the robe away. He cupped her face. "Using you. Forgetting who I was fucking and why. I barely even *kissed* you."

He corrected the oversight and she sighed into his mouth. Wrapping her arms and legs around his body, she hugged him with all of her.

"Take whatever you need from me, Harper. There are no conditions on the offer." Kissing his face several times, she whispered, "Come inside me. Relieve the stress and pressure. Let me have the honor of taking it away for a little while."

Arms tight around her, he started to thrust again. Building in force and speed, he didn't break eye contact.

The intensity of it drove her over the cliff of orgasm faster than she expected and she groaned his name as her body spasmed.

Only then did he let himself go, driving furiously into her body as he gave her everything he had. Crushing her almost painfully to him, he breathed raggedly against the side of her neck.

At his ear, she whispered, "Thank you, Harper."

Raking her fingers through his hair, she let his body settle. When he lifted his head, she kissed him deeply.

He helped her off the desk and she took a seat in his chair, naked. Pulling his hips closer, she sighed happily.

"I need to clean your lovely cock."

Sucking his semi-hard dick to the back of her throat, she moaned when his hands went into her hair. They stared at each other while he thrust shallowly.

"Are you ready for us, Gabriella?" She nodded around him. "Thank you for relieving the painful vise around my balls." He pulled from her lips and lifted her to her feet. Wrapping the robe around her, he bent to suck her nipple before he covered it.

"Harper?" He looked into her eyes. "Will you suck the other one as well? It feels neglected."

Grinning, he sat and pulled her between his knees. Separating the robe, he went back and forth between her breasts, sucking and nibbling her nipples as he plumped the mounds with strong hands.

She braced her hands on his shoulders. "Feels so good."

Then Elijah was behind her, his fingers raking through Harper's black hair as he suckled her.

"Watching him fuck you made me harder than I've ever been in my life." She moaned and pushed her ass against him. "Did he make you feel good?" He raked his palm over her belly, moving beneath the robe to shove two fingers deep from behind.

"He made me feel incredible. Fucking you individually is more than I imagined. I can't wait to fuck you together."

"Hmm. You have so much come in you now." He pumped deeper and faster, making her breathless. "We've never filled a woman up together. You're *soaked* and you deserve to come again while he feasts on your perfect nipples."

He lifted her face to the side and claimed her mouth until she was shaking from all the stimulation.

When she came, Harper helped hold her up.

"Such a welcoming pussy." Then he smoothed back and pushed slick fingers against the little pucker. "I think you need to have your ass filled as well."

"Yes. Yes, Elijah."

Stroking shallowly, she dug her nails into strong muscles as he went harder. "Do you want to experience Brie's remarkable ass, Harper?"

The two men stared at each other over her shoulder. Releasing her nipple with a soft pop, he let his hands grip the globes in question. He spread the cheeks and pressed them together.

She gasped in response.

Reaching between her legs, he pressed inside and her legs almost gave out at the dual penetration. "Please. Now."

"Mm." Elijah kissed his way up her neck. "Too easy, Brie. I have to make you work for what you want."

Barely able to form sentences, she managed, "Okay. Let's make that happen. I'm ready to work. I'm *such* a hard worker."

Elijah held her tightly against the front of his body while they fucked into her from the front and back with strong fingers, sending her careening into pleasure that didn't seem real.

As she regained her senses, he whispered at her ear, "The next time you come, you need to have permission." She nodded, feeling drunk. "Let's pull you together and go upstairs."

"Gabriella." Opening her eyes, she stared into Harper's and he winked. "Things are about to get interesting."

Chapter Thirty

After the three of them cleaned up enough to make it out of the office, the men escorted her up the same staircase in the robe. They passed the floor that contained her art studio. At the small third floor landing, there was a locked door leading to the fourth floor.

Brie realized it was the attic space of the house.

At the top of the stairs, a small foyer featured a crystal chandelier and a comfortable seating area. On the other side of the narrow space, there was a carved door, painted black, that looked like wood but she thought might be metal.

Elijah stopped and turned to face her. "I've lived on this estate since birth. My father was Hunter Delkin's head of security. Originally, I lived in his home in the security barracks."

Softly, she asked, "What about your mother?"

"She was killed a few weeks after my first birthday. I have no memory of her and I was an only child."

"I'm sorry, Elijah."

"I came to live here in this house when I was eight and Harper was six. My room was on the third floor at the opposite end of the hall from his." He crossed his hands at his back. "When I graduated high school, I went on the payroll as his official bodyguard. I thought to move to the barracks but Hope demanded I remain in the house."

Brie nodded. "I'm sure they were attached to you like a son and you inspire feelings of safety."

His eyes widened. "I honestly never considered that." She smiled and was glad when he returned it. "I requested to be placed in the basement. She insisted on the attic for better light and air flow."

"You also don't put people you love underground," she quipped. "Just saying."

This time, his smile held laughter. "This estate is approximately twelve-thousand acres and houses many buildings, both residential and otherwise. The mausoleum on the grounds holds three generations of Delkins. There are gardens, aviaries, greenhouses, stables, and ten acres at the southernmost edge that are dedicated to farming."

She rolled her eyes. "Money. Land. Possessions. *Awesome.* You know I don't care, right?"

Smiling slowly, he bent to drop a kiss on her lips. "I'm aware. I mention them to explain that the space beyond this door is all that belongs to me in all of the Delkin holdings." He crossed his hands at his back. "When the work was completed to my specifications, Hunter and Hope deeded it to me as a separate residence in thanks for my service. It spans the attic of the entire north wing. The attic space in the south wing is the training space for Harper and myself. Both are *tightly* secured."

"I wouldn't try to go inside without you."

"You misunderstand. Only Harper has *ever* been inside." Hiding her shock was pretty much impossible. "There are only three people on the planet I trust without reservation, Brie. Two of them I've known since they were born. The other is you."

Instant tears welled in her eyes and she pressed her hand over her heart. "*Elijah.*" She inhaled carefully. "Thank you."

His hand slid along her neck. "You've accepted everything we've revealed to you without reservation, without judgment, and you've given selflessly. I ask for more of the same now."

She nodded without hesitation.

"Where's your cell phone?"

Blinking in confusion, she gestured at her body. "Well, since you've both administered a thorough cavity search, I can say without a doubt that it isn't *on* me." They laughed. "I texted Hudson when we landed and shut it off. It might be in my art bag, I think." She frowned. "I was *sketching* so I honestly don't remember."

Bending, he kissed her lips and she melted into him. "Do you want to know why I asked?"

"Nuh uh. I'm sure it's a good reason."

He held her to his side as he opened a keypad with his thumbprint, typed in a long code, and waited. The door unlocked and she frowned.

"That was kind of anticlimactic. Damn it. I was hoping it would be like the movies and the whole room would spin around to a secret *lair*."

Harper petted her head. "Out of your mind."

"Are there lasers?" She *pew pew'd* them. "Freeze rays? Tank of sharks? No?" She sighed. "You could have at least had a secret handshake or provided decoder rings. I guess I'll have to make do with awesome cocks." She raised her brow. "There better be snacks. Vitamin deficiency is a thing."

They were laughing as they gestured her inside.

Three steps past the door, she took in the open space and froze. "I take it all back. This shit is *awesome*."

Elijah was *probably* Batman.

Most of the area was visible from the door. The décor was a blend of black, silver, and blue that worked. She felt them watch her explore.

Starting at one side, she scanned his library, touching the spines. Exclaiming several times over shared favorites, she let her fingers trail over the fabric of the chairs and trace the pattern on a glass lampshade.

In the corner, there were three beautiful violins on sophisticated stands. Leaning close, she could smell wood and resin. It made her smile but she was careful not to touch them.

The other side of the room held a fantastic kitchen. It didn't look like it had ever been used. Frowning, she opened the fridge and wasn't surprised to find it practically empty.

"Man, that secret hope for a juice box is looking pretty bleak." They chuckled behind her and she shook her head. Beside the kitchen was a *tiny* dining area.

Really, who needed to eat?

A private theater space made her laugh and she figured there was a probably a screen that lowered from somewhere if he wanted to watch a movie. Pressing up against the wall, she imagined the biggest speakers on earth hidden as well.

Men were men were men.

A full gym wrapped in an L-shape in one far corner and she murmured, "He might not use the kitchen but the man uses the *fuck* out of the gym equipment. As Tawny would say, a-fucking-men."

More laughter from her observers.

The opposite L-shaped corner was his massive workstation. A dozen screens featured places all over the world and streaming data. Several keyboards and other equipment that was foreign to her was positioned across the extended desktop.

Large screens on either side captured and held her attention. One had a slideshow of Harper, the other a slideshow of her.

She found herself enthralled by photos of Harper she'd never seen. "Oh, that's a good one. Holy shit, okay, that one's hot. I'll need a copy for my uh, personal collection. I'll need some of both of you for...reference and entertainment. Never mind, I'll draw my own. Mine are *way* dirtier."

Standing in front of the screen showing photos of her, she blinked when some flashed of her before she'd gone to New York. One on the back of her horse in the vineyard, another at a wine tasting event, and another of her in college.

"Man, your intel doesn't play. I didn't even know these existed. I wish they didn't."

There were several of her with friends, alone when she'd first arrived in Manhattan, and many after she went home from the hospital. She looked and acted *very* different from the people she hung out with, her friends, her lovers. Her sparkling personality must *truly* be awesome.

Turning to the two men who hadn't spoken, she smiled. "I love your place, Elijah. However, I see no bed, no bathroom, no way to shackle me to a wall or suspend me from the ceiling, which I know is on the list of things to do." She crossed her arms. "There has to be some *naughty as fuck* in your nice digs."

Neither moved nor spoke. They stared at her with their arms crossed and blank expressions.

It was a game.

Beside the entry into the attic was a solid black wall. At least it *appeared* to be solid. Passing them, she approached it. Standing a few feet away, she stared at it intently.

"Clever darling."

Then she walked through the illusion and found herself in a hall. Turning to the left, she entered a bedroom with the biggest platform bed she'd ever seen.

There was nothing on the walls or surfaces. A similar illusion concealed the entrance to a closet that featured floor to ceiling drawers and closed cabinets.

Walking to the other side, she found a large and simple bathroom. Back in the bedroom, the men leaned against the wall the bed was on, watching her.

Flicking her eyes to what was assumed to be the rear wall of the attic, Brie tilted her head. Up close, there were no openings. Placing her palms on it, she inhaled carefully.

She smelled *leather.*

"There are whips and restraints on the other side of this wall."

"Is that a guess?" Harper asked her with a smile.

"Since I was little, I've used my sense of smell more than most people." Glancing over her shoulder, she winked. "Now you *could* have horse tack on the other side of this wall but I'm betting on toys."

Inhaling deeply, she tilted her head. "I also smell gunpowder so I hope those spaces are mutually exclusive."

Elijah approached and stared down at her. "I don't know how you continue to surprise me." Reaching above her, he pressed the wall and a door slid in and to one side. "The armory."

She didn't walk in but as soon as the door opened, lights in the room illuminated more guns, knives, and what appeared to be small explosives than she'd seen in most action movies.

A long rack held bulletproof vests, tactical gear, and survival items she couldn't identify.

"Whoa."

He closed it and she exhaled roughly before clasping her hands under her chin and squealing, "I pick the door on the *right*. The door on the *right*! That's my *final* answer!"

Elijah bent until they were nose to nose. "You're *sure*, Brie?"

Harper murmured at her ear, "There's pain behind that door, Gabriella."

"There's also *pleasure* and I came for a party." She winked. "All your cloak and dagger hasn't scared me off. I need a quick shower because I *literally* have semen running down my legs and it's starting to squeak me out."

"It sounds so interesting." The laughter in the darker man's voice was obvious.

"The closer to my feet it gets, the less interesting it is, I assure you. A shower and then I'm ready to earn my granola bar, gentlemen."

Taking her hand, Elijah led her to the bathroom. "Oh *hey*, a second entrance. Convenient." She raced to the only space in the entire attic with a low-profile doorknob and was giddy to find the toilet. "Thank you, little baby Jesus."

Dropping the robe from her shoulders, she hung it on the door to the toilet closet. After using the facilities, she washed her hands, walked to the shower, turned on the water, and waited for it to heat.

Her eyes roamed the shelves and widened when she saw her favorite specialty shampoo and conditioner. Looking over her shoulder to mention it, she caught both men staring at her ass.

Elijah's eyes met hers and he didn't hide his hunger.

"You really do have come most of the way down your legs." Harper sighed. "If you wash it off, we'll have to start all *over*."

"Yes, I'm a harsh taskmaster. You must *produce*, Harper."

"Shower *quickly*, Gabriella."

She winked and stepped into the enormous glass enclosure. It was hard to pretend they weren't staring at her while she took care of washing her hair.

"Are you coming in? This isn't awkward. I feel like the most bizarre exhibit at a futuristic zoo." She worked to rinse her hair and said in a high-pitched voice, "Here we have the artist chick we took from that adorable blue planet. She consumes insane amounts of coffee and enjoys bantering with zoo patrons. Let's see if we can get her to interact today."

Both men laughed the entire time they stripped. She conditioned her hair and watched them. Once they joined her, they hit several places on the wall and multiple jets of water descended on them.

"Oh, hell. That's lovely." They soaped her from neck to feet, paying special attention to her breasts and other hotspots. Pressing a tile, an adjustable showerhead pulled from a small compartment. "I was *looking* for that."

Harper held her steady, the back of her knee in his hand, as Elijah played the spray over and just inside the entrances of her body. Several strategic jets of water made her struggle not to come.

Especially when he crouched and licked her from pussy to clit. "There. All clean."

He and Harper quickly showered, slicked back their hair, and got out.

Cabinets on either side of the shower gave up the towels. She watched them dry efficiently and found herself fascinated at how rough they were on their own skin.

The way they dried *her* skin was far different. Almost delicately, they took their time removing every drop of water. Then Harper wrung out her hair and led her to the counter.

"It's so long. Let's bring your beautiful curls back. I miss them."

Removing a hair dryer from the vanity drawers, he started drying her hair by playing heat over the tresses and running his fingers through it.

Elijah squirted her favorite lotion in his palm. Rubbing it between his hands, he worked it into her skin until she was trembling from their combined attention.

At her ear, Harper murmured, "I've never seen a woman soak up physical attention like you do."

"I *really* want to earn that granola bar. I hear you guys have chocolate chip and I'm a sucker for chocolate chip."

Such a sentence shouldn't have held breathless sexuality but they had her entire body tingling. They kissed her gently.

In the bedroom, Elijah pulled brown leather pants over his lower body but didn't button them. Harper dressed in thin cotton sleep pants.

Not offered clothes, Brie didn't ask for them.

Elijah held out his hand and she placed hers in it. Leading her to the rear wall, he stared at her for a long moment.

She returned his gaze in silence.

Then he reached above her, pressed the wall, and watched her face as the door slid away.

Expecting dark and almost paranormal like most of the BDSM playrooms she'd seen, Brie smiled at the choice of a pale apricot paint on the walls. The floor was terracotta tile and much of the ceiling was open to the sky above.

Recessed lights every few feet lit enclosed glass displays like the ones Hudson and Natalia possessed in their recreation room. Walking around the large room, she ran her fingers over everything and couldn't look at all of it fast enough.

There were a few pieces of small furniture she didn't recognize. Other pieces she'd seen in random internet searches and felt her heart speed up at the prospects they represented. There was a huge bed in one corner and a professional massage table in the other.

Walking to the center of the room, she looked up, closed her eyes, and absorbed the late-afternoon sunshine that slanted into the space from overhead.

Lowering her gaze, Brie relaxed her arms at her sides and inhaled deeply. Harper looked tense about her possible reaction. Elijah stood still and unblinking.

Staring into Elijah's green eyes with a smile, she said, "I'm yours to command."

Chapter Thirty-One

One side of Elijah's mouth lifted in a smile.

Harper exhaled roughly.

Brie didn't move or speak. The time for silliness and verbal quips was over.

Now began the exploration.

The silence dragged out for more than a minute but she'd learned from the best about what was expected. Utterly still, silent, and relaxed, she waited for the man she loved with all of herself to explain what he wanted from her.

She trusted Elijah. She trusted Harper by association. Naked to them, scars and all, filled her with anticipation rather than self-consciousness.

For her night of decadence and education, she'd always be grateful to Hudson and Natalia. Skills they taught, questions they answered without reservation, and the confidence they helped her find would benefit these men.

One minute turned to three and then to five but she liked the waiting, the building excitement, and did nothing but hold the gaze of beautiful green eyes.

"You're *magnificent*, Brie." Unable to hold back her blush, she was careful not to respond.

They approached her slowly and she kept her eyes still as they circled her. Stopping behind her, she felt one of them gather her hair carefully into a ponytail and tie it with something.

Warm hands settled on her shoulders. "What's your safe word, Brie?"

"Whale."

"When should you use it?"

"Real pain or fear."

"Specifically explain what I want you to pay attention to."

Swallowing carefully, she replied, "My bones, joints, and other areas that sustained injury."

"If you feel something isn't right, it stops instantly. If I suspect you're lying to me about your pain, I'll forbid you to come in any way for a *month*. Do you understand?"

"Yes. I understand."

His hands massaged the muscles of her neck and shoulders before smoothing down to her hands.

"You aren't to come until I give you permission."

"I understand."

Four hands moved slowly over her skin, smoothing oil over every inch of her body from her neck to her feet. It smelled of almonds and prickled slightly. They smoothed extra into the crease of her ass and through her folds.

Focusing on a glass figurine in one of the displays, she walked herself through meditation to calm her breathing and ease a body that already throbbed for them.

Their hands disappeared and she remained still another minute, staring at the glass.

Elijah appeared in front of her and she met his eyes happily.

"I like you in the sun." From above, she listened to the quiet slide of metal on metal. "Give me your hands."

She held them out to him without hesitation. He skillfully wrapped each of her wrists with supple leather. His thumbs smoothed over the pads of her palms and there was the distinctive sound of metal clicking into place.

As her arms rose over her head in a V, he stared at her face with clear tension. The restraints tightened enough to draw her completely erect on the balls of her feet without forcing her to her tiptoes. Most of the stress was in her upper back and arms.

"Brie."

"I'm okay." He reached out to cup her jaw. "I won't lie to you, Elijah. I'm okay. I swear it."

Harper appeared beside him. "You look stunning, Gabriella." She looked at him but didn't speak. He gave her a slow smile. "I tried to trick you. You're better at this than I was. Took me *years* to behave."

She pressed her lips together to keep from laughing.

"You've been suspended before." It wasn't a question but she met Elijah's eyes as he stepped closer to her. "Something tells me you embraced it then as well." He raised his hand to hers and slipped over the inside of her arm and down her side. "You're so relaxed."

"I was *never* relaxed, Gabriella."

Elijah stared at her. "What Harper *wants* and what he *allows* himself to have are often in discord. Why do you think that is, Brie?"

"Even though the need causes no harm and he's always safe with someone he trusts, he doesn't think he's *allowed* to have what he wants. Primarily because he's male."

"Explain."

"Society wants, even demands that *women* be submissive to the will of *all* men. Throughout history, we've been broken and abused to obtain it. No matter the situation, we're expected to obey, to bow, to take what we're given without question. Submission that's forced is abuse and that's *wrong*."

She wrapped her fingers around the leather that bound her. "The expectations for men are different but *also* wrong. It's harder as a submissive. Acting *like a girl* is apparently the worst fucking thing a male can do because they have to follow the fucking *be a man* mantra at all times." Growling, she added, "Fuck *all* that shit. Let's do what we want."

Closing her eyes, Brie took several deep breaths to calm down. When she opened them, they stared at her in shock.

"Sorry," she whispered.

"Don't you *dare* apologize for an eloquent rant on human rights, Gabriella."

Silver eyes stared into hers and she could see his inner struggle. Drawing a heavy breath, he didn't look away from her as he held out his wrists.

In silence, Elijah bound Harper in matching restraints. Moments later, he was extended less than a foot in front of her body. Placing his hand in the middle of the darker man's chest, Elijah murmured at his ear.

Brie panicked. She started to speak when Harper shook his head over the other man's shoulder.

Moving behind her, Elijah placed her on a block of some sort before drawing the ceiling restraints snugly.

She found herself eye to eye with Harper.

The first lash on her back made her rock forward with a sharp inhale. Allowing the sting to flow through her, she relaxed her body and let herself process. The second across the cheeks of her ass made her pant softly. Her nipples pebbled sharply on the fifth. By the tenth, she *wanted* friction on her clit but stepped out slightly to prevent it.

Then she lost count of how many times the whip landed. Breathing through parted lips, she stared into silver eyes and allowed her mind to drift.

She imagined Harper looked at her with love, the way she so desperately wanted him to look at her. She pretended he wanted her to be *his* as much as she wanted him to be *hers*.

Her entire body hummed and it was unlike how it had been with Hudson and Natalia because it wasn't one night and she didn't have to protect herself from love.

It's different because I already love them.

Elijah was the man who nurtured her light and fed a darkness she'd sampled and found fascinating. Harper was the man who shared her darkness, her need to be the *center* for another person sexually.

That it wasn't *her* was okay. Elijah was more than worthy.

She wondered what it would feel like when they took her together. Both of her brief encounters with ménage featured a woman and a man. She wanted to know the joy of two men, *these* men, taking her because she loved them.

Love them, want them, need them.

"Brie."

Eyes opening, she took in the brilliant colors of twilight through the skylight above her. Bringing her head forward, Elijah stood there, his hands on her face.

Such a beautiful man.

"Brie."

"Elijah. Will you kiss me?"

Exhaling roughly, he cupped the back of her head and claimed her mouth until she was moaning. Supporting her weight on her good leg, she wrapped the other around his hip.

Breaking the kiss, he asked, "Would you like to come, Brie?"

"I'll wait for Harper."

"You're a remarkable woman."

"More please."

Elijah smoothed more oil on the back of her body. It made her skin warm pleasantly.

Then a different leather connected and made her moan.

She regained her focus on Harper's eyes and thought about the stress he was under and how hard it must be to have so much depending on you. To have so many people looking to you for answers and money and results.

You want to just be but you don't think you're allowed.

The lashes were softer material. They laid over the original design Elijah placed on her back and ass. She wondered how it would feel during sex.

Slight bite while you fuck me…worth it.

"Brie."

I love the way you smell, Elijah. I love the way you taste. I love the way you touch me. Touch me, touch me, touch me.

"Brie, what's your safe word?"

"I'm not telling you."

Staring at the darkening sky, a few stars were out. Then he brought her head forward from where it had fallen back on her shoulders.

"I love you more than the sky."

"Safe word, Brie."

"I will *not.*"

"Why?"

"Harper needs it."

"Needs what, Brie?"

"He'll take the same lashes…"

"Brie!"

"I know that's what you told him. He doesn't take what he *needs.* Now he *has* to take it."

"Take her down. *Take her down,* Elijah."

"No…"

Elijah freed her arms and held her on the step. Slipping one arm around Harper's waist, the other up to cup the back of his skull, she rested her head on the inside of his arm.

"Gabriella."

"Take what you need, Harper. Feed the darkness."

"Stay with me." She nodded against him.

"Brie." She blinked and found Elijah's eyes. "You can't stand up. Let me help you."

He slipped a silken strap over her head and around her ribs while he supported her with one arm. It ran up between her body and Harper's, where it looped around the back of his neck.

"He'll be okay like this?"

"Yes." Elijah stroked his palm over her head. Behind Harper, he removed the lightweight pants.

She petted Harper's face. "Give him what he needs. Show him how much you love him, Elijah."

Then he was gone and Harper kissed her temple as the first lash landed on the back of his body.

She felt him tense but it left him by the ninth strike of the whip.

Brie played with silken black hair and pressed her cheek to Harper's so she could be near without him having to look at her as he took the same lashes she'd taken.

Zoning out, she allowed her mind to wander.

You're a good man, worthy of love.

As it darkened outside, it dimmed inside their sanctuary. Her eyes adjusted to the golden glow of the displays.

Every time the whip landed, he pressed against her and she welcomed him, accepted him, loved him.

I'm proud to love you. I love you, love you, love you.

She rode the lashes with him, knowing how badly he needed them but ashamed of the need. It had always been *Harper* who warred with the dual sides of himself. Elijah was the only person he trusted enough to help him, to purge him.

Trust in his love for you. Let him take it all away.

The stars moved across the skylight and she held him as hard as she could until the last stroke fell.

When his hands were free, Harper would've fallen if Elijah hadn't caught them both, leading them to the bed in the corner.

"On your stomachs, that's it. I'll be back."

Flat on the bed, their faces turned to one another, Harper whispered, "Thank you, Gabriella."

Slipping his hand over the satin, he wrapped it around hers.

She told him, "It's no hardship to love you, no sacrifice. It's an honor."

"You're beautiful."

"So are you, Harper."

She had no idea how long Elijah rubbed them down with oils that smelled wonderful and tingled warmly. Sleep drifted up to take her and she embraced it.

Chapter Thirty-Two

The room was tinted pink when Brie opened her eyes. Elijah stared at her from inches away.

"You're stupidly sexy." Reaching out, she stroked his face. "Good morning."

"Are you alright?"

She frowned. "Of course. Why wouldn't I be?"

He had her in his arms, gripping her to him painfully hard, his hand pressing the back of her head to his chest.

"Elijah…"

"Had you not already taken more lashes than any female I've ever met in my life, I'd paddle your *ass*, Brie."

"That sounds promising."

Rolling her over, he was suddenly inside her and she gasped in pleasure laced with a bit of pain as her tender back met cool sheets. His fist tightened in her hair and he pulled her head back to look at her eyes.

Hard, fast, he drove his cock into her until she was on the cusp of an orgasm that threatened any hope of control.

"M-may I come?"

"No." His hand wrapped around the knee of her good leg, raising it to his hip and granting him deeper access as she tightened around him. "Look at me, Brie."

Not realizing her eyes had closed, she opened them and stared into glowing green.

"You will *never* do that again. Do you understand?"

She wanted to come but she couldn't agree to something that wasn't true. "I can't promise that."

"Tell me why. Do *not* come, Brie."

Struggling to find coherent words as he stole her ability to think, she managed, "I-I want Harper to know peace."

"He has to find his own way. No matter how beautiful your heart is, you can't endanger yourself for him."

Reaching up with shaking hands, she held his face. "You do it every day." He stumbled in his thrusts. "I'm useless as a fighter. I've got *one* weapon. You can't tell me not to use it to protect men I love, Elijah. It's one command I won't obey."

He fucked her harder and Brie fought not to come as her muscles and skin tensed.

Staring into his eyes, she forced her mind to focus on the striations of green. To breathe through the want, to deny the need by diverting her mind.

"Brie!" She snapped back to the moment and her body tried to defy her. Elijah wrapped his arms around her and whispered, "Come for me, Brie."

The climax tore through her and he held her tight as he sealed them together and pumped himself dry. When she could breathe, she stared into his face with a smile.

"You hypnotize yourself." She frowned. "You withdraw from the surface of your mind. Why did you learn such a skill?"

She blushed. "I've always had a high tolerance for pain, even when I was little. I'd never had surgery until I-I had my breast reduction. I was afraid to get addicted to the pain medication so I'd take half and practice meditation."

"You meditate often?"

"I can't always draw. Sometimes I *need* to but circumstances don't allow it. I have to calm my mind to focus." One side of her mouth lifted. "I've got to *appear* normal." He smiled. "It helped when I was…suspended the first time. It allowed me to separate the sensations so I could take everything in."

"It heightened it for you. You liked the way it made you feel." She nodded. "Then you had the accident."

Nodding, she inhaled carefully. "When I came out of the hospital, it felt like someone was raking a fucking saw against my bones. I was losing my *mind* with it, leaning more and more on the pain meds so I could function. I felt weak."

"You aren't weak, Brie."

"I couldn't control the pain itself so I worked harder to disconnect from it when it got too bad."

Harper's voice beside them made her turn her head. "It's why you knew not to risk sex before the stress tests." He reached out to smooth his fingers through her hair. "You knew you'd compartmentalize any pain and we'd hurt you accidentally."

Brie nodded. "It was hard to wait."

He stared at her for a long time. "You gave too *much*."

"No, Harper. Each time Elijah brought me up, I took stock of my body, knew I was fine, and that I could handle more."

"What if he hadn't brought you up?"

"I trusted him to know. Elijah sees both of us clearly. He watches for signs, ensures we're never in danger. It's why you trust him with your life. It's why I trust him with mine."

Turning her face, she grinned at the man watching her intently. "I must ask that you remove your weight from my bladder before this becomes the kind of kink I'm not into…"

Laughing, he pulled away and stood on the floor in a single smooth movement. He held out his hand.

She whispered, "That was…really hot." He laughed and helped her up. She walked to the bathroom without looking back.

The heat of their eyes on her ass didn't need confirmation.

* * *

Elijah met Harper's eyes as he stepped into the pants he'd worn the night before and settled them over his hips. "Are you alright?"

"Better than I've been in too many years."

Getting off the bed, Harper half-dressed as well and stood in front of him, his silver eyes clear, the familiar tension eased at last.

Lifting his hand, he stroked through black hair and smiled when his thick lashes lowered in response. "You used to crave touch as much as Brie. I let you become too isolated when you married Danielle. I let you hurt yourself. I failed you, Harper."

Opening his eyes, he shook his head. "I didn't give you a choice. I didn't know how to get back to where we were. I didn't know how to tell you I was sorry for choosing a life I didn't even *want* over what we've always been." Lifting one broad shoulder, he whispered, "I pushed you away, changed too much. I regret *every* woman I forced you to endure in the years since."

"Had we not shared them, we might not have seen her."

Harper lifted his hands and cupped his face. "That *never* would've happened. She's the piece we didn't know we were missing."

Claiming the mouth of the only man he'd ever loved, Elijah hoped it was the start of a new chapter between them.

A chance to begin again and get it right.

He sensed rather than heard Brie's return but he didn't break the kiss. Gently leading Harper into trusting her was critical to melding *all* of who they were individually into the whole.

Something new and different.

Raising his face, he turned and met the eyes of a woman who touched every part of who he was as a man.

Harper tensed.

Her freshly scrubbed body was flushed, her nipples furled, her thighs pressed together. Elijah loved how easy it was to read her response to stimulus.

"I could come watching you kiss." She placed her hand over her belly and said breathlessly, "I realize it'll take time to have trust and ease with me here but I'd like to officially say *yes* and *more please*. You know, whenever you're ready to show me all the hot man on hot man action. Sign me up."

A rough exhale and the tension drained from the man in his arms. Hugging him tightly, Elijah wrapped his arm around his shoulders and turned them to face Brie.

The fingers of her drawing hand tapped her upper thigh. She zoned out for a minute and shook her head to clear it.

"May I politely request a protein shake or field ration of some sort? I just realized I haven't eaten anything or hydrated at all."

"Holy *fuck*, Gabriella. I'm sorry. Let me call downstairs."

Moving to break from Elijah's hold, he held him back. Meeting his eyes, he took a deep breath and kissed him lightly.

As he passed Brie, she said, "*Hey...*"

Harper stopped in confusion and she wrapped her arms around him, lifting her face. One arm went around her. The other lifted so his fingers could smooth along her neck.

"Elijah was trying to fuck me into behaving." With a wink, she whispered, "As if *that's* going to work. I'm not going to tell him though because I'd like him to keep trying."

The laugh he gave her made Elijah feel amazing.

"I was supposed to wait for you. I was distracted. Because of my outrageous orgasm, I didn't say good morning to you properly."

"You fucking *earned* it."

"May I have a kiss pretty please, Harper?"

"Your oddness is growing on me." Then he grabbed the hair at the back of her head and kissed her roughly. By the time he lifted away, she was boneless.

"Forget the food." She rubbed her fingertips over his nipple and trailed down to cup his cock through the sleep pants. "Breakfast of champions."

"You're so fucking tempting, Gabriella."

"You say that like it's a bad thing. I know you'll both be gone in a day or two. Let me overdose now to hold me over."

"Brie." She turned her head, her hair everywhere, and stared at Elijah. "You need to eat."

"I can eat *after*." Staring into his eyes, she pushed the fabric over Harper's hips. Resting her face on his chest, she stroked her palms over his ass. "He didn't *get* to come, Elijah."

He walked to them, stroking his hand over her hair. "You have no survival instincts, Brie." Smiling, he wrapped his arm around the other man and told her, "Harper is familiar with waiting for those things that mean more."

She whimpered.

"At this rate, we'll have you addicted by sundown."

"Too late."

He bent to kiss her. The way she opened to him, sliding one arm around his back, giving everything she was to the kiss while he hugged the two people he loved…it blew his mind.

When he lifted away, she followed. Eyes fluttering open, she rested her head on Harper's chest.

"You have to eat, Brie."

"Semen has lots of nutrients." Neither of them could hold back their laughter. "It really does though."

"Not enough."

He picked her up and her legs wrapped around him, one arm around his neck. She held Harper as well. Puckering her lips, she stared at him until he smiled and kissed her again.

"You have a gorgeous mouth, Gabriella."

"You should…"

"You're eating *first*, Brie. Cock doesn't count." Slapping her sharply on her bare ass, Elijah shook his head and she grinned.

Walking through the sanctuary and his bedroom, he set her on one of the leather barstools in his kitchen.

Chin in her hands, she watched him move around the kitchen. "Elijah?" He glanced over his shoulder. "Your ass looks *amazing* in those pants. I kind of want to bite it."

He made her a bowl of microwave noodles, setting it in front of her with a bottle of water.

Frowning, she took a bite. "Don't be offended but, this stuff is disgusting. I'm eating it so I get naked play time but I'll make the next meal."

He grinned. "I don't cook."

"Thank god you microwave like a motherfucker. At least you haven't starved." Tilting her head, she choked down another couple of bites. "I could show you a couple of easy recipes. I know you're not home much but you have to feed that fine body."

While she watched, he drank a packet of liquid nutritional supplement that distance runners used. He had many such products in his cupboards.

She shivered. "That's not food. That's like…slime. Please let me help you." Laughing, he walked around the counter and tilted her chin up for a kiss. She wrinkled her nose. "Water first."

"Do you *know* what fluids we've shared, Brie?"

"That's *organic*." She lifted a brow. "The stuff you just…swallowed? Slurped? I'm not even sure. That's a totally different animal. We shouldn't cross-contaminate."

She always managed to make him laugh. He winked and downed most of her bottled water. Then he kissed her smiling lips before walking to a phone on the wall and ordering the poor thing some real food from the kitchen on the first floor.

"Stop eating that before your system freaks out." He didn't have to tell her twice.

Twenty minutes later, three stacked and covered plates were delivered through an old dumbwaiter system that had been fully upgraded.

She looked like she was in heaven as she ate stuffed chicken breast and salad. He and Harper finished first and he returned their plates to the tiny box that was designed small for a reason.

Harper stood behind her stool, lightly stroking his fingertips over the pinked skin of her back.

"For such a delicate woman, you took a *lot* of pain, Gabriella. I've never seen anything like it with another female submissive." Sliding his palm along her shoulder, he asked, "Had you ever dabbled before Winters?"

"No. I barely touched *myself* before I met them." She cleared her throat carefully. "I didn't understand my own body. I didn't know…much at all." Shrugging, she added, "I was ashamed about what I *did* know because I'd been taught to feel that way."

The admission floored Elijah and he saw Harper was similarly surprised. He sent up a silent prayer of thanks to Winters.

She finished what she could, they ate the rest, and he took her plate.

Wiping her mouth daintily, she drank her water and smiled. "Thanks. Better than the post-apocalypse food." He winked and watched her mind working. "You always mention Hudson; ask about him specifically. Natalia was as important to me sexually. In some ways, definitely more."

"Why?" Harper was genuinely interested.

"She was the first woman I'd ever met who embraced her sexuality openly and without apology. She was confident. When I asked her questions, she answered them and didn't make me feel bad that I didn't know or dirty for *wanting* to know."

Elijah hated that she'd clearly encountered those attitudes before meeting her friends. "You should never feel ashamed of wanting to know things, Brie."

She shook her head. "It's different for women and I know you know that. When I was in high school, I was tormented *constantly* about my breasts. Every degrading thing boys could come up with, I heard them. Yet, I was almost suspended when I argued with my health teacher for discussing male ejaculation but not female climax."

Shrugging, she took a deep breath. "I accepted the way it was. Then I met Natalia. She was the first woman to look me in the eye without blushing and say words like *cock* and *pussy*. The first person to discuss topics like *trust*, *orgasms*, and *need* in a context that fit who I'd crushed down all my life."

Nodding, Elijah admitted, "I've never been so grateful for her existence."

It made her smile. "I'm glad you didn't get her. She belongs with Hudson."

"Agreed."

"With him, she's *completely* submissive. Stunning in her stillness and calm. As the focus, she's *so* beautiful to watch." Her eyes met his. "I learned from watching her."

Elijah planted his palms wide on the countertop. "You're an outstanding pupil, Brie." He meant it.

"Thank you." She blushed. "She taught me many things."

Harper lowered slowly onto the stool next to her. His face was filled with curiosity. "She was *different* with you. She was *dominant* with you."

She met his eyes. "Yes." Elijah watched her choose her words. "When I was the focus, Hudson was in control, but she sort of...facilitated at specific points. I know she was generally dominant with women."

It explained her knowledge of switching with Harper.

"Brie." Her eyes lifted. "You're comfortable in any role as long as you feel you're *giving* something to the interaction."

"Does it bother you that I'm submissive, Gabriella?"

Turning her head sharply, she frowned. "Hell no. If I was bothered by *your* natural tendencies, that would imply that for us to be *alike* is a bad thing. Do *you* think that's bad?"

He shook his head with a small smile and Elijah knew Brie's mind would never bore him.

Her hands cupped his face and Harper stared at her with incredible focus. "I find you strong, brilliant, and beautiful. I don't give a damn which end of the whip you're on or whether you're giving or receiving cock. None of that *matters*. You have to *know* it doesn't matter before you understand how I feel about you, Harper."

That she'd said it so plainly stunned them both.

"I'm afraid, Gabriella."

"I know. I'll never push and you might never feel comfortable. You've had your relationship forever. It fascinates me, stimulates me, to think of you and Elijah together but I don't have to be included if you don't want me to be."

"It would hurt you. Eventually, it would hurt you to be left out of that aspect of our lives."

Elijah watched her face and how she considered her answer.

"Maybe it would long-term. We'll have to see. If I get to that point, I'll talk to you about it."

There was no doubt in his mind that Brie didn't expect to be part of their lives for long. Harper's eyes locked with Elijah's and he saw that he understood what she wasn't saying.

Gathering her in his arms, Harper pulled Brie into his lap. Her entire body wrapped around him and her pleasure in the simple attention was awe-inspiring.

"I like you, Gabriella. I trust you more than any woman." He rubbed her back.

"Thank you."

"Twenty years ago, I wanted to be with Elijah publicly. Hudson and Natalia witnessed an interaction between us and for weeks after, the stress of how he'd *use* the information weighed on me. Though he *never* did, I didn't forget the way I felt. Most aren't as honorable."

"The ones that aren't can fuck off. I'll never give you any reason to regret your trust." Her smile was gentle as she traced his face. "No matter what happens, Harper. *No matter what*, I love you and *nothing* would make me betray you."

There was a long silence. Elijah straightened slowly and watched Harper process what she was telling them.

"If you're ever in danger, if you must make a choice between withholding details about me and saving your life, *save your life*, Gabriella. Elijah guards my back."

"Who guards his?" She shook her head and Elijah thought his heart would stop with the implication. "I'd never take the risk. I'd rather die knowing you still have each other."

The loving and *stubborn* expression on her face told him they wouldn't get anywhere *talking* to Brie about appropriate responses during crisis situations.

Harper had no clue how to handle the new information.

Elijah *believed* she'd give her life for theirs. That couldn't be allowed to be considered as an option if she were ever taken.

They'd have to *fuck* some sense into her.

Chapter Thirty-Three

Harper stared at the woman in his arms and wondered where the fuck she'd come from and how she'd developed into a small female willing to give her *life* to protect men she'd known for such a short time.

That she *said* it was bad enough, that he could truly *see* her making such a choice if faced with it made his mind contract in horror and something else he couldn't identify.

He wanted to *shake her* until she took back the words.

Glancing at Elijah, he could see the vibration of wildness in his stance, on his face. Normally, it was evident when he prepared to fight.

Harper knew he was about to fuck Gabriella Hernandez until she swore to never put her own life on the line in such a way.

"*Brie.*"

After dropping her statement like a *bomb*, the little kitten had curled up against Harper's chest without a clue about what was going to happen to her.

She sat up and looked at Elijah, the command clear in his voice.

"*Come. Here.*"

Sliding off his lap, she kept her hand on Harper until he was out of reach. He found it amusing that she'd been naked for a full day and hadn't questioned it.

As she stopped in front of him, Elijah looked at Harper. "Chair and necessary supplies."

Nodding, he walked swiftly to the sanctuary and pulled a heavily padded curved chair from the side of the room into the center.

Dropping a heavy linen sheet over it, he opened the closet and gathered lube, wipes, and a special cream.

Gabriella wasn't getting away easily.

Placing them on a small side table, he carried it within reach of the chair. Stripping the sleep pants away, he tossed them in the closet hamper and waited.

The object of their focused sexual attention practically *bounced* into the room. Unlike most women he'd known in his life, Gabriella showed the world her inner self without reservation and ended up hurt more than others for her honesty.

She had *zero* survival instincts.

Harper admitted it was adorable.

The moment she saw him standing naked in the middle of the room, her eyes lit up and she smiled happily.

Elijah came into the room as exactly what he was as well. A powerful male animal prepared to assert his dominance. It was a sight that inspired a prickle on the back of the neck.

Two feet from Harper, his best friend commanded her to stop.

She did so instantly with her shoulders back and her chin up. Barely five-three or so, she was small and curvy but carried herself with a grace rarely seen anymore.

Her features, so different from the women he normally chose, were what initially drew him. Full breasts and a gorgeous ass competed with her incredible curly hair and caramel skin.

It was odd that he'd never wondered more about her.

Only seen from a distance, and only ever briefly, he now knew she was responsible for the overwhelming success of a niche winery that could've struggled to survive. Her mind was almost as impressive as her heart.

Elijah circled her slowly.

Watching the man move was incredibly erotic. The first time Harper noticed it, he was barely sixteen and ashamed of the fact that he'd become hypnotized by watching his bodyguard spar with several bigger and more physically imposing opponents.

For months after, he masturbated to the memory.

Walking, fighting, fucking, or standing still, Elijah had a presence about him, a *will* that was difficult to define and impossible to deny.

Harper watched as he turned that will, all the power he possessed, on a small, pretty woman who loved him – *both of them* – more than she valued her own life.

"Brie." She met his eyes. "If you were to be kidnapped off the street right now, if you were told that you'd be raped, tortured, or killed if you didn't provide information about Harper Delkin or his life, what would be your response?"

"Fuck you."

"Incorrect. The response would be to spill your guts…*slowly.* Allowing us time to find you and get you to safety. You'd tell them anything you know."

"I would *not.*"

"Brie. We need to come to an understanding before we leave this room. You're a gentle woman. The methods used to extract information from you would be extreme physically, mentally, and sexually."

Harper saw the instant she realized Elijah was furious.

She swallowed and murmured, "And my guilt would be *less* extreme?"

Elijah tightened his hands into fists. It was his *tell.* Harper knew he was having difficulty navigating the emotions of the woman in front of him. "Once we *had* you, we could put measures in place to protect everyone involved."

"It might be too late."

"I need you to believe that I'll do everything possible to keep you from harm's way, Brie. I'd destroy anything or anyone necessary to get you back safely."

"I know, Elijah."

"Do you trust me to protect you?"

"Of course."

"Would you give information to save your life?"

"I'm sorry."

"Your reasoning, Brie?"

"You can't control everything. Things would probably move quickly. You *only* know how you and Harper will react at any given time. You can't determine other people, places, or situations. If I were to give up information, it could be *acted on* before you even know I'm missing."

"You're *infuriating.*"

"I know." She added in a whisper, "I'm also right."

"We're *trained*, Brie. We can defend ourselves. It doesn't fall to *you* to protect us from…"

"You aren't fucking *immortal*, Elijah!" Harper's eyes widened at her scream. "I won't be the cause of someone knowing information that allows one of you to be shot in the fucking head!" She pressed her palms to her temples. "I won't. You can't make me do that."

"Brie…"

"Do your fucking worst. I can take it."

Stepping close to her, he murmured, "Ah, but can you handle my fucking *best*, Brie?" She blinked up at him in confusion. "You belong to me because you love me. Not out of obligation or greed or status. You placed yourself into my care and keeping because you trust me, you love me. Is that right?"

"Yes. I love you so much."

"I love you, Brie." Her eyes filled with tears. "Do you *believe* in my love for you?" She nodded. "If anything happened to you, I would obliterate entire *cities* in retaliation. I would carve a path of death to the people who hurt you. There would be *no* hesitation, *no* guilt as I bathed in their blood."

"Elijah..."

"Silence." He gathered a handful of her hair and tilted her head back. "You are Gabriella Lenora Hernandez. Many things to many people. Artist, friend, lover. You are not a lamb to be *slaughtered*. I am Elijah Mathias Eklund. I am also many things. Protector, friend, lover. I am *he who slaughters* in our relationship, Brie."

Tears flowed from her eyes.

"You sharing information to save your *life* has a *slim chance* of resulting in the death of Harper or myself." Gabriella sobbed painfully hard. "If you do *not* share information and unknown persons *take your life*, I give you my *word* that it will result in the brutal death of hundreds, if not thousands, of people. I will see it done *personally*."

She broke, throwing herself against him, hugging him hard.

"You can dig in on *anything* but this, Brie. I love and respect your mind and heart. I'll consider your thoughts on all but your safety. You *will not* take my place. You *will not* take Harper's place. Tell me you understand."

"Please, Elijah."

"Tell me you understand, Brie."

"I understand what you're saying."

"Clever, Brie. Tell me you understand that *your life* is as important to *me* as my life, Harper's life, is to *you*."

"*Elijah...*"

"Bring it, Harper." Carrying a small tub of cream, he stopped beside Elijah. "To avoid chafing tender skin."

They worked together to smooth the organic blend into the soft flesh of her nipples, cheeks and pucker of her ass, inner thighs, outer folds, and inside her pussy.

The change of course made her sway on her feet.

"It'll also stimulate the nerves," he added when she was coated thoroughly. "It will feel more like a curse than a blessing by the time we're done."

They cleaned their hands carefully and stood staring at her. She blinked up at Elijah and he used his thumbs to wipe her tears.

"You're a beautiful woman. Brilliant and kind in ways I've never experienced. You don't know death, torture, and pain as I do. In this, you *will* allow me to lead."

Bending, he kissed her fiercely. As he lifted away, his smile was slow. "You'll come as many times as your body allows, Brie."

Harper returned to the chair, reclined, and held out his hand to Gabriella.

Confused and heartsick, she glanced at Elijah who nodded once. Then she walked to the chair and let Harper pull her astride his body.

"Put his cock inside you, Brie." With shaking hands, she did and started to lower herself, her hands on Harper's shoulders. Elijah gave her a sharp spank on one rounded ass cheek. "Wait for instruction."

"I have you, Gabriella." With just the head inside her, he held her waist, supporting her weight since only the tips of her toes touched the terracotta tile beneath the chair.

Then the cream started to do its' work and her eyes widened.

"Do you feel it, Brie?" Elijah asked. "Do you feel the blood moving closer to the surface? It's a similar effect to spanking without the wait."

"I-I...yes."

He gave her a spank on the opposite cheek and she put her head back to inhale deeply.

Stroking the flat of his palm over her throat, to her breast, and down her torso to her clit, Elijah delivered another spank to her clit. The orgasm took over and Harper felt warm wetness coat the tip of his cock.

"I said as many times as your body allows, Brie. You're not to hold them back. You're not to breathe through them. Stay in the moment.

Stay with us."

Shaking as her body did what it wanted, she nodded with her teeth gritted.

"Very good." Elijah stroked up to roll her nipple and asked, "Do you want more of Harper's cock?"

"*Please.*"

Green eyes focused on him intensely. "Give her all of you." Harper lowered her until their bodies sealed snugly. She pulsed around his shaft and his eyes rolled up in his head. "Don't move."

Gabriella's hands alternately squeezed his shoulders and massaged them. She stared at him and Harper lifted his hand to cup her face.

Her hips reflexively rolled on him and Elijah slapped her ass. "Don't. Move. Brie."

Petting her hair, he bent to kiss her forehead. "You *are* loved. You *will* be protected. You *must* understand, Brie."

"Elijah…" She raised her face to look at him.

"Ssh." He claimed her mouth and Harper wanted to move as badly as she wanted him to move. Against her lips, he murmured, "Take her, Harper. Show no mercy."

Bracing her hips in his hands, he withdrew enough to drive hard inside her. Short, brutal strokes that worked their groins against each other, causing friction on her clit that caused her to flex around him.

With a sharp smack to her ass, Elijah commanded, "No holding back, Brie." A shiver worked its' way over her. Inhaling sharply, she stared at him as he crouched beside them. "Watch."

A strong hand slid along the side of his neck and Elijah's mouth devoured his own until he was desperate for *everything*. Licking inside, coiling their tongues together as Elijah gripped his hair, the feel of Gabriella's pussy pulsing around the length of his dick as he fucked her.

So much stimulation.

The orgasm that took her made her hands grip him roughly. They broke the kiss to watch her in the clutches of it. Panting, whimpering, her heart rate through the roof, she stared at them through half-lidded eyes.

The way she felt around him was incredible.

She started to lift her hand, caught herself on his chest, inhaled deeply to gain control over her body, and tried again.

Raking fingers through Harper's hair, she cried, "*Please…*"

Gathering her close, he kissed her until she was moaning into his mouth and then supported her so Elijah could kiss her as well. Touching them both was strangely important to her in ways it had never been with their women in the past.

Already, she could barely lift her arms.

"You love me, Brie." She nodded against the side of his face. "You love Harper." Another nod. "I love you both with all of me. I need you to understand the strength of it."

"I do. I *do*, Elijah." Her voice was barely audible.

Their faces were close, the three of them huddled as Harper continued to thrust inside her. He could feel the way her body spasmed, coiling for another climax.

"You matter to me, Brie. You *matter*. Your life is not forfeited to save ours. Tell me you understand."

"Please. *Please*, Elijah."

He exhaled slowly and looked at Harper with a small shake of his head. When he stood, she tried to hold him, collapsing on Harper as she fell down the rabbit hole of physical pleasure while her emotions raged out of control.

Gripping her tight, he drove her through to the other side and she petted his skin, kissed his shoulder, and murmured words he couldn't hear.

Watching Elijah drizzle oil across the top of Gabriella's ass cheeks was one of the most erotic sights he'd ever seen. The force of his thrusts made the rounded bubble ripple.

Elijah took his time rubbing it in, smoothing it along the crease, and all around the pucker he imagined was clenched from the stimulation of the cream and her orgasms.

Entering her with two fingers, pushing deep, Gabriella gasped and bit Harper's shoulder. Then she came and the slickness of her body was audible in the quiet room.

Pulling from her, she sobbed as Elijah explained, "When two men take a woman at the same time, it's important to be careful, Brie. The inner flesh of your pussy and ass is tender, easily chafed, bruised, and torn. Harper and I will *never* harm your body."

Her fingers kneaded Harper's chest. She murmured quietly and he felt her tears on his skin. Pressing deep, he stilled. Her entire body trembled.

Elijah watched her as he used a wipe on his hand and stripped. Harper held his breath watching him lube his length.

Crouching over them, he growled, "However, we *will* take you hard and repeatedly. We *will not stop* until you forget where you end and we begin. There will be *no quarter given* until you *submit* to me, Brie."

Placing his cock at the entrance of her ass, Elijah's eyes met his. The wolf that lived inside him prowled the green depths. It had never failed to make Harper breathless.

Then he pushed hard and deep in the first thrust.

Gabriella gasped with a long wail and her entire body tightened like a bow as she absorbed the pressure and the fullness.

Since the morning they talked to the only woman in their history to capture Elijah's interest, he'd refused to touch anyone else, including Harper himself.

Feeling him through the thin layer of skin that separated the two entrances of her body was spectacular. Holding Gabriella tight to his body, he let his head drop back on the chair so he could catch his breath.

Filling her completely, they remained still. She panted between them, her body shaking hard. Elijah kissed her shoulder.

"From the time Harper was a small child, I've worked with him in self-defense. Until he was almost eleven, he believed the lessons were games. That was the first time a faction attempted to take him in retaliation for his father's work. Working together, we disabled two full grown men, killed another, and captured one for questioning."

"*Please.* I love you."

"I know, Brie." Pressing deeper, he lowered his chest to her back. "There have been more than twenty attempts on his life since he assumed leadership. At all times, he's able to aide in his own defense. I made sure of that to improve his chances of survival." She tried to hug Harper but she was physically and emotionally drained. He held her hard. "Should anything happen to me, I know he has a better chance to save himself."

"*No, no, no.*"

"Over the years, others have been taken to use as leverage. Some broke quickly while others took days. *All of them* gave up crucial information about Harper, the company, and the workings of his security team. Every single one of them, Brie."

Harper said softly, "The methods used range from amputation to gang rape. Some are barbaric in their pursuit of information, of access." He kissed her hair. "Do you think *less* of those innocent people for saving their own life, for stopping the pain they were in, Gabriella?"

She turned her face to his chest, weeping.

Resting his head against hers, Elijah said, "If you're taken, you'll be traumatized. The less damage you sustain before we get you back, the fewer people I'll have to gut once you're safe. Play dumb, share meaningless information first, but if you're threatened, you tell them *whatever the fuck* they want to know."

Inhaling carefully, he turned her face and kissed a cheek that was wet with sweat and tears. "Tell me you understand, Brie."

"You'll be careful."

"I'm the best at what I do, Brie. Harper has been personally trained by me for thirty-five years. He's *also* good at what he does. Trust me. Tell me you understand."

There was a long pause and her heart pounded against Harper's. "I understand."

"Do you submit to me, Brie?"

"Yes, Elijah."

He watched as Elijah closed his eyes and exhaled quietly. After several deep breaths, their gazes locked over Gabriella.

"Now you receive only pleasure, pretty girl."

Harper was as thankful as the woman between them.

Chapter Thirty-Four

It was rare for Elijah to feel exhausted.

Forcing a woman with a heart like Brie's to submit in such a way had not been easy for him.

However, it had been necessary.

The moment she casually stated she'd rather *die* than endanger them, it drove home *how different* she was from the women they'd known in their pasts.

Everything inside him had recoiled in true *fear*, an emotion he didn't recognize at first.

That she *meant* what she said without understanding what it would do to him if anything happened to her told him that she didn't give herself much of a priority in his life.

She believed she was disposable.

Such a belief could *not* be allowed to stand.

All his life, he'd known and accepted that he'd die to protect Harper. His lover, his friend, the first person to make him feel love, Harper shared space inside him.

They were broken for different reasons.

It was a reality they'd always recognized and, for the most part, ignored until Brie started putting those shattered pieces back together accidentally.

For Elijah, it changed his entire outlook.

Away from her, he worried, ached, and was often distracted. Near her, he felt a calm he'd never experienced. She settled the rage he'd carried since his first memory and slowly knitted together the wounds that continued to bleed.

Unwilling to risk Harper's safety, he'd taken the best men from each of his teams and started training them to back him up.

Those watching Brie were equally competent. Two of the team she didn't really understand that she had were already bonding to her. They'd requested permanent assignment to her detail.

Elijah understood.

Many thoughts filed rapidly through his brain as he regained control of his mind and his heart. Tears slipped from beneath her closed lids to Harper's chest.

Gaining her submission had cost them both. He'd broken her down. Now it was time to build her back up.

"Brie." Thick black lashes fluttered open. As the sun moved into the skylight above the sanctuary, it made her skin glow and made the blue of her eyes more obvious. "Are you alright?"

She nodded. Her fingers petted Harper's skin.

Carefully gathering her in his arms, he brought her back to his chest. Harper reached over and pulled a wipe from the box. Sitting up, he wiped her face while Elijah gathered her hair to one side.

When he was done, Harper bent his head to suck her nipples and her head dropped back. They were seated deep in her body, throbbing against each other as her muscles spasmed around them.

Hypersensitive to stimulation, Elijah stroking his fingers over her belly to her clit slammed her into another climax.

Moaning, shaking, as her body responded, Harper released her nipples and reclined again. Together, they lowered her to rest on him. He braced her as they started to move.

Elijah withdrew until only the head of his cock was clasped by the snug muscles of her ass. As he pushed deep again, Harper stroked out.

The friction of her body and their friction against each other wasn't unfamiliar. They'd taken more women than Elijah cared to remember in such a way.

Familiar, yet different in every way that mattered.

They took her up gently and heard her sigh as another orgasm crashed over a body primed for them. Moving with her, supporting her bodyweight, he stared into Harper's eyes.

"Have you missed each other?" The barely audible question took the men by surprise. "How lonely you must have been, Harper. I'm sorry."

"It's better now."

"I'm glad. You deserve to be happy. I want that for you."

"What about you, Gabriella? What about your happiness?"

"I'm blissfully happy in this moment, right now." She reached back with a shaking hand and stroked her fingers over Elijah's thigh. Turning her head, she kissed Harper's chest. "I feel grateful to have you both inside me, filled up with touch I've craved for months."

The women who'd found themselves between them over the years were cold, disconnected. Touching them, *being* touched by them, hadn't been expected or desired.

Without speaking, the friends took Brie slowly and they touched her. Hands slid over her hair and skin, massaged muscles taut with tension, and kissed flesh they could reach.

She soaked it up, giving back as much as she could, as tired as she was. Brie touched them with her heart and communicated it through her body.

Another climax stole control and she went limp between them. Still they took her, fucked her, loved her. Gave her what she deserved as Harper met his gaze and smiled.

Elijah returned it and they braced her as they went harder, faster, deeper in the body of a woman who welcomed what they offered.

Pushing her, pushing themselves, she shook powerfully between them as they provided counter thrusts.

Inclining his head, they ramped up the force and she moaned low in her throat.

"You're so hard and hot. *This*, I could get *addicted* to this." The words were murmured almost incoherently. "I've never felt as complete as I feel right now."

"Focus inward, Brie. Absorb every sensation. Hold back if you can. Let it build."

"Yes."

The sun was fully over the sanctuary, bathing her in light that turned her skin caramel and made her hair shimmer. She panted, whimpered, as she let them drive her higher.

Open, exposed in a way *no woman* had ever been with them.

Harper's eyes glowed silver as he struggled to hold back, to wait for Elijah's signal. His jaw was tight, clenched against the very real stimulation from Brie's repeated orgasms.

A few minutes later, she whispered, "Elijah, h-help."

Circling her upper body, Harper wrapped her close to his chest. Elijah slid his arm between them, crossing to Brie's shoulder and wrapping his hand there.

Their heart rates were through the roof, pounding against the sides of his forearm.

"Bring your thighs in, Brie." Harper grunted as she followed instruction and sealed herself to his sides. "Feel every inch of Harper buried in your pussy. He's desperate to come, to fill you up. Do you want him to fill you?"

"Please. Please."

He stilled his own thrusts and smiled at Harper with a small nod. Taking her harder from beneath, Elijah braced her for the force of his thrusts. "Watch his face. Tell him, Brie. You can give him permission."

"I want to feel you. I want your come. Please, Harper. Let me have it. Let me please you."

"Gabriella..." Upper body rising from the chair, jaw clenched, he gasped as he let go after hours of holding back. Pressing her hips to him, he groaned as he gave her everything.

Harper was a beautiful man.

He was even more so in the grip of passion.

Jerking against the chair, he held her to him, trying to breathe as pleasure stole the ability and her body milked him dry. Slowly recovering, nostrils flaring, he moved enough to cup her face and kiss her aggressively.

Raking her damp hair away from her face, Harper murmured, "Rest here. Hold on, Gabriella. You're strong. One more."

Laying back, he scooted his body lower to give Elijah better access to her. "I can feel how he throbs in your ass. He wants to coat you, fill you up."

Weakly, she replied, "Let's enjoy him fucking me together."

Hugging her hard, Harper stared at him. Feet flat on the floor, Elijah placed his palm in the center of Brie's back, stroking her gently. She glistened with sweat, panting with her lips slightly open as she held back until he gave her permission.

Pulling back, he thrust forward until his pelvis met the cheeks of her ass. Gradually, he raised the tempo until she was shaking, mumbling, and trying to hold on, hold back.

Every stroke was as deep as he could get in her ass. Hot and tight around his cock, his balls pressed against Harper's with each push. She was so tight with tension and he forced himself past natural resistance.

"Tell me how you feel, Brie."

"Loved. Safe."

The words sank deep, clawed their way into his soul, and he dropped his head back on his shoulders. Inhaling deep, he bent over her body and nuzzled against her ear.

"I want to feel you take your pleasure, to feel you fall apart for me, so

I can pump my come into your stunning ass. Come for me, Brie. Come for me."

The feel of her removing control over her muscles fascinated him. He watched her inhale slowly as she allowed herself to feel the effects of their attention.

Then she screamed his name and he drove hard into flesh that tightened like a vise. His climax crawled through his thighs, his ass, his low back, and around to his groin as he gave her every scalding drop. Thrusting, thrusting, thrusting.

Brie passed out cold.

When he trusted himself to move, he carefully pulled from her body, lifted her from Harper, and carried her to the bed.

Quietly, they worked together to clean her of their combined fluids and covered her in satin as they straightened the room and walked to the shower.

In the enclosed space, Elijah slammed Harper against the tile and claimed his mouth with force.

Moving back slightly, he stared into eyes filled with renewed passion. "I won't push you. You'll know when you're ready."

"I throb for you."

"Eventually, you'll let me soothe you as Brie watches. She'll come harder than ever before, no aphrodisiac cream required."

Breathing rapidly, he whispered, "How do you know?"

"She loves me, loves you, and desires us both. Her reaction when we touch each other is open and honest. I trust her."

"I'm…not there yet."

"When you are, I'll destroy you with pleasure." He smiled tightly at the thought, a spasm in his balls. "I wonder if she'll touch herself while she watches us."

Harper rested his head against the tile and closed his eyes. "To have a woman who *accepted* us. I refused to hope for such a thing."

He ran his hands up Elijah's chest and opened his eyes. "Give me more time."

He nodded. "Wash. Rest a few hours. Then we take her downstairs for food and to prepare."

"She won't be pleased with me. She won't like being forced to interact publicly. Not here in Washington."

Grinning, Elijah replied, "She protects *you*, not herself. Going public with her is different and you know that."

He nodded. "Let's show her why it isn't necessary for her to protect me."

Stepping from the shower, they kissed again before drying and returning to a woman who slept soundly in the room they'd always called a sanctuary.

It had never felt more of one until she entered it.

Chapter Thirty-Five

Blinking against the fading light of the room, Brie took stock of her surroundings, her body, and the men on either side of her in bed.

She felt incredible.

Sitting up, she raked her hands through her hair and pronounced herself gross. Careful not to wake them, she went to use the bathroom and shower.

Without company, she took her time scrubbing her skin and deep conditioning her hair. They'd made sure to include her favorite products.

In the main space, she wrapped a towel around her body and took her time detangling and drying her hair.

By the time she returned to the sanctuary, she felt sparkling inside and out. Both men were gone.

In the living space, the men met her at the door. They were fully dressed in slacks and dress shirts.

Harper took her towel and wrapped her in another silk robe. As he tied it snugly around her waist, he bent to kiss her.

"You have clothes downstairs. We'll move some here." His palm stroked inside the robe, over the skin of her side, and added, "Or not."

"I can paint naked." Silver eyes flared. "Kiss me stupid again. I like when you do that."

Grinning, he gripped the hair at the base of her neck and pulled her up on her toes to claim her mouth. Curling her fingers around his forearms, she took him deeper into herself.

Elijah slipped powerful arms around her midsection and bent to kiss his way up her neck as Harper lightly bit her lower lip.

"How are you, Brie?"

Leaning back against him, she said honestly, "Better at this second than any other in my entire life."

Lifting her face up and back, Elijah ate at her mouth. "We have to take you downstairs. First, you need to eat. We ordered real food."

They sat at the tiny table and enjoyed fresh tuna steaks, vegetables, and fruit salad. Receiving a glass of one of *her* wines made her smile.

When they were done, they moved closer, watching her eat. She sighed in happiness and consumed every bite.

"We're going to have to figure out this food thing. I need fuel to keep up with the two of you."

"You're a machine, Gabriella. No one else received more than a few hours of our time and far less of our sexual attention." Laughing, Harper added, "You remain fresh and lovely."

"Do what you love, love what you do," she quipped. It made them laugh. Leaning her elbow on the table, she rested her chin in her hand. "Does it bother you that I represent many firsts for both of you with women?"

Harper tilted his head. "You represent *every* first aside from actual marriage." Her eyes widened. "I didn't like Danielle. It's something I'm not proud to admit. I didn't eat with her, sleep with her, fuck her more than what I deemed necessary, and I wasn't faithful."

"Did she know?"

"Possibly. I was cold to her, Gabriella. The moment her pregnancy was confirmed, I put her out of my mind and went about my life. Looking back, the isolation and lack of care made things so much worse. I drove her to kill herself."

"Every person makes their own choices, Harper. She could've left you. She could've called a friend. She allowed it to go on, just as you did. She chose to ignore it, to sacrifice happiness for a standard of living."

Reaching out, she held his hand. "You may have been cold and unfaithful to her but you didn't shove her over that railing. It wasn't your fault. In the end, it was the culmination of bad choices, chemical imbalance, and simple sadness that did it."

He stared at her for a long moment and tugged her closer. "Thank you."

She kissed him, smoothing her hand along his face.

They cleaned up and Elijah took her hand, leading the way from his space to the third floor.

Harper opened the door to a room at the end of the hall. "I meant to show you this room yesterday." Glancing over his shoulder, he grinned. "You distracted us."

"Amen," she said deadpan.

He laughed and told her, "This was Elijah's room until he graduated high school."

"I *love* that you put me in here."

"No one else has used it. The staff knows it remains closed."

Blinking rapidly, she whispered, "No one has slept here since Elijah slept here?" He shook his head and she hugged him tightly. "That means so much to me. Thanks."

Walking with her to the closet, her eyes widened. "You'll find everything you need in here. Riya and Natalia ordered what they thought you'd need and instructed we not judge your need for leggings and t-shirts while you paint." She snickered softly.

Clearing his throat, he added, "We laid out what you need for tonight. Natalia had the gown designed to your measurements. A woman will be here to do your hair and makeup in half an hour. She'll help you dress as well."

In the closet, spread across a circular bench, was a gorgeous silver ball gown shot through with deep blue threads.

"Harper…"

He turned to her, his hand along her neck. "What did you say to me, Gabriella? *Fuck all that shit. Let's do what we want.*" His fingers tightened. "Did you mean that?" She nodded. "Then get dressed and show me how brave you are."

Kissing her roughly, he left the room.

Staring at the floor, she took several deep breaths. She felt panicked.

Elijah hugged her from behind. "You've got this." She nodded. "Tell me why you're afraid."

"You know why." Turning in his arms, she hugged him tightly. "Let's not talk about it."

He cupped her face, kissed her slow, and waited for her to ease. The moment she relaxed, he lifted her into his arms. She wrapped around him and rested her head on his shoulder.

"I love you, Elijah."

"I love *you*, Brie."

Lifting her face, she stared into his eyes. Dragging her fingers through his hair, she massaged his neck and shoulders.

"I-I need, will you to stay with me for a few minutes?"

Walking into the bedroom, he sat down in a comfortable chair near the window and held her close. She hugged him as hard as she could.

"Brie." She sat up to look at him. "I'll play for you tonight."

It was impossible to stop the tears that welled in her eyes. All she could do was nod and grip him in desperation. "That would mean so much to me, Elijah."

He held her, stroked her back, and finally, she found stability. She asked herself the worst that could happen by attending a gala. Taking a deep breath, she kissed him until he moaned in her mouth and started to slide his hands beneath the robe.

"We don't have time." Leaning back with a smile, she tugged her lower lip between her teeth. "*Unless…*"

"Nice try." Standing, he set her on her feet. "Get dressed. Take your time and let me know when you're ready."

She nodded and he left her with a wink.

Dressing quickly in the outfit they'd chosen for her, she smiled at the lovely underthings and hissed at the delicate flats. The gown draped to the floor, hugging her curves, and crossing her back while leaving most of it bare. If she knew where her cell phone was, she'd text Natalia a "woot" and a photo.

Answering a knock on the door, she opened it to a lovely older woman carrying a stylist's kit.

"Aren't you *pretty*?" she exclaimed and sauntered in.

She arranged Brie's hair in a waterfall style that flowed down her back. Dramatic eyes and a light gloss on her lips was all she said was needed.

Thanking her, she took in her appearance before walking to the window. She crossed her arms and inhaled deeply. Then her eyes registered that across the manicured lawn, there was a mausoleum featuring stunning scrollwork and *gargoyles*.

Grabbing her sketchbook, she took the stairs and searched for a door to the side of the house. Approaching the courtyard in front of the stone structure, she smiled at a marble podium that provided the ideal surface at the right height.

Brie took her time outlining the primary columns and statuary. She was filling in the central details when movement in her peripheral vision startled her.

Several men took up positions around her, standing at attention. Still holding her charcoal, she turned to see Elijah crossing the grass in her direction. He didn't look pleased.

"Brie."

"Hi. Um, I shouldn't wander off?"

Raking his eyes over her from head to toe, he said, "You look stunning." She watched as he inhaled carefully. "How would you feel about being fitted with a tracking device?"

It felt like her smile took over her entire face. "If you *really* think it'll help."

He glanced past her at her book. "That's amazing." Going to attention, he bowed slightly and extended his arm. "Miss Hernandez, the party started twenty minutes ago. Shall we?"

Grabbing her book, she slid her hand along his forearm. "Sorry. I didn't mean to lose track of time."

"We thought you were still getting ready."

The idea that she'd take longer than half an hour to fully prepare for *any* occasion made her laugh. When she explained to Elijah, he shook his head.

"We're in *such* unfamiliar territory with you."

She nodded with a sigh. "I know."

Just inside the door she'd used to exit the house, Harper waited. He held out his hand and she placed the sketchbook in it with a sheepish grin.

Taking her in, he winked, "Absolutely worth the wait. You look even better in that dress than I imagined."

Elijah kissed her hand with another bow and placed it on Harper's arm. As they passed Harper's office, they set her book on his desk. She hated to leave it but didn't tell them.

Instead of returning immediately to the hall, the darker man removed a box from one of the drawers.

"Before you throw a fit about this, I want you to know I asked Riya to help me select a simple set she thought you'd be willing to accept without kicking me in the dick." He grinned. "We opted for custom, designed and created by arthritic natives."

It was impossible to contain her snort of laughter.

"Now, I wanted to use gold and she insisted on silver. I tried to counter for platinum and she rolled her eyes and told me Mexico creates some of the most stunning sterling in the world and to stop being a pretentious douche."

Brie laughed so hard she thought she'd pass out.

"I tell you all of this so that you understand this wasn't bought in bulk, stored in stacks in my safe, to be used in payment of services. It's important that you know this was made for *you*. One of a kind like the woman you are."

Opening the box, he held it out to her and Brie took in the intricate feathers in varying lengths that formed a triangle of aged silver. There were matching earrings with a single delicate feather that would almost touch the top of her shoulders.

"Harper. They're *beautiful*." Blinking back tears, she added, "Thank you for thinking of me." She hugged him tightly.

He hugged her back carefully at first and Elijah took the box so he could return it with both arms.

"You're welcome, Gabriella." Tilting her face up with the side of his hand, he murmured, "Only my mother was ever touched by gifts." His smile was gentle. "I'd forgotten how it felt to give them to such a person. Thank you for reminding me."

"An even better gift is how relaxed you look." She trailed her finger over his forehead. "I love that one most."

They pressed into her from the front and back. "If there weren't sixty guests in my house, you'd already be naked."

Hopefully, she suggested, "I could strip down and wait here. You could pop by for intermissions and refreshments."

Nose to nose, he said, "Not happening, Gabriella."

"After the party, Brie." Elijah stroked his hands over her through her gown.

Sighing, she nodded. "Alright. Let's get this over with so I can have more naked time in the bat cave. Hustle."

Laughing, Harper clasped the necklace and they watched as she put the earrings in. Whispering about the things they'd do to her later, they led her through the house.

Chapter Thirty-Six

Dozens of guests milled in the ballroom when the three of them entered and many didn't bother to hide their shock.

There were several faces Brie recognized and could well imagine what they thought about seeing someone like *her* walk into a Delkin party with Harper and Elijah.

She remembered the first time she'd danced at Riya's Christmas party, how her friends had made her feel welcome and showed her she belonged. Channeling that memory, she decided she'd wallow in every wonderful moment for as long as she had them. She lifted her chin.

Fuck what these elitist assholes thought about her.

"Excellent," Elijah murmured.

She circulated as she'd been taught, made small talk she'd learned from Isabella, and smiled no matter the expressions of the people she spoke to or their impertinent questions.

An hour into it, her head started to pound. Harper told her quietly, "You're so tense, Gabriella."

"Not gonna lie. I'd rather be alone with the two of you."

A voice behind her said loudly, "Little mouse…?"

Fuck me running.

Turning, Brie met the shocked gazes of her *parents*. Plastering a smile on her face, she said, "Mom. Dad. Hello."

"You are in Washington. How long have you *been* here, Gabriella? When did you plan to see your family?"

The look on her mother's face promised a battle royal if the answer provided wasn't what she wanted to hear.

"Gabriella flew in a few hours ago," Harper interjected smoothly. "It was intended to be a surprise but I wasn't informed you'd arrived." Leaning, he kissed her mother's hand and shook her father's.

Frowning, Cabral said, "You came *here* first?"

"I've been commissioned to paint the estate. I agreed to meet with Harper before he leaves on business."

"Harper…? I was unaware you were acquainted."

Fuck. A social misstep.

"We became friends throughout the wedding preparations for Hudson and Natalia. He liked the painting of the building I did for Winters Enterprises."

"Ah, yes. I heard Harper was the best man. We couldn't get away to attend. I was sad to miss it." There was a slight pause. "I like *that* Hudson far better than the *other* one."

Brie stiffened with a small gasp but her mother didn't notice. In Spanish, she began to rant. "That was *quite* the mess. I still don't understand why you…"

"Mom." Their eyes met. Also in Spanish, she told her, "I'd rather not discuss this. Now is not the time."

"I'm sorry. It still makes me angry, Gabriella."

"It makes me feel *many* things. English." Her heart rate continued to rise. Thankfully, her mother changed topics.

"Isabella said the painting you did was good, Gabriella. I had no idea you still enjoyed your little hobby. You should paint the winery."

Touching her temple to relieve the pain there, she reminded herself *where* she was and *who* she was. "I've painted it, Mom. Many times."

"You have?" Brie nodded as the pressure built. "You always drew pretty flowers for your grandmother. I didn't know you painted other things."

"Yes. I dabble. It's still just a hobby." Inhaling carefully, she kissed their cheeks and hugged them tightly. "I'll see you later this week. I need to get photos of the estate while the weather is good."

Cabral smiled. "Hmm. You'll go to the winery next. I know how you are. They miss you, little mouse."

"I know, Dad." Swallowing hard, she smiled. "I see one of the clients for the winery and I need to say hello."

They hugged her again. "Of course. You can give us your annual report when you come to the house. I like how the numbers get bigger every year."

Mechanically, Brie replied, "They've grown again. You'll be pleased. I love you." In general, she said, "Excuse me."

Making her way out of the ballroom, she didn't know where to go. She was unsure what part of the house she was in and was grateful to find a small seating area along a deserted hall.

Lowering to it carefully, she caught her breath after one of the most awkward conversations of her life. She wasn't surprised when Harper and Elijah sat on either side of her.

"Your parents hurt your feelings. Regularly, it would seem. I'm sorry, Gabriella."

"They aren't emotional like me. They don't realize they do it." She met Harper's eyes. "I'm sure your parents had many expectations for you, Harper. You met and exceeded all of them." She shook her head. "In a family of hyper-organized and ambitious people, I'm a *continual* disappointment."

"They don't know how important your art is to you?" Elijah's voice was quiet.

"When I was seven, my grandmother wrote a cookbook. She asked me to illustrate the foods. A year later, she wanted me to help her catalog our family tree and fill it with sketched flowers that were native to her village. Always, to my parents, it was a hobby, a *silly thing* I did."

"Why did you get a master's in marketing?"

"It's a *real* job. They wore me down through high school and I let them because I was tired." Inhaling deeply, she explained, "When I was instructed to choose a corporation to assume, I was offered construction, real estate, restaurants, and hotels."

She twisted her fingers together. "I chose the winery because I thought if I had to have a job they approved of, I wanted to be close to beauty, to things that grow, so it would ease the agony of it." She met Harper's eyes.

"I built it bigger than they ever dreamed, nurtured strong relationships with staff and clients, and established the brand across the United States. Since I was sixteen, I've worked on or in the winery every day other than the time I was in the hospital. It comes easily *to* me but it isn't easy *for* me."

Turning to Elijah, she whispered, "I feel like a spoiled bitch complaining when, I'm sorry."

He held the side of her neck and said, "Pain is delivered in many ways, Brie. That yours was *different* doesn't mean it hurt you *less*. You're neither spoiled nor a bitch."

Harper stood and lifted her to her feet. "You won't hide. You can't hide, Gabriella." He stroked his finger along her temple to her chin and raised her face. "Eyes up. Give no fucks."

He dropped a kiss on her lips and Elijah did the same. He stared into her eyes and said in excellent Spanish, "You're a magnificent woman whose past does *not* define you."

Blinking back tears, she nodded.

As they escorted her back to the party, Harper said quietly, "As for your art, it isn't a fucking *hobby*. It's your goddamn *calling* and should be treated as such."

Local business owners didn't hide their surprise that she was in public. Several times over the course of the evening, she fielded questions about the *diet* that finally helped her lose weight, had she received *therapy* for her introversion, and was she still *working* at the winery for her parents.

Harper was abrupt and protective, bordering on acidic. It startled more than one of his guests when he came to her defense in ways that would've made Hudson proud.

A woman with whom her parents had done multiple real estate deals snidely remarked, "I heard a little rumor that you left Washington for a *man*. I didn't believe it, of course. You were such a chubby little thing. Whatever cosmetic surgery you received seems to have done the trick." She chuckled. "I thought perhaps you'd gone off to hide an unwanted pregnancy."

Stunned, Brie found herself speechless, frozen in mortification.

Stepping close enough so that no one beyond them could hear, Harper said coldly, "Your lack of class tells me your success to date is due to luck. One more word and there will be a sharp reversal."

He added with a smug smile, "Gabriella didn't *leave* Washington for *a* man. She *visits* Washington for *two*." The woman's eyes went wide. "Get *out* of my *house*."

Elijah stood close enough that she could feel his body heat on the bare skin of her back.

A glass of champagne appeared in her hand and Harper said quietly, "Drink this, Gabriella. You're shaking."

Blinking against tears of embarrassment and fury, she focused on Harper's tie. Allowing herself to zone out, she meditated long enough to slow her heart rate and calm her nerves.

Meeting his eyes, she whispered, "I told you. I've *never* fit in your sphere, Harper."

He took her empty glass and handed it to a passing server. "And yet, here you are. Beautiful, successful, talented, and the sexual focus of two men who have allowed you closer than any other." Lowering his head, he added, "These functions are necessary and you know that. Trust Elijah to guard your back. Trust me to guard your delectable front."

Unable to resist, she gave a trembling laugh.

"Now, we circulate. I'll piss people off as you wow the men, and more than a few women, with that dress. Elijah will glare them into silence. A good time had by all."

They were several hours into the party when Marciella Canfield entered with the Ghonim cousins to the shock of several guests. All three were known to be practically reclusive outside the charity circuit.

Making a beeline for their threesome, the cousins shook Harper's hand and nodded imperceptibly to Elijah.

Marci hugged Brie tightly. "It's so good to see you fully mobile. You look *damn* good, Brie."

"Thank you. So do you. Your shoes make me want to cry with envy." She wore a pale gray sheath and truly fabulous heels. Her strawberry blonde hair was perfectly coiffed in an up-do. "I'm also giddy to see a familiar face."

"Let me guess, the catty bitch socialites giving you shit?" One brow lifted. "I love to scare them."

"You're so lovely and sweet. I can't *imagine* you scary."

Harper gave a small bark of laughter. "You haven't been in negotiations with her. She's downright terrifying."

"No," Brie breathed. "I don't *believe* it."

Marci nodded seriously. "In business, I'm a stone-cold bitch and I never, *ever* apologize. I have Hudson to thank for honing my natural skill." Leaning closer, she whispered, "Harper liked me before I started giving him fits and referring to him as *Delkin* in talks."

Hand on her hip, Brie giggled. "I've got a vision of Harper in his office, shaking his fist and growling *Winters*." Elijah stifled a laugh behind her but Marci didn't hold back. "I might have to create a graphic novel now. Hudson would love it for his birthday." She winked. "I can do one for each of them with the roles reversed."

"You're definitely an original. You get into graphic novels and all of us are ordering our own."

The cousins stepped forward and bent as one to kiss Brie's cheeks. Each took a hand and bowed slightly. She loved the way their black eyes sparkled with happiness.

Fahad told her, "Your gift was spectacular, Gabriella."

"I'm so glad you liked it."

Nuri laughed. "You captured the night we found our Marci again. I don't believe *like* is the appropriate word."

She grinned.

Fahad turned serious. "How would you feel about spending a few days at a small winery we own in Southern California? We purchased it and hired highly recommended managers who can't seem to figure out why it turns no profit."

Accepting a glass of champagne, Brie asked, "Are they riding the fields? You wouldn't believe how much waste I found in the fields and processing divisions when I took over."

The cousins shared a look. Nuri frowned. "You ride the vineyard on horseback?" She nodded. "Does your security detail also ride?"

She was confused. "For the most part, I've always ridden alone." Brie watched the cousins glance at Harper and realized their concern. "My first job was picking grapes but I've worked every position. I'm safe there."

Sipping her wine, she changed the subject. "You've got such a diverse collection of businesses. I only have one but I know everything about it so I'd be happy to tour your facility and tell you what I see."

"Allow us to compensate you for your time."

"Absolutely *not*. I'm glad to do it. I'll send you a report." She grinned. "Don't worry, I won't ruffle any feathers."

That made Marci laugh. "As if you would. You bring out the soft little kitten in everyone. Sashay in there, smile, and they'll have no secrets." Arm around Brie's waist, she tugged her away. "Let the boys talk because I'm *done* with business for today."

A dozen feet away, her friend took her hand. "You're glowing. I promised Hudson and Natalia I'd report back."

"They're on their *honeymoon*," Brie moaned.

"I know but they have to eat sometimes. Not every meal can be consumed *on* the human body." Brie struggled to contain her laughter. "I got the call today at brunch." She rolled her eyes. "For god's sake, *eat*."

"They're going to come back sleep deprived and malnourished. Tell them not to worry."

"Gabriella." Her mother's voice behind her startled her badly. "An introduction please."

No breaks. Not a single break on this night from hell.

Carefully, she made formal introductions and Marci wrapped her arm around Brie's waist as she shook her parents' hands.

"How lovely to meet Brie's mother and father. I'm honored." She hugged her closer. "She absolutely *saved me* earlier this year with her redesign of my company graphics."

Her mother blinked and a small frown appeared between her eyes. "Gabriella did this?"

With wide eyes, Marci gasped, "Her insight on our web design increased consumer interaction by more than sixty percent. You must be incredibly proud."

Turning, she smiled as her men approached. "Do you know Fahad and Nuri Ghonim?"

Marci made introductions and Brie thought her mother was going to pass the hell out from the opportunity.

"They bought a small winery in California to save a brand they love but it flounders. We usually book Brie months in advance but she's agreed to take a look at the facility for them. The way her mind works is so refreshing."

Cabral smiled. "Our little mouse *knows* wine. When she was small, she was always covered in juice from the grapes." He reached out to tap the tip of her nose. "She has the best sense of smell I have ever seen."

"Her mind is sharp as a blade but we forget the gentleness of her heart." The compliment from her mother literally *stunned* her. Smiling at Marci, she said, "She did *not* get such a heart from her parents. My mother, I think."

"We're leaving, Gabriella." She looked at her father. "Are you cleared to ride?"

"I'm sure I'll have to work my way back to hours in the saddle but yes. I can't wait to ride again."

"Excellent. We will go together." He kissed her cheek. In Spanish, he told her, "You hide your bright light under dark bushes. Stop that, yes?"

She nodded with a small laugh. "I'll call you in a few days."

Moments later, her parents were gone and Brie looked at Marci. "How did you know?"

"Your mother reminds me of mine without the sociopathic genes. Such driven women rarely see past the layer of sweet to what's really going on."

"Thank you, Marci." She quirked her brow. "You realize my mother is going to blow your shit up now, right?"

She winked. "She's an astute businesswoman who has access to several opportunities I've been scoping out this way. I'd have met her eventually and now she'll be nicer to you. I love to win."

The rest of the evening passed quickly and Brie hugged the threesome in sincere gratitude when they prepared to leave.

At two in the morning, she looked at Harper and Elijah. "I'm out. Whenever you're done, I'll be painting. I love you. Thank you for an odd but also lovely evening."

Smiling, she turned to leave but Harper caught her hand, bent, and kissed the corner of her mouth.

She stared into his eyes. "You…can't do that, Harper," she said in a whisper.

"On the contrary. We'll see you soon, Gabriella. You've been a pleasure." He kissed her hand and winked. "I'm proud of how you handled these assholes."

Nodding numbly, she made her way to the third floor where she undressed and searched the insane amount of clothing until she found leggings and a t-shirt.

Leaving the gown laid out on the circular bench, she placed the jewelry on the table by the bed and went to her temporary studio.

Her mind was on fire with stimulus and she needed to subdue the flames. She exhaled slowly and dropped into the canvas.

Unknowing how much time passed, she was surprised when she turned and saw Elijah sitting on the sofa across the room. He wore nothing but sleep pants. Harper was stretched out, dressed similarly, with his head in Elijah's lap.

"You're a stunning creature to watch, Brie."

Quickly cleaning her brushes and paints, she washed her hands and walked to them. Bending, she kissed Elijah and then Harper, stroking her hands over his shoulders to wake him gently. Confused at first, his face spread into a smile.

It would break her when she had to leave.

Chapter Thirty-Seven

For three blissful days, Elijah and Harper crawled over her body and allowed her to crawl over theirs.

They carried her small easel to the sanctuary so she could sketch them. She instructed them to get comfortable in a position they could hold and made a couple of adjustments.

"Normally, I take a photograph or sketch really fast but I won't photograph you and I want to take my time." Sighing, she stepped back and took them in. "So lovely."

While they posed for her, she talked to them about anything and everything. They made her laugh and she did the same.

After almost two hours, she said, "This one is specifically for you. I'll *never* sketch you like this outside your protected sanctuary. You have my word. I really, really wanted to bring it to life though." Pausing, she smiled and gave a small nod. "I'll fill it out and add some color. The finished product will take me a couple of days. You can look."

Standing, they walked to her and stood at her back as they took in the charcoal drawing she'd done of them.

Elijah leaned against the dark wood headboard with his arm around Harper who reclined against his shoulder. Shirtless, their naked lower bodies concealed by artfully placed linen, they stared from the sketch intently.

While they watched, she filled in a few more details and shading. To herself, she murmured, "I like the rawness of the charcoal. Hmm, I'll have to decide."

Leaning close, she darkened Harper's hair and brows. "I don't know that it *needs* color." Across the canvas, she used the edge of her finger to blur and smooth lines.

Taking a step back, she took it in from several angles, added a couple of lines, and smiled.

"What are your thoughts?" When they didn't answer, she glanced at them. Their eyes were locked on the sketch.

"Sign it, Gabriella."

"What?"

"Sign it. I want your name on it."

"Brie. Sign it."

"Okay." Bending, she signed her first name to the bottom. "Does that mean you like…?"

The rest of her question was lost as they all but pounced on her. They didn't even seem to notice her hands were covered in charcoal.

* * *

On her fourth dawn in Washington, Brie was awakened to their hands and mouths on her body.

They wrung pleasure from her for a solid hour and when she was limp from it, Harper told her, "We have to leave, Gabriella. We fly out in an hour."

Nodding, not trusting herself to speak, she kissed them deeply and hugged them as hard as she could.

Taking a few minutes to breathe and wrap a robe around her body, she finally managed, "Be safe. I'll be around."

A short while later, they came to say goodbye dressed in the suits she'd been most familiar with before joining them in Washington. She took her time kissing them and then hugged them tight.

"I'll miss you and I love you."

Then they were gone and she soaked for a long time, thinking. She didn't know where they were going or when they'd return. Brie wasn't about to spend the time moping.

She had plenty of shit to keep her ass busy.

* * *

The first week they were gone, Brie completed every single pending project for her various clients.

She delayed her visit to the winery but held several virtual meetings with her staff and management team to make sure they understood they were still a priority to her.

Two small paintings she wanted to gift Hudson and Natalia were done, curing in the studio. It would be months before they were cured enough for framing. She hoped Harper wouldn't mind her leaving them. She'd done several smaller ones as well for her other friends, her parents, and the men who took up so much space in her thoughts.

When she realized their absence was likely to be one of the long ones, she decided to start her gift for Harper.

Dressing in jeans, a t-shirt, and trail runners, Brie pulled her hair into a bun and went to the first floor with her art bag.

Harper's assistant greeted her warmly in the small office she used across the hall from her boss. "How may I help you, Miss Hernandez?"

"Phyllis, you're gonna *have* to call me Brie. I'm going to bother you about the most ridiculous stuff so less syllables."

Laughing, the older woman said, "Alright, Brie. What can I help you with?"

"I could really use a camera with a decent memory. I need to take photos of the house and mausoleum, the gardens, and the stables I glimpsed. I'll need them for reference when I start the canvas."

"Absolutely. I know we have one. Give me just a minute." Brie sat on her little sofa and gazed at a pretty sphere with color patterns inside it. "Here you go."

"You're damn fast. Okay, not sure if I'm supposed to tell someone but I'm going to start from the furthest point in each direction and work my way back. It's clear and pretty today."

Smiling slowly, Phyllis replied, "I appreciate that. Harper threatened *head rolling* if we lost you on the grounds."

"You can tell him I responded with *eye rolling* since I'm a grownup. I'll pop back in later." She turned to go and the woman saying her name made her turn back.

"The kitchen made lunch for you. They'll pack it up so you can work and eat."

Snickering, Brie nodded. "Those guys don't think about food. Like, ever. You're awesome."

With a wave, she stopped by the kitchen for a fantastic care package. Then she took a hike to discover what the Delkin estate had to offer as far as inspiration. Several men shadowed her at all times. She engaged them in conversation if possible but they took *stern* to a whole new level.

The first day, she took more than two hundred photos and emailed those she needed to Phyllis to print. Positioning a huge canvas, she clipped the photos along one side.

Elijah called just after dark and she was giddy as she answered the phone. Collapsing on the sofa in her studio, she asked about his day and he asked about hers. Harper provided commentary in the background that made her laugh.

"I'll call you tomorrow, Brie."

"I miss you guys. Remember that someone who loves you would like you back in one piece. Please and thank you."

"I love you, too."

The following day, she hiked in the opposite direction, clicking away. Her phone calls from New York were ridiculous. Wearing headphones with her phone in her back pocket, she caught up with Riya while she was consistently distracted.

Finally giving up, her friend laughingly shouted, "Call me when you break, squirrel!"

"Will do. Sorry, Riya!" She'd taken several photos during the call and wondered at an image in them. "Hey guys, where are we?"

Jim was the man in charge of her personal detail and stepped forward. "East side, a mile from the main house and three-quarters from the entrance, ma'am."

Hand on her hip, she grinned. "You give me *way* too much credit. I meant are we close to working parts of the estate? Like stables and stuff?"

He nodded. "Yes, ma'am. We're less than a quarter of a mile from the security barracks."

A chill crawled up her back. "Okay." She turned the camera and showed him the image. "Is that part of it?"

Jim frowned. "No, ma'am. If I recall, that's the original cold storage. Where they used to cure meat when the estate was built by the first Delkin to settle here."

"Thank you," she said softly. "I'm going to get some photos."

"Yes, ma'am."

The security team followed as she took an overgrown trail to the wooden structure. There were no windows and the door hung at an angle. There was an old padlock on it.

Twenty feet away, her entire body was cold. Her arms and legs felt like lead. Walking closer, she picked up a rock and paused for a moment.

Then she busted the lock and swung the door wide.

"Ma'am. You shouldn't explore it. The structural safety of that building is unknown."

"I'm going in, Jim. I'll be fine and please wait here." When he started to follow her, she added more forcefully, "I insist."

Then she shoved the panel wide, lit the flashlight on her phone, and stepped across the threshold.

It took thirty seconds to confirm her suspicions.

She'd stumbled on the scene of Elijah's childhood torture. What was horrifically referred to as his *training*.

Up one panel on the inside of the door was a record of his growth. The first entry was when he was two years old. The last was when he would've been about seventeen.

She trailed her fingers over the heights carved into the wood and cried silently. Further inspection of the room made it clear that he'd been chained to the wall, the ceiling, the floor, as well as a heavy rack once used to cure animal hides.

On a table that stretched down one wall were horse whips, chains, and canes. Several switches still had thorns on them.

At the small fireplace, she knelt and felt fury unlike *anything* she'd ever known. The upper scroll and tuning pegs of a violin were all that remained of an instrument that had been incinerated deliberately. Also among the ash were pages of books and corners of photos.

Running her light over the ceiling, she found what she hoped for and yelled for Jim. He was through the door in under two seconds.

"I need all of those please."

Frowning, he raised his arm and took down several lanterns that hung from a center beam.

"Thank you for your help. I'll be right out. Please call down to the security barracks and ask them to bring fire containment gear immediately."

"I'm sorry, ma'am. What did you say?"

"This shack is getting burned to the ground in the next two minutes. We *will not* put out the fire until all that's left are the stones from the chimney. Understand that it's *going* to burn. Make arrangements so it doesn't spread, please. Thank you."

Then she proceeded to upend each of the lanterns that still contained kerosene in the tanks.

Jim scrambled to the door, talking urgently on his radio.

The wood was old and it didn't look like anyone had been inside the building in a long time. It was dry and it was going to go up quickly.

She hoped the man who used it to torture a little boy had gotten what he deserved. Either way, she wasn't leaving the goddamn building standing where he'd whipped Elijah bloody for *years*.

Fuck that shit.

When every lantern was empty, she walked to the exit and opened her art bag. From one of the pockets, she removed a box of matches she always carried to soften her pencils.

Without turning around, she called, "Jim, tell me safety measures are in place."

"Yes, ma'am. Are you…"

Then she lit a match and flicked it inside. Backing slowly from the vicinity, she watched as the building was engulfed in less than a minute.

Absolutely livid, she put both her middle fingers up at it and murmured, "You didn't *win*, motherfucker. I hope you're rotting in hell."

The flames were so hot that it blew like a breeze in her direction but she refused to move until it was leveled.

Only then did she give the signal that the team could check for stray embers.

"Do you have a bobcat on this property?" Jim nodded, clearly in shock at her actions. "Every fucking piece needs to be removed. Every stone, every stick. *Today.* I mean it. I'll help. All of it needs to be put in a truck and hauled *off* this property. I'll pay whatever it takes to make it happen." She ground out, "Are we clear, Jim? *Off the goddamn property.* Every *scrap*."

"Y-yes, ma'am."

When there was no movement beside her, she looked at the poor man who probably thought she was out of her fucking mind. "Now. Right *now*, Jim. Make this shit *happen*. Get me gloves and let's get to work."

Several hours later, the sun was setting when one of the security team insisted on driving her back to the estate in the Kubota. She was approaching the front of the main house when a limousine barreled down the drive at top speed.

The man driving her pulled a huge gun from beneath the seat and barked, "Get down!"

Skidding to a halt, the headlights flashed in a signal and her assigned protection lowered the weapon.

Then Elijah and Harper stepped out of the interior and stormed in her direction.

Brie climbed out and set her feet, ready to rage like a fucking *lunatic*. Elijah grabbed her roughly and claimed her mouth until she felt faint.

All the fight went right out of her.

Chapter Thirty-Eight

Without speaking a word, Elijah carried Brie through the house to his space on the top floor. Harper followed with an expression on his face she couldn't translate.

In the bathroom, they stripped her down roughly. Then they each held her tightly while the other pulled away suits that were probably ruined from the soot and mud she'd been covered in.

Under the water, they used soft cloths to wipe the skin of her face. It was tender to the touch. Scrubbing her head to toe, they washed themselves fast and tensely.

They dried her carefully and applied lotion over every inch of her body. Another cream was applied to her face. Together, they dried her hair. In the mirror, she noticed her face seemed a little red.

Taking her hand, Elijah pulled her quickly to the sanctuary.

She was a little nervous that they hadn't said anything in the thirty minutes since getting out of the limo.

Expecting to be strung up and interrogated, she was shocked when Elijah followed her down to the bed and drove his cock deep in a single stroke.

He took her hard and fast, never taking his eyes off hers. The first climax happened embarrassingly quick but she didn't care because she'd missed them touching her.

Planting himself as far inside her as he could get, he stilled and stroked her hair away from her face as it turned her loose.

She was afraid to speak because she was angry, hurt for him, and horrified that the scene of his torture hadn't been obliterated from the face of the planet.

Then she wept bitterly and hugged him as hard as she could.

Returning the hug with the strongest arms of anyone she knew, he let her cry out all her pain for him.

"You're strong and beautiful, Elijah." Her hand stroked the back of his head. "I'm sorry. I'm so sorry. You survived and I'm so goddamn happy you did. I hate what happened but I'm so relieved you're still here. I love you. I love you. I love you."

Lifting to look at her, he whispered, "I love *you*, Brie."

Her fingers traced his face. "H-how did you know? What was happening?"

"When you insisted on going into the building, Jim didn't want Elijah to kick his ass. They're equipped with cameras." Harper said quietly, "We were in the air when you lit it up."

Setting her jaw, she turned her head and ground out, "I'm not sorry I did it. I don't care if it was a fucking historical monument, Harper. I don't *care*. It was evil. It had to fucking go."

"I didn't know it was *there*, Gabriella." There was no way to hide her shock. "I've lived here all my life and didn't even know it existed until today. I realize now he kept me away from that side of the estate. I never wondered why." His eyes closed. "I'd have *never* left it there had I known." Reaching out, he held her face. "I'll *never* question your instincts again. You really *are* that perceptive."

Exhaling roughly, she kissed his palm. "I was *so* angry with you. I should've known better. I'm sorry."

"I understand." He leaned close and kissed her for a long time. "For a gentle woman, you certainly have a warrior's spirit, Gabriella. Thank you."

She nodded and pulled them both close, hugging them hard. "I missed you both so *much*."

Then they deconstructed her with pleasure.

* * *

Elijah watched her sleep, held tight to his body, knowing the nightmares that would haunt her. Several times before the sun tinted the room, she shook uncontrollably in her sleep.

Each time, he and Harper would press close and whisper to her, calm her, until she slept deeply again.

They were boarding the plane for home when Jim sent him a text that Brie was photographing the estate and all was well.

An hour later, he texted again when she discovered an abandoned building. Moments later, his text held a tinge of panic when Brie refused to remain outside the structure.

Instructing the man to go to live feed, every nerve in his body went tight when he glimpsed the woman he loved investigating a door frame he knew *well*, on one knee, clearly distraught. Instantly, he knew what else she'd discover.

He hated that she'd have it in her mind, that it would bruise her tender heart.

Harper moved to sit beside him when he was unresponsive. The silence drew out as he watched the feed on Elijah's phone.

"Elijah...? Is that on the fucking *estate*?" Unable to speak as he watched Jim take lanterns down from the ceiling, Elijah gave a single nod. "Gabriella. Oh god *no*."

Then she set the goddamn building that was haunted by the ghost of his childhood on fire and burned it to the fucking *ground*, standing close enough to ensure no one stopped it.

For two hours after it was incinerated, they watched as she barked orders, all sign of *sweet little Brie* crushed in her fury and sadness.

The chimney leveled, every piece of charred wood dumped in the back of a truck, and hauled off the land.

"Take it at least twenty fucking miles from here. Dump it and cover it the fuck over." Then she got quiet for a long moment. "He better be *dead*. He better be fucking *dead*."

Jim shadowed her, both of them filthy, while she paced.

Gentle Brie, a woman *everyone* knew had a heart softer and kinder than most, called Hudson Winters.

"Hudson. I have an unusual request." There was silence as she listened. "I need to know if someone is still alive." Another pause and she glanced at Jim before murmuring indistinctly. Then she hissed, "I can't *tell* you. Just know that if he is, he doesn't get to *keep* breathing!"

She went quiet for a long time and sat on a fallen log while Hudson worked to calm her, to find out why she was so upset.

From the messenger bag she carried everywhere, she removed all that was left of Elijah's first violin.

Holding it in her hand, crying, she begged, "Hudson. Please help me." She closed her eyes. "Yes, I can! I *can* live with it. At this moment, I'd slit his fucking throat myself. Okay."

She hung up and paced angrily.

Several minutes later, her phone rang. "Hudson." She listened. "You're *sure?*" With a hiss, she told him, "I hope he went fucking *screaming*." She nodded and rubbed her temples.

"Thank you, Hudson. Apologize to Natalia. Ignore all calls from me henceforth on your honeymoon." Exhaling, she laughed shakily, "They're wonderful. Mm hmm. Not telling. Not telling that *either*."

She tried to smile as she scrubbed at tears. "I'm okay now. Thank you. Love you guys."

Walking around the barren space where a building had once stood that instilled him with terror, Brie knelt and touched the rich soil exposed by fire and scouring with heavy equipment.

"New again. Grow quickly." Then she stood and stopped in front of Jim. "I realize I seem insane. Let's get the fuck out of here. I need a shower and several drinks."

His first sight of her when they left the limo was her entire body covered in dirt, her hair wild around her, and her face lightly burned from the heat exposure. Then she planted her feet, lifted her chin, and clenched her fists, ready to go to *war* over injustices done to him decades ago.

It made him harder than he'd ever been in his life.

Less than twelve hours later, they held her sleeping form between them, soothing her from nightmares her empathetic nature guaranteed she'd have.

* * *

Harper stared at Elijah as he drifted back to sleep when Gabriella settled. He'd been in almost every dream he'd ever had. Lately, another face appeared frequently when he closed his eyes. He pressed his face to her hair, inhaling deeply of oranges and goodness he'd never encountered.

He wanted to cry knowing the building that housed the horrors of Elijah's childhood had remained standing for two decades. On his land. A mile from the fucking home where he slept.

The fucking thing should've been destroyed when the man who used it to torture his son had his twisted heart stopped. He was ashamed it had gone undetected for so long.

He was goddamn grateful to Gabriella for burning it to the ground.

She was such a puzzle to a man like him. Soft and sweet, gentle in ways that soothed pain she didn't even know another person had. Smart and world savvy enough to capture the interest of people who weren't easily impressed. Loyal to the point of being willing to commit violence to keep the people she loved safe.

It was while she was ordering estate personnel that Harper understood how she'd grown the winery to such success. She wasn't rude, she didn't raise her voice, but there was no mistaking the authority she possessed.

Every man working with her while she destroyed the structure and had all traces of it taken off the estate listened to her, respected her, and moved quickly to follow her orders. Especially when she *helped* get it done.

Watching her command hardened fighting men and staff responsible for the grounds made him painfully hard.

When he'd seen her standing beside the Kubota, he knew without a doubt she'd go toe-to-toe with him if he *dared* to question what she'd done.

The little woman was prepared to *fight* anyone who got in her way.

She had so many interesting qualities.

Carefully getting off the bed, he walked around and laid down on Elijah's side. Curling against his body, he smiled when the man he loved wrapped his arm around him, pulling him closer in sleep.

With his face resting on Elijah's chest, he watched Gabriella's face in the same position on the other side. He covered her hand, spread over Elijah's heart, with his own.

More relaxed than he'd been in too long to try to remember, he drifted back to sleep.

* * *

The sun filled the sanctuary with pink and orange light when Brie woke. Harper's face was a few inches from hers on the opposite side of Elijah's chest.

He had the longest lashes.

As she had the thought, they fluttered open and eyes that glowed silver in the light stared at her. He squeezed her hand.

Quietly, he started to talk. "When I was eighteen, we were attacked on the way to the airport. Elijah killed seven men protecting me. As the dust settled, I realized he'd been hurt."

Moving their hands together, he stroked her fingers over an old scar beneath his ribs. "He remained standing until backup arrived. The moment I was in an alternate vehicle surrounded by a dozen armed men, he passed out from extreme blood loss."

"You already loved him," she whispered. "You must have been terrified."

He nodded. "I dreamed about him every night for two years. I didn't tell a soul, of course." Inhaling carefully, he went on. "Of all the injuries he's taken over the years, that one, the first serious one, almost killed him. I refused to leave for college. I stayed at the hospital until he was released. He raged about being weak but I didn't care. He fought recovering in my wing and I ignored him."

She smiled. "I would have, too."

"Even wounded, he was a powerful man. At twenty, he was even leaner. He remains the fastest and best trained fighter but I didn't care about any of that." He gave her a soft smile. "I loved that for all his ferocity, for all his skill to protect and kill, he played the violin."

Brie nodded seriously. "I get that. It ramps up the hotness."

Harper laughed. "I'd never *seen* him play but I'd *heard* him. I already liked and respected him as my best friend, as my personal bodyguard who'd kept me safe many times. His love of music, his gift for something so gentle, that's what made me love him."

"That's beautiful, Harper."

"He never told me what happened to the violin he used to play. I realized I hadn't heard him in a long time." His eyes held hers. "I bought him another one and brought it to him while he healed. He sat up enough to play it."

"It helped him."

"Yes. It cooled his rage. I asked if I could sit with him while he played and he didn't understand. I told him it was wonderful to listen to him, that he was incredibly talented." His fingers tightened around hers. "Watching him, seeing how it affected him, it pushed me fully over the edge."

He shrugged his shoulder lightly. "I whored my way through high school. I wasn't interested in men, I never even noticed them. Wanting him like I did fucked me up mentally but I couldn't help myself."

Brie reached out to stroke her fingers through his hair. "Wanting Natalia shocked me at first, too. Anyone who isn't attracted to *Elijah* is in denial."

It made him laugh and she returned to holding his hand. "I don't remember crossing the room to sit on the bed. He put down the violin and stared at me. I stretched out beside him and went to sleep. When I woke up, I was laying like this on his good side. I thought he was asleep. I *told* myself he was asleep." He murmured, "I wanted to touch him. I'd wanted to touch him for *so* long."

Harper moved their joined hands over Elijah's chest. "His heart beat slow and steady. I held my hand over it for a long time." Her own heart started to race as he moved their hands to Elijah's abdomen. "I couldn't believe his fitness. It was even more obvious touching him. It made my mouth water."

"I feel like that with both of you."

"We feel the same about you, Gabriella." He moved their hands back and forth across his waist. "His hair is so *light*, I never realized he had it. I liked the way it felt under my hand."

Her entire body tingled with need. His eyes held hers. "He was hard. I could see him outlined under the cotton sleep pants he wore. I wanted to know how it felt."

"I need to know, too."

Their hands moved over the ridge of Elijah's cock through the sheet that covered him, up and down, and Harper whispered, "I *needed* it, Gabriella. I'd never felt such need in my life and I didn't understand it. No matter how much it confused me, no matter how wrong it was, I *had* to touch him." His eyes held hers. "I *had* to taste him."

Moving together, they pushed the sheet away, exposing Elijah to their eyes, hands, and mouths. Sliding lower on the bed, she watched as Harper licked over the throbbing head, damp with pre-come, and then she did the same.

With their palms over him, they leaned closer and Brie kissed Harper. Moaning into his mouth, she said against his lips, "Tell me the rest. I *love* this story."

He rested his forehead against hers as they lightly stroked Elijah together. "I had no idea what I was doing. I knew I wanted to make him come. I didn't ask, I didn't discuss it, I just took what I wanted." One side of his mouth lifted in a smile. "I'm lucky he didn't kill me."

It made her laugh softly.

"I sucked the head for a few seconds but I wanted to take more." Bending, he wrapped his lips around the crest and sucked it with his eyes closed in pleasure. Moving away, he waited for her to do the same.

With her mouth around him, Harper said, "Then I felt his fingers in my hair." Brie moaned as Elijah raked through her tresses. "I thought he was going to pull me away. I was so afraid of his reaction." At her ear, he said, "He *didn't* pull me away. He pushed me closer and said…"

"Deeper."

Brie was in danger of having an immediate orgasm. Elijah applied pressure on the back of her head and she took him deeper.

Harper whispered, "I sucked him and I couldn't believe how long he could last. I didn't have the same control. I explored him while I moved over him and I was harder than I'd ever been." He moved their joined hands lower, cupping Elijah's balls in their palms. "Then he held me still and started to thrust between my lips and I almost came."

Fingers tightened into a fist at the back of her head and Elijah used his hips to fuck her mouth in shallow strokes.

"I felt like I was going to pass out from the pleasure and it was surreal because it was quiet and the room was filled with sunshine. It didn't seem like I could be sucking the cock of the man I'd been secretly in love with, but I was." Brie shook with need. Harper ground out, "Then he told me…"

"Take every drop and I'll make you come," Elijah said.

"He went still and started to spurt in my mouth. It was unlike anything that had happened to me before and I drank him down greedily."

As the first jet of Elijah's release filled her mouth, Brie whimpered. He came for a long time and she reveled in it.

"I worried about what would happen next. He pulled me off his cock and dragged me up his body." Seconds later, she found herself staring into Elijah's green eyes. Her arm wrapped around Harper's neck kept him close. "I loved the look on his face. He told me…"

"This changes everything."

Brie nodded and he devoured her mouth. When he broke it, she roughly pulled Harper to her and kissed him for a long time. Then they traded Elijah's mouth between them.

Focusing on silver eyes, she groaned, "Tell me the rest. Show me what happened next."

"Brie." She looked at Elijah. "Scoot over." She did and he powered Harper over his body to lie between them on his back. "I wanted to fuck him but I was injured. I knew I'd have to be careful with him, ease him into who I was."

She stretched out beside Harper with her head in her hand. "He's so beautiful, it must have been frustrating to not be in peak condition to show him everything."

"I can't explain the frustration." Stroking his hands over the front of Harper's body, he smiled. "I shoved his clothes away and touched him. He absorbed it, craved it." Glancing up, he met her eyes. "Much like *you*, Brie."

It made her happy. She reached out to help him stroke over Harper's skin.

"I took his cock in my fist." He licked the inside of his palm and fisted the throbbing length. "I didn't look away from his face because I needed to be sure of his thoughts. I worked him, palming the head, and watched for signs that he was getting close. Back then, it didn't take long when I didn't command him to hold back."

"I'm going to come, Elijah."

"I wanted to see it on him. Splattered over his skin. I wanted to add mine to it. Then he was coming and it was the most stunning sight of my life."

Pearly white release painted the skin of Harper's stomach and chest. Brie leaned over to lick it from his nipple, down his chest. Raising her face, Elijah claimed her mouth.

Then she dragged her fingertips through a stream on Harper's flat stomach, laid on her back, and put them over her clit. Replaying the experience through her mind drove her to climax quickly and she worked to calm her breathing before she opened her eyes and turned her head.

"You're the hottest men on the planet. Holy fuck."

Rolling back to her side, she kissed Harper desperately. "Thank you for including me." She smiled gently as she held the side of his neck with her palm. "I love your love story."

Then he was hugging her hard enough to hurt and part of her wondered if…

Maybe, she wouldn't have to give them up after all.

Chapter Thirty-Nine

Last week of July 2015

Elijah and Harper left for China the same day but Brie was glad for the time she had with them to settle her hurting heart.

Explaining to Phyllis that she needed to get to the winery, the woman coordinated with her team to get her back and forth, shadow her while there, and basically make it *super* awkward.

Her staff didn't ask questions but she could certainly see they wanted to.

She spent a solid week going back and forth to the vineyard and processing facility. It was great to catch up with her staff and she promised to be around more.

When she realized reviews and raises hadn't been implemented by her plant manager, she corrected the oversight and approved bonuses across the board.

Elijah confirmed they'd be gone another week so she contacted Marci about taking a trip down to the Ghonims' winery. The following day, she stepped off their plane in a business suit.

Walking the grounds and engaging the staff in relaxed conversation over several days made it possible to find the waste and where they'd been losing money in overhead.

She sat in an interim office when Marci poked her head around the door. "Don't you look uber professional?"

"Hey! Give me ten minutes to finish these numbers or I'll be lost." Rolling her eyes, she murmured, "I don't adult well."

Without glancing up again, she typed rapidly on her laptop. Marci sat in one of the chairs and checked her messages.

Done, she saved the initial report and forwarded it to the cousins. Sitting back with a smile, she said, "They'll see a substantial bounce if they change the things on my list. I can't wait to see it. This is such a pretty location."

"I'm taking you to lunch." Marci was more relaxed than she'd ever seen and Brie mentioned it. Grinning, she explained, "Orgasms and two men who know how to help me simplify. I'm finally to a point where I can take time off."

Lunch with one of the richest people in the world wasn't what most people would imagine. Though they were covered by ridiculous amounts of security, they giggled and gossiped like girls in high school.

The next day, Brie returned to Washington and realized Elijah and Harper were *still* gone. When she asked Elijah if there were delays, he seemed perplexed.

"We should've been back by now. It seems something comes up every time I think we're on track to return. Not too much longer, Brie. I'm sorry."

"It's okay. I know you're both really busy."

They talked for an hour and she felt a little better when they hung up. She texted Harper to tell him she missed him and loved him. He responded with, "Really busy. Miss you, too."

Sighing, she got to work on the paintings for the estate and crushed down her loneliness.

* * *

By the time she'd finished the painting of the main house and set it up to cure, she was ready to crawl out of her own skin.

Pulling on jeans, a t-shirt, and the cowboy boots she'd grabbed from her old place above her parents' garage, she decided to go riding.

Harper possessed a fantastic stable and she'd chatted with the manager several times about their shared love of riding. They had a pretty mare saddled and waiting when she made the walk across the fields. Mounting, she nodded at the two men who insisted on riding with her and lit out across the wide fields behind the corrals.

Prolonged riding made her hip ache and she listened to her body when the pain started. A mile from the stable yard, she was surprised to see a woman on horseback waiting for her.

It was Harlow Delkin, Harper's little sister. They were similar in age but certainly not in temperament. They'd never really gotten along.

Coming alongside, the female version of the man she loved stared at her intently. "Gabriella. I haven't seen you since we were children."

"You look lovely as ever." The woman wore professional riding gear. For a moment, Brie felt self-conscious and then decided more people in the world rode in the clothes she was wearing. "How have you been?"

"I need to talk to you."

"Alright."

Silver eyes glanced at the security men who rode alongside. "You can leave."

Jim shook his head. "I'm sorry, ma'am. We have our orders."

"I'm a fucking *Delkin* as well."

"True. However, you're not the Delkin I report to nor are you the Delkin who will have my head if Miss Hernandez comes to harm."

Rolling her eyes, Harlow nudged her mare in the direction of the stables. Brie wondered at the other woman's sudden interest. She steadied herself for a discussion about how inappropriate she was to be involved in Harper's life.

"It's partially my fault, Gabriella."

Frowning, she asked, "What do you mean?"

"Scott focused on you because of me. I told him you'd be his type." It took a long moment for her to realize she'd called him Scott. "I didn't know he was running a con. H-he told me he wanted to twist Hudson up, play a prank on him. I…was still angry and hurt."

Realization dawned and Brie stopped her horse.

"We spent a weekend together years ago. I fell hard, Hudson didn't.

He was the first man in my life who didn't and he was the only fucking one I wanted."

Inhaling carefully, she said through gritted teeth, "Harlow, you purposely let Scott Truing humiliate me to *get back* at Hudson?"

"I wasn't thinking clearly, I…"

"Let me guess, woman scorned? Poor little hurt feelings?" Brie shook her head. "You should've raged at *Hudson*. You should've thrown a tantrum in *his office* or maybe, fuck, *talked* to him like a *grownup*. Instead, you wrapped me up in your little revenge scheme that almost got me killed."

"I know. I acted like a child."

"Clearly, you're *still* a child so the behavior fits. Grown women don't sabotage other women. They don't take petty vengeance when a man doesn't want them."

She leaned closer and Harlow flinched. "I knew when I *met* Hudson that he wouldn't be *able* to love me. He can *only* love Natalia because she's his fucking *soulmate*, you silly bitch. I happily took my orgasms and walked away."

Sitting up straight, she couldn't believe the rage boiling through her. "Hudson is the most honorable man I've ever known. You can't tell me he made promises to you, that he in any way led you on. You spun that tale in your own mind. For getting me involved, I'd like to say *thank you*." Harlow's eyes went wide. "Going to New York, meeting Hudson and all the people in his life, was the best thing that ever happened to me."

She turned her horse, lined them up, and looked in the other woman's face. "That's the only reason I'm not kicking your spoiled ass, Harlow. You *ever* fuck with me *or my best friends* again and I give you my word, my reaction will be quite different."

Then she nudged the horse and took off toward the stables, bent over the neck. Her security detail was two seconds behind. Dismounting, she nodded to the stable hand and walked toward the main house. Jim and Davis walked at her sides.

"Are you alright, Miss Hernandez?"

"Pissed, Jim. Really pissed. I'm going to paint it off. I promise not to leave the studio so you guys take some time to chill out, eat, watch reality television. You know, whatever badass security guys do when they aren't doing badassery."

He laughed. "Understood. We'll make sure you get food."

Glancing at Davis, she grinned. "You're younger than I realized and armed to the teeth."

"Yes, ma'am. I'm training with Elijah. My dad arranged it."

"You like this sort of thing then?" He nodded. Given his age, Brie asked quietly, "Is your dad nice?"

"He's the *best*. He's trying to talk me out of the military because my mom will worry and not get to see me when she needs to. She's real gentle. You remind me of her."

They entered the house and she paused. "I imagine it would be hard to let your child go into danger on purpose. Not sure I'd be strong enough either." She sighed. "You won't find better training than with Elijah and his men. He'll teach you how to stay safe. That way, even if you go into the military, you can still get back home to your mom."

The young man was blonde with pretty copper eyes that practically glowed from his face. "My mom would *love* you. Enjoy your painting. I'll sit outside in the hall in case you need anything."

"You don't have to do that. I'll be zoned out for hours."

"I don't mind. Jim is the team lead and does lots of reports and things. Someone will have to and I'd like to be the one."

Smiling at both men, she nodded and took the stairs to her studio.

At the window, she replayed the conversation with Harlow Delkin in her mind. She'd never liked the woman but for her to stoop to such a level just to get revenge on Hudson for not falling at her feet. It was utter bullshit.

In fury, she painted until she was too tired to sleep anywhere but the couch there.

Looking at it the following day, she determined that the result was one of the best pieces she'd ever done.

Grinning, she put another canvas in place and let Phyllis know she was going to need more.

* * *

Mid-August 2015

When Elijah told her Harper's birthday was a few days away, she planned an extravagant dinner to celebrate.

She commandeered the estate kitchen and cooked all day.

Elijah texted her when they landed. She dashed around so she was ready when they arrived. She hadn't seen them in three *weeks*.

Her body missed them. Her heart so much more.

As arranged, Phyllis sent her the signal when they stopped in front of the house. She greeted them at the door with hugs, kisses, and smiles.

Elijah returned them warmly. Harper seemed upset.

"Welcome back. I made dinner."

She led them through the house and encouraged them to sit. When she found out that amaretto cream cake was Harper's favorite, she texted Natalia and got a recipe from the woman who did all the baking for *Trois* events.

It sat in the middle of the massive dining table.

She poured them glasses of wine and raced to the kitchen to plate food. Harper's tension lines were in clear evidence and she silently promised to make him feel better after he ate.

Setting down his plate, she bent to kiss his cheek. "Happy birthday, Harper. I hope there are *many* more filled with happiness in your future." She took Elijah's plate from the little cart and walked around the table.

The darker of her lovers glared at her. His fists were clenched on the surface of the table. "You can't *do* shit like this, Gabriella."

Brie saw Elijah stiffen in her peripheral vision and was genuinely confused as she bent to put his plate in front of him. "Do what?"

Harper's expression was cold as he replied, "Play *house*. That isn't what this is."

Dropping the plate she held the last few inches to the hardwood, she heard it break but didn't look or care. Her heart felt like lead.

She whispered, "Harper, *wow*." There was a pause. "I see."

Elijah was silent as he stood.

Walking into the hall, she grabbed her messenger bag from Harper's office and headed for the front door.

Harper grabbed her arm and spun her around roughly. "Where the fuck are you *going*?"

"Harper!" Elijah's voice was low and dangerous.

She stared into a face she knew better than her own and held back the hurt. Reaching up, she rested her palm on his cheek. Going up on tiptoe, she kissed his beautiful lips.

Then she carefully extracted her arm from his hold and backed toward the door.

"Thank you for clarifying my position. Consider this my resignation as your whore." He took a step in her direction but she held up her hand. "You said all there is to say in a single sentence. The paintings of the estate are in the studio." She bowed slightly, "Thank you for an experience I'll never forget and know that I love you anyway."

To Elijah, she said softly, "Keep him away from me. I've never been more serious in my life."

She watched Harper turn his head at the same moment his best friend, lover, and employee cold-cocked him. He caught Harper as he fell.

"Brie. Don't go. Please don't go."

She walked to him and pulled him down for a kiss. "If I stay now, I really *am* a whore, Elijah. I don't want to be that. Don't ask me to. I love you. I love both of you so much and I don't regret it. Not one minute."

Running her fingers through Harper's black hair, she kissed his forehead. "He may not love you more than I do but he's loved you *longer* and he *needs* you more. Love him. Keep him safe." She gave Elijah another kiss and said against his lips, "I love you. I'm sorry."

She went through the front doors, smiling when she saw Harper's car still parked on the drive. Phyllis ran out on the front steps of the house as she walked toward it.

"Miss...Brie! Where are you going?"

"Home, Phyllis. See you later."

Slipping in the back, she smiled at Deville. "I need a quick ride to the airport, kind sir. I hope you're not busy."

He grinned and started the engine.

As they pulled onto the main road, she focused on breathing and calming her heart rate. Through the drive, the waiting, and the flight, she fought hard to hold it all back.

* * *

Elijah lowered Harper to the floor of the foyer gently and stood over him. He'd never been so conflicted in his life.

Watching through the front doors as Brie got in the car and drove away, he felt ripped in half.

In the dining room, he picked up a glass of water and returned to the main entry where he threw it in Harper's face.

Sputtering, he reached his feet and glared at Elijah in fury. He said nothing as he walked to the stairs.

"We're not going after your little obsession?"

"You're not."

Following, he shot back, "I'm going, Elijah. She doesn't get to win."

Livid, he slammed Harper against the wall by his shoulders. "You're cruel and petty. You've learned *nothing*." He released him and backed away. "I need to know she arrived, I need to know she's safe. Then I'll *let her go* because it's the only thing that will ever be *enough* for you."

* * *

Hours later, when Brie exited the airport, she took in New York with a smile. "I've missed you, lovely lady."

When the cab let her out in front of the building, she was swarmed by armed men on the sidewalk.

It scared the hell out of her before it pissed her off.

"Miss Hernandez. We've been instructed to keep you in sight until Delkin and Eklund arrive."

The fucking nerve.

She put her hand on her hip. "You've seen me, confirmed my safety, and may now wait in your command center for your bosses. As a grown ass woman, I'll be going to my apartment, taking a shower, and then a nap. Have an awesome day, men."

Henry and Carlo stood by the front door, unsure what to do.

"I missed this place." She kept her voice cheerful. "You wouldn't believe how much *work* I've gotten done." The men hadn't dispersed and she glared at them. "Go away now."

Naturally, they did *not*.

Hudson's car pulled to the curb. Leonard opened the rear door and her best friend stepped from the back. Shooting his cuffs, he took in the scene calmly.

Approaching their little gathering, the men around her stiffened. Leonard unbuttoned his jacket.

"Guys, Leonard is Hudson's Elijah. Be nice and don't move suddenly. Also, he's dressed so pretty and I don't want your blood on his suit." Squeezing through their ranks, Brie hugged Hudson tight. "Hey you."

Lifting her face, he stared at her for a long moment. She shook her head as tears filled her eyes. He kissed her cheek and wrapped his arm around her shoulders.

352

"Leonard, you're with me. Carlo, please instruct a valet to move the car."

"Right away, sir."

Over his shoulder, he said, "Tell Delkin she's fine. Either of them may call me directly." Then he escorted her into the building, through the lobby, and up to the penthouse.

As they left the box, his phone vibrated. "Winters."

He listened in silence as he walked to the kitchen and poured them glasses of wine.

"I'll stop you there, Delkin. Perhaps she simply missed her own home? You've kept her in the ivory tower for two months. I've seen you more in the last several weeks than Gabriella. She has many friends here."

Clinking their glasses, he took a long sip as she sat on the barstool. Leonard pulled a deck of cards from his jacket and dealt them a game of rummy.

"She's having a glass of wine and playing cards with Leonard. They're buddies." He grinned. "Yes, she does make the most *interesting* friends." There was another silence as he listened.

Straightening, he said sharply, "She hasn't said a *word* nor have I asked. However, I don't interrogate my best friend when she returns to her *home*."

Hanging up, he took the stairs to the second floor and Brie sighed. "I swear, Leo. I'm like a bad penny."

"Nonsense. You're a *lucky* penny no one knows how to apply properly at first. You may be an heiress, run in the circles of the uber rich, and have untold opportunity, but I can see you as comfortable in a tiny cottage with unlimited painting supplies and a few nice neighbors."

"Thanks. That's an awesome thing to say." He grinned.

"Gabriella." She turned at Hudson's stern tone. "Is there anything you'd like to share?" When she didn't reply, he sighed. "What happened to bring you home or your run-in with Harlow Delkin perhaps?"

"Well, *no*. I handled it." Her eyes narrowed. "Wait, how do *you* know about Harlow?"

"Apparently, your security detail takes live feed of situations where you could become…unpredictable. None of them want to be on the receiving end of Elijah's wrath if you shake the world and end up hurt."

"Lord. They've been gone for *weeks*. I accomplished a shit ton of stuff and it was time to hang out in my own space." She swallowed around the partial lie. "I-I missed my friends, I missed my home, and I didn't want to run into Harlow and accidentally kick her bratty ass. When we were kids, she liked to refer to me as Flabby Gabby so this new layer to her personality isn't exactly surprising."

Raising a brow, she added, "You had *shitty* taste in women other than Natalia. For fuck's *sake*, Hudson."

Smiling, he approached and kissed her forehead. "Harper was putting Elijah in Natalia's way rather more than I liked. I thought Harlow was far more hardened than she ended up being."

"Totally your effect, and that of your superhuman penis. She's a bitch mostly." He laughed. "As for the rest, our time together is o-over. I'll be fine. I haven't had a chance to process. I sketched the entire trip to keep my mind occupied."

Wiping at tears she resented, she asked cheerfully, "Where's your lovely wife, by the way? I'm gonna hug her hard enough to break her."

"Darling." She glanced up to see Natalia descending in a silk robe. "I drastically overslept. I've taken your advice too far."

Jumping up, she met her at the bottom of the stairs and hugged her as hard as she could.

"You smell like brown sugar and oranges. How I've *missed* you, Gabriella."

"You smell like *Hudson*. I've missed you, too." Brie managed to hold back her tears but had a hard time controlling the way her body shook. "Help me be strong," she whispered.

"Always, darling." Wrapping their arms around each other, they returned to the bar.

Hudson answered his phone. "Hmm. That was quick."

Disconnecting, he placed Brie on the barstool and handed her the glass of wine. "They made excellent time. Steady."

The elevator doors slid open and Leonard moved deliberately to stand behind Brie.

Elijah and Harper stepped from inside, took in the scene, and walked to her. Harper had a dark bruise along his jaw and she could see his tension.

Their eyes slid over her slowly.

Leaning in, Elijah took a deep breath, growled, and glanced over his shoulder at Hudson. Her best friend sipped his wine with a wink.

Setting down her glass, she lifted her shirt, inhaled, and laughed despite the stress she was under. Shaking her head, she hopped off the barstool, walked around the men, and went to kiss Natalia.

Bending, she inhaled the fabric across her breasts and confirmed it was coated heavily in Hudson's cologne.

"I'll call you later and that wasn't nice. Funny but not nice."

Natalia cupped her face. "Then they must stop acting like you're a tree in their yard that they can mark whenever they happen to pass." She kissed her lips.

"They *still* don't quite understand how your heart works. Don't you *dare* settle for less than *every* goddamn thing you deserve or I'll spank your pretty ass myself."

Forcing a smile, she hugged Hudson. "I smell more like you than *you* do. Love you guys. I'll be around. You have to tell me everything about your honeymoon."

"We're returning to Washington tonight." The cold statement from

Harper made her still. "You'll have to reschedule."

"Harper. *So help me god.*" The words from Elijah had a clear effect on his lover.

Brie faced him, her heart heavy that he'd push at her again. "Perhaps *you* are. I'm staying in New York." He started to speak and she clasped her hands in front of her tightly. "Submission is the *will*, not the *rules*. I willingly submit to Elijah but make *no* mistake. No one *owns* me."

Swallowing past a painful lump, she said as firmly as she was able, "You've made your feelings about me clear, Harper. I won't wait around an abandoned estate for weeks waiting for the two of you to show up to fuck me. I know that's all you've offered from the beginning but I have a life, friends, clients, and a company of my own. It's time I get back to them."

Grabbing her bag, she walked to the elevator and pushed the button. "I can *play house* by myself. I'm not a fucking call girl, damn it." Stepping inside, she kept her eyes on the floor. "You didn't have to *do* this, Harper. I told you I'd leave when you let me know it was time. You didn't have to be cruel."

The doors closed and she choked down a sob. Back in her apartment, she ran a tub and stripped down.

Sliding into the warm water, she let herself feel the chaos from the last hours. That Harper treated her in such a way between the three of them was bad enough. That he'd done it again in front of her *friends* was embarrassing and hurt so much worse.

It looked like he wasn't going to let her keep the good memories in the end.

Brie cried hard.

Chapter Forty

Elijah struggled not to physically *hurt* the man he'd sworn to protect. The man he'd loved more than half his life.

Natalia stared at Harper with a frown as Brie left the penthouse. "Do you understand that you're three *couples* as well as a threesome?"

"We *aren't* three couples. We're *one* couple and a threesome when opportunity presents itself." Harper straightened his jacket. "In case you're wondering, I'm *not* part of the couple. There's *Elijah* and *Gabriella.* On occasion, I'm included."

His smile was bitter. "Forgive me, Natalia. You wouldn't have stood for that shit either."

"You regret less access to Elijah but *not* to Gabriella." She sighed. "Let her go *now*. This isn't going to work."

To Elijah, she added, "Harper *refuses* to love her despite her obvious love for both of you. Her safety and happiness are *your* responsibility. You *have* to let her go."

He gave a single nod. The thought of losing Brie caused him *unbelievable* pain. He doubted he hid his emotional turmoil.

Hudson raked his hand through black hair, he walked to the elevator and hit the call button. "You've gone too far, *hurt* her badly, Harper. Now she must save herself."

Harper raised his chin. "Gabriella is fine. We'll smooth things over and Elijah will have what he so *desperately* wants."

Winters snapped. "She's not fucking *fine*! Unlike the next woman you'll bed, Gabriella has class and self-respect. She was attempting to retain her goddamn dignity."

Looking directly into Elijah's eyes, he added, "You can't *make him submit* in this. I'm *truly* sorry for the pain I know this will cause you, Elijah." Exhaling roughly, he said, "We'll help her pick up the pieces."

As the doors closed on them, Elijah remained silent.

"You fucking win. You've made it clear I'm to have no access to you without Gabriella's presence." Harper laughed bitterly and it hurt Elijah's heart to hear it. "I concede. I'll put everything I am on the line to be able to touch you again. You choose to blackmail me to receive my consent. I choose to pay the ransom."

"Harper…"

"I'm *alone*. I'm fucking trying but you keep me at a distance as if I'm goddamn *new*."

"I said I will *let her go*."

"Elijah…"

"It's what you want. It's the only way to keep you from repeatedly hurting her. I'll break you *both* if I don't."

The elevator opened and he stepped into the lobby, signaling the team. "Escort Mr. Delkin to his apartment and stay with him."

"Elijah!"

He went through the doors and started to run. He ran for hours. He ran until he knew he was on the verge of damaging his body.

Staring out at the river, he gripped the railing and accepted that letting Brie go would be like carving out a piece of his flesh.

He was unsure he'd survive it.

Much like the day his father shattered his violin and made him watch, chained to the wall, as it burned.

Harper was *not* like his father. So many mistakes had been made where their relationship was concerned. Elijah didn't know how to fix them but he knew one thing was real and true.

Brie would eventually break under the pain of Harper's methods of retaliation. He knew the best ways to wound her and lashed out in anger, sadness, and neglect.

There were *so many* sins at his door. Brie would be the one that hurt the worst.

* * *

Harper paced the floor as Elijah entered the apartment and stilled when he saw the condition he was in.

Soaked to the skin with sweat and more exhausted than he'd ever seen him.

"Elijah…"

Without looking at him, he said, "I'm going to shower and talk to Brie." The door to his bedroom closed quietly.

By the time he came out, Harper wondered if he could lose his mind with the worry, the regret, he felt. Elijah emerged, showered and in clean clothes. He held his violin case.

"Elijah…"

"When I return, it will be done. Give me time to heal and things will be back to what you need."

"Wait. Wait and let's…"

"No, Harper. I waited too long to end it. I pushed when I should've pulled back." Bowing his head, he whispered, "I wish you'd never noticed Brie. I wish I didn't know the beauty of her. I wish she'd never touched me."

Then he was gone.

When he hadn't returned by morning, Harper texted Natalia for information. Her immediate response chilled him.

"Elijah left Brie at midnight. She's with us now. We'll take care of her. I'm sorry for you, Harper."

None of the security team had contact with him. Elijah disconnected from his life and walked away.

Harper begged every being in the universe to bring him back.

* * *

The knock didn't surprise Brie. She opened it to Elijah and stepped back to let him in. He wouldn't use the key to do what had to be done. He placed his violin case on her foyer table.

As the door clicked shut, she rested her forehead against it.

"Before you say anything, I know and I understand." She swallowed hard. "You tried to *make* me fit. I know you wanted it to work and that you didn't think it would come to this."

Turning to him, she took his hand and he gripped her fingers hard. "I knew Harper wouldn't accept me and I don't *blame him*, Elijah. There were a few times I hoped but…"

"I'm sorry, Brie."

She met his eyes. "He *never* lied to me. He *never* pretended. He was honorable. I knew the price and I paid it willingly to-to have the memories."

Sliding his palm along her neck, he brought her to his chest. "I won't ever touch another woman, Brie."

"Don't…"

"You have my word." She hugged him hard and stifled her sob. "You're the *only* woman I've ever loved. The only woman I'll *ever* love."

Fisting his fingers in her hair, he pulled her head back and kissed her. She held him, shaking apart on the inside, and wished for so many things to be different.

"Once more, Brie. Let me love you."

Right or wrong, she nodded and he carried her to her bedroom. Removing his own clothes, he took his time removing hers, worshipping revealed skin.

When she was naked, he knelt at her feet and hugged her with his face pressed to her stomach.

Allowing herself the freedom to take everything she could from the last chance she'd have, she stroked her fingers through his hair and held him to her.

Laying her down, Elijah kissed and massaged every inch of her body, front and back.

She knew he was memorizing her by *touch* and the similarities to the last moments she spent with Natalia and Hudson sent her pain to the bone.

When he rolled her to her back and slid deep, she sighed in pleasure. Tears slid silently into her hair but she held his gaze and shared everything she had, all she was, with the only man who'd truly *wanted* it.

He thrust slowly, steadily as she watched him, touched him, loved him. Strong hands stroked as much of her as he could reach and she soaked up his warmth and the love she knew he wanted to give her but understood why he couldn't.

The first climax rolled over her in a gentle wave and she sighed his name. His arms went around her and held her tight.

Best hugs ever.

Rolling to his back, he held her while she rode him. His thumb smoothed over her clit while his cock hit deep, filling her completely. When she came again, her head dropped back on her shoulders and she prayed she'd survive without him.

He sat up and lifted her from him, gently placing her on her stomach. Entering her from behind, he held her and planted kisses on the side of her face as another orgasm stole her ability to hold back her sob.

On and on Elijah made love to her and Brie somehow loved him more with every touch he gave her to say goodbye.

When she was sheened with sweat and shaking, he held her tight and fucked her hard.

The resulting climax made her scream his name, gripping him tight as he filled her with his come. He never broke eye contact and she whispered, "I'll always love you, Elijah."

"I'll always love you, Brie." Rubbing his face against hers, he told her, "I'll play for you."

She nodded against him and her tears fell faster, harder. He pulled from her body and she wrapped her arms around herself at the loss.

From her bathroom, he brought a washcloth and gently cleaned her as he kissed her face.

Tucking her in snugly, he went to get his violin. As he played the first notes, he murmured, "Let it carry you to sleep, Brie."

For more than an hour, he played for her and she fought sleep to watch him, to hear him. The pleasure he'd given and the emotional upheaval of the day took the choice from her hands.

The last thing she remembered was the image of Elijah playing his violin naked as he sat on the side of her bed. It was the most beautiful sight she'd ever seen.

An extraordinary gift from the man who *saw* her.

* * *

The first rays of sunlight filtered into Brie's room and she opened her eyes knowing he was gone. Rubbing her heart, she turned her head.

Elijah's violin rested on the pillow. The combination of the instrument and the note he left on her bedside table made it impossible for her to see to find her phone.

This belongs with the woman I love.

Forgive me, Brie.

Elijah

On her knees, fumbling for it blindly, she managed to dial. It rang once before it was answered. "Please, *please*, Natalia."

"I'm coming, darling."

Moments later, her friends picked her up from her bedroom floor, helped her dress, and held her while her heart shattered.

Chapter Forty-One

Elijah watched Brie fight for a long time and even when he knew she was deeply asleep, he continued to play for her. As the last note faded into silence, he placed the violin on the pillow beside her.

In her studio, he wrote her a note on a piece of heavy parchment and took in art projects she'd been working on before they took her to Washington. There were dozens of quick sketches of him, Harper, and the two of them together.

It was telling that Brie never placed herself in them.

Returning to her bedroom, he wanted to kiss her but he didn't. If he had to look into her eyes, he'd never have the courage to walk away.

When he realized she continued to cry in her sleep, he backed from the room before he started screaming.

Taking the cash he concealed in his violin case, he descended using the service elevator, ducked under the loading bay door, and walked into the bustling streets of Manhattan.

* * *

End-August 2015

Harper thought he'd lose his mind with worry.

He'd cancelled every business meeting until further notice and turned every personal resource to locating Elijah. He dialed his last resort and was surprised the man answered his call.

"Hollow."

"Help me find him. I'll do anything you want."

"He doesn't want to be found, Harper." There was a pause. "He's bleeding out internally. Let him stop the hemorrhaging and he'll resurface."

"Tell me where the fuck he is!"

"I'm not telling you shit. You never learned to share a goddamn thing. Firstborn, royal heir, protected at the cost of everything and everyone around you. That *me first, mine* attitude is what got you here."

Calming his thoughts, he asked, "Is Elijah safe?"

"Yes. He's the most lethal human on the planet. He's not likely to get mugged, Harper."

"You know what I fucking *mean*."

The silence drew out. "He's doing penance."

Oh, fuck no. "Get him out. Get him the fuck out!"

"I'm going to need you to calm down. He's fine and winning every round in under ten seconds." There was a bitter chuckle on the other end of the line. "Once again, the international champion. Betting against him is just *stupid* but people continue to do it. I'll never understand."

"Get him out or I go get him myself."

"As if you could *find* him…"

"I don't have to. I found *you*. Shall I recite your address?"

"Harper, I swear to god."

"You get him out. Give him a message from me. *I submit, Elijah.* You fucking tell him and get him out of there."

The line went dead and Harper nodded at the security team. "There's a hard lock. Do we prepare to breach, sir?"

"Are you out of your fucking *mind*? Elijah trained him." Turning to the window, he stared out at Manhattan. "Besides, I promised my mother I'd look after him."

* * *

In all his years of guarding Harper, Elijah had only removed himself from active duty twice.

The first was when he executed his father at seventeen.

As a child, not excelling meant *penance*. Most of the time, his father delivered it personally.

After he turned ten, he decided to let his son's skills earn him some cash. He'd take him during breaks from school and bring him back barely standing.

There was a time the matches were to the *death*. However, people trained like him weren't easy to replace. When the betting pool dwindled, it was changed to *incapable of continuing*.

In all the matches he'd fought in such horrific places, only *one* involved a man the underworld now knew as Hollow.

His shock when the *boy* of eleven was thrown into the ring with him turned to cold-blooded rage when his father smiled smugly from the spectator railing above.

Scaling the pit wall faster than the fight promoters could prevent, he grabbed his father by the back of the neck and power bombed him to the dirt floor twenty feet below. He dropped easily there himself.

To the boy, he growled, "Look away." With blank eyes, he refused. "So be it."

The fall broke Rolfe Eklund's ribs, punctured his lungs, and blood gurgled from between his lips. Reaching into the man's boot, he removed the knife he always kept there.

Leaning close, he whispered, "I see from his eyes what you did to him. *It will not stand.*" Then he said loud enough for the stunned and silent crowd to hear, "I am Elijah Mathias Eklund. I am your son and I am your *destroyer.*"

Stabbing the long knife into his throat, he dragged it to his groin, opening him to the audience above. He watched him take his final breath before wiping his fingers on the blade. Staring up at the crowd, he painted lines across his face in his father's blood and roared with his arms back.

"This boy is *protected* on penalty of death. Any who touches him will die screaming." He kicked the eviscerated body of his father. "Bring my next opponent and drag this piece of shit out of my sight."

He willingly stayed to fight for another week to earn the cash he needed to get them back to Washington from South Africa.

Hollow remained with him and they were given a wide berth by the other fighters, spectators, and promoters. Upon their return, he explained that his father had disappeared.

The second time he freely performed penance was when he broke the woman he loved.

Walking to a ferry, boarding a ship, Elijah made his way to the newest location for the Games in Greenland.

He allowed each rival to land two hits before he wiped them out and sent them from the pit unconscious.

Every hit that connected was punishment he deserved for what he'd done to her. Selfishly seeking one thing for himself, he'd inflicted damage it would take Brie *years* to recover from.

As another limp man was dragged from the ring, Hollow appeared in the threshold that led from the pit. Their eyes met and shared horror would always be there.

"He submits. The exact message was *I submit, Elijah.*"

"It isn't *about* his submission."

"You can't stay here, Elijah."

He stared at the stone wall. "How is she?"

"She doesn't leave the building." Elijah's eyes closed in pain. "Harper hasn't returned to Washington. He also doesn't leave the building." Hollow shook his head. "It's like a fucking *hive* over there. A message?"

"I need two more weeks." He rotated his neck on his shoulders as his next challenger was let into the pit from the other side. The man was massive with dark skin and blue eyes. "I atone for my sins."

He stepped into the circle, allowed the man to hit him in the side and the back.

Then he destroyed him with focused strikes and watched as he was dragged away.

Glancing over his shoulder, he told the man who still stood there, "It's going to take some time."

Chapter Forty-Two

Mid-September 2015

Brie painted and slept for the most part. Her friends kept her from falling into complete despair but their worry was clear.

When Tawny and Riya called, she was happy to soak up their natural effervescence. They wanted to visit but, more often than not, she told them she wasn't up for company.

Knowing they were getting increasingly stressed about her state of mind, she invited them to the apartment for brunch. She'd done her best to hide evidence of her incessant crying before she opened the door.

Tawny took her in quickly and wasted no time. "We leave for Dallas in two days and you're *going* with us."

"I can't. Not yet. I don't need to be around people."

"You've wanted to see the club forever. KiKi wants to meet you in person and I know you're done with her mock-ups. You need to get the fuck *out* of this apartment, Brie."

She shook her head, unsure about seeing a place she knew had history for Elijah and Harper. A place she'd hoped to visit *with* them one day. "You guys don't need me around right now. I'm ridiculous."

Riya took her hand, "We hardly *see* you." The brunette chose her words carefully. "You have to start getting out, getting back into the world, Brie. It'll take time to heal but it'll take more if you stay in seclusion."

Glancing across the living room, she stared at the whale sculpture and the violin. She'd had a special case delivered that was lit and sealed to display it.

"I have the means to go somewhere but I've got no idea where I should go. I feel wrong in my skin, sensitive to the touch. Unable to think clearly." She swallowed hard. "I always knew so I should've expected the pain. Somehow, I never really saw it coming. Not when and how it did."

Lowering to the dining chair beside her, Tawny said gently, "Come to Dallas. You know you'll have fun and we love having you with us. Just the ticket, I think." With a wink, she added, "Riya has been so worried. I hate seeing her cry."

"The Riya card. You're *such* a bitch."

The friends laughed and Tawny nodded seriously. "Acknowledged. Pack a bag and let's get our drink on in a place where I don't have a record."

"Yet, Tawny, you don't have a record *yet*."

"Your mouth is moving but I can't *quite* understand." Standing, Tawny grabbed a plate. "Stop working all the fucking time and have some fun."

"I like working. It keeps my mind occupied."

For an hour, they ate and Brie honestly did feel better by the time she walked them to the front door.

"Thanks. You guys are incredible."

"Duh. Oh, I bought you a leather skank outfit to wear."

Then she pulled the door closed before Brie could question the strangeness of the statement.

* * *

Elijah was gone twenty-six days when the security team on the ground floor reported he'd entered the building.

Harper waited as he opened the door to the apartment.

He sobbed in sadness and shame. There were bruises, scratches, and abrasions all over him and it looked like he'd lost twenty pounds. His lips were cracked, both hands were torn up.

"I'm sorry. I'm so sorry, Elijah."

"Do you even understand why you're apologizing?" There was a long silence and he shook his head. "I thought not."

He moved to pass him and Harper put his hand on his shoulder. "I missed you."

"You missed me as one misses a tool that's formed to the palm after years of use. Comfortable, familiar, easy to pick up when you have need of it. Just a tool."

"No, Elijah. *Never.*"

Without another word, he walked to his bedroom and locked the door.

Harper knew the wound he'd caused between them might never heal. Gabriella would've been able to help Elijah but Harper didn't know what to say to make things right.

Then again, if he hadn't lashed out at her in selfishness and fear, the three of them might even now be together in the sanctuary instead of struggling with their pain separately.

In his own bedroom, he mourned the loss of her, the way she'd always known what to say, the love that would've healed so many hurts over time.

Filled with self-loathing, with loneliness, Harper wept.

* * *

"Eklund."

"Hollow." There was a pause. "She's meeting with KiKi."

"When?" He recited the date and time. "For what purpose?"

"Website upgrades. New graphics."

"She goes alone?"

"Chadwick, Scottsdale, Riya, Tawny, and the java boys."

"Winters and Natalia?"

"Unknown if they're aware of the trip."

"Keep me posted of changes."

"Done."

* * *

Brie's initial impression of The Playground wasn't at all what she expected. It was done in deep jewel tones and dark woods, well-lit, and welcoming. Every surface sparkled and the staff seemed happy to be at work.

Kikiama Espinosa greeted their party at the door with a huge smile. "Welcome to The Playground." Introductions were made and she told them, "Call me KiKi."

To Brie, she said, "I've heard incredible things about you. I look forward to picking your brain. We'll have time for business later. Right now, Misery's show is about to start. Let's get you good seats and drinks."

She seated them in an alcove with several comfortable couches. Riya and Tawny settled with their men on either side of them.

Brie chose a seat alone. The sleek leather portfolio in her lap held the mock-ups she'd done for the club. It felt odd to be having a business meeting the way she was dressed.

Tawny had presented her with leather pants that felt like they were painted on, a stunningly detailed corset tank in royal blue, a bolero jacket that matched the pants, and black riding boots that ended at her knees.

Her hair was pulled back in sparkling blue clips and fell down her back. Her makeup was heavier than any she'd ever worn.

Riya and Tawny wore chokers that matched their leather outfits. Several times during the trip, Tawny attempted to get her to wear one as well.

Filled with sadness, she refused. "No. I don't belong to anyone."

Micah tried to explain. "Brie, it's a safety precaution..."

"It's a *lie* when it comes to me, Micah. No. I can't."

Self-conscious and wishing she hadn't come, Brie stared at a painting across from her. Standing up, she walked to it and realized the detail was incredible. She wondered at the medium used and gently touched the edge.

"Come with me."

Glancing up in confusion, she looked at a man standing beside her. "Hello."

"*Come with me*," he said more forcefully.

A stranger was trying to give her a *command* as if he'd earned the *right*. "I'm sorry, *what*?"

He grabbed her upper arm roughly and Micah appeared like a dark demon, positioning himself between them.

"She's off limits, mate." His tone left no room for argument.

The older man hissed, "Bullshit."

Drawing himself to his full height, Micah growled, "She's *off* limits. Back the fuck away or I *make* you back away."

The fingers around her upper arm tightened sharply before releasing her. The look the stranger gave her caused a shiver of fear to skate up her back.

He clenched his fists and walked away.

Micah led her back to their group and she lowered into a chair. He crouched in front of her with a gentle smile.

"Brie. Some of the members are more aggressive in this environment. Stay with us so we can run interference."

"They think..." She swallowed hard. "It's assumed I'm available for sex, isn't it?" He nodded and she closed her eyes. "I didn't understand, Micah. I should've listened. I was hurt but it was foolish."

He patted her hand and gave her a wink. "Stay with us. You'll be safe in KiKi's care while you talk." She nodded and he returned to Riya's side.

Unable to look at any of them, uncaring about the show taking place, Brie rubbed her hand over her heart and tried to get her shit together. She gripped her portfolio tightly and struggled not to cry and humiliate herself in public.

She missed Elijah and Harper. She wouldn't have felt so out of place if she'd come with them.

The thought brought tears she couldn't fight. Avoiding looking at her friends, she made her way to the closest bathroom.

Using tissue, she blotted away the damage to her makeup and took a deep breath. Pressing her fingers to her temples, she closed her eyes and tried to center, tried to find her way back.

When she reopened them, the same man who'd thought she was available stood behind her.

He grabbed her hair and wrapped it around his fist several times. At her ear, he whispered, "You'll fucking *obey* or I'll make you hurt."

"The fuck I will." She rammed her elbow into his sternum but he didn't let her go. "Get *off* me!"

Slamming her against the wall, he bounced the back of her head off the tile. His fingers gripped her throat tightly, limiting airflow and preventing her from screaming.

He glared at her. "Did you think to see what the lifestyle was all about? Did you read your steamy erotica novels and think you knew what the fuck to expect? Silly bitch."

Dizzy, she tried to kick him but he pressed himself against her, limiting her movements. His other hand roamed over her breasts and between her legs.

"I chew up little girls like you every week. I'm a kid in a candy store with this lovely new trend."

Gasping, Brie managed, "*Stop.*"

"I'll stop when I'm *done*. You want to see what the thrill of submission is all about, honey? I'm *happy* to show you."

Tighter and tighter, he squeezed her throat and she distantly heard him unzipping his pants. Then he was gone and she felt herself falling. Arms caught her, held her, as she tried to focus.

Reality was confused as she watched Elijah systematically obliterate the man who'd tried to rape her.

Releasing her bodyweight, she slipped through the hands holding her and landed on her knees. Crawling toward him, she placed her hand on his shoulder.

"Elijah, stop…stop." Her voice sounded like ground glass. He turned and the man she usually saw in his eyes wasn't present. He returned to punching her attacker in the face and she tightened her grip. "I *love* you. Don't kill for me, Elijah."

He blinked and she saw he was back. Her head dropped between her shoulders and blood dripped on the floor as arms lifted her from behind. It was only then she realized it was Harper who held her.

Elijah tore his shirt over his head and held it to her face. She was shocked at how quickly her blood soaked it.

She passed out and regained consciousness in the back of a limo.

They pulled under an emergency room canopy and she gasped, "None of you can go in with me."

"What the fuck are you *talking* about, Gabriella?" Harper looked livid.

"They're going to think I'm a hooker." He started to speak and she shook her head. "I'm a Mexican woman dressed in leather who looks like I just got beat up by my john. Trust me on this."

Tawny leaned over her face. "I'll take you in."

"Your men…"

"I'm *never* photographed with them, Brie. No one knows me."

"She's not a goddamn…"

"Shut the fuck *up*, Delkin," Tawny hissed. "You run a company that's publicly traded. You're on the boards of several prominent charities, as are the *rest* of you. You don't know the goddamn preconceptions people have about women just like her all over the motherfucking planet. Stay in the fucking car. I've got this."

She settled her eyes on Elijah. "Your hands are fucked up and *your* shirt is soaked in her blood. Stop. *Think.* You know I'm right and you *know* I'll keep her safe."

Fists clenched, vibrating with fury, he gave a single nod.

Tawny wrapped Brie's arm around her shoulders and sat her up. When the driver came around, he helped them from the interior.

Over her shoulder, she commanded, "Get them the fuck out of here."

Brie stumbled beside Tawny through the emergency room doors and the nurse at the desk rolled her eyes.

The redhead barked, "She's not a hooker, you cunt. Do your fucking job or call the police to save your old ass."

Over the next hour, the doctor on call managed to stop the nosebleed that raged completely out of control due to eighteen months of blood thinners. He confirmed her vitals were stable and put her on an IV.

At one point, security handcuffed Tawny to the chair beside her bed. The moment the pissed off guard left the room, the redhead slipped them and stuck them in her back pocket.

Quietly, her friend asked, "How do you feel, bitch?"

"Weak but alright."

"We're leaving. Where do you want to go?"

"Anywhere that isn't *here.*"

Carefully detaching the IV like a fucking nurse, she helped Brie sit up and get her bearings.

When she nodded, she supported her as they made their way from the hospital. A block away, the redhead hailed a cab.

The sun was lighting the sky when a woman Brie would've sworn was familiar the day before climbed into the pilot seat of a small plane and took off.

Drifting to sleep several times, she came to as Tawny set the plane down on a private airstrip in the middle of nowhere. She cut the engine and took a deep breath.

"Welcome to my bolt hole, Brie. You're the only person in the real world to ever see it."

"Where are we?" The entire situation was surreal and more than a little fascinating.

"Not far from the Canadian border. Vermont specifically." Tawny climbed down and helped Brie to the ground. "Come on, bitch. Let's get you out of the BDSM Barbie getup."

Chapter Forty-Three

Learning the day after he returned from penance that Brie would be going to a BDSM club filled Elijah with dread.

Elijah had no intention of interacting with the woman he loved.

In the weeks since he left Brie's side, there hadn't been a single photo of her from any source. He needed to confirm with his own eyes that she was alright.

Harper insisted on joining him.

Brie was *not* alright. Despite the stunning way her friends turned her out to help her blend in for her meeting with KiKi, she was clearly wrecked.

She wore no collar. Elijah knew Chadwick would've tried to convince her. He understood her refusal, it made him love her more, even as he worried.

In the time it took Elijah to circle the stage for a closer look at her face, he lost her.

Panicked after her earlier run-in with the sort of man he despised in their circles, he knew he needed to find her quickly. Seeing her leather portfolio on the chair, he knew she hadn't left with KiKi.

The ladies' room. Avoiding being sighted by her friends, he made his way there quickly.

The vision he walked into made his entire mind go red.

A man held her against the wall by her throat, her feet just off the floor, as he worked at the closure of his pants.

She was choking and her nose was bleeding.

"Catch her," he said coldly to Harper.

Then he whipped the man away from her and drove him hard to the marble floor. His plan was to beat the man to death with his bare hands and watch the last breath gurgle out of him.

"Elijah, stop…stop." She'd crawled to him. Hearing the way her voice scraped because of the scum *choking* her, he went back to hitting him. "I *love* you. Don't kill for me, Elijah."

He blinked and realized the lower half of her face was now covered in her own blood. Harper lifted her and Elijah pressed his shirt to her nose as she lost consciousness.

He made his way through the club with Brie in his arms, ignored her friends' panicked questions, and remained silent as they all climbed in the back of Harper's limo.

Hollow's top lieutenant insisted on taking her into the emergency room and he agreed she was the best choice. She was also capable of keeping her safe in ways others in the vehicle could not.

Unlike Harper, he knew it was likely he'd be arrested and Elijah couldn't leave him unprotected.

Watching Brie disappear through the doors of the emergency room caused him to punch a hole through the glass of the limo bar.

Everyone in the car was silent as Harper wrapped his bleeding hand. "Drop everyone off. I need to change."

Harper gave the driver instructions and an hour later, they were finally on their way back to the hospital.

"Elijah…"

"I need to confirm. I won't talk to her."

"Elijah, you *need*…"

"What I need is *irrelevant*, Harper."

"Gabriella…"

Closing his eyes, he said quietly, "Don't say her name. Don't."

Harper sat back slowly and rested his head against the seat. "I lost you anyway. What difference did *any* of it make?" His voice was filled with sadness but Elijah closed his heart to it.

"As soon as I can fucking *breathe again*, I'll readapt to the lifestyle you prefer, that's so *fulfilling* to us both, Harper. I'm unable to simply forget Brie a mere *month* after breaking her heart when I *swore* I wouldn't hurt her."

"I'm the one who hurt her, Elijah."

"You did…and I delivered the killing blow by *walking away* from everything she offered despite her love for me and knowing it would break her."

A few minutes later, he discovered Tawny had removed Brie from the hospital after they managed to stop the bleeding caused by her medication.

The redhead didn't answer her phone. Brie's was still at the club. The two of them simply disappeared.

His phone rang. "Eklund."

"Hollow." The man cleared his throat. "She's going off-grid."

"Why?"

"Red said she was tired of seeing a gentle woman fucked over by men and Brie needs time to breathe before she slits her goddamn wrists."

Elijah let the words sink in. "She's safe?"

"You know better than to ask." There was a long silence. "She needs to heal. I've…known someone like her before. Pushed much further, she could break in a way that ends in her death."

"Protect her." He pressed the bridge of his nose. "When she's back on grid, I'll assign security. Harper's public display with her will keep her on the radar for a long time. She can't pay the price for our callous treatment of her."

"Understood."

"Keep me updated."

"I will." Hollow sighed. "Elijah, I'm sorry."

"So am I."

Hanging up the phone, he walked back to the car with Harper a step behind him. As they pulled away, he asked, "Where do you want to go, Elijah?"

"Washington. When she returns to New York, she'll be stronger. Tawny will make sure of it." He could see the questions but he slid shades in place and ignored everything.

When they boarded the plane and took off, he sat opposite Harper as he always had. The man stared at him.

"I shouldn't have appeared with her."

Without looking at him, Elijah replied, "No, you shouldn't. It made things far more difficult for her. She had enough obstacles before your public display." He shook his head. "She fucking warned you."

"I thought, I don't want her in danger."

Well at least there's that. "I'll keep her safe but I'll have no contact with her."

"Maybe with time, I could…"

"For a *year*, she's been on the receiving end of our needs and our lust. Every absence, no matter how extended, was borne with understanding. Every hurt, every mixed signal, *every fucking thing* we did, she continued to give. She has given until she has nothing, *absolutely nothing*, left. I'll take no more from a woman whose only sin is loving two men who are too broken to appreciate her. Neither of us deserve her."

"You deserve her, Elijah."

"No. A *good* man would've left her alone. A *good* man doesn't break something he loves." He looked out the window. "I'll never touch another woman. Enjoy them at your risk and at your leisure. I won't be involved."

Harper frowned. "Elijah, you made a vow to her?"

"It's a vow to *myself*." He met gray eyes. "Equal to the vow I made for *you*, Harper. As you said, I'm *better* at self-denial." Returning his gaze to the passing landscape, he added, "The thought of touching another woman makes me ill."

"It…isn't the same without you."

"Then find a man to play the game with you." Harper gasped. "In our first conversation, Brie defined us clearly. I ask for nothing, expect nothing, and am not surprised when that's exactly what I receive. You've made no vow to me."

"Do you hate me?"

"I don't hate you, Harper. I love you as I've loved you for most of my life. I'm hurting, I'm angry, and I'm painfully tired. Allow me time to adjust and our days will get back to the way they have *always* been."

Harper moved to sit beside him and he stiffened.

He wrapped his arms around him and whispered, "I'm sorry, Elijah. I'm sorry you're hurting. I know how much you love her. I don't know what to do. Tell me what to do."

"Let me grieve. If she must be dead to me, let me grieve."

"She doesn't have to be, Elijah. She loves you so much."

"She told me you've loved me longer and you need me more, that you were honorable, and she understood why you couldn't accept her." He struggled for air and pressed his hand to his heart. "Even as she *broke*, she thought of us. After everything that's happened, I can't even ask her to be my friend."

Elijah hadn't shed a tear since he was two years old. That Brie reactivated the ability did not surprise him. As they slid down his face, he stared at Harper.

"Let me grieve."

Silver eyes wide, a shaking hand lifted to touch his cheek. Then he slowly wrapped him in a hug and held him close.

There was nothing else to say.

Chapter Forty-Four

Brie's Birthday - End-October 2015

After six weeks at Tawny's hideaway, Brie accepted that while she might have many things in her life, a love of her own wasn't to be one of them.

As a child, she'd dreamed happily about *true love*. As a teenager, she hoped for someone to at least be *nice* to her. As a grown woman, she realized that love was far more *brutal* in reality than it was in fairy tales.

She reached the conclusion that she was likeable, she was many positive things to wonderful people. She was *not* loveable.

It was a painful truth but one she could no longer keep from herself. She was tired, isolated in a way she'd never envisioned for her future. She floundered in some bizarre place between friend and lover, finding herself alone again and again.

Elijah was the only man to love her, *truly* love her, but he belonged to someone else. That she'd hoped for the outcome to be different was her own fault.

It was time to be *alone*.

Ménage was clearly the wrong path and the thought of touching another man or woman while Elijah lived vibrantly in every cell was physically sickening.

It felt like every beat of her heart brought a memory, a moment with him, and so *many* of the most beautiful ones included Harper. The other man she loved, the man she'd hoped so desperately would love her in return.

She'd *allowed* herself to hope.

Tawny stayed with her the first two days, brought in basic things she needed, and told her to unplug her brain.

"Everyone knows you're fine. Focus on getting better, stronger. I won't take you back until you're ready. Make a plan for *you*, Brie. What it is doesn't matter. All that matters is that you know your own path."

Nodding, Brie was quiet for a long time. "I need art supplies."

"Done."

Tawny hooked her up to a secure system so she could continue to run the winery. Her staff believed she was still in New York. The people in New York had no clue where she was.

On her first morning, she emailed her best friend.

> *Hudson, I'm sure you're freaking out. I'm okay. I promise. Another of those bizarre things I seem to attract. Tawny decided to help me get some breathing room. I miss you and I'll stay in touch so you don't worry. Hug Natalia for me and tell her I love her so much.*

He'd written her back immediately.

> *Gabriella, don't tell me not to worry. When I look into your eyes, I'll know if I should worry. Natalia says she loves you and to please hurry back. I love you, too.*

An email from KiKi raging about the actions of the man who'd tried to rape her scared her a little bit. Brie immediately responded, asking her *not* to have the man killed.

After several responses back and forth, she felt the club owner was firmly off the ledge and told her she'd contact her about business when she was back in circulation.

On one of Tawny's rare visits, she said, "I need you to show me how to protect myself, Red."

Eyes wide, at first, she didn't reply. Then something flickered over her face and she gathered Brie close. "I forgot the rest. I was so worried about your physical state. I'm sorry."

Suddenly, Brie was sobbing and Tawny didn't let her go until she'd cried herself out.

"Everyone always thinks I'm weak. Until that night, I didn't believe it, Tawny."

"You're not *weak*. Even *trained* women can forget during a sexual assault. As common as it unfortunately is, it's still a shock."

Pulling back, she smiled and smoothed her hair away from her face. "I'll teach you a few basics but I want you to remember something important. Not *everyone* is a fighter. You're a good and gentle woman, perfect as you are."

Brie used Tawny's gym to relieve stress, exhaust herself for sleep, and drown out the almost constant memories of Elijah and Harper that seemed to haunt her.

Every day, she slept, sketched, worked out, and considered the next step in her life. Some days, she felt as if she was crawling out of her own skin.

Sitting on Tawny's deck, she stared out at forest as far as the eye could see. She felt as if she was vibrating on the inside.

Walking inside, she changed into leggings and a t-shirt, stepped into sneakers, and went for a walk. The physical therapy had not only healed her injuries, it had increased her cardio stamina to a level she'd *never* had before.

She walked *alone* for *two miles* before returning to the house.

It was the first moment of true physical freedom she'd felt since the day Scott Truing used a car to express his rage and run her down in the street.

The first time she could envision grabbing her backpack and going for a long walk on the city streets again.

Over the next few days, she tested her body, pushed herself, and tried to figure out what she was capable of physically.

The morning of her birthday, she woke devastated at the memory of Harper flaunting a perfect woman in front of her the year before.

The day Elijah told her to seek comfort elsewhere.

She'd already loved him but hadn't yet fallen as deep as the following months would take her.

She cried for a long time.

* * *

Beginning November 2015

Stepping back from her latest piece, Brie took a deep breath.

After careful evaluation, she'd mentally flipped through the work she'd done over the years to determine which truly filled her up with joy. She liked to paint when the sun was highest.

Disconnecting from her life, stepping back from the people in it, allowed her a perspective she'd been missing. Every choice she'd made was influenced by someone other than herself.

It was a bad habit she needed to break.

She went for her walk, proud of the progress she'd made over several weeks. She went almost five miles before she had to turn back toward the house.

As she approached the deck, a man stood there and she turned to run. He called, "I'm Tawny's friend. It's okay, Gabriella."

Maintaining her distance, they stared at one another from two different levels.

He gave her a gentle smile. "My name is Hollow. I've heard a lot about you." Tilting her head, she looked into his eyes and her own went wide. "Yes. I see you know who I am in the real world. I'd *never* hurt you. Not in any way. No one knows I'm here. You have my word."

Taking slow steps, she walked up the stairs and faced him with a few feet between them. A few months after her accident, she questioned Hudson about the events following the hit and run.

She had a hundred questions after he mentioned a man who existed on the fringe of society who took care of things no one else could.

He was truly beautiful. He was also familiar.

Her mind spun with so much information and emotional stress. The *similarities*...she blinked back tears.

"I'm sorry, Gabriella. I don't want to cause you pain."

Inhaling carefully, she tried to be strong. "I'm okay. Tawny w-works for you."

He held her gaze. "With me, yes. I recruited her more than a decade ago."

"Why did you come?"

"Gabriella, in my work, I see *many* horrible things. I've experienced some of my own. I've also committed my share."

He lowered himself into one of the deck chairs and gestured for her to sit in the other. She did, perching on the edge.

"Years ago, when you were still in high school, you affected a dramatic change in my life." She frowned and shook her head. "To *you*, it was likely small, inconsequential. A part of the person you are, as familiar as breathing. To me, it changed everything."

"I don't remember. I'm sorry."

"I was in a dark place, darker than any other time in my life. I was at the winery, forced to be there for a family event, hiding as I usually did from the prying eyes of others." His expression was sad. "I was high. A habit I'd been trying to break since my return from the streets."

She placed her fingertips over her lips and he nodded. "You remember. One of the staff was gossiping, speculating on my mental instability. She suggested my family would be better off if I was dead and I should kill myself."

Thinking back to that day, Gabriella remembered. The rage that filled her was uncommon but she'd embraced it, releasing it without hesitation.

"You told the woman she didn't know my pain, she didn't know my story. You told her to get out and said if it was up to you, she'd be forced to live a day in my shoes."

Leaning forward, he took her hand. His were long and well formed, cool to the touch. "Thank you. That's something I've wanted to say to you for a long time. That's why I came. To make sure you were alright and thank you for caring about a person you didn't know, defending what appeared to be nothing more than a drug addict without a future."

"You're welcome, H-Hollow." She smiled.

He returned it and the sight made her close her eyes for a moment. *Too much, too much. I can't take it.*

When she opened them, he stared at her. "I'm so sorry."

She shrugged sadly as tears slipped past her control. "It'll get better. I-I hope it gets better." Clearing her throat, she told him, "Clearly, you made a *wonderful* future for yourself."

"I try to do good things. When I learn of people like you, Gabriella, I know there's hope." Taking a deep breath, he added, "Perhaps not for *me* but hope in general."

Staring off into the distance, she whispered, "Listen to the violin. It always makes me feel hope."

An expression of pain crossed his face and she asked him to tell her something interesting about his life that wasn't sensitive. Surprised at her understanding, he complied.

They talked for hours.

When Tawny appeared in the clearing at a full out run, Hollow quickly put her mind at ease. "I'm alone, Tawny."

The redhead stared back and forth between them as she joined them on the upper level. "You're okay?" Brie nodded. "Wow. Oz came out from behind the curtain. Trust me, he doesn't do it for just anyone."

Leaning up, she kissed Hollow's cheek. "How've you been?"

"Receiving non-stop calls about your lovely friend." He smiled carefully. "How long will you hide, Gabriella?"

Lifting one shoulder, she told him, "I have many beautiful things in my life. It's time to accept love is one I'll have to live without. I'll go back, ease the minds of my friends, and wait for my heart to heal."

He stared at her in silence for a long time. "You truly think it a lost cause?"

"Yes." Her voice broke on the word. "I understood the risk and made a conscious choice to ignore the warnings."

Inhaling carefully to control tears she was tired of crying, she added softly, "I'm grateful for the moments. I *hoped* but it wasn't meant to be. I need to heal and change direction."

"Hope is a funny thing, Gabriella. Sometimes, it's realized when you think all is lost."

Approaching him, she wrapped her arms around him and was surprised at the strength in his arms as he returned it.

"You're living proof and I'm glad to see it. Your secret is safe with me. I give you my word. Thank you for your trust."

Turning, she pressed her cheek to Tawny's. "We can go back whenever you're ready, double-oh-seven."

Chapter Forty-Five

November 2015

Brie's return to New York City following seven weeks in absolute seclusion was accomplished quietly.

After hugging her tightly, Carlo keyed her up to Hudson's penthouse and the couple was waiting just outside the elevator when it opened.

They hugged her so hard that it hurt and she let them because she understood. "I'm sorry you were worried. I needed to stop the world for a minute."

Letting her go slowly, Natalia stroked Brie's hair away from her face. "Where to begin, Gabriella?"

"At the beginning." Taking a deep breath, she let them lead her into the living room where they settled beside her on the couch. "I've missed you so much."

They asked her about her attack at the club and though she was certain they already knew, Hudson slowly tensed, his fists clenching on his thighs.

He watched her intently. "You're one of the strongest people I've ever met. I'm proud of you." Stroking his hand over her head, he murmured, "That someone *again* touched you in violence *destroys* me. I'm sorry, Gabriella."

"I'm...stuck in a weird loop." She shook her head and twisted her fingers in her lap.

"There's no doubt you've been through the ringer in the last couple of years, Gabriella." Natalia squeezed her hand. "I've never seen one person endure so much, so close together."

"It *has* to be something I'm doing; a vibe I'm putting out there. I don't know what it is and I don't know how to stop it."

Hudson disagreed. "You're a gentle person. Those who are *not* gentle are drawn to you. Some are intrigued, most are naturally protective toward you, and then there are those who seek to use you. It's bullshit to think you've *done* something."

"I have to be stronger. No more relationships. No more ménages. No more of the lifestyle."

"Gabriella…"

"I'm not suited. In the end, *they* aren't doing it. I did it to myself. I'm too emotional, I don't fit." She shrugged. "I don't *know* where I fit but…I'm confused, hurt."

Quietly, she added, "I need to talk to Scott. I need closure. It's time to move on."

Inhaling carefully, he gave a single nod. "Anything you need, you know we'll help you."

"I know. I love you both for that."

* * *

Several days later, they met at her apartment. She dressed carefully and pulled her hair snugly to the back of her head.

In the living room, her eyes landed on the sculpture and the violin. "Are they okay?" Hudson grunted. "I need to know they're still breathing."

"Yes. They're okay."

Natalia held her shoulders. "We see them often. Is there a message, darling?"

"I…" She took a deep breath and started again. "Tell them I gave freely, without condition, and I'll never use it against them. I regret *nothing*."

Wiping stray tears, she grabbed her bag. "I want to close the door on the past. Maybe then I'll be able to think clearly about my future."

In the lobby, she remembered the day of the attack and suppressed a chill, pressing her heart.

Leonard held the door to the car and as she approached, he gave her a hard hug. "I'm glad you're okay, Brie. I'm sorry I wasn't with you."

At her ear, he added in a whisper, "The man had half a kilo of cocaine in the back of his car. When he's released from the hospital, he'll be going to prison."

"He's...still in the hospital?"

"Eklund is rather good at destruction." She nodded and moved to pull back. He held her a moment longer. "Men such as us don't give up easily. Don't lose hope."

Staring into his eyes, she tried to smile and failed. He kissed her forehead and nudged her into the back of the car.

"Cocaine?" she asked Hudson when the door closed.

Brushing imaginary lint from his slacks, her best friend met her eyes. "He had to go for *something*. The sentence for drugs is harsher than that for violence against women. A fact that *sickens* me." He faced forward.

"I wanted him punished without involving you. Leonard is imaginative. I never appreciated the range of his skills until you came into our lives. I've given him a substantial raise."

"As did I," Natalia told her with a wink. "He *adores* you and I do so enjoy a man with excellent taste."

Brie hugged them and loved them for so many reasons.

* * *

They drove for an hour to a luxury apartment building. "You put him in New Jersey?"

"He *was* being punished," Hudson replied deadpan.

Despite the mood, she laughed.

At the curb, Leonard let them out and winked at Brie. Her friends flanked her as they entered the building.

"Mr. Winters. Good to see you again, sir." An older woman manned the concierge desk. "They're expecting you."

As the elevator rose, Brie worked to center her mind, to calm her thoughts, to ease the pressure in her heart.

In the hallway, there were armed men on either side of an apartment door. Their heads turned to take them in.

Hudson took her hand. "Are you alright?"

"I will be." She gave him a shaky smile. "Let's do this."

One of the men opened the door. "Mr. Winters."

Hudson nodded and they walked into a gorgeous space. On the other side of the room, Scott Truing stood in front of the windows. Men stood on either side of him. She knew they'd subdue him if he tried to hurt her.

She stared at him for a long moment. His light blonde hair was longer and he was leaner. He was still a beautiful man.

Squeezing Hudson's hand, she let him go and approached Scott slowly. His eyes were clear, pale blue. He met her gaze directly and she could see the pain in them.

Tears slipped from the corners of his eyes and he said quietly, "I'm glad you're alright. I'm sorry. I'm so sorry, Gabriella."

Stepping closer, she wrapped her arms around him. He gasped and hugged her hard. They stood like that for almost a minute.

Finally leaning back, she asked, "Are you better now?"

He nodded, more tears slipped over his cheeks.

"So am I. I forgive you." Scott sobbed brokenly, tightening his hands on her. "Why you did all of it doesn't matter. Why you were so angry, that doesn't matter either."

"W-what matters?"

"That you move on. That you stop hurting people. That you know Hudson loves you and would give his right arm to protect you. That you *matter* to someone, to *many* someones, and they want to see you safe and happy. That you understand where you *were* so you don't go back."

He lifted his hand to brush his fingers over her face. "I hurt you in so many ways. I almost *killed* you, Gabriella. How can you forgive me?"

"How can I not?" She shook her head. "I believe in second chances, in starting over. If I don't believe in them for *you*, then I c-can't believe in them for myself."

Lifting one shoulder, she whispered, "I'm also grateful that a bizarre and sometimes painful chain of events brought so many wonderful people into my life. I can't regret it."

"You're a *spectacular* woman." He inhaled carefully. "I want you to know I introduced myself to you originally to fuck with Hudson. I wasn't running the con then. I had no intention of falling in love with you but I did. I fell hard. I knew you *wanted* to love me, that you tried, but you didn't."

"I'm sorry, Scott."

He shook his head. "You'd have stayed with me anyway because you give so fucking much. A few months after I met you, I started using and lost my mind. You were an easy target because you always expect the best of people. I imagine they continually disappoint you."

"Not always."

"I was so high the day I hit you that I don't remember driving to that corner. There was a moment of clarity where I tried to stop the gruesome thing I was doing but…it was too late." He swallowed hard and more tears fell. "The rage, that Hudson had what I wanted so badly, I went insane."

"I'm not in love with Hudson, nor he with me." She sighed. "He felt responsible for me, for how I showed up at his door. He and Natalia are my best friends, the best people I know."

Scott's hands tightened on her shoulders. "Is there someone? In your life?" She nodded and he closed his eyes. "How could there *not* be?" He swallowed hard. "Is he good to you?"

Shaking, she whispered, "Yes."

"Does he love you as much as you love him?"

"That's a hard question to answer."

Scott frowned. "That's the *easiest* question in the world." Her eyes filled with tears and he hugged her. "You deserve love more than any person I've ever met. I'm sorry my version of it was so fucked up."

Nodding, she hugged him back. He lifted her face and kissed her lightly on the lips. "Thank you for your forgiveness. You have no idea how much I needed it."

"Have you been okay here?"

"For what I did, I should've been beaten to death in a prison shower, Gabriella." He shook his head. "I've lacked for nothing. It gave me time to think and I needed that."

She held his gaze. "Make the rest of your life amazing, Scott. Let go of all the resentment and old hurts." After one more hug, she let him go. "Get out of this apartment and start over, find your path. I believe in you. I always did."

As she turned to go, he said her name. Looking over her shoulder, he smiled. "You still have the most *incredible* ass."

It made her laugh and he winked. "Bye, Scott."

"See ya, pretty girl. Later, Hudson. Natalia, *still* hot."

In the hallway, Hudson grabbed her in a hard hug. "You have the most beautiful fucking *soul*, Gabriella."

She started crying and couldn't seem to stop. They got her to the car and held her between them firmly.

"Get it all out, darling. God knows you need it."

* * *

"Eklund."

"I'm sending you footage. Gabriella met with Scott Truing today. Winters and Natalia were with her."

"Received. Is she alright?"

"She's…amazing. The safe house is being shut down. Scott is staying with his mother for a few weeks." There was a long pause. "I'll keep an eye on him for now. Make sure."

"Thank you."

* * *

The next morning, Brie was severely sick and wondered if her new medication to help her blood clot properly was freaking out her system. She made an appointment with her doctor.

Leonard took her there and insisted on waiting.

Hours later, he escorted her to the penthouse and she leaned heavily on him. She was shaking *apart* on the inside.

Natalia took one look at her and froze in the act of taking a sip of her wine. She murmured, "*Hudson.*"

He glanced up from reading the financial papers.

"I-I'm pregnant. I'm so scared. I don't know what to do." Her friends were across the room in seconds. "The birth control…maybe the other meds?" She shook her head and the pain was excruciating. "I don't know. I don't know *anything.*"

Then she started to laugh hysterically until the laughter dissolved into wracking sobs.

Brie was four months along, knew Harper had to be the father, and wondered what the fuck was going to happen.

* * *

Harper stiffened as Hudson and Natalia entered the charity gala. Elijah stilled behind him.

In a distant part of his mind, Harper remembered the gown and the jewelry he'd had commissioned for Gabriella to wear to the event and his heart trembled in true pain.

The couple made a beeline for them and he steeled himself to endure their contempt.

"Winters. Natalia, you look lovely."

"Thank you, Harper." The blonde glanced back and forth between them with a frown. She asked softly, "Are you alright?"

He didn't know how to respond.

"Ask me, Delkin." Black eyes held his resolutely.

Clearing his throat, he murmured, "How is Gabriella?"

"Healing slowly. She asks about your safety." Harper closed his eyes. "We told her we see you often and asked if there was a message."

"Did she...have one?"

Part of him was afraid to know. With the sort of women Harper was accustomed to before her, he couldn't imagine her having anything positive to say.

"Yes." Natalia tightened her hand on Hudson's arm and told them, "She said to tell you she gave freely, without condition, and that she'd never use it against you. She also said she regrets nothing."

Behind him, he heard Elijah's small grunt of pain and inhaled carefully to calm his own reaction.

Winters held his gaze. "She said we aren't to hold you accountable. That condemning *you* would be like condemning *Natalia* for her ability to love only me."

"That's a correct statement, is it not, Harper?" Electric blue eyes met his. "Are we alike in our ability to love only one?"

He blinked. "I haven't examined our similarities too closely, Natalia." He smiled. "I'm *glad* to say I never had that chance because you're *exactly* where you belong."

"Thank you. I agree."

Smoothly changing the topic to the small Utah town they'd purchased together, Harper engaged Winters in their first civil conversation since he'd set a chain of events in motion that he couldn't take back, and didn't know how to fix.

His choices haunted him.

Elijah's continued silence was devastating.

Chapter Forty-Six

Beginning December 2015

When Brie was twenty-one weeks pregnant, she started to slip getting out of the shower in her apartment, grabbed for the frame, and felt everything give way inside her.

She hit the panic button in her bathroom and struggled to calm her body, to mentally save her child.

Two minutes later, Natalia entered her bathroom with paramedics. Brie was sobbing, lying in a pool of her own blood, and she *knew.* Her friend knelt at her side, held her hand tightly, and murmured soothingly as she cried with her.

Listening numbly as the paramedics confirmed she'd lost her baby, Brie wasn't able to verbally respond. Natalia spoke for her and rode in the ambulance that waited in the loading bay.

She wouldn't remember the trip to the hospital or what the paramedics looked like who worked over her. She wouldn't remember saying several times, "I give up. I fucking give up."

All she could do was shed tears that seemed *endless.*

* * *

"Eklund."

"You get that selfish piece of shit to her side *right fucking now* or I'll do it myself!"

Immediately on alert, Elijah stilled. "What happened?"

"Lenox Hill. Get him there and if he doesn't show some goddamn *compassion*, you tell him to expect a visit from me!"

Hollow disconnected and Elijah busted into Harper's room.

He was climbing naked from his bed. On the other side was a doe-eyed nameless woman who fit every stereotype.

"Shower the whore off your body and dress. You have three minutes, Harper."

"What the fuck happened now?"

Elijah grabbed him by the throat. "Two minutes and fifty seconds."

He shoved him in the direction of the bathroom and kicked the frame of Harper's bed. The woman screamed.

"Get the fuck out if you don't want to be riddled with bullet holes. Move your ass."

He texted Winters.

Four minutes after Hollow's call, they were descending in the elevator. "Elijah, what the *hell* is going on?"

"I've been told to get you to Lenox Hill and that if you don't show compassion, Hollow will be paying a visit."

"Oh, for god's sake. We're racing around on *his* orders? Fuck that shit. He *lives* to be obnoxious."

In the car, his phone vibrated and he read a short reply from Winters. Closing his eyes, Elijah searched for strength, for patience, for a clear head.

"Before we make some *charity* visit, let's have breakfast."

Elijah stared into silver eyes that had grown colder, crueler than he remembered. Quietly, he asked, "How was your date, Harper?" His expression shuttered. "Was it fulfilling? All things beautiful? Everything you needed?"

"Why? Jealous?"

"If that's your intention, I have no choice but to disappoint you, Harper. I've spent twenty *years* watching you fuck hundreds of women. I'm immune to it now."

"I'm sorry, I…"

"I was curious. Does every pussy feel the *same* to you? After so many, do they all blend together? Just another hole? Your type all make the same sounds, the same motions, and supply appropriately appreciative gestures when given gifts."

Harper rubbed the back of his neck hard. "I don't know what you're asking me, Elijah."

He was unable to keep from screaming. "In all your goddamn *life*, of all the women you've *fucked*, are they all the fucking *same?*"

"No."

"Explain!"

"She was different. You know she was different."

"Do you mean Brie?" Harper nodded. "Hmm. That's good to know. In a few minutes, I want you to hold onto that understanding, Harper. I want you to keep it close to yourself." Elijah watched as realization dawned.

"*Gabriella* is in the hospital?" He said nothing, he didn't blink. Harper whispered, "What happened?"

The driver opened the door and Elijah moved to get out.

Pausing at the last moment, he said over his shoulder, "She just miscarried your *child*, Harper."

Guiding him through the hospital, Elijah noted that all color had drained from Harper's face.

Winters stood as they entered the waiting room, feet planted and fists clenched. Natalia sat behind him, her face in her hands, her shoulders shaking with her sobs. She wore pajamas, a robe, and running shoes.

The fabric from her knees down was covered in blood.

Harper walked to the nearest trashcan and vomited.

For two hours, Elijah stood beside the chair Harper sat in with his head in his hands and waited.

When a doctor entered, he went to the other side of the room. "Mr. and Mrs. Winters?" Hudson nodded and helped Natalia to her feet. "You're the contacts in her paperwork." The words filled Elijah with shame. "I'm cleared to update you."

"Do it faster."

"Of course, I'm sorry. Miss Hernandez is stable. We stopped the hemorrhaging. We couldn't save her baby. The good news is that she should be able to conceive again at some point in the future. It was touch and go. With the various medications listed in her records, her pregnancy was *extremely* high-risk from the beginning."

"She didn't *intend* to get pregnant. In fact," Hudson glared at Harper, "*every* measure was taken to prevent it."

"Certainly. Without her body's ability to clot properly, it could've been much worse. As it was, she required several units of blood." The doctor crossed his hands in front of him. "Our main concern at this point is her full recovery."

Elijah knew there was more.

Hudson did as well. "Tell me."

"Mr. Winters, we had to sedate her. We…have her upstairs." Hudson frowned. "She's extremely distraught. It's important not to upset her."

Natalia whispered, "Did she try to *hurt* herself?"

"She…fought receiving medical attention. Rather violently. I don't think she was fully coherent." He took a deep breath. "I'm sorry for your loss but she's young and strong. She should make a complete recovery."

Hudson held Natalia. "The child."

Brie's baby…

"Arrangements can be made. I'll send in a counselor to handle that for you. Again, I'm sorry. We'll get her back on her feet."

The man left and Natalia pressed her face against Hudson. Elijah looked down at Harper. He gripped his hair with both fists and tears dripped between his feet on the floor.

Crouching, Elijah held him while he sobbed. "I wouldn't have let her go through it alone. I'd have helped. I'm a horrible person but…not in *that*, not in that, Elijah. I'd have helped."

Hudson's voice was calm. "She wanted to wait until the end of the second trimester before she told you. She found out a few weeks ago but she said she didn't want to bother you if she couldn't carry the baby to term."

Didn't want to *bother* them. Elijah's regrets compounded.

"She took *every* precaution," Natalia whispered. "She was terrified when she found out but she *wanted* her baby. L-last week, she felt him move and…" Unable to continue, she gripped Hudson and cried as he held her.

Elijah screamed in his mind, his heart in tatters, as he maintained the appearance of detachment to the outside world.

Hudson picked Natalia up and sat on the sofa with her in his lap, holding her close to his body and murmuring softly to her. She hugged him hard and nodded.

Sitting beside Harper, he wrapped his arm around his shoulder and kissed the top of his head. He responded by putting both arms around him and crying bitterly. Barely controlling his own shakes, Elijah held him hard.

Over and over, Harper murmured, "I'm sorry. I'm sorry."

"Ssh, Harper. It'll be alright." He shook his head. "Yes. We'll help her in any way we can."

"You'll hate me, she'll hate me. I've lost *everything*." He gasped for air. "I didn't *mean* it. I was afraid. I didn't *mean* it."

Stroking his hand over his head, Elijah asked with a frown, "What didn't you mean?"

"That I couldn't love her. Gabriella scared me, I felt pushed by both of you, I wanted you back, and it was too much. All of it was too much." Elijah stilled. "I didn't *want* to love her. I thought it would go away if I got away from her."

No. No. No.

Holding the side of his face roughly, Elijah lifted it to look into his eyes. "*Harper.*"

"I know. I know. I'm so fucking sorry."

There was a part of him that wanted to snap the other man's neck. "I *left* her, Harper. I *hurt* her and left her alone."

"I'll do anything to make it right. Tell me what to do. I'll do anything. Forgive me, forgive me, forgive me."

Throwing himself against Elijah's chest, his body shook as he cried raggedly. Staring at the ceiling, Elijah struggled, *fought* to understand what to do.

Then he lowered his head and met the eyes of Hudson Winters. Pools of black stared at him and Elijah's mind cleared with a snap. He lowered his hand to the back of Harper's head and the sound of his sobs increased.

"Harper." The other man moved back to look at him. Elijah removed a handkerchief from his suit and wiped his face gently. "You and I are going to come to an understanding. As of today, *this moment*, your days of unchecked *fear* are finished."

Nodding, Harper took several deep breaths.

"For more than half your life, you've given me your submission in some ways while doing whatever the fuck you damn well pleased in others. Your actions have hurt people, including *yourself*, and it can't continue."

"I'm sorry, Elijah."

"Your remorse is admirable but it isn't enough. You see that, don't you?" He nodded. "Words are no longer enough. It's *actions*, Harper. Actions are what *define* you."

Holding him by the back of his neck, he stared into his eyes. "If you *lie* to me, if you act as if nothing fucking matters, I'll rescind my vow and walk away. Do you *understand* me?"

"I understand."

In the waiting room of the hospital where his beautiful Brie coped with the loss of her baby, Elijah issued a command.

"Tell me how you feel about Brie."

Inhaling carefully, he said shakily, "I love her. I've loved her since the day she understood what I needed and put her own body on the line to see that I received it."

The pain that arced through Elijah was intense. Gripping Harper tighter, he growled, "You fucking *hurt* her. You let *me* hurt her."

He whispered, "Penance. I'll do penance."

"Yes, you fucking will. If we've lost her due to your selfishness and cruelty, I'll lock you the fuck down. You'll *withhold* for a year and not be able to sleep on your back for a month. At the end of that year, you'll *never* see me again."

"I-I understand."

Releasing him, Elijah stood and paced. The synapses in his brain were brilliantly lit as he put together a plan.

He was going to need Winters' help.

* * *

"Hudson." It was the first word Brie uttered in two days. Her best friend sat beside her bed in a suit. He looked beautiful, capable as he always did.

"Yes, Gabriella?"

"I need to bury my little b-baby."

"It's already done. Rest."

"You're the kindest man I know. I need somewhere to go. Far away, off the grid. I don't care what it costs. Will you arrange it for me?"

"Stay here. Let us help you."

"I can't. As much as I love the two of you, this *should not* and *cannot* be on your shoulders." She swallowed and her throat hurt. "I'll be okay. I'll stay in touch so you don't worry."

He sat up and gripped the rail of the bed. "Gabriella…"

"Hudson, you've done *enough*. From the first *hour* you met me, you've had to protect me from the results of my mistakes. You've done so much, *too much*, for me. I'm one fucking mess after another."

"You're *not* a mess. Nothing about you is messy."

"My heart hurts so bad. It feels heavy and useless."

"It *will* get better. I promise."

"Hudson, *I really wanted my baby*." She fell apart and he bent to hold her tight as she sobbed against him for a long time.

Gasping, her fingers tightened on him. "He moved and I thought he w-would be okay after all, despite the medications and everything. I knew he'd make the pain better and I wouldn't be alone. I'd have someone to love, who would love me back. Someone of my *very own* to love."

"I know, I know, Gabriella. I'm so sorry."

"I'd have been a *good* mother."

"The *best* mother and one day you will be."

"No. I wanted *this* baby. This baby was Harper's and that's like having a baby from both of them. I'd have loved him extra to make up for all the love Elijah didn't have as a little boy. He'd have been part of the three of us, from the happiest time in my life. Wickedly smart and beautiful like his father. Maybe creative like me. I'd have bought him a violin and ached a little when he played…"

She wept bitterly and Hudson cupped her face. "You're strong, Gabriella. One of the strongest people I've ever met. You *will* make it through this."

"I'm tired, Hudson. I'm so *tired*."

"I know, but you have to fight. I need this *one thing* from you. Look at me." She met his black eyes and saw his pain for her. "Fight. Don't you fucking *quit* on me. I didn't quit and you can't either."

"You're *you*...I'm just *me*."

"You listen to me. There are too many people who will *break* if you give up. We can't lose you. I know you're in pain. You need to grieve and get strong again. Then you have to get your ass back to your *life*."

"It hurts *deep*, Hudson." She choked back her tears.

"It'll always hurt but you *will* make it. You're our *best friend*. You hold that position because you're kind and loving but also because you're strong. You have to be strong for me again."

She whispered, "I-I don't want to let you down."

"You could *never* let me down." He pressed a kiss to her forehead, pulled back, and stared into her eyes. "*Swear it*, Gabriella. Swear to me you won't quit and if the pain gets too bad, you'll call me. You can't lie. If you swear it to me, I'll put my trust in you as you've *always* put your trust in me."

Tears streaming into her hair, she managed, "I swear I won't quit, Hudson."

"Good girl."

"I need to breathe in a place where no one knows me. I need to grieve my b-baby. My soul feels bruised, broken. Will you help me?"

Hudson smoothed her hair. "*Always.*"

* * *

When Gabriella fell asleep, Hudson stepped into the hall and stared at Elijah for a long moment.

Harper saw his determination, his rage, and his sadness.

Listening to her had been the hardest thing Harper had ever had to do. Elijah demanded he know her pain.

As they stood outside the room, the man he loved stared into his eyes and endured every word with him. Holding him against the wall with his palm on Harper's chest, he was utterly still as tears slipped over his cheeks.

He wondered if either of them would ever forgive him.

Hudson rubbed his hands over his face. "If you hurt her, if you break her again, both of you will answer to me." His voice was quiet, deadly. "I help you only because I need her to keep breathing. If she stops, I swear on my life, I *will* destroy you."

"Understood." Elijah's voice was equally quiet.

He shook his head. "I should get her behind the highest walls to protect her from both of you."

"I would *scale* them and you *know* it. Nothing will keep me from her now."

Harper didn't blink when Hudson turned his fierce gaze on him. "Learn from her pain, learn from your own."

He stepped closer and said softly, "You're *better* than you have been, Harper. You're *stronger* than this. Gabriella found you *worthy*. Prove her right."

Natalia walked into Hudson's arms, her eyes swollen and red from crying. "I once told you she was too good for you and I stand by that statement. She *chose* you, Harper. She *chose* Elijah. Her love will make you stronger. Accept it."

Looking up, she told her husband, "They're going to release her tomorrow. I found the perfect villa in Croatia. Easily fortified and defended. There's an apartment across the courtyard that overlooks it."

"Take them both."

"Already done, darling."

"Call Vi."

"I left her a voicemail."

Hudson kissed her lips and rested his forehead on her hair. "That was the most painful conversation I've ever had, Natalia. I feel ripped *apart*."

"You were the only one Gabriella would've listened to at this point, darling. I-I couldn't have been half as strong. Thank you." She stroked his face. "How I *love* you, Hudson."

"I love you." He met Natalia's eyes. "You were as excited as she was. I'm sorry."

"It's our *Gabriella*. I may fear children but *she* doesn't. I could've enjoyed him with backup." She blinked against tears. "She was trying to *will* her body to save him. *If I can just focus hard enough, if I can calm down.* I just, the *blood*, Hudson."

"Natalia." He wrapped her as tightly to his body as he could and stroked the back of her head. "She's strong. She'll make it through this." She nodded against him.

Harper felt utter devastation. While Elijah watched the couple, he slipped into Gabriella's room.

Her curly hair was tangled around her, her skin gray from blood loss. She looked too fragile.

She'd spent too much time in hospitals over the last two years.

Bending, he pressed a light kiss to her temple and whispered, "I'm sorry, Gabriella. I'll make it right. I love you."

As he straightened, Elijah stood beside him. His expression as he took in her still form made Harper's stomach cramp with shame.

He bent to kiss her and said softly, "I love you. I'm sorry I left you alone. Forgive me."

Then Elijah wrapped his arms around Harper and hugged him tighter than he had in years.

Chapter Forty-Seven

Mid-December 2015

A few days later, Hudson and Natalia sat in the limo and held Brie's hands. She couldn't stop shaking. It felt *wrong* that the sun was shining, that the day was so beautiful.

"You'll call the moment you land."

It wasn't a request and she smiled at Hudson despite how strange it felt on her face. "I will."

"We'll miss you *terribly*. I hate not knowing how long you'll be gone, darling."

Blinking against tears, she struggled to find words. "Until the pain stops. I'm not sure."

Natalia held her hand and brought her forward to rest their foreheads against each other. "Right now, I know life seems dark but you have a natural radiance. It's something you were born with and it'll fill you up again if you welcome it, Gabriella. When the time is right, open your heart to the light."

She nodded and swallowed hard as Natalia sat back. "When I come back, I'll be stronger. I won't lean on you so much."

Hudson squeezed her hand and she looked at him. "Every day I've known you, in *every* situation, you've given so much more than you take."

"Thank you, Hudson."

"Remember your vow to me, Gabriella."

"I won't forget. I'll c-call if it gets too bad."

Leonard held the door and they got out together. The driver gathered her carefully to him. "I believe in you, Brie. Give yourself time to heal so you can smile again. You owe me a rematch when you get back."

"You always let me win, Leo." He laughed and let her go with a wink. "Take care of them."

"I promise."

Attendants came to take her bags while the plane idled on the tarmac. Hudson and Natalia hugged her tightly and she hugged them back even harder, inhaling deeply of the strongest and most loving people she'd ever met.

Pulling back, she took a deep breath. "I love you. Thank you."

"We love *you*, darling."

"Gabriella." She looked into black eyes that sparkled. "Come back. Your presence makes me happy."

Nodding, she hugged them again and got on the plane.

While she waited for takeoff, she wrote the men she thought of constantly. It was a crucial step for herself, to end their time together with positive words, thoughts, and feelings.

> *Elijah, I want you to remember that someone in the world needs you to keep going, to keep breathing. Knowing you're out there helps me. Please don't be angry with Harper. Love him and forgive him. See the man you've always loved, the way you saw me. Show him how the heart works. You have that knowledge now. Your heart is so beautiful. I love you always, Brie*

She sent it and gave herself a moment to calm down before she wrote the words she'd wanted to say months ago.

> *Harper, I understand why my presence was so hard for you. I'm sorry for the pain I know I caused, for intruding on something that has always been vital to your happiness. Please love Elijah in all the ways he deserves and let him love you just as hard. Don't be afraid. I regret nothing and will forever remember our moments fondly. I see your love for Elijah. Don't forget to also love yourself because you're worthy. Gabriella*

Struggling, she pulled herself together.

She turned off the secured cell they'd never asked her to return, slid her sunglasses in place, and got the fuck out of the western hemisphere.

* * *

At the apartment in Manhattan, Elijah read the short message from Brie several times. He felt the *pain* in her words. He also felt her *love*. She'd always be unshakeable.

How he missed touching her, breathing her in, loving her.

He received a second message from Winters that outlined her itinerary.

When Harper leaned his head back against the sofa and put his hand over his eyes, there was no doubt he'd received a message of his own.

Moving to sit beside him, Elijah brought him to his shoulder. It was the first time he'd touched him since the hospital and the low sounds of pain he made affected him deeply.

"I love you, Harper. I'm sorry for many things." He stroked his hand over silken black hair as he wept against him. "It's only when you're awakened that you realize how long you've been sleeping. I'll make it right."

"I've been a horrible person, Elijah." The words were barely audible. "I've put you through so much bullshit." He lifted his face. "You've loved me better than I've loved you and I'm sorry, so sorry, for never seeing what I was doing."

Elijah pressed his lips to his forehead, his cheeks, and claimed his lips in a way that reminded both of them of the first time they'd kissed.

Testing the waters, expressing untapped desires, and embracing love that was scorned by most of the world.

When their love was new and beautiful.

As their tongues coiled together, he stopped and experienced everything. Harper's fingers tightened on his arms. He took his breath and gave it back. The strength of his hands, the warmth of his skin, the softness of his hair. Elijah *saw* the man he had in his arms for the first time in a long time.

When they pulled apart, they stared at one another.

Taking a deep breath, Harper whispered, "I'm going to thank Gabriella for days when we have her back." His hands lifted and he cupped Elijah's cheeks. "You *see* me again."

Stroking his palm along his neck, he confessed the words he'd held back for two decades. "It…hurt me. The way you were. There were so *many*, Harper. I had to pull back."

"I was selfish. I didn't know I was hurting you."

He shook his head. "There are two people in all my lifetime whose touch I've welcomed. With you and Brie, I give and receive touch willingly. To make my vows was no hardship to me. It *isn't* self-denial. It's an *honor* to preserve who I am for the only people I love."

Harper put his palm over Elijah's heart. "When I was eighteen, the first time I touched you, I *knew* there'd never be another man. I thought you knew that, that you knew you were unique to me. I should've told you."

He swallowed hard. "I thought from the start that women would fill a place that was empty inside me. In the beginning, I tried to talk to them, to know them, but they were so shallow."

His smile was self-deprecating. "You know my type. It was about the money, the power, the position. I started to hate them, to use them, to *punish* them for the emptiness I felt."

Elijah watched him breathe deeply. "Then we met Gabriella. She was different. She made me *hope* and it made me furious. I didn't want to try again at *forty*. I fought her but she's fucking *relentless* in her nature."

"She twisted you up." He lifted his hand and brushed his fingers through Harper's hair. His lashes drifted closed at the simple contact. "Tell me, Harper."

"The morning after she burned down the building, I-I shared myself with her and I felt incredible, free for the first time."

His face contorted in pain. "We left a few hours later. I started thinking, wondering, *doubting* her. The entire time we were gone, I obsessed over it. I felt vulnerable. I kept finding reasons not to go back to her. It built and I resented that she had access to you that I didn't."

"My fault, Harper. I handled it wrong. I see that now. I wanted to establish a bond between the two of you. To have you *include* her. I thought *we* were strong. Gabriella and I were strong. I wanted to give you time to see how you could be with each other. You have so much in common."

"I thought…you needed *her* to want *me*."

"No. I wish I'd understood."

"When we got back, sh-she did more for my birthday than any woman other than my mother. I didn't know how to deal with it. I treated her the way I treated Danielle when she wanted to go on vacation together. With my dead wife, I knew it was so she could shop. Gabriella just wanted to be good to me. By the time I realized, she was gone. You were so angry."

"It reinforced what you already thought." Harper nodded. "I'm sorry. It was never about that." He sighed. "For years, you've had so many women in and out of your bed, I figured you were fine. You didn't seem to miss me, to need me, unless we were in the sanctuary or you needed a third."

Harper's face contorted in pain. "*Elijah.*" Hugging him hard, he whispered, "I always miss you. I always need you. I love you. I know I haven't shown it but I *always* love you."

Gripping him tight, he inhaled the scent of him. "Thank you."

Leaning back, Harper smiled and it was as heart-stopping as it was when he was eighteen. "I'll eventually have to get back to work. I've taken more time off in the last months than I have in more than twenty years." He traced the lines of Elijah's face. "When do we leave for Croatia?"

Elijah powered him to his back on the couch. Harper was shocked, staring up at him. "After I remind you how much I love you, Harper."

"Gabriella…"

"Is going to need us solid, strong. Natalia was right that we must be *three couples* as well as a threesome. Brie tried to tell me the same thing months ago. I wasn't paying attention."

He gripped Harper to him. "I almost lost the *only* two things on this fucking planet that really *matter* to me." He shook his head. "I won't repeat my mistakes."

"I can wait, Elijah."

"You shouldn't have to. I'm sorry I hurt you."

Claiming his mouth, he rocked himself against Harper, holding him roughly, touching him more forcefully than he touched Brie. One day, if they had the chance to be with her again, he hoped to show her the differences.

He had no doubt it would fascinate her, stimulate her.

Rising from the couch in a single movement, he lifted Harper to his feet, took his hand, and led him to his bedroom.

Tearing at their clothes, Elijah felt like he could breathe again when they were naked together. He shoved him to the bed, followed him down, and soaked up the sounds of pleasure Harper made.

Kissing him, touching him, he reconnected to the man he'd always loved. He needed to remind himself, to remind Harper, of how strong they'd once been together, how hard they'd loved for so many years.

He had to heal the breaks they had between them before they could include Brie. It would never work otherwise.

The past couldn't repeat itself.

Elijah remembered the pleasure Brie felt at simple touch and how similar they were to each other. They were male and female equals. The only difference was that Brie exposed herself to the world while Harper hid behind expectations.

Moving from his lips, he traced his mouth along his jaw. "When you were seventeen, I was training you in Krav Maga."

Breathlessly, Harper murmured, "I remember…"

"I was showing you a cross-body technique and you were bowed across my torso. It was the first time I noticed you were hard. I started paying attention." Kissing down his neck, he massaged his shoulders firmly. "I'd never voluntarily allowed another person to touch me. I wanted *you* to touch me."

Warm hands started to touch him back and it made Elijah smile. "I didn't care that you were male, I didn't define it. At the time, I didn't have much emotional capability to do it, even if I'd tried. All my life to that point, I'd been trained to fight, to kill, to protect. I didn't know what love was."

Sliding further down his body, he bit a tight nipple and Harper moaned, his hands raking through his hair and holding him close. "The night before the attack when you were eighteen, I walked the house after midnight. Your mother's dog had pushed your door open. I watched you stroking off."

A low groan and Harper lifted his hips, pressing himself against Elijah's belly. "I'd never been so hard in my life. Then you came and whispered…"

"*Elijah…*"

"It made me more aggressive the next day. While I'd always been worried about your safety, I felt as if fate would snatch you from me. I'd already lost so much."

He rested his cheek on Harper's stomach, defined as it had always been from the brutal workouts Elijah insisted on. He'd never risk his survival on a lack of fitness.

"Then you kept me in the room near yours while I recovered. It was the most time I'd ever spent with you outside of training or school. All our time together had been scheduled."

Kissing one hip, he trailed his lips across his lower abdomen and kissed the other. The underside of his chin brushed the head of Harper's cock and made him gasp. His hands massaged the muscles of his thighs, around to the firm cheeks of his ass.

"Then you brought me a violin. I don't know why I never thought to replace the one my father destroyed. I didn't know you knew I played. The look on your face, that's when I knew what love was, Harper. That's when I knew I was meant to love you."

He sucked the head of Harper's cock between his lips and he cried out, curling his fist in his hair and gripping the bedding.

"Elijah, I'm not strong enough, it's been too long."

Releasing him, he rubbed his face over the bend in his hip, "Hold back. You're strong enough. Let me suck you."

He took him deep and swallowed around a cock he'd learned better than his own over the years they'd spent together.

The first ten years, they'd *hungered* for one another. It was after Danielle's death that they began to drift apart.

That was when the rotation of random women in and out of his bed truly started to become a problem. More often than he liked, he was requested as a third. Looking back, he realized Harper needed *help*.

Brie would've *known* how to help him. Elijah hadn't.

Now they needed to find their way back to each other, to the love they'd always shared.

Sucking him slow and deep, he took in the way Harper's hands shook as they touched his hair, the pressing of his thighs against his shoulders, and the groans he made from deep in his chest. Breath sawed in and out of his lungs.

Accustomed to Brie and her need for touch, Elijah ran his hands over the first skin he'd ever wanted against him. He worshipped a man he'd loved long before a sexual element was part of their relationship.

Higher and higher, he pushed Harper through pleasure that made his entire body tighten, his balls draw close to his body, and his fingers fist in his hair.

Gripping the length, he said against the head, "Come for me, Harper. Let me drink you down."

Jaw clenched, he breathed out Elijah's name as he let go of the control he'd fought to maintain. Jets of hot come hit the back of his throat and he wrapped his arms under Harper's body to hold him close. Hugging him as he took him deeper still.

Only when he had nothing left did Elijah release him and rest his face on his thigh. Harper raked his fingers through his hair as he struggled to settle his system.

"I love you, Elijah. I'll always love you."

Crawling up his body, he stretched out beside him and held him to his chest. "I love you, Harper. Until death."

They laid like that, stroking over each other's skin, for a long time. When Harper fell asleep, Elijah raked his fingers through his hair and stared at a face he'd always found beautiful. Kissing his temple, he pulled the blankets up and held him closer.

Only with Brie had he ever slept so deeply.

Chapter Forty-Eight

End-January 2016

Brie spent the first six weeks in a pretty villa on the coast of Croatia trying to reconcile her grief over the loss of her baby.

A child would've complicated her broken heart. It would've been difficult seeing Harper and Elijah, being unable to touch them.

Still, she had no doubt Harper would've taken an active role as a father. For herself, once she discovered the pregnancy, she loved the child.

Her doctors warned her from the start that there were great risks due to the powerful medications and that her blood didn't clot correctly.

Again, though she'd known the risks, Brie *hoped*. The loss of the little boy she'd so looked forward to bringing into the world cut her to her core.

For her, in all ways, the conception was one of love.

While she was still in the hospital, Natalia booked the place and had it stocked with things she knew she'd need. The blonde had Tawny set up a secure system so she could work.

It was Hudson who staffed it.

The woman who acted as her personal driver, chef, and assistant struck her as the type to know hand-to-hand combat and probably had the ability to disassemble a weapon in ten seconds or less.

Obviously, her friends felt she needed a bodyguard. Brie thought maybe she needed one for her heart.

The calls to and from her parents, her friends, her staff, and her sister were filled with unasked or unanswered questions.

Hudson and Natalia called her every couple of days. She always picked up the phone. She tried to be strong. Every conversation ended with her reassuring them that she was getting better.

Many of her days were spent in memory, in reflection. Those days were harder to bear and she hated the tears she couldn't stop crying.

She worked on healing from two years of chaos, injury, and loss. She stared out at the water and tried to decide what she was going to do with the rest of her life.

Sometimes, she'd press her hands to her stomach, remembering the first and only time she felt her baby move.

During those moments, it felt as if she was broken in two.

Vi would bring a glass of infused water and stand guard at the rear door leading to the expansive second floor balcony with a view of the sea.

She never spoke but Brie felt better with her presence.

Vi wasn't chatty so Brie figured she probably drove the poor woman nuts. Sometimes, she watched her with a tilt of her head as if confused. She listened the way Hudson did. Absolutely still with every ounce of focus.

During the day, Vi prepared shakes and meals meant to put her charge's system back in balance. Brie cooked for them at night and always insisted the woman join her when she ate.

A local woman did their shopping and light cleaning. She wasn't ready to leave the house and her hired protector insured she didn't have to.

One day while cooking, Brie slipped and cut her hand. It bled profusely. Without an instant of hesitation, Vi removed a medical bag from the cabinet, covered the wound with a powdered clotting agent, then cleaned and bandaged it.

"Thank you. I usually end up going to the hospital."

"I'd like to avoid that if possible. Your blood is still too thin. We need to make a few changes to your diet." The woman gave her a careful smile.

"Whatever you think." A few minutes later, she plated food and they sat quietly. "Vi, can I do anything for you?"

"Explain."

The way she said it reminded her of Hudson and made her smile. "I bet you lead an exciting life. Am I keeping you from things you enjoy? This seems pretty boring."

"I needed a change of pace." The woman looked at her intently. "Perhaps you did as well." Brie nodded and stared out the window. "Is there anything I can do for you?"

"You're doing it. I wanted to be alone but having you here keeps me from being *too* alone." One shoulder lifted in a shrug. "It helps. I'm kind of embarrassed to be around my friends right now. I've made a lot of mistakes."

"Mistakes don't define you. How you deal with them does."

"I don't know how I deal with them." One side of her mouth lifted. "I haven't gotten much of a break between mistakes."

"Then this change will help you in many ways."

Looking into pretty light blue eyes, Brie nodded. "You say a lot with few words. You remind me of my best friend."

"The man who hired me?"

"Yes."

"You consider him your best friend?"

"The very best. Hudson changed my life."

Vi nodded but Brie could tell she wasn't sure what to make of her relationship. It certainly wasn't a unique reaction.

They cleaned up and Brie went out on the second-floor balcony with a glass of wine. Lifting her face to the setting sun, she sent positive vibes out to Elijah and Harper, wherever they happened to be.

Vi stood a step behind her and to the side.

"I should get a treadmill or something. I was starting to walk again. I wonder if I could take up running someday."

"Why don't you try something that will strengthen your core but not stress bones and muscles that sustained so much trauma?" The bodyguard came alongside her and stepped close. Her muscle tone was incredible. "Come."

Brie turned to face her and felt shorter than usual. Vi was as tall as Natalia in heels. She took her glass.

"Let's try some simple movements. See how you feel."

Already wearing leggings and a t-shirt, Brie used the tie on her wrist to secure her hair. The blonde worked with her for half an hour in the fresh breeze off the water.

Though she wasn't jostled or jumping around, Brie's skin was damp and she was surprised at the effect of the isolated movements. She liked the way it made her feel.

"You have excellent balance. Stick with tai chi and yoga. Build your inner core without wear and tear on your joints."

"Thank you, Vi."

"You're welcome, Gabriella."

* * *

Mid-February 2016

Every day, they worked out together and then the bodyguard would send her to shower while she blended her a protein shake. One morning, she came out and sat at the counter to watch the other woman chop fruit.

"I bet most clients don't require you to be so gentle. Thank you for helping me."

"You're a unique experience for me. You've been restless."

"I used to walk *everywhere* if I could. I loved the freedom of just tearing up the miles. After the accident, being still was the hardest part. For a couple of months, I couldn't even sketch. I'd say that was the closest

I ever got to true insanity."

"You were immobile for a long time."

"It could've been worse. The wheelchair made me feel trapped. The walker made me feel old. The cane made me feel ridiculous because I was *almost* there, but not quite." She smiled. "I worked hard to get back on my feet again."

"The man who hit you, do you hate him?"

Brie shook her head and gave a small shrug as tears filled her eyes. "No. He had his own demons. I believed every word he said to me because I was so desperate for someone to love me, to be nice to me. He was in trouble and I was naïve. Neither of us escaped unscathed. I hope he'll be better now."

"The way you think, I don't always understand it. I'd have killed him if he'd done that to me, Gabriella." She *meant* the words.

Brie took a deep breath. "The hurt was *always* worse than the anger. I felt…dumb. My sister always questioned things about him and I figured she was wondering how someone so good looking was with someone like me. She was just worried."

"What do you mean?"

"Scott is *very* beautiful. We didn't really fit. I-I don't really fit in with most of the people in my life. I'm kind of goofy and awkward. I'm chubby among a bunch of lean, gorgeous types. I tend to be scattered a lot." She shrugged. "I'm glad they overlook my oddities."

Vi blinked. "Perhaps they don't *overlook* them. Perhaps they *love* them. You're hard on yourself." She frowned. "I think you're lovely."

"There are a few people who have made me *feel* beautiful but it never works out. I think I'm better alone."

"I'm sorry about what happened to you."

"I think…I *know* everything happens for a reason. If Scott hadn't gotten me wrapped up in what I thought he wanted, I'd have never met my friends. His choices created a domino effect in my life." Staring out at the sea, she added softly, "So many good things happened because I went to New York."

Vi handed her the protein shake. "I've never met someone like you, Gabriella. It's…refreshing."

"Hudson said that a lot in the beginning. He and Natalia thought I was an interesting puzzle."

"You're *very* close to them. I didn't understand your relationship to them at first."

"More than anyone else in my life, Hudson had the biggest influence. He shook me out of my comfort zone. Through him, I met people I can't imagine my life without now. Natalia is my best female friend. I love the way she moves through the world. Maybe I'll be like her when I grow up." She grinned. "I call Hudson a redwood. *Deep roots.*"

There was a long pause. "I'm his sister."

Brie almost dropped her glass. "What?"

"I'm Hudson's sister, Scott's twin. When Hudson asked me to watch over you, I expected someone different."

"Holy fuck. No *wonder* you focus like a ninja."

Vi chuckled. "You have *no* idea."

"I can't believe I didn't see it. You *look* like Scott. Wow." Another thought came to mind. "He was detained for eighteen months. Hudson insisted and I agreed. I was…afraid at first."

Vi rested her palms wide on the counter. "Had my little brother been charged, he'd have done much harder time and a lot more of it." She shook her head. "You were far more lenient than I'd have been, Gabriella. Thank you for showing mercy. I would've been incapable of it."

Brie stood up and walked around the counter. "You grew up to be a badass." She hugged the bodyguard who hugged her back awkwardly. Taking a step back, she smiled. "I'm glad to meet you officially. Thank you for agreeing to stay with me."

"I kept hearing your name from my brother, Natalia, and my mother.

I was curious."

"Your mom is awesome."

"Yes. Gentle and easily hurt, much like you. I understand my older brother's protectiveness and Scott's fascination. Hudson wanted a woman guarding you. He said you make men kind of stupid. I see what he meant now."

"I think, that's a bad thing, huh?"

"No. That's totally on the idiot men. If they can't think around you, that's their fucking problem. If they don't know how to treat you, they can fuck off."

"You're really strong."

"I'm also a bitch, Gabriella. After a lot of years and a lot of men, there's one I can't shake from my psyche and it infuriates me like you wouldn't believe. I don't tolerate shit from swinging dicks anymore."

Hands on her hips, she smiled. "You don't want to be like me but you do need to get a little, I don't know, meaner?" She winked. "We'll work on it."

Unable to stop her laughter, Brie said, "That would really come in handy. I'm a wimp."

"Bullshit. You attract really strong men who mow you over and leave you mangled in a fucking ditch filled with your own tears."

"Jesus, what an image. Also, accurate." Tilting her head, she smiled slowly. "Natalia talked to you."

"Yup. She knows I'll *fuck up* a man faster than I'll *fuck* him. She thought I'd be a good influence once you started healing."

"She's damn good."

Chapter Forty-Nine

End-February 2016

The routine at the villa was an easy one. Their days were relaxed and Brie encouraged Vi to open up about her childhood with Hudson. The things she learned made her respect her best friend even more.

After more than two months indoors and on her balcony, she knew she couldn't keep the bodyguard locked up with her forever.

She entered the living space drying her hair and smiled at the woman making a grocery list.

"Let's walk the market or something. I don't feel like I'll shake apart now. I can't keep you cooped up here all the time."

"Excellent, Brie. I've lived underground for almost a year so this doesn't bother me. You *definitely* need fresh air."

She watched as Vi stripped down to her tank top and panties, then armed her body in layers from a storage container she hadn't wondered about under the bar.

It seemed like a lot of trouble.

"Nobody knows I'm here and it's been more than seven months since Harper was seen with me in public. I'm sure everyone has forgotten about me."

Vi froze. "Gabriella. Do you know what Harper Delkin does? Do you know what his company does?"

"Not really. He travels a lot."

"You were involved with him and didn't have him checked out?" She put one hand on her hip. "You're an heiress."

"Yeah but it's nothing compared to their holdings."

"No. No, that's not what I mean. Thirty seconds with you and I knew you didn't give a fuck about money." Inhaling carefully, she said, "Delkin Acquisitions rebuilds war zones."

"I don't…know what that means."

"Let's say a little village in *Bumfuck Nowhere* gets taken over by a guerilla faction. They terrorize the villagers, destroy shit, rape women, and kidnap kids. Maybe on their way out of town, they burn it to the ground."

"Oh *god…*"

"DA goes in after that faction is wiped off the planet by the government or hired mercenaries. They rebuild. They take over businesses run by dictators, mobs, and drug cartels all over the world. They build homes, create new companies, throw up a school, maybe a hospital…boom. Back in business and therapy is included. As you can imagine, it pisses off the bad guys pretty hard."

She stepped closer. "You *never* fall off the radar. You'll *never* be forgotten, Gabriella. You're at the center of a group that includes Delkin, Hudson, the Ghonim cousins, Marciella Canfield, and so many fucking others. They're rich, powerful, and wanted dead by a lot of people."

"I'm the weakest link."

"Not at all. Something tells me you'd die rather than compromise any of them. What you are is *valued*. Every single one of them would pay the price of a small country to get you back if you were taken. Those things don't go unnoticed."

Smiling slowly, she added, "However, that you're also the darling of people like Eklund, Hollow, Leonard, and *moi* might make them pause…a little bit."

Trying to process a heavy load of information, Brie watched as Vi pulled her long blonde hair snugly to the base of her neck and stepped into running shoes with her track suit.

She felt woefully unprepared in her sundress and sandals. "Should I change?"

Vi took her shoulders. "Gabriella. You're you and that's okay. If you learned how to hurt someone, you'd feel *horrible* about it. Let's go over the rules. I tell you to do something, you do it. Don't try to help me and don't argue."

"Okay. I won't panic."

"Let's get you some fresh air and sunshine."

There were lovely stores and an open-air market that they strolled together for hours. The bodyguard didn't rush her. Brie insisted on having lunch and Vi clinked their glasses over the table.

"To breathing when you think you can't."

The words made Brie smile. She wondered if she'd ever be able to spend an entire day, even an hour, without thinking about her time with Elijah and Harper.

Heading back to the villa in the afternoon, Vi went quiet and tense.

"Are you okay?" Brie asked her softly.

"Something feels *off*. I don't like it."

As they prepared to cross the street to her gate, Vi yanked her back forcibly and shoved her into the threshold of a shop.

"Don't move."

Two black cars pulled from opposite directions and several men piled out of them, yelling in a language Brie didn't recognize, their weapons trained on Vi.

She took a single step and Vi said without looking at her, "Don't *move*, Gabriella."

Still, relaxed, the bodyguard waited for the first man to grab her, clearly planning to put her in restraints. The moment he touched her wrist, she reacted so fast it startled Brie to press herself harder against the wall.

In three strikes, she had the man on the ground and his weapon in her hand. Shooting two, she used the weapon as a bludgeon to another's face.

When one tried to shoot her, she pulled his colleague in front of her and used his weapon after he took the bullet.

Vi moved almost effortlessly through their ranks, rapidly destroying one after another.

Occupied, she didn't see four men filing in silence, low to the ground, from the alley beside Gabriella.

As she started to scream a warning, *Elijah* landed among the four and snapped the necks of two before the others realized there was an additional threat.

A shadow moved over her as a man blocked Brie's body from the street. She recognized the shape of him, the black hair that was a little longer than the last time she'd seen him. Her small gasp made him look at her over his shoulder.

"Harper...?"

He gave her a gentle smile and returned his attention to the street.

The fight wrapped up quickly with Elijah and Vi dispatching the remaining men, pulling the drivers from inside the vehicles. A van pulled to the curb and Elijah's men climbed out.

He gave instructions for detainment of the attackers already bound on the pavement as well as the cleanup of the rest. She wondered how such things were explained to foreign governments.

Speaking to his team, Elijah never looked away from her face.

Reaching back, Harper wrapped his arm around her. It made her stiffen in recognition and pain.

"I won't hurt you, Gabriella. We need to get you off the street." He tugged her gently. "Come with me."

Numbly, she let him lead her out of the threshold as Vi glanced up from restraining an unconscious attacker. Pointing her finger at Brie, she said, "I'll be with you in ten minutes."

With a nod, she stayed beside Harper in a circle of several men who looked ready to invade something. He held her hard.

They passed within six feet of Elijah and she thought she might faint trying to get air.

Back in her villa, she could breathe again. Pulling from Harper's grasp, he hesitated before he let her go.

Walking into the kitchen, she tried to pour wine but her hands shook too badly. Harper took the bottle and poured a glass for each of them. He held her hands so she could take a sip.

"I'm sorry for the violence." His words were gentle.

"I'm getting used to it, actually. Everyone else seems to know what they're doing so I try not to freak out." She inhaled carefully and placed her glass on the counter. "I-I...what are you both *doing* here?"

"Gabriella." The sound of him *saying her name* made her entire system freak out. She pressed her fingers to her temples. "Look at me. Please."

She managed to meet his eyes. It made her heart hurt.

"I'm sorry, Gabriella. So fucking sorry. Knowing you, I can't imagine the pain you've been in. We should've been with you...*I should have been with you.*"

Realization that he *knew* about her miscarriage was too much for her to handle. She backed away, tears streaming down her face. "I don't, I don't want to..."

Shaking horribly, she whimpered when he took her in his arms and held her tightly.

"It's going to be alright."

"It *won't...*"

"Yes, it will. I won't stop, Elijah won't stop, until it is. Tell me what you need. Tell me what you want. I'll do anything." He pulled back to stare into her eyes. His were dark gray with emotion.

"I don't know what to say...how to talk to you."

Lifting his hands, he cupped her face and used his thumbs to wipe her tears. "Would you have told me? About the baby?" Closing her eyes, she nodded. "You'd have let me be a father?"

Shocked, she murmured, "I wouldn't have kept...your ch-child from you. You know me better than that."

"I do. I wanted to hear you say it." Leaning close, he rubbed his cheek against hers. "Did you want to be a mother, Brie?" The pain of her quiet sobs made it difficult to nod. He held her harder and she missed every moment they'd shared. "Even with our dynamic, you'd have faced the world?"

Until he asked the question, she hadn't considered what lengths she'd have taken to protect her child.

It wasn't a far stretch to imagine her parents' anger and disappointment. She might have lost the winery.

None of it would've mattered.

"A child comes before anything, *everything* else. Nothing is as valuable and I'd have gladly paid the price to have him. I-I wanted him so *badly* and I failed. I failed at everything."

"You've failed at *nothing*, Gabriella. Nothing. I'm so sorry you lost him. I know it crushed your beautiful heart."

Unable to stop herself, she wrapped her hands around his waist and held him while she sobbed out the hurt she could have only shared with Harper and Elijah.

She cried for a long time and he held her, stroking her hair, and murmuring soothing words.

When it began to ease, he kissed the top of her head. "We took him to the estate, Gabriella. I insisted and Winters agreed. He's with my parents, my grandparents."

Leaning back, she stared up at him. "You...claimed him?"

"As I'd have claimed him had he lived." He smiled sadly. "I would've been proud to be a father to our child. Prouder still to have *you* as the mother. There could be *no one* better."

His hands held her face, fingers stroking through her hair, and he exhaled. "I did *everything* wrong. I hurt you deeply and my regrets haunt me."

He rested his forehead against hers. "I want to see you smile again, to hear you laugh. To be one of the reasons for your happiness. Tell me how to earn your forgiveness."

The feel of his lips on hers was so familiar, so desperately missed, that Brie didn't hesitate to return the kiss. He held her close, stroked his hand over her back, and made love to her mouth in a way he never had before that moment.

Everything inside her wanted him, wanted Elijah, wanted what they represented to her. She was *terrified*.

Inhaling deeply, she told him. "My heart wants you, both of you until I can't think. There's no emotional distance with you and Elijah. For months after it was o-over, I felt like I couldn't breathe. I'm not *strong enough* for this."

"You are. I know that even if you don't. I want you happy again. Let me help you get there."

Confused, she tried to pull away. "What do you *want* from me? You've already gotten the *only* thing you ever wanted from me. I don't understand, Harper."

Their eyes locked. "I love you, Gabriella." Blinking back tears, she tried to get away from him but he held her firmly. "I was afraid. I made horrible mistakes. I love you."

"*Harper...*"

He shook his head. "Let me finish. You confused me from the moment I saw you. I wanted you. There was never any doubt about that. Then you got under my skin so fucking fast I couldn't adjust. I acted like an ass. I was cruel and I said shit I didn't mean." He held her shoulders and looked deeply into her eyes. "I didn't *mean* it, Gabriella."

All her life, she'd eased the pain of others. Her initial reaction was to forgive, to crush down her own hurt, to move on. To take what she was offered under no conditions of her own.

Protecting and loving everyone but herself.

"Of all the people in the world, you and Elijah have the greatest ability to wound me. Everything I am is *bare* to you. I have no defense mechanisms in place. I love you as I've never loved anyone or anything until my b-baby."

He nodded and she was shocked at the tears that tracked down his cheeks. "I hurt you. I hurt Elijah. I know you need time. I know you need me to show you I learned from everything I did wrong."

Then he kissed her again and she fell into him, into everything she wanted so much. She was dizzy by the time he broke it and stared at her with complete intensity.

"I'll wait for you, Gabriella. As long as it takes." His arms tightened around her. "You'll see I'm different now and you'll forgive me. You'll let us spend the rest of our lives loving you." He put his palm on her chest. "This heart is constant. This heart loves hard. It needs *us* as much as we need *you*."

"I'm afraid."

"I know a *lot* about fear. I'll help you." Another kiss and he released her but didn't step back. "We're not going anywhere."

"I don't…aren't you working?"

His smile made her hold her breath. "Things are on autopilot for now. Elijah and I made you our full-time job until we have you back." Bending, he said at her ear, "We discovered that wherever *you* are, there also is sanctuary."

She inhaled sharply with a low moan. He planted a kiss beneath her ear and breathed in the scent of her hair.

Then he walked out of the villa to the men waiting outside.

Pressing her hand to her heart, her eyes met Elijah's from where he stood still on the outside steps and she wanted to run to him.

The pain was *unbelievable*.

Brie took several gasping breaths and used the counter to hold herself up. Vi entered and closed the front door.

Through her tears, Brie managed, "Thank you for keeping me safe. I'm so glad you weren't hurt."

Strong arms helped her to her couch.

"You're welcome, Gabriella. How about you stop worrying about everything in the world other than yourself?"

The shock of their presence, her complete confusion about Harper's words, and the strength of her own *want* had her flipped inside out.

"Love is supposed to make you feel *stronger*. I feel so fucking weak I can barely stand myself."

"It's hard to reconcile asshole behavior sometimes. Hard to tell if someone is *really* an asshole or just plays one on TV."

Despite her aching heart, Brie tried to smile. "Harper can be abrupt but he's a good man. I was too different, shook things up too much. I hurt him without meaning to do it."

"Well, he got you back for your supposed sins so, now what?"

Hugging her torso, she bent over her legs. "I want them so much I'm *sick* with the need to touch them."

"Natalia mentioned you're a touch junky. She warned me that you hug a lot and not to freak out."

Brie snickered shakily.

"You've been through hell. I'm sure your friends hugged you a lot but it's not the same, huh?"

Shaking her head, she whispered, "Only *they* ever helped me be truly calm inside."

"Excellent. Let's talk about rules." Brie glanced up in confusion. "You know *exactly* where to get your fix, Gabriella. They're *here*. They *want* you."

"U-use them? I can't do that."

"Yeah. You can, and you absolutely should." Her bodyguard outlined ground rules before she made two calls. "Let's go."

"Go where?"

"Get you some touch. You need it and god knows you fucking deserve it. It's time you get some shit *you* need out of this lopsided equation."

Chapter Fifty

Brie wasn't surprised to see several armed men outside her front door when Vi escorted her through it. She *was* shocked that they simply walked across the street and climbed stairs to a third-floor apartment.

The security detail waited at the landing. Vi stayed by her side all the way to the door.

Elijah opened it before she could knock. Glancing at the female bodyguard, he waited.

She wasted no time. "She's under my protection, Elijah."

"I'd *never* hurt her." Harper joined him at the door.

"When she cries, it means she's *hurting*. I've personally seen her cry far too much over you two. If I get her back broken, you deal with *me*, Elijah. We both know I might not win, but I'd make you work pretty fucking hard to beat me."

"Understood."

"Sylvia." She looked at Harper. "Thank you."

"That's a first in all the years I've known you. You're welcome. Okay." Vi turned to Brie and took her shoulders. "Remember our talk. Call me when you're ready to leave. Do *not* leave alone or I call Hudson. Don't make me do that. He's such a *dad* sometimes and I roll my eyes like a teenager."

Brie smiled shakily. "He doesn't care about having kids of his own because he considers you and Scott his children. Don't fight it." She shrugged. "He always wins."

"Maybe with *you*. You're spun sugar. See you later, Gabriella."

With one more glare at the men, Vi returned to the stairs and jogged out of sight.

Swallowing carefully past the lump in her throat, Brie turned to the two men she hadn't seen side by side in months. Her heart felt like it was going to pound through her breastbone.

"I don't want to talk. I-I can't handle it right now. My heart hurts. I just..." She tried to breathe through her stress. "I'm really lonely. I need you to touch me."

Elijah moved so fast to pick her up it startled her. Harper slammed the door and followed them through the living space to a bedroom. Setting her on her feet, they worked together to remove her sundress, underthings, and sandals.

When she was naked, Elijah held her close and kissed her. She felt the way his entire body vibrated, knew his desperation in the way he gripped her, and tasted a man she'd missed more than it was possible for her to express.

Then she was in Harper's arms, his body naked, as he ate at her lips. Elijah's body pressed tightly against her back, closing her between them. He moved her hair away and kissed his way up her neck.

She had no idea how long they stood there, trading her mouth between them. Drunk on the way they touched her, she wrapped her body around Elijah when he picked her up.

Caught up in touching him, kissing him, loving him as she had from the start, she barely registered when he laid her against cool linens.

Inside her, thrusting deep, she stared into eyes she'd sketched a thousand times since she'd been close enough to see the striations of green. Touching his face, she didn't realize she was crying until he kissed away the tears at her temples.

His strokes were steady and strong, driving her to a powerful climax while she struggled to breathe, to steady her heart, to take what she needed.

What only these men could provide.

With another searing kiss, he pulled away to lay beside her as Harper took his place. Eyes of silver gray stared into hers and she continued to cry as he held her gently, kissed her with every ounce of focus, and *made love* to her.

A second orgasm crashed over her body and Harper rolled to his back as Elijah kissed along her spine. As she rode waves of pleasure, he positioned himself at her ass and pushed inside.

They filled her, kissed her, touched her and she wanted to remember *everything*.

No matter what the future held for her, she knew she'd have this perfect memory as a buffer between the night she was attacked, the loss of her baby, and the non-stop grief she'd been under like a dark cloud.

For a long time, they took her, holding her between them as their cocks shuttled in and out of her in tandem.

"Harder," she whispered. "I want to feel you when it's over."

Bracing her, they fucked her without mercy, driving deep with every synchronized thrust. She started to shake, moaning low in her throat, and they didn't slow, didn't hesitate to take her harder still.

As the orgasm slammed into her, she felt lightheaded. They stilled and she absorbed the sensation of their release coating her tissues, deep and hot.

Resting her face on Harper's chest, she murmured, "Thank you. I n-needed...I'm sorry."

"We're not done, Gabriella. Rest and catch your breath." Harper's hands petted through her hair. "Never apologize for what you need."

Elijah pulled from her carefully and she heard him in the bathroom. When he returned, they lifted her from Harper and took her into the shower. They cleaned her, taking turns kissing her, and she was afraid.

Drying her gently, smoothing lotion into her skin, they returned her to the bed and stretched out beside her.

Pressed tightly to her front and back, she let herself take the strength and warmth she needed. She cried purging tears without talking and they held her hard.

She fell asleep and it was the best rest she'd gotten since the last time she'd slept between them.

It was dark when she opened her eyes and registered that candles flickered around the room.

Hands and mouths seemed to touch her *everywhere* and an orgasm was there before she even knew who'd given it to her.

Crawling up her body, Harper shared the taste of her before Elijah turned his face to kiss him deeply, his fingers gripping black hair tightly.

It made her hips rock into Harper, seeking friction to relieve the stimulation they provided. She let herself stroke her fingers over them and they kissed her again.

Pushing his cock deep, sealing them together, Harper stared down into her face. "I love you, Gabriella. I'm sorry I was afraid. I'll never doubt you again."

Over his shoulder, she met Elijah's eyes.

They were *including* her. She could tell the moment he gained access to the tight entry because Harper's cock flinched inside her, going somehow harder, as his eyes drifted shut in pleasure.

Brie couldn't control her instant, *ferocious* climax. "*Yes...*"

She gasped for air, held Harper as hard as she could, and tried not to bite through her lower lip to keep from screaming. It held her for a long time and their eyes were waiting when she opened them.

With a smile, she stroked Harper's face and whispered, "Let's enjoy him fucking you together."

Elijah kissed his shoulder and didn't break eye contact with her as he said, "Don't come until Brie gives you permission."

Each withdrawal pulled Harper slightly from her. Each forward thrust drove them together. The result was short, brutal strokes that made her pant for control.

"Harper, oh my god, it's beautiful to watch him take you." After she kissed him, she added in a whisper, "You're *so* hard. It's amazing."

He hugged her *tight*. "I can't explain, Gabriella."

"Just feel…just *feel*, Harper."

She touched him everywhere she could and reached around him to rest her hand on Elijah's thigh. The way it flexed with his thrusts made her crazy with the need to come.

Brie could barely talk. "I won't come until you're r-ready. We'll come together. Drag it out. Experience everything. The way his hand holds your shoulder. The feel of him going deep, raking over that special little hot spot in your ass, again and again. How warm and hard he is. The way your body craves him. The sound of his breathing. The way it feels when he loves you. Soak it up."

His hand fisted in her hair, tilting her head back so he could rake his teeth over her neck. He moved his knee forward, opening her legs wider, tightening them both and she sighed.

Between kisses, Harper told her, "The way you smell, the sound of your moans, the way your pussy grips my cock in a velvet fist, the softness of your skin, the way your eyes sparkle in candlelight, the joy of your touch, the pure beauty of your love. I'm soaking up *everything*, Gabriella."

At her ear, he asked, "Do I have permission?"

"Yes, yes. Come for me, Harper. I'll die if you don't."

Elijah drove harder and faster into his lover's willing body and pushed them both over the edge of pleasure. When they were at the peak of it, he came with a growl, his head thrown back in what could only be described as *victory*.

It was such a powerful image that it sent Brie into another climax before the first released her. Her body tightened like a bow and she couldn't get enough air.

She didn't fear the darkness that rose to claim her.

* * *

Staring down into her sleeping face, Harper smoothed wild curls away. "I've never encountered a soul so beautiful."

Elijah turned his face and kissed him with all the love they'd rediscovered as they waited for Gabriella to heal enough to reach for them.

They'd known from the beginning that touch would be the key back to her. She craved it, required it to make it through her life without shaking apart.

Her belief that she was *using* them gave her the emotional distance she required to take what she needed without conditions or apology.

"How do you feel, Harper?" Elijah's voice was low, sensual as his teeth clamped down on the muscle between his neck and shoulder.

"Loved. Safe." He gasped as Elijah's barely softened cock pressed more firmly into his ass and he moaned as it pushed him tighter into Gabriella.

"We fucked her into a coma. Let's revive her and do it again. I want her overdosed on pleasure. She's been through so much and alone far too long."

Harper nodded. "I want her to suck me while you take her. To watch your cock disappear inside her." Elijah's cock flinched inside him. "Then we can trade places. I want to fuck her until she can't move. Until I can't move." He chuckled. "It's useless to say until *you* can't move. You could fuck us both for the next week and barely end up winded."

Nuzzling his face against him, Elijah whispered, "Let's test the theory, Harper. Let's see how long I can keep going."

"There are two of us so that helps."

"I enjoy long odds."

* * *

Brie opened her eyes on the third day in their apartment a few hours before dawn and felt as if she'd been through intensive physical therapy again.

Pleasantly sore, interestingly sticky despite multiple showers, at peace for the first time in her life, she stared at the men next to her.

During their last session, Elijah talked her through sucking Harper as he fucked her from behind harder than he'd ever taken her. Then she and Harper changed places and she came too many times to count.

Collapsing, they slept where they fell. Harper was in the middle and she grinned at how entwined the three of them were with each other.

They hadn't talked about the past or the future. They hadn't discussed the loss of her baby. There were no hurts revisited.

They'd touched her. They'd healed her.

Sliding from the bed, she used the bathroom to pull herself together and texted Vi. When she received a reply message, she quickly dressed and left them a note.

Then she walked out of the apartment and allowed her bodyguard to escort her home.

* * *

When Elijah woke, he knew she was gone.

His heart contracted in visceral fear until he saw the confirmation from Vi that they were safely at the villa on his phone.

"Do you think she'll come back to us?"

Harper's voice was scratchy primarily from lack of adequate hydration and possibly a bit from how hard Elijah had fucked his mouth the night before as Brie rode him.

The memory made his balls draw up close to his body but he sent a signal to his cock to calm the fuck down.

"I know she will. Let's shower and dress."

They found her note as they entered the living room.

I love both of you so much more than you know. Thank you for helping me heal from the greatest loss of my life. Thank you for every moment but more for your trust. I hold it close to me.

I can't love you more than I love myself. It's not healthy and I don't want to hurt anymore.

I've said from the beginning that you don't need me. You may want me but you're strong together.

Love each other hard. Be thankful every day for the opportunity you found and take pride in the fact that you healed a relationship that was broken. You belong together, need each other, and I'm beyond honored to have been part of what you have for a little while.

I don't mind being a bridge. Know I take every touch with me. Brie

Harper frowned but Elijah wasn't concerned.

With a reassuring smile, he said, "She's being stubborn. She doesn't quite get it. Let's explain." He turned to go and paused. Running his palm along Harper's neck, he asked, "You're sure? This is the most important choice you've ever made. She's breakable."

Rolling his eyes, his best friend, his lover, replied, "Yes, I'm fucking *sure*. Don't tell me *you* doubt how I feel about her after the last few days?"

"No. I just wanted to confirm. I'll never push you again."

"Elijah, I rather *enjoy* when you push me."

He blinked. "Remember that later."

"As if I'd forget." Harper kissed him roughly and said against his lips, "Let's go get our woman."

Epilogue

Gabriella tried to ignore the sound of everything she'd *ever* wanted outside her window.

Tears streamed down her face as gentle beauty drifted on the air at the hands of the world's most dangerous man.

Shrugging a light sweater over her tank top, she stared at the front door for a long time.

"Are you sure, Gabriella?" Vi asked softly from behind her.

"No but I so want to be."

"Then you have to take the chance." The bodyguard smiled. "Sometimes, the biggest risks have the greatest rewards. You're strong. You must be a priority in their lives. Don't forget."

The blonde unlocked the door but didn't open it.

Brie took two steps, paused, then took another and placed her palm on the carved wood. Closing her eyes, she whispered, "Please don't hurt me. Please love me."

Then she opened the door and stepped out on the stoop.

Less than a dozen feet away in the small gated courtyard, Elijah played the violin while Harper's hand gripped his shoulder.

She approached slowly, breathing deeply to settle her mind.

Arms wrapped around her torso, she stared back and forth between men she'd fallen completely and irrevocably in love with faster than she ever expected and harder than she thought possible for so many reasons she couldn't explain if asked.

Elijah brought the song to a close and lowered the violin. His natural radiance glowed from his eyes, enthralled her yet again and made her *want*. All of him, always.

Harper's hand tightened on his shoulder and he had a fierce expression on his face. After time spent with him, she knew it was fear that inspired it. She wanted to love him, soothe him.

Both looked as if they held their breath.

Reaching up, she smoothed the lines on his forehead. "You should smile more, Harper."

"Perhaps you could help me do that." His features relaxed. "You're the only person who's ever had the power to make us smile, Gabriella."

The silence drew out between them. Three days of pleasure behind them, she had to say the words.

"You broke my heart."

"I know I did. I'm sorry. Forgive me, Brie. Let me try again to get it right."

Looking down at the ground, she told him, "You can't take away the water." His gray eyes were lighter when she met them. "Be sure this time. Be certain you want *who* I am, *how* I am. I'm still me."

"All I want is the woman you are, Gabriella. I love you more than I've ever shown you, for longer than I admitted. I want you as desperately as I want Elijah. Come back. Let me love you as you deserve. Let me show you the man I really am."

Moving her eyes to Elijah's, she whispered, "You're a *beautiful* soul. I love when you play for me."

"You're the only woman I've ever played for, the only one I ever will." He blinked against tears that stunned her. "I want to stop breathing to stop the pain. You don't understand how much I *need* you, Brie. How I've missed you. I need you to love me as much as I need Harper to love me."

Through sobs, she answered, "I can't *help* loving you. You're the only men I've ever loved. I don't want to feel weaker for it. I want to feel stronger."

"Let us make you strong, Brie."

"Take our love, Gabriella. Freely given, without condition."

For almost a minute, she stared at them, thinking. The sun was coming up, a light breeze lifted her hair across her face.

Finally, inhaling carefully, she asked, "Would you like coffee?"

"Yes." Harper scooped her into his arms and stared down into her face. Startled, her arm went around his shoulders. "You're a *stunningly* beautiful woman, Gabriella."

Burying his face at her neck, she felt him take several hitching breaths. When he lifted his head, he gave her a brilliant smile.

It made her heart thump hard in her chest. Reaching up, she traced her fingers from his temple to his chin.

"You slay me when you smile, Harper."

Then she sat up and hugged him hard. He returned it as he carried her inside. Elijah followed closely behind and when their eyes met over his shoulder, he winked.

Vi waited in the entry with her bag when they walked into the villa. "I'm going to give you privacy."

She stepped close to Brie and brushed her curls away from her face. Firming her expression, she glared at Elijah.

"Anything happens to her and I hold you responsible."

"Understood."

The woman with deadly skills grinned. "Don't let them get away with a fucking thing, pretty girl. See you next week." When she started to ask, Vi explained, "Hudson is anxious to see your face and confirm personally that you're safe and no longer being *fucked with emotionally*." She shrugged. "His words, not mine."

"I'll call him."

"Good plan. He'll give no fucks about your privacy."

With a laugh, she hugged the other woman's neck. "Be safe, Vi. I like having my friends come back in one piece."

"I'll be based in the city for a while. I have interests there." Bending, she kissed Brie's temple. "Thank you for showing me a different life, Gabriella. I'm glad of the knowledge. However, I admit to being more terrified of your gentleness than an assailant with a gun. See you soon."

She went through the door, the courtyard iron gate clinked into place, and she walked down the cobbled street toward the intersection. Her tech bag was slung over her shoulder.

Elijah closed and locked the door when she was out of sight.

She met his eyes. "One day…"

"Not today."

Then the men she loved carried her into her bedroom and showed her how much they'd missed her. Again.

When she'd forgotten her own name, lost buckets of fluids, and took a short nap, she woke exhilarated.

She called Hudson while she watched Harper and Elijah sleep side by side.

"Gabriella, your ass is spanked. What the *fuck* is happening?"

She grinned. "Hi, Hudson. I'll be back in a couple of days. I've missed you. Catch me up on everything."

After a low growl, he did.

Curling up in a chair near the window that looked out on the azure sea, she chatted with her best friend and waited for her men to wake up.

It was the perfect way to start the next phase of her life.

She embraced the light, welcomed it, and it filled her up again.

Excerpt — Hollow's World

September 2016 — New York City

Brie laughed with Riya and Tawny. Their inner circle was in attendance to celebrate the launch of Marciella Canfield's new grassroots programs to address hunger and homelessness.

Her ideas were wonderful, realistic, and doable. Brie was proud of her involvement in the marketing material designs.

Harper and Hudson were gradually easing up on their open hostility and her best friend confided that he needed to know *Delkin* was serious about his life changes.

It made her laugh and she kept the information to herself.

Glancing across the room, Brie looked at her men. Harper was involved in an intense conversation with a man who didn't look pleased with his responses. Elijah stood closer to Harper's back than usual and though his expression was blank, she read the tension that surrounded him.

"Bitch, those heels are hot," Tawny told her with a raised brow.

Sighing, she glanced at the platforms that seemed higher than the two inches they really were. "I have to work my way up. They're better than *flats*."

"You make it sound like a dirty word. You'll get there," Riya chimed in with a chuckle. "You look incredible."

After leaving Croatia, Brie insisted on taking things with Elijah and Harper slow. She lived in New York to be closer to her friends and they made a greater effort to take time off.

Absences were usually no more than a week, a fact for which she was grateful. Her doctors inserted a non-hormonal birth control device in her uterus to prevent pregnancy.

She knew losing another child would destroy her.

Excusing herself, she walked into the hall and found the luxurious ladies' room. Using the facilities in formalwear was never an enjoyable experience.

Washing her hands, she took in her appearance. Her black raw silk gown was a halter style that clung to her upper body. It draped perfectly from beneath her breasts to the floor and was shot through with silver threads.

Most of her back was bare to just above the crack of her ass and when Harper presented it to her, she told him, "You *love* exposing my back so you're lucky Elijah is so skilled with the whip or people would talk."

Stepping close, he'd responded, "Fuck them. I love seeing as much caramel skin as you're willing to expose in public so I can imagine touching it when we're no longer required to be appropriate."

He'd promptly separated the robe she'd slipped on after her shower and taken her hard against the wall of her closet. Time between them alone had done much to heal old wounds and grow the love they had for one another.

She thought about the way Elijah entered, kissed Harper and then her passionately, and led them to the shower…again.

It gave her a pleasant shiver.

In the small foyer of the restroom was a seating area. She perched on the edge of the loveseat there to adjust the strap of her heel. As she straightened, a gorgeous woman lowered to the seat beside her.

Turning her head with a smile, the woman sprayed something in her face.

* * *

Brie's skin felt sticky and she was completely disoriented. She tried to open her eyes to see who carried her.

"You have bandages on your eyes until I can flush them again. The light makes the effect worse."

"Elijah…?" They were in an elevator.

"Trust me right now, Brie. Will you do that?"

"Of course. Is everyone alright? Can you tell me?"

"You were the target, Brie. Tawny contained the situation."

"Gabriella." Hudson's voice spoke close to her. "You're alright. Elijah is going to help you."

"I know. Go back to the gala."

"Darling," Natalia sniffed back tears, "I'll personally spank you if you don't stop saying such outrageous things."

Elijah lifted her close and whispered, "Everyone is panicked. Let them recover and I'll fill you in when I know you're safe. Alright?" She took a deep breath and nodded. "Good girl."

"I feel…Elijah, I'm going to be sick."

"Excellent. We need it out." She felt the floor beneath her feet and he placed her hands on a trash can. "I've got you."

She'd never vomited so hard in her life. The elevator stopped moving and she could tell the doors were open but Elijah stayed with her while it felt as if she threw up everything she'd eaten in her lifetime. He gently patted her mouth and placed an open water bottle in her hand.

"Drink all of it. More will be necessary."

He lifted her again and walked quickly. Doors opened and closed, people murmured, but she couldn't get anything solid.

Then she was in a bathroom. "I'm sorry, Brie. I need to dilute any remaining residue. I've got to put you underwater. Hold your breath and tap my wrist when you need me to bring you up. Do you understand?"

"Yes. Hurry."

He lowered her into lukewarm water fully clothed and braced his palm on her upper chest to hold her under. She panicked the first time after only a few seconds and tapped him.

"I'm sorry. I-I can hold it longer. Sorry."

"It's alright. We have to do this a lot."

It seemed like *days* but it was worse when he removed the bandages and told her to open her eyes when she was under. He drained the tub several times, held her under the running tap as it filled, and continued to submerge her. Each time she came up, he sprayed something cool on her skin.

She vomited several more times during and he forced her to drink more water each time.

Finally, he lifted her up and held her on his lap. She registered that he was still in the shirt and slacks from his tuxedo.

"The lights are dimmed, open your eyes for me, Brie."

She did and murmured, "I-I can't see."

Elijah growled. "I need to spray your open eyes. I'm so fucking sorry, Brie."

"It's okay."

He held her lids wide and sprayed the cool liquid in them. It burned like *fire* on the surface of her eyes. Her instinct was to rub them and he hugged her arms against her body.

"You can't, sweetheart." That was when she started to cry. "I know. I know it burns." He kissed her hair. "You're being so strong. Trust me. Please trust me."

"Of *course*, I do. Of course, Elijah." She forced the words through sobs she couldn't help. "Keep going."

He nodded against her head and put her back in the water.

She had no idea how long the process went on but by the fourth time he sprayed her eyes, she could make out other people in the room with them. A few more treatments and she saw their worried faces clearly.

"I can see. I can see."

Hudson held a quietly sobbing Natalia and Harper's fists were clenched at his sides. *Hollow* stood in the doorway with his arms crossed and Tawny vibrated in fury beside him.

Then Elijah pulled her to his chest and cried brokenly against her neck. She hugged him tightly as her stomach cramped and her head pounded painfully.

"Thank you for keeping your head, Elijah." Her throat was raw from vomiting. She brought his eyes up to hers. "I love you. Thank you for powering through it. I know it was hard."

Harper held himself up by the vanity.

"What else has to happen?"

Wiping his face on his sleeve, Elijah said hoarsely, "We have to get you on an IV drip. I need to pump a lot of fluid through your body."

"Can I wear dry clothes or at least take this off? I'm freezing."

"As requested." Two of his team entered with bags. "Mrs. Winters provided the sizes, sir."

Glancing past them to Natalia, Brie whispered scratchily, "Mrs. *Winters*. Oh my god, I never get tired of that."

Stomping across the room, Harper lifted her from Elijah's lap and held her soaking wet body against him. "Everyone get out so we can get her in dry clothes." Closing his eyes, he added more calmly, "Please. Please give us a minute."

When the door shut, Harper stripped her dress away with shaking hands. She didn't know where her shoes were.

"Harper…?"

"We just, we have to fucking warm you up. Let me focus." She heard fabric tear and placed her hands over his. "Getting a fucking gown off shouldn't be so goddamn *difficult*!"

"Harper."

"Stop being fucking understanding for a second so I can…"

"Harper. It wasn't your fault. I'm fine but even if I hadn't been, it *still* wasn't your fault."

"You could've been blinded. Taken. Killed."

"I wasn't but you didn't *do* anything, Harper." Wrapping her arms around him, strange shivers wracked her frame. "Take a deep breath and help me undress."

He nodded and got her out of the gown. As she bent over to strip the wet panties away, she vomited water.

"That's not embarrassing at all."

"Slow, Brie. Slow."

Elijah finished undressing her while Harper rubbed her down with warm towels. Wringing the water out of her hair as much as possible, they worked a soft t-shirt over her head, pulled stretchy pants up her legs, and sat her on the counter to put warm socks on her feet.

She glanced at her reflection and gasped. Her eyes were almost solid red and the skin around her eyes, nose, and mouth looked as if she'd burned to the point of blistering.

"I...will it heal?"

"Yes. Yes. Don't worry, Brie." Another bottle of water appeared and she took it. "Ready?"

She nodded and Harper took her off the counter and into the main room of the hotel suite.

Throughout the night, they cycled several bags of fluids through her and carried her to the bathroom to vomit or pee.

When the sun came up, she was sore all over and exhausted.

She croaked, "I'm *pissed* my night of debauchery was cancelled. Otherwise known as a day that ends in *y*. I had so many lovely things planned."

Elijah gave a hesitant laugh and kissed the top of her head. "Your debauchery has been rescheduled. Rest."

Brie drifted off and smiled when she opened her eyes to Tawny crouching in front of her.

"Hey, Red. I hear you saved my life and shit."

"Shut the fuck up. I just needed my drinking buddy." Her green eyes took in the skin of her face. "You look *fucked* up."

"How's the person who sprayed me?"

"Breathing through a tube. Ask me if I feel bad about it? You don't have to ask. I don't." Tawny picked up her hand. "Let them get you behind walls for now. Don't fight them even though you'll hate it sometimes."

"We're going to Washington?" She looked at Harper and he nodded. With a heavy sigh, she murmured, "I wish I was more like you. More like Elijah."

"No, you don't, Brie. Don't ever wish that." The redhead leaned forward and pressed a kiss to her hair. "If people like you and Riya weren't around, people like us would suffocate and eventually die."

"I don't know anything. I can't even help. I'm also like a newborn calf stumbling around, loving everybody, and making friends." She swallowed hard. "What would've happened if you hadn't gotten to me so fast?"

"I did so we're not going to fucking discuss it." She gave her a smile. "Hang out, sketch, get your fucked-up skin under control…"

"Thanks for that, really."

"No worries. I'm here to boost esteem." Tawny stroked her fingers over her hair. "I'm sorry, Brie." Then she left the room.

A minute later, Elijah placed her in Harper's lap and kissed her gently before following Tawny out into the hall. Glancing up, she met silver eyes that stared at her with true pain.

"Harper, is everything okay?"

"No. It isn't but it'll be." He held her close and she felt him shaking. "I'm sorry. I'm so sorry, Gabriella."

She hugged him. "Listen. I love you, I love Elijah, and I love the life we're slowly building together." Leaning back, she looked into his eyes. "Every risk, every threat, is worth it to be able to touch you, to talk to you, to share my love with you."

He kissed her carefully. "You're magnificent."

"So are you. In every way." Sighing, she added, "I have to pee again. Damn it."

* * *

Hollow hugged Tawny tight enough to hurt. "You saved her, Tawny. You diluted it before the acid in the compound had time to work."

Then she was crying against his chest and he knew how deeply she felt things wasn't something most people would ever know about this woman.

"It's alright. You got there. You got there."

"I don't like these fucking things. Too many valuable people under one roof."

"Hiding makes them more determined." He lifted her face and wiped her tears.

Elijah stepped out of the room and walked up to the redhead Hollow had always wished he could love but knew he was incapable of it.

Gathering her carefully in his arms, Elijah hugged her and planted a kiss on her forehead. She took several gasping breaths. Leaning back, he stared at her for a long moment.

"I won't forget." Turning his face to Hollow, he said, "I'm in. We need to meet at the estate. It isn't secure here."

The men held one another's gazes for a long time. "Are you sure, Elijah? I don't...want to take you back to that time. You have so much now."

In a low growl, he replied, "Then he shouldn't have tried to destroy the only woman I've ever loved. Now, I'll have his *head* on a fucking *pike*."

Tawny sniffed. "That's like, a figure of speech, right? Because it's kind of a gross image."

Elijah looked down at her and winked. "If that helps you sleep at night. Sure, it's a figure of speech."

"Lord. Dealing with both of you might be too much."

"Nah," Hollow told her, wrapping his arm around her shoulder and leading her to the elevator, "This is going to be awesome."

Over his shoulder, he grinned at Elijah. "Glad to have you. I'll try not to covet."

Then he took his second-in-command downstairs so she could reassure her men she was okay.

Hollow left through the kitchens, hailed a cab, and changed to another cab that took him in the opposite direction.

When he was still miles from home, he got on the subway.

Getting off three exits before his own, he took to the roofs and dropped to his building with a tired sigh.

Some days, the chaos and stress of it all didn't seem worth it. Then he remembered what Rolfe Eklund had put him through until he was eleven and what he put Elijah through.

The man who'd tortured and abused them was merely a puppet and Elijah had made sure he'd *never* hurt either of them again.

The man been *behind* Elijah's father was still breathing.

It was time to change that.

© Shayne McClendon

The Barter System Series

Read the entire series now!

The Barter System Prequels

The Barter System (Book One)

Hudson (Book Two)

Backstage (Book Three)

Liberation (Book Four)

Radiance (Book Five)

The Barter System Companion – Volume 1

The Barter System Companion – Volume 2

About Shayne McClendon

If you're looking for stories that tug at your heart, make you laugh out loud, and sometimes make you cry so hard you need a giant box of tissues...look no further than books by Shayne McClendon.

She's a prolific author (more than 8 million words and counting) known for dramatic, steamy, enthralling fiction that will grab you and not let go until the last page.

A nomad at heart, Shayne currently lives in America's heartland with her dog, cats, and two grown children.

She listens to the voices in her head because their ideas are (almost) always awesome. Coffee consumption is too high, amount of sleep is too low, but the words always feel just right.

Be sure to like her <u>Always the Good Girl Facebook page</u>, or visit her at <u>Always the Good Girl</u> and join for your free story!

Shayne currently has more than two dozen books that range from heart-wrenchingly romantic to captivating non-stop heat. Explore them on the next page!